The Norman Maclean Reader

The

Norman

Maclean

Reader

EDITED BY O. ALAN WELTZIEN

The University of Chicago Press CHICAGO & LONDON

Norman Maclean (1902–1990) was born in Clarinda, Iowa, and grew up in Missoula, Montana. He worked for many years in logging camps and for the United States Forest Service before beginning his academic career. A scholar of Shakespeare and the Romantic poets, Maclean was the William Rainey Harper Professor of English at the University of Chicago until his retirement in 1972. He is the author of the acclaimed books *A River Runs through It and Other Stories* (1976) and *Young Men and Fire* (1992), both published by the University of Chicago Press.

O. Alan Weltzien is professor of English at the University of Montana Western, in Dillon, Montana. He is the author of *A Father and an Island: Reflections on Loss*, a memoir (2008); coeditor of *Coming into McPhee Country: John McPhee and the Art of Literary Nonfiction* (2003); and the editor of *The Literary Art and Activism of Rick Bass* (2001).

The University of Chicago Press, Chicago 60637
The University of Chicago Press, Ltd., London
© 2008 by The University of Chicago
All rights reserved. Published 2008
Printed in the United States of America

17 16 15 14 13 12 11 10 09 08   1 2 3 4 5

ISBN-13: 978-0-226-50026-3 (cloth)
ISBN-10: 0-226-50026-8 (cloth)

Library of Congress Cataloging-in-Publication Data

Maclean, Norman, 1902–1990.
  [Selections. 2008]
  The Norman Maclean reader / edited by O. Alan Weltzien.
      p.   cm.
  ISBN-13: 978-0-226-50026-3 (alk. paper)
  ISBN-10: 0-226-50026-8 (alk. paper)
  I. Weltzien, O. Alan (Oliver Alan) II. Title.
  PS3563.A317993A6   2008
  818'.5408—dc22

                                    2008014519

Contents

· ·

Introduction, by O. Alan Weltzien vii

THE CUSTER WRITINGS
Edward S. Luce:
   Commanding General (Retired),
   Department of the Little Bighorn 3
From the Unfinished Custer Manuscript 9
   Chapter 1: The Hill 11
   Chapter 2: The Sioux 26
   Chapter 3: The Cheyennes 40
   Chapter 4: In Business 55
   Last Chapter: Shrine to Defeat 62

A MACLEAN SAMPLER
"This Quarter I Am Taking McKeon":
   A Few Remarks on the Art of Teaching 69
"Billiards Is a Good Game":
   Gamesmanship and America's First Nobel Prize
   Scientist 78
Retrievers Good and Bad 93
Logging and Pimping and "Your Pal, Jim" 101
An Incident 116
The Woods, Books, and Truant Officers 130
The Pure and the Good:
   On Baseball and Backpacking 136
Black Ghost 141
From *Young Men and Fire* 150
Interview with Norman Maclean 166

SELECTED LETTERS
Letters to Robert M. Utley, 1955–1979 183
Letters to Marie Borroff, 1949–1986 212
Letters to Nick Lyons, 1976–1981 234
Letters to Lois Jansson, 1979–1981 246

Acknowledgments 257
Suggestions for Further Reading 259

A gallery of photographs appears following page 104.

Introduction

O. ALAN WELTZIEN

In 1976 the University of Chicago Press published an original work of fiction for the first time in its history. It was an unusual compilation, two novellas with a short story placed between them, and its author was a legendary English professor at the university who had recently retired after a career of forty-five years. The Press hedged its bets by binding up three thousand copies of a five thousand–copy first printing, but from its very first notice—by Nick Lyons in Fly Fisherman magazine—the book had rave reviews and sales followed accordingly. A River Runs through It and Other Stories made Norman Maclean famous far beyond his adopted city of Chicago and native state of Montana, where he spent his summers. The book helped inaugurate the contemporary literary flowering of the Rocky Mountain West and, in ways that would have both horrified and pleased Maclean, introduced a broad public to the hitherto cultish, hidden sport of fly-fishing. A generation later, River enjoys a global reputation, one enhanced by numerous translations and Robert Redford's sensitive film adaptation, which was released soon after Maclean's death in 1990.

Where did this astonishing book come from? Maclean had to reach, as he was fond of saying, his biblical allotment of threescore years and ten before he could write it. As he approached his retirement—having weathered several bouts of extended illness—he followed the suggestion of his son, John N. Maclean, and daughter, Jean Maclean Snyder, and began writing what he called "reminiscent stories" about his youth in western Montana. A story about his summers working in the Forest Service turned into a long one, and only after completing that did he turn to fly-fishing and his long-lost younger brother, Paul Maclean—his only sibling. In many letters from the period 1973–75, Maclean speaks of writing a story about his brother, whom he considered one of the great fly fishermen of his time. He wanted this story to be the best he was capable of writing, and his standards were unforgiving. By 1975 he had finished the book he wanted. It was a triptych, the title novella already promising to overshadow the short story and novella that follow it. Maclean knew it was an odd package, but he always favored structures and rhythms composed in threes, which for him echoed, however faintly, the Holy Trinity he grew up knowing from his father, for many years minister of Missoula, Montana's downtown First Presbyterian Church.

So Professor Maclean became famous during our Bicentennial year, and for the remaining fourteen years of his life he followed with pride the career of his book. He hesitated about a movie version, calling the Hollywood people who had begun to pursue him "jackals" and fearing they would "prostitute" his family. It was only after rebuffing several directors and screenwriters that Maclean optioned the film rights to Robert Redford. Maclean was less pre-occupied with movie negotiations than with his next book, which concerned a 1949 Smokejumper tragedy little remembered outside Montana, or at least outside Region One of the U.S. Forest Service. Maclean devoted over a decade to researching and writing this fire book, which he still had not finished to his satisfaction by the time of his final illness. After his death in 1990, University of Chicago Press editor Alan Thomas, working closely with John N. Maclean and Jean Maclean Snyder, edited Maclean's manuscript, and two years later the Press published *Young Men and Fire*. This second, longer book received the National Book Critics Circle Award for best nonfiction and has considerably broadened his literary reputation. *Fire* is a strange and haunting and eloquent book—part autobiography, part "fire report," part classical tragedy, part el-egy, part philosophical statement. It resists easy classification but is both sub-lime and, to use Maclean's favorite word, "beautiful," its beauty deriving in large part from its somber poignancy.

. . . .

Maclean then published only one slender book during his lifetime, and a sec-ond, longer book followed posthumously. In addition, he published a hand-ful of essays during the 1970s and early 1980s, several of which appeared in a 1988 Confluence Press anthology of writings by and about Maclean. How did Maclean's youth and long academic career lead to this late achieve-ment, and why didn't he publish more? The two questions overlap, but the simplest answer to the second concerns his severe habit of self-criticism. Writers know that rewriting entails a good deal of subtraction, but Maclean was perhaps too ruthless in this respect. He learned to be hard on his own writing under the harsh tutelage of his minister father. As Maclean has writ-ten in "The Woods, Books, and Truant Officers" (reprinted in this volume), he never attended public school until age eleven. Up to then, his entire cur-riculum consisted of reading and writing, carried out in a room across from his father's study. When he crossed rooms with a written composition, his father read it and then told the boy to return with the composition half that length. And so on, until the reverend had him tear it up.

Maclean looked back affectionately upon this early school of hard knocks, however, because he had afternoons free to roam the woods surrounding Missoula while other kids his age sat in classrooms. Maclean was born in Clarinda, Iowa, on December 23, 1902: his family didn't move to Missoula until his sixth year. Because *River* and *Fire* contain so many autobiographical elements, Maclean's readers already know some pieces of his life story, though significantly compressed and rearranged. In 1917 Maclean began working summers for the Forest Service—a big federal institution, particularly in the western states, founded in 1905 and so a bit younger than Maclean; throughout his life, Maclean liked to say that he and the Forest Service were contemporaries. After earning his B.A. at Dartmouth (where he took a writing seminar with Robert Frost) and spending two years there as a teaching assistant, Maclean returned to Montana in 1926 to work for the Forest Service. Maclean's years as a Forest Service employee did not end until he took a job as a graduate assistant at the University of Chicago in 1928. Yet he never imaginatively surrendered the idea of a Forest Service career; it was always his road not taken. His novella USFS 1919: *The Ranger, the Cook, and a Hole in the Sky* condenses and shapes experiences from at least four Forest Service summers into a coming-of-age story, and he based his short story "Logging and Pimping and 'Your Pal, Jim'" on those Forest Service summers as well. Also, without his own experiences in wildland firefighting, Maclean would never have become obsessed with the deaths of the twelve Forest Service Smokejumpers and a recreation guard killed in the 1949 Mann Gulch tragedy.

During his college years in New Hampshire, Maclean would take the long train ride home every summer. Beginning in 1921, he helped his father build what became the family cabin on the shores of Seeley Lake, Montana, fifty miles northeast of Missoula. That cabin became his cynosure in his native state. After the spring term at Chicago ended and many of his colleagues had left for London, to study and write in the British Museum's Reading Room, he and his wife, Jessie Burns Maclean, and their son and daughter would drive west to Seeley Lake and the mountains of home. Those migrations west and back defined Maclean, who relished playing the Montana exotic in the intellectual circles of Chicago's Hyde Park. After retirement, he spent more time at Seeley Lake, staying on until autumn snows drove him back to Chicago. He liked to remind friends that the cabin was only sixteen miles from glaciers, and that the fishing kept his "wand" bent.

Looking back on his early years at the University of Chicago, Maclean recalled the miserable load of assigned compositions that needed attention every weekend. Yet he quickly became a first-rate teacher and in 1932, only a year after being promoted to instructor, won the University of Chicago's Quantrell Award for Excellence in Undergraduate Teaching, a distinction he would win twice more during his career. Maclean was a legend in the classroom: that rare professor with such gifts that he marks students for life. His status was acknowledged by the endowed chair (William Rainey Harper Professor of English) he held during his final decade at Chicago.

In 1940 he became Dr. Maclean, having completed his Ph.D. at Chicago. R. S. Crane, chairman of the English department and spokesman for what became known as the neo-Aristotelian school, served as his mentor and something of a father figure. Maclean taught Shakespeare and the British Romantic poets—Wordsworth, Coleridge, Shelley, and Keats—favoring close readings of the poem or scene. Though scholarly, he never published much scholarship: he thrived at Chicago even as "publish or perish" became the byword at American research universities. Over the course of his career, Maclean produced two scholarly articles, both of them in a landmark volume of literary criticism, *Critics and Criticism: Ancient and Modern* (1952), edited by R. S. Crane. The first, "From Action to Image: Theories of the Lyric in the Eighteenth Century," explains Maclean's views of lyric poetry in British eighteenth-century literature. Deriving from Maclean's dissertation, it is a long, erudite performance that shows his aptitude as a literary scholar. The second essay, devoted to Shakespeare's tragedy *King Lear*, anticipates the concerns of his later writing. Dauntingly titled "Episode, Scene, Speech and Word: The Madness of Lear," it unfolds Maclean's theory of tragedy, which he deemed the highest literary form, and to the discerning reader tells as much about Maclean as about Shakespeare.[1]

It could be said the "the problem of defeat"—a phrase appearing in a letter to Robert Utley in the early 1960s—became Maclean's consuming theme. It served as his contemporary expression for that welter of tragic forces he found best distilled in the ancient Greek tragedies and Shakespeare's tragedies. Certainly he wrestled with this theme in his book manuscript, eventually aban-

---

1. "Episode, Scene, Speech and Word: The Madness of Lear" is available at www.norman maclean.com.

doned, about George Armstrong Custer and the Battle of the Little Bighorn, whose final chapter was to be titled "Shrine to Defeat." Near the beginning of the *Lear* essay, he announces the essay's scope:

> We propose to follow Lear and Shakespeare across the heath to the fields of Dover on what for both was a unique experience, and then to be even more particular, considering the individual scenes leading to this meeting of Lear and Gloucester when in opposite senses neither could see. And, for smaller particulars, we shall consider an incident from one of these scenes, a speech from this incident, and, finally, a single word. In this declension of particulars our problems will be some of those that were Shakespeare's because he was attending Lear and at the same time was on his way toward a consummation in the art of tragic writing. (*Critics*, 599)

This prospectus describes, in various ways, Maclean's approach to the Seventh Cavalry at Little Bighorn, to his doomed brother, Paul, and to the Smokejumpers in Mann Gulch. Influenced as he was by Aristotle's *Poetics*, which defines tragedy as the epitome of literary art, Maclean always held that the "the most composed" writing illuminates "the disorderly" forces within us, whether in an eighty-year-old king gone mad or a younger brother out of control. In his essay, he describes the old king's philosophical dilemma in terms that go to the core of his own later writing: "The question of whether the universe is something like what Lear hoped it was or very close to what he feared it was, is still, tragically, the current question."

At Chicago and elsewhere, he was known as Norman. In addition to teaching his popular courses, he took on many service roles at the university, including, from 1942 to 1945, the job of dean of students. In 1942 Maclean coauthored a *Manual of Instruction in Military Maps and Aerial Photographs*, and from 1943 to 1945 was acting director of the university's Institute on Military Studies. After the war, Maclean founded the Committee on General Studies in the Humanities, a highly successful interdisciplinary program he oversaw for fifteen years. His pride in the committee is clear in several of his letters to Robert Utley included in this volume.

After his third year at the university, Maclean married his sweetheart of several years, Jessie Burns, whose family ran the general store in Wolf Creek, Montana. Wolf Creek lies at the mouth of Little Prickly Pear Canyon, near the Missouri River, and only a few miles from Mann Gulch. After his wife's death, Maclean scattered her ashes atop a mountain near Wolf Creek that Burns family members had named for Jessie. Maclean was fond of recounting how his tough, hardworking wife described him in his late twenties: "Norman, I knew you when you were young and you were a goddamned mess." Their daughter, Jean, was born in 1942 and their son, John, followed the next year.

Four years before he became a father, though, Maclean's younger brother, Paul, was murdered in a Chicago alley. This remained perhaps the single most shattering event of Maclean's life, and it haunts his most memorable writing. Robert Redford's film version of *River* plays up contrasts between the older, quieter brother, Norman, who observes closely and constantly, and the talented, reckless younger brother, always the life of the party and of the family. Both the novella and the movie obscure Paul's actual history. In the movie's adaptation, when Norman goes east, Paul stays behind in Montana, as though incapable of leaving the great trout rivers of home. In fact, Paul Maclean followed Norman to Dartmouth and, after his own graduation and several years of working for Montana newspapers, to Chicago, in hopes of landing a job on a big-city daily. Given these facts, it is tempting to speculate about whether Norman felt personally responsible for Paul's death. But in *A River Runs through It*, readers face only Maclean's silence as they ponder the tragic ramifications, in life and literature, of being one's brother's keeper.

. . . .

Maclean was built like an early twentieth-century halfback, which in fact he was in high school in Missoula—short at five feet eight and a half inches, but solid at 165 pounds, a weight he maintained for most of his life. At Dartmouth his nickname was Bull Montana, after a movie character of the day. He spoke with an unhurried voice, choosing his phrases as carefully as he crafted his tight, ironic sentences. His mobile, deeply lined face registered his moods as swiftly as changing light over a mountain lake's surface. He did not suffer fools gladly. His Chicago reputation rested in no small measure upon his other life in a big rural state where cowboys and loggers and miners worked hard and cussed easily. Maclean's research partner during the *Young Men and Fire* years, Laird Robinson, once said that Maclean was "frequently profane but never vulgar"—a key Montana distinction. This is a writer who, as we see in one of the letters to Marie Borroff, delighted in reading aloud a story with "pimping" in the title to a select University of Chicago group called the Stochastics. This also is a writer who savored the word "beautiful," parsing it one syllable at a time, and who might call somebody he disliked a "prick" or "pig fucker," though rarely to his face. In Montana such names don't qualify as vulgar. And beer isn't alcohol.

Maclean embodied the tough-but-tender formula in his own distinct fashion. A student who knew him well described him as owning a tensile grace, as though he were a coiled spring always controlled with some effort. He lived his own version of the Hemingway credo, grace under pressure. He had been in fights as a "town" kid and weathered several rough logging camps. He favored metaphors from boxing and, of course, memorably describes Paul as fighting right to his end. USFS 1919 climaxes with the hilarious brawl between the Forest Service crew and several card sharks who judge them easy pickings but who are themselves fleeced by the crew's cook, a card pro. Looking back on his childhood and weighing the respective influences of his father and mother, Maclean concluded he was a "tough flower girl," which gives us a clue to the sensibility that makes him so distinctive on the page.

One suspects that Maclean sought, but ultimately didn't find to his satisfaction, this same sensibility in the larger-than-life figure of George Armstrong Custer. By the mid-1950s, Maclean was a full-fledged Custer aficionado, one who sleuthed Custer Hill in southeastern Montana—the Little Bighorn Battlefield National Monument, as it's been known since 1991—with like-minded enthusiasts. Maclean conceived and taught for years a course about Custer and the Battle of the Little Bighorn. He was soon at work on a book manuscript, an unconventional, "pretty introspective study of a battle, one involving a study of topography of certain exposed portions of the surface of the soul," as he wrote in a letter to Robert Utley. Maclean found a valuable interlocutor for his project in Utley, a younger man about to embark on a writing and publishing career that has since made him one of our leading historians of the nineteenth-century American West. Utley's own obsession with Custer started earlier and lasted much longer than Maclean's, as his book *Custer and Me: A Historian's Memoir* (2004) attests. His first book, *Custer and the Great Controversy: The Origin and Development of a Legend* (1962), focuses upon the Custer myth in ways that overlapped with Maclean's interests. Maclean acted the part of writing tutor to Utley and, through many letters, shared with him his hopes and frustrations as he struggled with his own manuscript about Custer and Little Bighorn. The correspondence shows Maclean defining and recommending "narrative history" to the talented historian—and himself. Maclean worked hardest on the manuscript from 1959 to 1963, drafting most of its projected chapters.

Maclean could not, however, see his way through to this odd kind of book—"a very strange and introspective thing," as he wrote to Utley. He was most interested not in the battle itself, which others had already chronicled repeatedly, but in what he called its "after-life," the myriad forms in which it was replayed or alluded to in subsequent popular art up through the present. His commitment to the battle as ritual drama baffled historians such as Utley. Maclean found that he could not shape the material to fit the tragic blueprint he had outlined in his Lear essay a decade earlier, and he had embarked on a genre of interdisciplinary, highly personal nonfiction that was well ahead of its time. "I don't have any models for the kind of 'history' I am trying to write," he told Utley in a letter. "I don't have any models of methodology . . . and I have no compendium of truths to rely upon, and yet I aspire for something sounder, more objective than 'so it seems to me.'" The same could be said, two decades later, for *Young Men and Fire*. It's likely that the Custer story finally proved insufficiently personal for Maclean, who as a writer would finally surmount many of the same challenges only when he opened the door upon his own past.

Maclean held a complex, ambivalent view of Custer. By the time he turned to writing about him, the cult of hagiographic veneration, maintained for decades by Custer's widow, had weakened. Custer had been mythologized as a monumental figure in this last white stand against hordes of reds, but his reputation began to crack in the 1950s, and novels such as Thomas Berger's *Little Big Man* (1964), and the subsequent film of the same name, completed the demolition. Maclean was under no delusions about Custer, a vainglorious fool who had graduated last in his West Point class and who didn't measure up as a tragic hero. Yet he remained fascinated by what he called "a certain type of 'leaders of horse' from Alexander the Great to Patton," and as late as 1971 he whimsically told Utley that he might "start back on Custer." In 1970 Bruce A. Rosenberg published *Custer and the Epic of Defeat*, a scholarly work in comparative mythology that covers some of the ground that most interested Maclean. But by then Maclean had let loose "the waters of memory," as he calls them in *A River Runs through It*, and had begun writing his "reminiscent stories." Within a few more years, the Smokejumpers who perished in the Mann Gulch fire—also young, elite, and doomed—had taken the place of the Seventh Cavalry soldiers as Maclean's subject for an exploration of tragedy in nonfiction form. The Smokejumpers, like Paul Maclean, died too young. As important, in those young Smokejumpers Maclean saw himself in his imagined, other life: a hurrying youth brandishing a Pulaski whom we fleetingly glimpse down his untraveled road.

For several years during the 1960s, Maclean suffered months of ill health—stomach flu, dysentery, kidney and prostate infections, fever—and spent over half of 1964 in the hospital. By then Jessie had contracted emphysema and never regained robust health, cancer finally claiming her in 1968. In the final sentence of *Young Men and Fire*, Maclean recalls Jessie "on her brave and lonely way to death," embodying, like the Smokejumpers, "courage struggling for oxygen."

By the time Maclean reached "three score years and ten" in December 1972, his physical health had improved and he turned up the lights on his youth. His sharp autobiographical focus enabled him to define the relationship of life—his life—to art. Maclean enjoyed talking about his aesthetic principles, particularly the way in which he construed his life to have occasionally, mysteriously, transformed itself into story: story with plot and characters that he didn't author or control. The British Romantic poet William Wordsworth remained one of Maclean's primary influences, since Wordsworth insistently addressed this conversion of life's random moments and raw materials into the charged, happily shaped textures and structures of poetry. It was Wordsworth who, in the "Preface" to his *Lyrical Ballads* (1798), famously changed the course of poetry by defining it as "the spontaneous overflow of powerful feelings . . . recollected in tranquility." Maclean came to see the genesis of art in similar terms, as the sustained, disciplined recollection in tranquility, and borrowed Wordsworth's notion of "spots of time" to describe those moments in his past when, looking back upon them, he felt his life had become a story. Maclean's writing expresses and confirms those Wordsworthian transformations of one's life. It is the outer sign of a hard-won, inner grace.

The idea of life shaping itself occasionally into story is one that Maclean elaborated in several essays and interviews, but he wrote about it most memorably near the beginning of USFS 1919:

> I had as yet no notion that life every now and then becomes literature—
> not for long, of course, but long enough to be what we best remember,
> and often enough so that what we eventually come to mean by life
> are those moments when life, instead of going sideways, backwards,
> forward, or nowhere at all, lines out straight, tense and inevitable, with
> a complication, climax, and, given some luck, a purgation, as if life had
> been made and not happened.

The passage amounts to an aesthetic credo. Maclean never would have adopted and expressed it in these terms had he not absorbed Aristotle's notions, in his *Poetics*, about the essential psychology of tragedy ("complication" and "climax" leading to "purgation"). The very shape of the sentence demonstrates how the drab bombardments of the mundane can give way to the superior *order* of literature, which possesses, as Aristotle urged, a beginning, middle, and end—what are sometimes called the unities. If life is *made*, it reveals rhythm and design.

Yet the most revealing words in Maclean's aesthetic, quoted above, must be "every now and then." Maclean's temperament and his writing oscillate between the hope that this is true and the fear it is not. He swings between conviction and profound uncertainty, as there is no telling what pieces of life might be apprehended and shaped into some form he can call literature, or whether that might happen at all. This fundamental tension offers an essential clue to Maclean's fiction and nonfiction. His prose never moves far from a sense of despair, a fear that life merely happens, incapable of being charged with meaning and grace. The statement from USFS 1919 expresses Maclean's idealism and desire, but also the doubt so characteristic of his voice.

Rhythm and design also form cornerstone aesthetic principles for Maclean. In fact, these principles fuse the aesthetic with the theological (derived from Maclean's Presbyterian upbringing) and the philosophical. Maclean wants to see literature rescuing life from randomness, above all the unfathomable chaos found in "the problem of defeat"—madness in old age, self-destructiveness in youth, or the premature arrival of death for elite young men. I earlier remarked upon Maclean's stylistic fondness for triadic series or cadences, which in their regularity suggest the kind of order observed in those Aristotelian unities. One hears that triadic rhythm when life "lines out straight, tense and inevitable," as indeed in the title "Logging and Pimping and 'Your Pal, Jim'" and the subtitle *The Ranger, the Cook, and a Hole in the Sky.* One source of Maclean's appreciation for design in the mountains of home was the landscape art of USFS photographer K. D. Swan (1911–1947). Swan taught Maclean how to "compose," that is, discover ordered visual structures in lines of peaks, canyons, and rivers that are analogous to what he sought to create in his stories. In USFS 1919 Maclean calls the mountains of Idaho "poems of geology," and he lyrically describes the Continental Divide in the Bitterroots as a dance in three parts with two geometric shapes: "It was triangles going up and ovals coming down, and on the divide it was springtime in August."

Because Maclean taught close analyses of Shakespeare's and the Romantics' verse rhythm, his students learned scansion, the method of parsing the metrical structure of a poetic line. Scansion used to be taught in schools generations ago, and through it Maclean's students would have learned the almost unconscious grip and power of Shakespeare's iambic pentameter (a line of five pairs of syllables, or "feet," with the second syllable of each pair accented). In fact, a discussion of iambic pentameter works its way into one of the funniest scenes Maclean ever wrote, in which the narrator of USFS 1919 eavesdrops on "a pimp and a whore screwing up and down the bed" and scans her indignant refrain: "You are as crooked as a tub of guts." (Perhaps no other passage in Maclean so well shows him cultivating his "tough flower girl" persona.)

Maclean sought the supple rhythms of verse in his prose because rhythm manifested, more than anything else, the presence of design. He subscribed to Chaucer's conviction that a poet is a "maker" (the root of "poetry" is the Greek *poiesis*, meaning "to make"), a wordsmith who forges his materials into something elegant and pleasing and enduring. Consider the opening sentence of USFS 1919, which Maclean rewrote several times and was quite proud of, citing it on occasion as an example of sentence rhythm. It is a poem of adolescence: "I was young and I thought I was tough and I knew it was beautiful and I was a little bit crazy but hadn't noticed it yet." Here Maclean strings five short independent clauses together with coordinating conjunctions, and the sentence's rhythms show him a direct descendant of a line of American writers running from Mark Twain through Hemingway. The sentence, which evidences an older narrator assessing his earlier self, summarizes the cockiness and intimates the gradual maturing of the teenage narrator, the autobiographical Mac, youngest member of Ranger Bill Bell's Forest Service crew. The clause Maclean was most proud of, "and I knew it was beautiful," captures the idealism of young adulthood when life's possibilities seem endless, and the novella's physical setting realizes this idealism. "Beautiful" was Maclean's talismanic word, one he claimed Presbyterians were shy about using but that he picked up from his father. For Maclean, beauty could be realized in the mountains and rivers of Montana or in the physical grace of his brother as he worked a trout stream, but it was also the aim of his carefully controlled sentences, which pulse as deliberately as the casting technique the Maclean boys learned "Presbyterian-style, on a metronome."

. . . .

How did Maclean's personal style and aesthetics shape the two novellas and longer book upon which his reputation rests? I have already referred to a couple of scenes and quoted a few sentences from USFS 1919, which functions like a bildungsroman, that is, the education of the protagonist into the greater world. As with the autobiographical narrator in "Logging and Pimping," Mac survives his harsh work detail, including some forced time alone at a fire lookout. More significantly, in the novella he learns a lesson in vulnerability and compassion through the cook, his antagonist. Mac's ego is checked, and by the summer's—and novella's—end, he emerges a bit less hotheaded and more thoughtful than he had started out. He acts less superior to the other, older crew members, and Ranger Bill Bell, the boss Mac admires deeply, suspected Mac capable of such growth all along. The experience is transformational because the narrator—and Maclean right behind him—sees his life self-consciously, for the first time as a story.

Maclean opens and closes USFS 1919 quoting two lines from Victorian poet Matthew Arnold's "The Buried Life": "And then he thinks he knows / The hills where his life rose . . ." At the beginning this topographic image of one's youth serves as an epigraph, but at the end Maclean declares these lines "are now part of the story." They ground the novella just as the Bitterroot Mountains of Lolo National Forest—particularly Blodgett Canyon and Pass, and Elk Summit beyond them—specify this writer's native topography. The novella circles back to its beginning to underline the changes in the main character. As in the more famous novella Maclean wrote after it, memorable scenes of low comedy balance passages reflecting Mac's growth and commemorating those expert with their hands in the woods and mountains. "Logging and Pimping" describes a logging camp and the rhythms of cutting old-growth trees with a two-man, six-foot crosscut saw. USFS 1919 celebrates the knowledge of Ranger Bill Bell, Mac's role model, who handles the pack mules, loading and balancing their panniers and deftly tying off these loads and the lines running between mules with particular knots. A pack train resembled a work of art. Bell ties and links his motley crew with similar finesse.

In its closing, after Mac shakes hands with Bell and watches him recede with his string of horses, Maclean illuminates the scene:

> Then the string swung to the left and trotted in a line toward Blodgett Canyon, with a speck of a dog to the side faithfully keeping always the same distance from the horses. Gradually, the trotting dog and horses became generalized into creeping animals and the one to the side became a speck and those in a line became just a line. Slowly the line disintegrated into pieces and everything floated up and away in dust and all that settled out was one dot, like Morse code. The dot must have been Morse code for a broad back and a black hat. After a while, the sunlight itself became disembodied. There was just nothing at all to sunlight,

and the mouth of Blodgett Canyon was just nothing but a gigantic hole in the sky.

"The Big Sky," as we say in Montana.

Maclean's geometric recession marks an epiphany for both character and reader. It is as though Mac's summer, epitomized by his crew boss, expands and diffuses itself across the entire visible sky, and his future. For the first and only time, Maclean cites the third part of his subtitle, which subsumes the human characters, the ranger and the cook, who most shape Mac. Maclean favored metaphors of geometry to symbolize that *design* essential to his worldview. The abstraction of geometry, that reduction to lines, forms a key signature in Maclean's writing. Though the shapes shrink and disappear, the vision expands because we understand, along with Mac, that his life now "lines out straight, tense, and inevitable." It's as though Bell has disappeared into one of K. D. Swan's black-and-white landscapes or through the lower center of a sprawling, glowing Albert Bierstadt canvas.

In Montana's Bitterroot valley, Blodgett Canyon, running due west until it curls south to Blodgett Lake, looms as one of the most imposing in the Bitterroot range. The walls of the lower canyon, hundreds of feet high, attract rock climbers, and its mouth, a giant V, yawns just west and north of the booming town of Hamilton. Maclean's visionary closing inflates and elevates the V into a figure, a hole in the sky, common in Native American tales of cosmogony. It also gestures to A. B. Guthrie's enormously influential historical novel, The Big Sky (1947), whose title became the official epithet for Montana after 1961: Montana is the only state whose license plate slogan derives from a novel. Years later William Kittredge, who had known Maclean for years through the project of writing a screenplay for River, used the same figure, titling his memoir Hole in the Sky (1991).

If USFS 1919 centers on Mac himself, A River Runs thought It puts Maclean's brother at the center of a family that eternally loves him but is eternally unable to help him. That homily, voiced by both Norman as narrator and by Reverend Maclean, marks Maclean's best fiction as a universal human fable and locates "the problem of defeat" agonizingly within the family. River borrows as it rewrites and darkens the parable of the Prodigal Son, and it relentlessly exposes the role of being my brother's keeper: a rack we cannot avoid but squirm upon as helpless witness. Certainly there is a great weight of painful confession in the autobiographical narrator, who fails to help let alone save this brother. And the failure is not entirely explained as Paul's refusal to be helped, proud and out of control though he is. Norman often talked about his family's Scotch restraint, in which emotions were rarely expressed. Paul was the only one who broke through that restraint regularly: as Maclean liked to recall, Paul was the only man in the family who openly held Mrs. Maclean in his arms, kissing her and laughing.

After its publication in 1976, Maclean enjoyed discussing the structure of *A River Runs through It* and otherwise playing literary critic of his own work, as the interview in this volume attests. He would gleefully paraphrase a reluctant student at Minnesota's Southwest State University who reduced *River* to a skeletal formula: these two brothers go fishing, then they go fishing again, then they drink, and later they fish again. Maclean claimed she got it right. But he also took special pride when fly-fishing guides praised *River* as an effective manual on fly-fishing. He had, indeed, structured the novella so that each fishing scene progressively elaborates the art of fly-fishing. The novella climaxes with Paul making "one big cast for one last big fish," and then his mighty struggle with a huge trout, "the last fish we were ever to see Paul catch."

This last scene, Paul's apotheosis, seals the connections between religion and fly-fishing announced in the novella's opening sentence. Early in the book, Maclean explicitly extends Reverend Maclean's judgment about our fallen nature to the reader—"if you have never picked up a fly rod before, you will soon find it factually and theologically true that man by nature is a damn mess." And he explains that the only redemption lies in the beauty we achieve by "picking up God's rhythms." "He is beautiful," Reverend Maclean remarks finally after Paul lands the big trout, but that glimpse of redemption is not enough to save Paul from the "damn mess" of the rest of his life. At the end of their final fishing trip together, Maclean writes, "It would be hard to find three men side by side who knew better what a river was saying." But a river "has so many things to say that it is hard to know what it says to each of us," and with that qualification he relates the sudden news of Paul's murder. The Big Blackfoot still harbors words, however, "and some of the words are theirs." *River* climaxes, then, between the desire to believe in redemption and immortality, and their elusiveness before the ultimately unknowable—a river, or a brother.

Maclean insistently employs the metaphor of "reading the water" in *River*. In doing so, he aligns himself with an American literary tradition seen, for example, in Hemingway's "Big Two-Hearted River" and Twain's *Life on the Mississippi*. Paul is an expert at reading currents and so, in other ways, is Norman. In a passage comparable to the discovery in USFS 1919 that life occasionally transforms itself into story, Maclean writes, "Stories of life are more often like rivers than books." Elsewhere, Maclean writes, "I knew a story had begun, perhaps long ago near the sound of water. And I sensed that ahead I would meet something that would never erode so there would be a sharp turn, deep circles, a deposit, and quietness." It is a statement that recalls his Matthew Arnold epigraph to USFS 1919 while shifting the geography of knowing from mountain to river.

. . . .

A River Runs through It closes perfectly with the utterance, "I am haunted by waters," but Maclean was equally haunted by fire. His interest in wildfire had smoldered during his early Forest Service summers, particularly when fighting the Fish Creek fire (cited in both USFS 1919 and "Black Ghost"), and flamed after the Mann Gulch tragedy of August 5, 1949. By the time A River Runs through It and Other Stories appeared in print, Maclean was hard at work on his book about Mann Gulch. His research took him repeatedly to Forest Service headquarters in Washington, D.C., as well as Region One headquarters in Missoula. Already in his mid-seventies, he also traveled by boat, horse, and four-wheel drive into Mann Gulch, sometimes accompanied by his research partner Laird Robinson and, on one occasion, by Robert Sallee and Walter Rumsey, the two survivors of the fire. Maclean was after an exact account of how the tragedy came about, including a minute-by-minute reconstruction of the fire's course. Along the way, he encountered cryptic or missing files, reluctant or uncooperative relatives, and, most significantly, his own relentless self-criticism. Letters to friends, some of which are reprinted in this volume, attest to his periodic doubts as well as his determination to finish and publish the large manuscript he initially called "The Great Blow-Up," and later Young Men and Fire. Maclean researched and revised for more than a decade, and by the last years of his life, when ill health all but ended his work, he had a full but still rough draft. His long labor and inability, or unwillingness, to complete it are thematically inscribed in the book. As editor Alan Thomas wrote in a publisher's note to the book, "Young Men and Fire had become a story in search of itself as a story, following where Maclean's compassion led it. As long as the manuscript sustained itself and its author in this process of discovery, it had to remain in some sense unfinished."

Young Men and Fire is structured it as a triptych, though part 3, only eight pages, functions as both climax and epilogue to parts 1 and 2, which are almost exactly equal in length. Maclean divided his manuscript into sixty-three short chapters. When he prepared the work for publication, Thomas faithfully observed Maclean's triadic structure but consolidated these mini-chapters into fifteen chapters, and added a prologue, "Black Ghost," that he found among Maclean's papers. Roughly speaking, part 1 narrates the minute-by-minute story of the blowup, part 2 narrates the story of Maclean's research and eventual understanding of the fire, and part 3 serves as an imaginative funeral service and benediction, as the men meet their death. Part 1 encodes physical knowledge, part 2 presents scientific and a kind of metaphysical knowledge, and part 3, spiritual knowledge. *Fire*'s achievement rests in the insistent way Maclean approaches, closely and personally, the unknowable: the final minutes and seconds when the Smokejumpers are running for their lives as the towering, suffocating inferno overtakes them. More generally, it rests in the way Maclean concedes and makes a theme of his uncertainty and doubt in the face of unrecoverable history.

Maclean was intrigued by resemblances between what happened to Custer's men at Little Bighorn on June 25, 1876, and what happened to the Smokejumpers in this dry box canyon August 5, 1949, and he evokes the Seventh Cavalry in *Young Men and Fire*, though without pressing the parallel. In both cases, the speed and seeming inevitability of disaster read like a Greek tragedy, and Maclean's attention in *Fire* to exact chronology—correlations by minute and location—reflects his admiration of Greek tragedy's concentration and speed. In these conditions, the players have no choices except how to face their already-determined destinies. As he says about the Smokejumpers in *Fire*'s opening, "They were still so young they hadn't learned to count the odds and to sense they might owe the universe a tragedy." Thus both in his own struggle and in his subject, Maclean voices "the problem of defeat."

The stakes in *Fire* are high: Is catastrophe beyond human ken? Can disaster be made to own some sense, or is the universe as capriciously destructive as mad old King Lear believes it to be? Fittingly, Mann Gulch belongs, as Maclean notes, to a geological zone that scientists call the "Disturbed Belt." *Fire*'s drama unfolds between faith and knowledge, the need to believe and the ultimate failure to know as much as we need. Maclean's articulation of these core questions takes by now familiar form and sustains his aesthetic principles: "This is a catastrophe that we hope will not end where it began; it might go on and become a story." Yet his uncertainty and the anguished irresolution of his nonfictional quest give the book an emotional power that is new in Maclean's work. He closes *Fire*'s first chapter by memorably summarizing where he hopes his quest will lead:

It would be a start to a story if this catastrophe were found to have circled around out there somewhere until it could return to itself with explanations of its own mysteries and with the grief it left behind, not removed, because grief has its own place at or near the end of things, but altered somewhat by the addition of something like wonder. . . . If we could say something like this and be speaking both accurately and somewhat like Shelley when he spoke of clouds and winds, then what we would be talking about would start to change from catastrophe without a filled-in story to what could be called the story of a tragedy, but tragedy would be only a part of it, as it is of life.

This passage paraphrases Aristotle's experiential definition of tragedy formulated in the *Poetics*: our witnessing tragedy on stage arouses pity and fear, which are purged from us such that we emerge cleansed and ennobled. *Fire* contains Maclean's most extended discussion of tragedy in the chapter reprinted here, and parts 2 and 3 model the kind of Aristotelian purgation he recommended. The passage also suggests that one kind of knowledge is never enough to translate catastrophe into story. It will not be enough, for example, to explain what happened in terms of the science of fire behavior. So Maclean invokes the "most Romantic of the Romantic poets," Percy Shelley, referring to two poems, "The Clouds" and "Ode to the West Wind," which he elsewhere describes as "mixtures of the poetic and scientific imaginations." Ghosts occasionally appear in *Fire*, and Maclean makes repeated references to the Stations of the Cross, the Via Dolorosa, and the Four Horsemen of the Apocalypse. *Fire* thus embraces not only the graphs and mathematical formulas of fire scientists, but poetry, Christian symbolism, and metaphysical speculation.

    Young Men and Fire is not as tightly shaped or written as *A River Runs through It*, and Maclean faced many more difficulties writing it. But more than *River*, it braids together the strands of Maclean's life as a woodsman, scholar, and writer. And it is a strangely moving and gripping book, one suffused with remarkable writing. *Fire* painfully registers the impasse suggested by the statement "it is all cockeyed and it all fits," and, seeking to restore "the key to the . . . eternal arch of Montana sky," worries continually that it cannot.

· · · ·

The Norman Maclean Reader includes six hitherto unpublished pieces by Maclean, five of them chapters from his uncompleted book on Custer. Readers for the first time will discover Maclean's obsession with Custer and Little Bighorn, and glimpse the unfinished book that foreshadows and informs both *River* and *Fire*. The anthology provides a comprehensive cross-section of Maclean's writing, arranging the material mostly chronologically across thirty-six years, from his 1956 essay on Edward S. Luce, coauthored with Robert Utley, to "Black Ghost" and the eighth chapter from *Young Men and Fire*. Seven of the pieces included here were written or published between 1974 and 1979—the years immediately surrounding *A River Runs through It and Other Stories*—and the interview dates from 1987, when Maclean was still working hard on *Young Men and Fire*.

The four sets of correspondence each highlight a different facet of Maclean the literary critic and writer. When readers turn from a writer's published work to his letters, they travel inside to more private, less guarded territory. The letters to Robert Utley begin before their collaboration on the Luce article and extend well beyond the time that Maclean gave up on his Custer book. The letters to Marie Borroff also cover a broad span of years. By contrast, the letters to Nick Lyons date from a shorter span in the late 1970s and track the growing reputation of Maclean as a writer. And finally, the letters to Lois Jansson cover three years (1979–81) when Maclean was most actively researching and rewriting what became *Fire*. Each set of letters demonstrates Maclean's capacity for friendship and conveys his distinctive voice with particular immediacy.

Here, then, readers can see the themes and characteristic style of *River* and *Fire* in new contexts and gain new biographical insights into one of the most remarkable and unexpected careers in American letters. As his third published book, published thirty-two years after his first and sixteen after his second, *The Norman Maclean Reader* provides the long-missing third panel in Maclean's biggest triptych.

The Custer Writings

Edward S. Luce

. . . .

COMMANDING GENERAL

. . . .

(RETIRED), DEPARTMENT

. . . .

OF THE LITTLE BIGHORN

. . . .

Norman Maclean & Robert M. Utley

Norman Maclean's 1956 profile of Edward S. Luce, coauthored with Robert M. Utley, pays tribute to a retiring superintendent of the Custer Battlefield National Monument. Until it appeared in Montana: The Magazine of Western History, *Maclean's only substantial publications were two scholarly articles and a military manual. Utley has said the article bears Maclean's impress much more than his own, and in it we first see Maclean's playful irony and wit, and tightly constructed style of writing. A biographical note accompanying the article notes that Maclean "has devoted years to an exhaustive psychological study of the golden-maned soldier, George Armstrong Custer. We look forward to its early publication."*

I t was in the year—even in the season of the year—marking the 80th anniversary of the Battle of the Little Big Horn that Major Edward S. Luce retired as Superintendent of the Custer Battlefield National Monument.

He and the Hill have long been closely connected. Indeed, like the Hill itself, he has become part legend, part history, and part an inseparable mixture of both. Some tourists have pointed him out as the sole survivor of the Battle, others as Captain Keogh, and one mother was heard to tell her son that he was Comanche. But no tourist since 1940 has ever been mistaken about two facts—the Superintendent was 7th Cavalry, and the Hill is a memorial to its dead.

"Edward S. Luce: Commanding General (Retired), Department of the Little Bighorn" is reprinted from *Montana: The Magazine of Western History* 6, no. 3 (Summer 1956): 51–55. Courtesy of the Montana Historical Society.

Since the 7th Cavalry was not organized in 1066, it may be irrelevant to trace the Major's ancestry back to Count de Luci, aide to William the Conqueror. More likely, genealogy proper begins with the Major's great-uncle, Andrew Jackson Smith, first colonel of the 7th Cavalry, with Lt. Col. George Armstrong Custer as second in command. In any event, the Major's post-natal connection with the 7th began early. His family knew both the Custers and Godfreys, and his memories of Mrs. Custer go back as far as 1890. Although Gen. Godfrey often bounced him on his knee, it was Young Corbett, then lightweight champion of the world, who gave him the bounce that started him on his way to the Custer Battlefield. Young Corbett was touring the country, offering $50 to any one who could stay with him for four rounds. Edward S. Luce lasted three rounds and a certain number of seconds about which there has never been any argument. Two months later, after the imprint of the canvas had faded from his back, he enlisted in the 7th Cavalry—on the strength of the first three rounds.

At Fort Riley, he was assigned to headquarters as a clerk where four survivors of Reno's command at the Battle of the Little Big Horn were present in the flesh compiling a history of the 7th Cavalry, now an item for collectors who don't ask about prices. The clerk's assignment was to take down the sacred words of Edgerly, Godfrey, Hare, and Varnum. So he was introduced to history almost as soon as to the saber-drill, and has never forgotten either. In 1939, he published *Keogh, Comanche, and Custer*, itself already a collector's item and invaluable for any close understanding of the 7th Cavalry at the time of the Battle.

But from the time of his first enlistment (1907) until he was gassed in World War I, he was soldier of fortune, with only a few months between enlistments. During one of these periods he became a motorman in Dorchester, Massachusetts, so that he could drive by his home and ignore the stop signals of certain members of his family who had disowned him. One day, while he was asleep in the carbarns, an organ-grinder came by, turned the crank, and out came Garryowen, battlesong of the 7th. Sgt. Luce awoke looking at a monkey that reminded him of the commander of E Troop. He gave the monkey a nickel, the monkey saluted, and the sergeant reenlisted, but the 7th had been sent to the Philippines and he found himself in the Coast Artillery.

Between hitches in 1914, he put in three months fighting with the Mexican rebels. American machine-gunners were at a premium, and it was safer to get captured than to escape. So he was kept busy changing hat bands from green to red to white and shouting "Viva Villa," "Viva Carranza," "Viva Madero," and sometimes just "Viva." Re-enlisting, he was assigned to the 12th U.S. Cavalry (known, but not affectionately, as the "Royal Siberian Uhlans") who had the job of guarding eight Mexican armies that escaped across the border—some of which he had just served in.

In 1917 he was commissioned captain in the Quartermaster Corps. His transport was torpedoed off the coast of Ireland and he was gassed in France, a disability that ultimately ended his active military career. For a while, he tried banking and acquired the long cigarette-holder which is the only visible part of him that does not seem to derive from the 7th Cavalry. But the banking experience has been important behind the scenes, for the growing popularity of the Monument has meant, among other things, that it has become big business. Before coming to the Hill, he also had experience in meeting pilgrims at a public shrine. For a short time he was Assistant Superintendent at the Arlington National Cemetery where daily he greeted the fathers, mothers, grandfathers, grandmothers, brothers, sisters, and wives of the Unknown Soldier. Not until coming to the Hill, however, did he greet pilgrims who wanted to know whether the Continental Divide was a WPA project.

Mrs. Luce says that she never did anything spectacular except keep out of trouble until she met Major Luce, and the Major adds that she has been in nothing else since. She wouldn't make this added comment herself, but might admit that she has never ceased to be amazed. She was teaching high school in St. Louis when they were married in 1938, and since then she has had to revise considerably the theories about educational psychology she learned at Drake University back in Iowa. The 1938 edition of the Major has also been subject to slight revisions—certain words have been deleted from the text, a gentle "Address to the Reader" has been added, and last year, when he was on a speaking tour, friends telegraphed ahead to each other the news that he was taking bubble-baths. Mrs. Luce's previous training in history has had even more important effects. She is one of the best informed of all those who have studied Custer, and was Historical Aide at the Museum (ten years without salary) where she spent most of each day cataloging collections, following leads that might bring new items of importance to the Museum, conducting the research necessary to answer the hundreds of letters from scholars and writers, etc. It is hard to see how she found time to make a home out of the big stone house down the Hill, and it is an even greater mystery how she made all who entered feel that it was their home, too. Mrs. Luce is very embarrassed when nice things are said about her.

Major and Mrs. Luce became custodians of the Hill in 1940 when Custer

Battlefield National Cemetery, as it was then known, was transferred to the National Park Service and the Major was appointed Superintendent. In 1946 its name was changed to the Custer Battlefield National Monument, but much more than the name has changed since the Luces arrived as is indicated by the increase in the number of visitors—from 80,000 in 1940 to 140,000 last year.

The accompanying changes on the Battlefield itself tell only part of the story, although certainly one problem has been to make the Battlefield accessible to the American public and to draw them to it. But pressure groups are always proposing changes that would leave the Battlefield with its story obliterated by California mausoleums, courthouse statues, and concessions selling hot dogs, moss agates, petrified wood, fool's gold, and warm beer. Perhaps the second is the harder problem—to keep the Battlefield so that it may be seen as it was by those who made it history.

To a greater or lesser degree, the National Park Service is always confronted by these two conflicting problems—to get Americans to see its history, walk in it, and touch it, and yet to leave its history intact. But there are always those who see only timber or grazing lands, or would just like to look around—for minerals or oil. Although the Battlefield is not without some of these economic threats, its greatest menace is the widespread belief that the dead should always be covered with domestic grass and the grass should be frequently watered. Yet what could be more becoming to these dead who fell on sand and sagebrush than the sagebrush that half hides the simple stones placed where their bodies were found?

The Major has instinctively assumed that he was given a military assignment, and he has held the Hill. He commands the post, and the Stars and Stripes float over it. It is more even than a military trust. It is the hill where the Ten Commandments were given to Moses—and to him, and a voice sounds out over the 750 acres of the enclosure when a tourist is seen removing a yucca plant or a clump of sagebrush.

But the ultimate justification for preserving history is that it may be seen and understood. In 1940, the road from the main highway extended just beyond the Monument, under which lie the bones of the enlisted men who fought in Custer's command; today, tourists can follow the 3½-mile flow of battle on an all-weather road which continues down the Battle Ridge, crosses Medicine Tail Coulee where Custer may or may not have first met the Indians, and ends at Reno Hill (although the Major hopes that funds will be found someday to complete the road to the main highway so that the tourists will not have to retrace their route). It was a fight to get this road, and it is a fight to keep it open in all weather with a small force and a small budget. Along the road there are interpretative signs at key points, and these did not come easily, either. The guide service established by the Major is as fine as will be found at any historical site. Before the Museum was built, the Major stationed the guides at the Monument and they were expected to have the same all-weather properties as his road. Scheduled talks are now given in the observation room of the Museum, from which a wide view of the actual scene of fighting is supplemented by a relief map of the whole battle area that cannot be seen from any one point near the Hill.

Of course, the Museum itself is the most important addition since the Major became Superintendent.[1] History grinds slowly and painfully in building a museum. It was not until 1952 that the Battlefield Museum was officially dedicated by Gen. Wainwright and Col. Brice C. W. Custer, but it was first envisioned by figures from another era—Mrs. Custer herself, General Miles, Governor Joe Dixon, and Senator T. J. Walsh. Major Luce worked with them, and, after their deaths, with Senator Burton K. Wheeler who continued the fight. In 1939, Congress authorized the construction of the Museum, but inscrutably failed to appropriate funds to construct it, and the war years that followed should have ended any hope whatsoever. Instead, Major and Mrs. Luce went on campaigning and planning and in 1947 completed their "Museum Prospectus," which is the basis of the present arrangement of exhibits. They not only made plans; they went out and acquired museum collections for a museum that might never get to an architect's drawing board, and to do this took much more than belief. It took a lot of the Old Army humor, sentiment, and dramatic sense to get owners to part with almost priceless historical possessions but fortunately many of these owners were themselves tied to the Old Army by family and by sentiment. For both tourists and historians the Museum today gives life and added meaning to the silent stones outside. For the tourists, there are dioramas of scenes from the Battle, displays of actual Battle relics, and uniforms and photographs of many of those who crossed the divide between the Rosebud and the Little Big Horn at high noon on June 25 eighty years ago. In addition, for historians and writers there are letters, diaries, official papers, newspaper clippings, and a library containing many rare and valuable works.

Undoubtedly, these changes on the Hill partly explain the increasing

1. For a full description of the Museum, see Harry B. Robinson's article ("The Custer Battlefield Museum") in the July, 1952 issue of this magazine.

numbers who come there, but the Hill has not stood waiting for the American public to come to it. The 7th Cavalry never believed in waiting around for somebody to find out about it. The Major has worked with local chambers of commerce, and state and national historical societies. He has eaten roast lamb, mashed potatoes, and green peas, and made speeches. He has written articles, unveiled paintings and statues, and appeared on radio. He has politicked with politicians, and ambushed writers who never knew what happened to them—even after Cheyenne and Sioux warriors began to gallop through their stories shouting Hi-yi-yi. It is little wonder, therefore, that in the year before his retirement he was given the National Achievement Award by The Westerners, or that at his retirement the National Park Service presented him with a citation for outstanding service.

Yet, of his many honors, he probably most cherishes the one he received long ago when he was made Sergeant, Troop B, 7th U.S. Cavalry. This is the honor that he has always worn, and he has worn it even in his unguarded moments. Often in the evening, for instance, the old Sarge of the 7th would sit watching the shadows of rabbits shyly appear from the sagebrush and grave markers. The name he called them were not poetical names but the names of old troopers. "Hey, Horseface Klotz," he would call, and an oval shadow would come toward him, stop, and then come on again.

Undoubtedly, too, he is on friendly terms with many other shadows that move in moonlight through the grave markers.

Sir, the Hill will miss you.

From the Unfinished

....

Custer Manuscript

....

For several years, primarily in 1959–63, Maclean struggled to
write a book about Custer and the Battle of the Little Bighorn. He
tried to define the battle as ritual tragedy and planned a book in
three parts: part 1, "The Battle"; part 2, "The Marks on Those
Who Survived"; and part 3, "Our Marks." Judging from this
blueprint, Maclean was most interested in the continuing story
of the battle, the myriad ways in which it remains a part of our
national mythology. Maclean saw Little Bighorn as one litmus test
of our changing attitudes about the American West, particularly
the frontier military campaigns that almost wiped out many tribes
of the Great Plains and Rocky Mountains. For many reasons,
including health problems, he was unable to complete the book he
envisioned. He knew he was writing about the battle—its principal
players and afterlife—in ways markedly different from western
historians, and finally could not make the material fit into the
conception of classical tragedy he held in highest regard. He drafted
and worked on fourteen of his projected twenty chapters, none of
which have ever before been published. Maclean's letters to his
friend the distinguished western historian Robert Utley poignantly
attest to his struggle to define and complete his project, and his
eventual abandonment of it.

   In these five extracts from Maclean's first, incomplete book, we
see Maclean's distinct style emerge, as well as ideas about tragedy
that receive full expression in Young Men and Fire. Included here
are three of the four chapters from part 2: chapter 1, "The Hill";
chapter 2, "The Sioux"; and chapter 3, "The Cheyennes." In the
first, Maclean announces his fundamental interest in the "after-life"
of the battle and focuses upon the subsequent changes in status of
the battlefield itself. The next two chapters tell contrasting stories of
dispersal and defeat of the primary tribes who fought the Seventh
Cavalry at Little Bighorn—their Pyrrhic victory. Also included
is the fourth chapter, "In Business," of the projected part 3. Here,
Maclean's irony rings loudly as he links the battle with subsequent

advertising, particularly the most famous popular art image of the battle, a favorite saloon lithograph, with the growth of a major American brewery, Anheuser-Busch. "In Business" shows a drier, more satiric side of Maclean, who savors the fact that Custer, a teetotaler, was elaborately deployed in saloons to sell beer. Finally, the opening two sections of what was to be his final chapter, "Shrine to Defeat," reveal Maclean drawing together several strands from his overall project under the aegis of Sigmund Freud's Civilization and Its Discontents, an excerpt of which serves as the chapter's epigraph. These pages elaborate the connections between that epigraph and some of Maclean's conclusions about the aftermath of the battle. In addition to Freud, Maclean cites George Orwell in exploring "our tendency to memorialize some of our disasters."

Note: Maclean's citations, however incomplete, appear here in his footnotes as they do in the original manuscript.

PART II

The Marks on Those Who Survived

"There are rewards for hawks and dogs when they have done us service; but for a soldier that hazards his limbs in a battle, nothing but a kind of geometry is his last supportation."—Bosola in The Duchess of Malfi, I, l

CHAPTER 1

· ·

The Hill

· ·

E very battle has something of a personality and a personal after-life. But it is true of battles as of men—only some have a deep personal life of their own with the capacity to affect permanently the lives of those associated with them and to be known everywhere by those who know almost nothing about them. The battle of the Little Bighorn, which from the ordinary historical point of view lacks any great significance, has been an immense personal force altering the feelings, beliefs, daily routines and larger destinies of those who survived it or were related to the dead. It has given a structure to their lives, however harsh the outlines, for (it seems that) the dead who continue to live become abstracted into patterns and are transformed and transform others, as it were, into a kind of geometry.

To the large world outside, the Battle has many personal traits that attract a wide diversity of personalities. It has the power of an endless argument, one of the world's battles destined to be fought forever. More has been written about it than about any American battle excepting possibly the Battle of Gettysburg,[1] and at times with as much fury and general confusion as darkened Custer Hill late in the afternoon of June 25, 1876. Some of its power, undoubtedly, is in its artistry. It is almost a ready-made plot with ready-made characters for that large class of writers who lack the power to invent plots and characters of their own. To painters of similar abilities, it is close to a finished composition—a hilltop in a big sky; repeating the circle of the hilltop, a circle of kneeling men in blue; within the embattled circle a central standing figure highlighted by blond hair; and, surrounding the circle of blue, larger circles of contrast-

---

1. Col. W. A. Graham, *The Custer Myth*, p. xi.

ing redskins. The Battle has also had the power to promote business, draw customers and sell beer. And it has had two powers perhaps deeper than all others—the power of horror and of jest. It shocked the nation as nothing had since the death of Lincoln, leaving permanent marks upon the individuals, families and tribes connected with it. Recently—but only recently—we have become enough at ease with it to make it into a joke. The joke has many variants, some of them dirty and all of them grim, but essentially it is one joke and underneath the many variants is a kindly undertone, as if some joke had been played upon the bluffs of the Little Bighorn for which there should be universal forbearance, on the chance that the joke played there is played some time on all of us. Clearly, our dead are delivered from oblivion when they become a joke on us.

The history of the personality and personal after-life of an event is not history of any commonly recognized kind, and this one, for lack of a classification, may be called the biography of a battle. That the Battle still lives and grows, however, is a fact demonstrable by the ordinary kinds of historical and even statistical evidence—by the number of books written about it, the number of times it appears visually in paintings or on the screen or TV, the number of times it is heard in such common sayings as "so-and-so made his last stand" or "too damn many Indians." But a reality of a somewhat different order has to be explored for the sources of its life, and observations about this reality cannot always be documented with footnotes, since life-after-death, at least in this life, depends upon patterns and geometrical extensions and may of course depend upon much more. Yet what lives beyond its natural self is clearly structured for remembrance. The patterns are partly in the natural thing which must have had a higher sense of form than that of most of the living matter surrounding it. The patterns are also partly superimposed and come from us, who strive or at least feel at times that we should strive to make something structural out of our own lives. The history of this life-after-death, however, involves much more than the matching of two sets of fixed patterns. As there is no life in fixities, so each who achieves immortality must retain something of his past and yet take on new meanings with the passing of time. Unless capable of such organic growth, even immortality dies.

The ground itself upon which the Battle was fought has its own history of death and transfiguration, and it seems right to begin with the reality of the earth and to trace first how this isolated piece of it soon after the Battle became known to the whole world and eventually was transformed into a National Monument. On the Hill itself, which is somewhat symmetrical, there are also lines to be traced. The lines are of white-stone markers and they correspond roughly to the Hill's contours and converge near its top. Each stone is indeed an abstraction of what was found there.

1. THE NEWS

News of the Battle was spread first by mysterious smoke signals in the sky and by mounted warriors, the "moccasin telegraph" of the Plains Indians, and days before news from Terry arrived, apprehensiveness deepened at Ft. Lincoln because the Indians there seemed to know that a big battle had been fought and that Indians had better be quiet about its outcome.[2]

It was by a newspaper scoop, one of the biggest ever made by small western newspapers—not by official report—that word of the Battle first reached the outside world and the War Department.[3] On July 1, Muggins Taylor, one of Gibbon's scouts, had been sent west from the mouth of the Bighorn where Terry had now moved his troops to carry the official sealed report to Ft. Ellis. But a newspaper man met him on his lonely way and it was Taylor's account, not the sealed report, that was the basis for the stories appearing in the Bozeman *Times* of July 2 and the Helena *Herald* of July 4. Since the white man's telegraph lines were down, it was July 6 before eastern newspapers told the country what at first seemed impossible to believe. When interviewed, Gen. Sheridan said, "It comes without any marks of credence," not from any information received by the War Department but from frontier scouts who have "a way of spreading news."[4] So the country paused in the midst of the Centennial Exposition, its pride momentarily supporting its disbelief although not removing its anxiety.

On July 3 at five o'clock in the afternoon the *Far West* left the mouth of the Bighorn with orders to reach Bismarck in "the shortest possible time."[5] For the wounded, the deck had been made into a large mattress with new tarpaulins spread over eighteen inches of marsh grass. The *Far West* also carried a

---

2. *Custer's Luck*, p. 484.

3. There has been controversy even about how the news first reached the outside world. For an authoritative discussion of this controversy, see Harrison Lane's "Custer Massacre: How News First Reached the Outer World," *Montana: Magazine of History*, Vol. III, No. 3 (Summer, 1953), pp. 46–53.

4. *The Conquest of the Missouri*, p. 311.

5. For a detailed account of this trip, see the chapter in *The Conquest of the Missouri* entitled, "The Far West Races with Death."

"confidential" dispatch from Gen. Terry very different from Terry's official dispatch carried west by Taylor to Ft. Ellis. A sentence from it may suggest its guarded import: "For whatever errors he [Custer] may have committed he has paid the penalty and you cannot regret his loss more than I do, but I feel that our plan must have been successful had it been carried out, and I desire you to know the facts."[6] Although meant only for Sheridan and Sherman, this confidential dispatch was soon to become public property and to arouse conflicting indignations. So Terry's "secret" was part of the hurried preparations being made to endow Custer and the Battle with immortality, a part of which depends upon the perpetual motion of a heated argument.

At full steam, the *Far West* slid over sandbars and caromed off the banks of the river on the sharp bends, tumbling the crew to the deck. Then, draped in black and with flag at half-mast, she tied up at Bismarck in the darkness of the night of July 5. "She had covered 710 miles at the average rate of thirteen and one-seventh miles per hour and, though no one stopped to think of it then, she had made herself the speed champion of the Missouri River."[7]

In the office of the Bismarck *Tribune* whose editor, Col. C. A. Lounsberry, was also correspondent for the *New York Herald*,[8] the telegraphers worked in relays sending fifteen thousand words in a day and holding the key between messages by clicking out passages from the New Testament. But again the white man's telegraph lines were down—this time east of St. Paul—so that it was July 7 before the messages reached the east, and the country and Gen. Sheridan received "the marks of credence."

Even before sunrise of the 6th, however, the *Far West* had docked gently at Ft. Abraham Lincoln with the wounded, although the wounded by now were not so heavy a burden as the news that had to be told to women. Of the sunrise of July 7, 1876, Mrs. Custer wrote one sentence, "From that time the life went out of the hearts of the 'women who weep,' and God asked them to walk on alone and in the shadow."[9]

6. The dispatch is quoted in full in *The Custer Tragedy*, pp. 196–97 and *The Story of the Little Big Horn*, pp. 110–14.

7. *The Conquest of the Missouri*, p. 306.

8. As such, he had planned to accompany Terry's column on the summer campaign, but had to cancel his plans at the last moment because of the illness of his wife, and sent Mark Kellogg, a reporter for the *Tribune*, in his place. *The Conquest of the Missouri*, p. 309.

9. *Boots and Saddles*, p. 269.

2. THE RECEPTION

It is not easy to become a part of the world that received the news of the Battle of the Little Bighorn, for any modern analogy is remote and the imagination is taxed to recover even the shadows of past feelings. Let us go back no further, then, than the early winter of 1950. A few years earlier our country had concluded its greatest war, in which we had finally assembled a military machine never before equalled in efficiency and complexity. One of the proudest generals of that war, Gen. MacArthur, had been directed to bring this modern might against some dark-skinned north Koreans and Chinese communists who in a semi-barbaric way had been annoying one of our distant outposts. As soldiers, they were known to be good when it came to crawling through the underbrush, suddenly appearing and disappearing, enduring hardships, living off a handful of rice, and torturing prisoners, but they were thought to be without modern organization, weapons, and generalship. Among the other units under Gen. MacArthur was the First Division of the Marines. The "end-of-the-war" offensive was on, and advance units had reached the Manchurian frontier. Then garbled accounts began to appear suggesting through the censorship that the front of the American army had been trapped and shattered and that few American prisoners were being taken alive.

The analogy is not very close. To transform the incredulity of 1950 into the horror of 1876, the imagination must place Gen. MacArthur in personal command of his advance units, kill him and all those directly under his personal command, leave their bodies mutilated upon the battlefield, and permit no survivor to return to mitigate part of the incredibility and horror with a factual explanation. There are still other imaginative additions that must be made. Like Custer, MacArthur was not only a proud but a political general, in deep trouble with the President of the United States, but the imagination must reverse the political affiliations and then send MacArthur to Washington prior to the Korean campaign to testify to corruption in the administration of President Truman—who must next remove MacArthur from command, arrest him, and finally give him a lower command. It also has to make the early winter of 1950 into the summer before a presidential election, with the Democratic and Republican candidates already nominated.

Both political parties saw the Battle as a political slaughter. To the Democrats, Grant was the butcher. "General Grant's administration has a heavy responsibility to incur for the reverses and sacrifice of life reported in these accounts," said the Charleston (S.C.) *Times*, a more moderate remark than was

being made by many Democratic papers in July of 1876.[10] Democratic indignation was flamed both by the President's treatment of Custer in the Belknap
case and by the unfortunate publication of Terry's "confidential" dispatch to
Sheridan, which implied that the annihilation of Custer and his troops was
the result of Custer's failure to obey orders. This dispatch was delivered to
Sheridan in Philadelphia where he and Sherman were attending the Centennial. Sherman wished to forward it by telegraph to the War Department, but
the man who represented himself as a government messenger proved "to be
a newspaper man by profession and a thief by incidental occupation," and
the dispatch appeared in print on the evening of July 7.[11] Then the President
entered the battle by repeating the charge:

> "The New York Herald has interviewed the President at Long Beach,
> and reports as follows: 'Correspondent: Was not Custer's massacre a
> disgraceful defeat of our troops?
> 'The President: (with an expression of manifest and keenly felt regret)
> I regard Custer's massacre as a sacrifice of troops, brought on by Custer
> himself, that was wholly unnecessary—wholly unnecessary. He was
> not to have made the attack before effecting the junction with Terry
> and Gibbon. He was notified to meet them on the 26th, but instead of
> marching slowly, as his orders required in order to effect the junction on
> the 26th, he enters upon a forced margin of 83 (!) miles in 24 hours and
> thus has to meet the Indians alone.'"[12]

So the Battle on the Little Bighorn almost immediately extended its lines
across the country and was on its way to being one of the longest battles ever
fought.

10. For some representative comments by Democratic newspapers, see *The Custer Tragedy*,
pp. 205–6.

11. *The Story of the Little Bighorn*, pp. 109–10. Dustin is wrong in giving the date as July 6 (*The
Custer Tragedy*, p. 205), for as noted above the messages sent from Bismarck were held up a day
because of line trouble east of St. Paul.

12. Quoted from *Did Custer Disobey Orders*, p. 25, because it is accompanied there by Dr. Kuhlman's interesting and probably valid conjecture as to the sources of the error in mileage (83
miles in 24 hours) upon which President Grant based the charge of disobedience. As for the
actual mileage, Dr. Kuhlman says, "The fact is that the greatest distance marched in any given 24
hours was 35 miles, and the whole distance from the Rosebud to the battlefield was, according
to Godfrey, 113 miles—which is not far from the truth."

3. THE BURIAL

Even the dead on the Little Bighorn were not destined for composure. In the public mind, they lay mutilated and unburied upon the battlefield, and deep in the mind of this modern age was the belief inherited from all our ancestors, that eternal peace of spirit is dependent upon decency and formality of interment and intactness of the body. There were horror stories about the general condition of the battlefield, but as usual the public imagination focussed upon the top of the Hill and took on concreteness as it approached Custer whose heart, so the stories went, had been cut from his body and then was circled by dancing Indians.

By July 25, Lt. Bradley felt impelled to make a public report on the dead as he had found them,[13] the bare fact being painful enough, as he said, without fictional exaggeration. He admitted that there had been "real mutilation" of Reno's troopers who had fallen near the Indian village, but of the dead on Custer Hill his account was very different. According to his account, most of the bodies (although not all including the body of Kellogg, the correspondent) had been stripped; possibly a majority had been scalped; there were only a "comparatively few cases of disfiguration"; and Custer lay as if in sleep, his body "wholly unmutilated."

Bradley's report, however, has not always been received as completely accurate, especially his description of the bodies on Custer Hill. There has never been any dispute about the bodies of Reno's men who fell near the Indian village. Even as Terry's troops moved through the deserted Indian camp on June 27 they found three burned heads threaded on a wire stretched between lodge-poles,[14] and what was found up the valley was not much better. On Custer Hill, it was not so bad, if for no other reason than that mutilation was primarily the sport of squaws and children who had enough to do closer to camp. Witnesses agree that nearly all the dead on the Hill were stripped, lying in bloody socks, that most were scalped and slashed on the right thigh by Sioux knives marking their dead, and that the axe had often been used to finish off the wounded. But only some of those who saw the battlefield agree with Bradley that the disfigurement beyond this was limited, others, both

13. First published in the Helena (Montana) Herald and reprinted in full in The Story of the Little Big Horn, pp. 162–67.

14. Custer's Luck, p. 466.

Indians and whites, maintaining that the mutilation was general.[15] Most certainly Bradley's intention in writing the letter was to say what little he could in the way of comfort to the anguished families of the dead, and certainly such an intention affected what he said and did not say; for instance, he gives no detailed or concrete description of mutilations whereas he describes in commemorative prose the unmarked features of his hero whose expression was that of a man "who had fallen asleep and enjoyed peaceful dreams." Such an intention, however, does not justify the often-whispered rumors that he and others lied about the dead to spare the living. Bradley as chief of Gibbon's scouts was a trained observer and so unyielding in his integrity and convictions that he sometimes irritated and amused his commander; McClelland's testimony about the condition of the dead coincides closely with Bradley's, and part of his assignment as Gibbon's engineer was to make an objective record. Others undoubtedly saw with their own eyes more horror than these did, since the threshold to horror varies with the observer, but probably the facts were substantially those reported by Bradley in words chosen to blur their visualization. To have seen these facts would have been something else. Nauseated troopers had to be excused from the burial details that crossed the Field on the 28th.

We can get an early glimpse of the mind's preference to construct history more by the principles of literature than by the canons of evidence if we observe briefly the construction that both Indians and whites have built upon the mutilated body of Tom Custer,[16] and the UNMUTILATED BODY OF THE general. No literary sense is deeper than the one that recognizes the emotions most inherent in an actual situation and then does everything in its power to preserve this emotional unity and to magnify its impact by addition, subtraction, and embroidery. It took only an ordinary instinct for plot to extend the horror done upon Tom's body into a horror story. One principle intrinsic to all plots—embryonic, amateur, or professional—is that prophecies are

15. For instance, see *The Story of the Little Big Horn*, pp. 167 f., but a much larger list could be drawn up by anyone interested in this unhappy subject.

16. Godfrey's detailed description of the body is reprinted in *The Custer Myth*, pp. 376–77. Dustin says that all officers who viewed the body agreed there was no sign that the heart had been removed. Sgt. Ryan's later story to the contrary Dustin regards as imaginative, stimulated by the legend then current and by distant memories of the actual slashings on the abdomen. The odds are all that Dustin is right in dismissing "the heart story" as imaginatively plausible but untrue. *The Custer Myth*, p. 185.

fulfilled ("foreshadowing," as it is called by teachers of fiction). A slight creative act was enough to connect the disembowelment of Tom Custer with the fact he had once arrested the Sioux warrior Rain-in-the-Face who, it was rumored or surmised, had promised vengeance. Rain-in-the-Face had therefore sought out and found him on the Battlefield. It probably took a little time and literary talent, but only a little, to make the revision that changed the bowels to the heart; the concluding scene in which Rain-in-the-Face eats Tom's heart also required little creative originality, since one of the oldest conventions of literature and magic has the avenger consummating his vengeance by taking some vital organ of the victim into himself. This was the version of the horror story believed by some of the nation, including Mrs. Custer,[17] and the one given out as "the true story" in 1894 by Rain-in-the-Face (who recanted, however, on his death bed).[18]

The other version of the horror story appeared as a special news release on July 12[19] and must have received immediate wide-spread acceptance, for Lt. Bradley's letter, written only a month after the Battle, was partly intended, as he says, to refute the nation's belief that the Sioux cut out Gen. Custer's heart "and danced around it." There is nothing extraordinary, however, about this artistic alteration of bodies—it is a simple illustration of the imagination's natural aversion to the lower echelons and of the hero's power to attract to himself the big stories that venture into his magnetic field. This version was given poetic permanence by Longfellow's "The Revenge of Rain-in-the-Face," and both versions are permanent in popular legend.

Still another set of stories preserves the fact that the General's body was exempt from mutilation of any kind, for the fact in this case makes a better story in many ways than the fiction of horror. This exemption from mutilation naturally suggests an intentional act of sanctification, especially since his naked body had been leaned against the bodies of two soldiers, "his right forearm and hand supporting his head in an inclining posture like one resting or asleep."[20] Stories have always been told, therefore, that Indians recog-

17. *Boots and Saddles*, p. 215. "It was found out on the battlefield that he had cut out the brave heart of that gallant, loyal, and lovable man, our brother Tom."

18. See below, pp. ___.

19. See below, pp. ___.

20. According to Godfrey, *The Custer Myth*, p. 376. But descriptions of the position in which the body was found vary somewhat (see for instance, *The Custer Tragedy*, p. 185), although all agree that the position was one of composure, perhaps arranged composure. The variations in

nized the body of the Big Chief and paid special respect to is bravery,[21] and one of these narratives adds a funeral procession of Indians who carried the General's body to Reno Hill, tried to deliver it to Reno and, when fired upon, carried it back some four miles to Custer Hill and gently arranged it in heroic posture.[22] Another narrative version adds many more elements of the tragic drama—fulfillment of prophesy, love interest, tragic kinship between protagonist and antagonist, and purification of the dead. This version, which is gaining in popularity, rests upon the testimony of one Cheyenne squaw who quotes two other Cheyenne women.[23] These latter, visitors from the Southern Cheyennes, claimed they recognized the General's body on the Battlefield because they remembered "the handsome man" they had seen in the campaigns of 1868–69. "Thinking of Me-o-tzi" (who, according to certain stories examined earlier, was "Custer's Indian wife"[24]), these two Cheyenne women announced to the Sioux warriors about to mutilate Custer that he was a "relative" of theirs, so the Sioux cut off only a joint of a finger. The Cheyenne women then punched holes in his ears with a sewing awl since he had not listened to what the Cheyenne chiefs had warned him would happen if he fought them again, and ever afterward they hoped that their ponies had kicked no dust on his body.

There is little or no historical plausibility to any of these accounts. It is doubtful if the Indians knew they had fought Custer's troops until they began to hear from agency Indians,[25] few of the hostiles would have recognized the General or his brother in ideal circumstances, and it is hard to believe that any of them would have recognized the General with short hair and red-beard and black with battle. As for Rain-in-the-Face, he may not have been anywhere near the Battlefield on June 25.[26] It intrigues the dramatic imagination, of course, that the body of one brother was horribly mutilated and the body

---

descriptions may well occur because Bradley or the parties coming later to the Battlefield probably moved the body in order to be sure of its identity.

21. Even Sitting Bull and Gall are quoted to this effect, *The Custer Myth*, pp. 73, 376.

22. *Custer's Luck*, p. 487.

23. *She Watched Custer's Last Battle*, last page.

24. See below, p. ___.

25. *Legend into History*, p. 212.

26. Edgar I. Stewart, "Which Indian Killed Custer?" *Montana: The Magazine of Western History* (Summer, 1958), p. 9. This article also relates Rain-in-the-Face's own confirmations and denials of the story.

of the elder was exempt from the surrounding violation, but nothing closely resembling authentic history remains to explain this drama or to explain it away. On the other hand, it is within the realm of psychological plausibility that the stories of the deaths of these two brothers are parts of one dramatic unity, the mind having a disposition to operate, in philosophy as well as drama, by "contraries that meet in one." The Custer brothers were men of battle, and their bodies at times seem to be viewed as a collective expression of man's contrary feelings about war—that it is both a horror and a god. Moreover, the opposite emotions of hatred and adulation which Gen. Custer had aroused throughout his lifetime seem dramatically validated by what remained of himself and of his other self. But almost no one, whatever he may feel about the General and his brother, fails to observe their approximation to unity in death. All writers dwell upon the fact that their bodies were found close together, and some of the more imaginative picture them as dying with hand holding hand. Sgt. Ryan who was there testifies that they were placed together in a common grave and covered with pieces of tent and then with fifteen to eighteen inches of light earth,[27] but neither they nor the others who died on Custer Hill had yet found a final resting place.

The dead on Custer Hill were buried on the 28th, although it was anything but a final interment. There were few tools among troops equipped to chase Indians, their first obligation was a heavy one—to transport Reno's wounded to the *Far West* which was tied up at the mouth of the Little Bighorn, and always there was the chance that the Indian retreat had been a ruse to get the troops spread out in an indefensible position. Reno's regiment was on Custer Hill one day only, each troop moving across an assigned piece of terrain in something like skirmish order. Certain bodies were missed altogether; others were covered by piles of sage brush; others buried by one of the details having a spade were covered by the ashy soil of the hillside and sometimes were left with a foot or hand protruding. For the officers, generally something shallow was dug, and each officer's grave was marked by a stake into which an empty cartridge shell was driven containing a number on a piece of paper,[28] and then Capt. Henry J. Nowlan made a field sketch showing the location of each officer's grave. No record was made of the identity of the enlisted men.

27. *The Custer Myth*, pp. 363–64.

28. "The bodies of Dr. Lord and Lieutenants Porter, Harrison, and Sturgis were not found, at least not recognized," Gen. Godfrey, *The Custer Myth*, p. 377. See also Sheridan's report, Ibid., p. 374.

These dead have been buried and reburied until their bones have acquired a restless history of their own determined by ruin, wolves, job not well done, and some strange power that resists finality. It is a history that will be touched on here only lightly for its outline. In the following summer of 1877, Gen. Sheridan instructed his brother, Lt. Col. Michael V. Sheridan, to proceed to the battlefield with Capt. Nowlan and Company I of the 7th Cavalry for the purpose of returning the bodies of the officers to civilization and of re-interring those of the enlisted men. Because of the stakes and Capt. Nowlan's sketch marking the location of the officers' bodies, presumably most of them were recovered, but, as noted above, four of them were never found and the hastily buried remains of others were now exposed and scattered. Under the ground, there was also confusion. Sgt. Caddle says that when they came to the stake marked Number One they first placed in the coffin a body that later was discovered to have been lying on a corporal's blouse: "I think," he says, "we got the right body the second time."[29] Tom Le Forge, squaw man and scout, who claimed to be only ten feet away when this body was put in a box, said it was a thigh-bone and a skull attached to part of a skeleton-trunk.[30] This constitutes what there is of reality under the General's monument at West Point.

The bodies of the enlisted men that remained buried over the winter were located by their mounds and by a richer vegetation, and those scattered on the hillside were separated from horses' bones; each was buried where found and marked by a willow cutting. But there is disagreement over the care given to the burial of the enlisted men in the summer of 1877, and certainly for many years there were bones of men upon the battlefield, and many further attempts to get them buried and to keep them from returning.[31] In 1879 Capt. C. K. Sanderson from nearby Ft. Custer erected the first "monument" on Custer Hill under which he placed "all the human bones that could be

29. *Conquest of the Missouri*, pp. 378–79.

30. James S. Hutchins, "Custer's Clay," introductory essay to *The American West: Emphasizing Custeriana*, Catalogue 56 (J. E. Reynolds: Van Nuys, California, 1960).

31. Part IV, Section 1 of *The Custer Myth* is devoted to accounts of the burials, and contains the first-hand accounts of Godfrey and Col. "Mike" Sheridan and two articles by Dustin. The chapter in *The Conquest of the Missouri* entitled "The Bones of Heroes" is also devoted to the same subject. Since the location of the grave markers is crucial to Dr. Kuhlman's analysis of the Battle, the "Foreword" to his *Legend into History* should be carefully studied. It will be noted that he and Dustin disagree considerably about the care given to the dead.

found," including "parts of four or five officers' bodies."[32] This first "monument" was a cordwood crib, which he filled with all the horse bones he could
find on the field, probably because he realized the large number of horses'
bones was one of the reasons for the persistency of sensational stories concerning the condition of the dead. In 1881, Lt. Charles Francis Roe erected
the present granite monument at the top of the Hill some six feet from the
grave marked Number One; and at its base the bones of the enlisted men
were reburied in a common grave. In 1890, Capt. Owen J. Sweet placed the
present white stone markers at the sites of the individual graves and on the
whole they mark the places where the bodies were found. On the officers'
markers the name is given; the markers for the enlisted men say simply, "7th
Cavalry, June 25, 1876."

Slowly, then, the horror, confusion, and remnants of one kind of reality
have become a kind of geometry, a hillside of white stone lines pointing to a
hilltop with a granite shaft that can be seen a long way off. Custer Battlefield
is now a National Monument, and, like Glacier and Yellowstone Parks, under
the direction of the National Park Service.[33] Over 130,000 people visit it annually, and they, too, somehow change when they turn off the main highway (US
87) on to the blacktop road leading to the Museum and the Monument and
continuing as far as Reno Hill, although most of the traffic goes no farther
than Custer Hill. There is a change even in their natural tone of voice, most
speaking in a distinctly lower key and cautioning their children. The change
in behavior is varied, but there are patterns to it. Those who talk louder than
usual generally have some original theory about the Battle, and are further
excited by the fact that never in ordinary life have they been surrounded by
so many quiet people willing to listen to them. On the whole, most of the
remarks overheard on the Battlefield sound foolish and irrelevant. A mother,
standing in front of the Museum case displaying the uniform worn by the

32. *Legend into History*, pp. xiv–v.

33. Not until 1930 were both Custer Hill and Reno Hill purchased from the Crow Indians
and named Custer Battlefield National Cemetery. The administration of the area was changed
from the War Department to the Department of the Interior, National Park Service, in 1940, and
in 1946 the area was given its present name, Custer Battlefield National Monument. Its splendid
museum, first conceived by Mrs. Custer, was officially opened in 1952. For a history and description of the latter, see Harry B. Robinson's article on "The Custer Battlefield Museum" in *The
Montana Magazine of History*, Vol. II, No. 3 (July, 1952).

General at West Point, whispers to her son that he must study hard in school if he expects to get anywhere in life. On the Field, some original genius with a suddenly admiring wife explains to silent people what really happened at the Battle. The explanation is usually simple and often ingenious: Gen. Custer reached the top of the Hill and was doing all right against the Indians with his dismounted troops until all of a sudden his wagon train appeared on Weir Point; just like that he ordered two columns to mount and move down the Battle Ridge so the wagon train could march safely through; there wasn't a shot until the columns got stretched out, and then bang, bang, bang and it was all over. Little of what is said on the Battlefield has much to do with events that happened there or with those who took part in them. The uniform which inspired the mother to inspire her son belonged to a cadet who was graduated 34th in a class of 34 and had other troubles before finishing West Point. The wagon train was left miles back at the mouth of the Powder river. Yet probably none of these remarks would seem foolish or irrelevant if one knew who made them. For instance, the original genius on the Battlefield is himself something of a type—usually cautious and fairly successful in life, and unknown for any original speculative efforts except when some recessive part of him accompanies incautious men on their way to disaster. Then he becomes different, more foolish and, in a way, better than himself. This particular one differs from the others in that he is in the supply business, and so probably his concern about the wagon train, even if it wasn't there.

Since what we see in the Battle is largely something in us, it is natural that behavior on the Battlefield is varied, though patterned. Many make a point of touching the white grave markers as they walk by, others just as clearly avoid doing so, and I have seen several standing in tears and probably not for anyone buried here. Nearly everyone finds himself wishing that there were no high fence around the grave markers of Gen. Custer and the circle who made "the Last Stand," and the guards are always on the watch against those, including perhaps you and me, who feel an impulse to carry away just a little piece of the hill with them, a chip of stone or a cactus plant beside a marker.

After the traffic of the day is gone and the gates are shut, the Hill takes on another appearance that again alters dimensions, proportions, and reality. In the moonlight, the Hill is very small, the sky enormous, and in a universe of white diffusion it is hard to tell where the Hill ends and the sky begins and there is no reason to. This is a reality more abstract than the others, in which geometry has almost faded except for the lines of white grave markers. Among the markers close by, rabbits appear moving like oval specters. An old friend,

Major Edward S. Luce, formerly Superintendent of the Battlefield and formerly and forever of the 7th U.S. Cavalry, had names for all these rabbits, and they seemed to know him, too. In the moonlight, his National Park Service hat looked like an old cavalry campaign hat. The names he called them were the names of old cavalry troopers. "Hey, Horseface Klotz," he would call, and an oval specter would appear from behind a grave marker, advance and tremble, and then fade back into white diffusion.

This, then, is Custer Battlefield, a slight and distant elevation on which men died in bloody socks and since have been transformed into a universe of other meanings by their own ashy soil, by identities established however irrelevantly with our own lives, and by a power that for a better word is here called spectral. It was the purpose of this chapter to record the transformations of the soil, but the Battle has two other histories far larger in scope and significance. The first is the alterations the Battle has made in the lives of individuals, families, and tribes connected with it, changes in many instances visible even in the present generation. The second is a history of the changes that we of the world at large have made in the Battle and in its participants as we have projected some part of ourselves into them, altering fact, feature, and tone for a gigantic image of something hidden in our own small lives. So the Hill as a hill we now leave behind, by preference in moonlight.

CHAPTER 2

· ·

The Sioux

· ·

*"Then he whom we had followed showed us his hands
and feet, and there were wounds in them which had
been made by the whites when he went to them and they
crucified him. And he told us that he was going to come
again on earth, and this time he would remain and live
with the Indians, who were his chosen people."*
—Kicking Bear, Sioux medicine man, reporting to
his people

I t is easy to point to spectacular illustrations of the power of the Battle
over those who survived it—to Sitting Bull as he toured the country
in Buffalo Bill's circus which featured a re-enactment of Custer's Last
Stand, or to the 7th U.S. Cavalry in Korea, motorized but still advancing
to "Garryowen," as they entered Seoul led by Col. Wild Bill Harris in a jeep
with a cavalry saddle cinched on its hood, etc. Although the Battle passes on
its flair for the spectacular, its profounder meanings must not be lost in picto-
rial moments that overlook the linear course of ensuing events. The Battle's
marks are clear and deep in the outline of the succeeding history of the Sioux,
the Cheyennes, the 7th Cavalry and the Custer family.

[1.]

When the Indians broke camp late on June 26, 1876 and moved majesti-
cally and indifferently up the valley of the Little Bighorn, the men on Reno
Hill could scarcely believe what they saw in the sunset. The line was half a
mile wide and three miles long, its pony herd estimated at twenty thousand.[1]
Reno's men stood up one by one from their dead, many still fearful, some
crying, but all finally uniting in three cheers as a salute to the Indians and
themselves. The Indians were still in sight when darkness came.

This moment was indeed their sunset. They were illuminated with glory,
but their power was soon to become a shadow and then to disappear. Few nations, however, even nations such as the Teton Sioux who regarded themselves

---

1. *Custer's Luck*, p. 428.

as the chosen people,[2] have collectively witnessed such a moment of self-glory, a glory evidently never to fade from our minds which almost instantly picture all Indians as mounted Indians of the Plains and most northern Plains Indians as feathered followers of Sitting Bull—at least in movies and TV few Indians go slipping through eastern forests on foot. Yet this moment of triumph was to have far different meanings to the Sioux who have left no songs, sagas, or dances to celebrate it.

With their twenty thousand ponies they continued up the valley toward the Bighorn Mountains. Then, in a short time, like other chosen people before, they began to disperse, although for special reasons of their own. It was too big a camp to feed except where grass and game were in superabundance; Indian organization was loose even at a tribal level and anything like a confederacy depended upon a crisis now seemingly passed; but it was also old Indian tactics to hit, run, and then disperse until the trouble was over and the Army got tired of looking and went somewhere else. So "agency" Indians in small groups slipped back to their reservations, trying to look as if they had been there all the time or had been gone a few days to call on relatives. Soon the "hostiles" were separating, the Sioux from the Cheyenne, and these in turn, breaking up into smaller camps, went hunting buffalo, for the most part back through the country where the Army had pursued them—down to Rosebud and across to the Tongue and Powder rivers. But this time when they dispersed they were going ways that in some senses were to be permanently separate, and such reassembly as they have since had has not been as chosen people. Their dispersal, though, did keep the image of their victory intact, frustrating a humiliated Army from ever delivering one blow that would dramatically restore the supremacy of civilization. The drama had been drained from the situation, at least for the white troops. The armies of Crook and Terry sat paralyzed on Goose Creek and the Yellowstone, waiting reinforcements, so for some weeks of a false summer all seemed as before to the buffalo hunters.

2.

While the Army was making its necessarily slow preparations, the public wanting full-scale drama did its best with the one dramatic incident it was furnished. In June, Buffalo Bill dropped all theatrical engagements and theatrically signed again as an Army scout; in July he was with Gen. Wesley

2. *Warriors without Weapons*, p. 85.

Merritt's 5th Cavalry on their way to reinforce Crook. At War Bonnet Creek,[3] a party of Cheyenne attempting an ambush were themselves trapped by that able commander and probably Buffalo Bill killed the first Indian, whose name actually was Yellow Hair although it has nearly always been mistranslated as Yellow Hand to be more in keeping with his dramatic role of Buffalo Bill's adversary.[4] This, of course, is powerful dramatic material—Gen. Custer, Buffalo Bill, and the first dead Indian appropriately called Yellow Hand—and almost immediately the public transformed it into permanent legend by screening it, as we do much of life, through literary conventions combining the Feudal Age with the Far West. In legend Buffalo Bill, wearing one of the black velvet Mexican costumes he used for his theatrical engagements,[5] rides out before the two armies, challenges Yellow Hand to a personal combat, topples his man and lifts his trophy with the shout, "First soul for Gen. Custer!" But for the rest of the summer the public was given little else it could dramatize.

It was August 5 before Crook broke camp and moved down the empty Rosebud, on the 10th meeting Terry's forces who had made an equally empty march; then more or less together they continued on their empty way to the junction of the Yellowstone and the Powder rivers. Here Crook left the Yellowstone to be guarded by Terry who was supposed to keep the Indians from escaping north and himself continued east following Indian trails, but not before incurring several interesting losses that were returned by steamer to civilization. Buffalo Bill left to resume his theatrical engagements, and during that winter, which "was probably the most profitable of his theatrical career," he appeared in a dramatization of the Yellow Hand incident and added considerably to the receipts by show-window displays of Yellow Hand's war bonnet, arms and shield.[6] Also on the same steamboat with the returning hero were

---

3. Actually at Hat Creek, thirty miles from War Bonnet Creek, but legend has shifted the incident to the more literary watershed.

4. This incident is examined thoroughly and with discernment by Don Russell in *The Lives and Legends of Buffalo Bill* (Norman, 1960), pp. 214 ff. Don Russell tells me that for a while he lost any belief in the story that Buffalo Bill killed Yellow Hand but his faith returned as he began to note how many of those claiming Buffalo Bill had not killed Yellow Hand ended up by claiming they had.

5. The part about the costume may well be true. See *Campaigning with Crook*, p. 42.

6. *Campaigning with Crook*, pp. 42, 94.

four of Crook's cavalry troopers on whose minds "the Custer massacre had so preyed" that they were relieved from further service in the field.[7]

Crook's column continued east on dispersing Indian trails discouraged by prairies left burning, then by cold September rains, and finally by starved horse-meat and dysentery. The column had called it quits and was heading south for the Black Hills when on September 8 the advance guard stumbled on a Sioux camp of about forty or fifty lodges under American Horse. What happened the next day when Crook arrived is called the Battle of Slim Buttes and is best known for the wild beauty of its setting,[8] its colorful literary coverage,[9] and the bravery of the Sioux warriors and women who made their last stand in a cave. American Horse finally surrendered, walking erectly from the cave with a squaw holding his intestines in a shawl. Crazy Horse, who was camped nearby, arrived too late to be of any real help, but he left a deep impression on Crook's troops who discovered, as Crazy Horse's warriors flashed by, that they were no longer in any condition to be looking for large numbers of well-mounted Indians.

3.

So the summer campaign ended, and what was to have produced a victory to compensate for Custer's defeat instead looked much like any summer the Army had spent chasing Indians and with luck catching a few trapped in a ravine. But, if the Indians had a feeling that all was as before, they learned otherwise with the coming of winter. The Plains Indians of the northwest had never been exposed to the theory, developed by Sheridan and Custer in the southwest, that winter was the time to catch Indians when their ponies were in poor shape from eating cottonwood bark and they themselves were necessarily scattered in small camps and less watchful than usual because of their remoteness. The Army surrounded them with their best Indian fighters—"Bearcoat" Nelson A. Miles operating in the north from Ft. Keogh where the Tongue joins the Yellowstone river (present Miles City), and Crook and Ranald S. Mackenzie

---

7. *Campaigning with Crook*, pp. 94–95.

8. The work that DeLand and others did in locating the exact site of the battle is described by him in *The Sioux Wars, South Dakota Historical Collections*, XVII (1934), 218–27.

9. This small battle was witnessed and dramatically described by two professional writers, the reporter, John F. Finerty (in *War-path and Bivouac*) and the soldier-novelist, Capt. Charles King (in *Campaigning with Crook* and *Stories of Army Life*).

operating in the south from northwestern Nebraska and Wyoming. There was nothing brilliant about the campaign—it was just relentless. The weather was bitter and to the Indians so also was the fact that the troops were often led to their camps by their own relatives who had surrendered and had then signed up with the Army as scouts. There were small Washitas—camps that were surrounded; their inhabitants killed, captured, or scattered into the winter; their lodges burned and their ponies shot.[10] Even the big camps escaping destruction had to fight all winter until "peace parties" began to develop, threatening unity. A medicine man who took the name of "Long Hair," claiming he was the bullet-proof spirit of Gen. Custer, was killed.[11] Altogether, it was a bad winter for the Indians and when spring came many knew it was never going to be the same again. By May, Sitting Bull and Gall had led their Hunkpapas across the Canadian line, and early in the same month Crazy Horse with nearly a thousand of his Oglalas surrendered to Crook at Ft. Robinson.[12] When soldiers there tried to photograph him, he replied, "My friend, why should you wish to shorten my life by taking from me my shadow?" Then on September 5 he was arrested because of rumors that he was planning to murder Crook and escape north to join Sitting Bull, rumors that well may have been started by a jealous Indian. At the cell door, he drew a hidden knife and came out of the guard house fighting for light. He was calling, but it was not his old battle call: "It is a good day to fight! A good day to die!" He kept saying, "Let me go! Let me go!" A soldier of the guard ran a bayonet through both his kidneys. It is generally said, that like Custer, he was thirty-six years old when he died.[13]

4.

North of the border, the old life lingered on, although it had no ultimate power of survival, even under the protection of the Queen and the Red Coats

10. The most smashing of those winter attacks was led by Gen. Mackenzie against the Cheyenne camp of Dull Knife. For a detailed account, see Grinnell's *The Fighting Cheyennes*, pp. 359–82.

11. [blank]

12. For a detailed account of the surrender and death of Crazy Horse, see De Land's *The Sioux Wars, South Dakota Historical Collections*, XVII (1934), 313 ff. and Mari Sandoz's *Crazy Horse* (New York, 1942).

13. Actually, he may not have been this old, since speculations as to the date of his birth vary from 1840–45.

of the Canadian Northwestern Mounted Police. The buffalo were about gone, on alien soil dissension began to spread through the camp, and many, listening to the promises of Indians and priests sent from the agencies, began to slip back home. Besides, though treated with justice, understanding, and courage by the Canadian government, they created a situation that could not be tolerated long. They hunted on both sides of the border, and south of the border they stole horses and killed more beef than buffalo. With the attempt of Chief Joseph and the Nez Perces to escape to Canada in 1878, the Canadian government began to realize that, in granting protection to Sitting Bull and his followers, they had set an example for all the dissatisfied Indians of the northwest to follow. So they took quiet steps to hasten the inevitable—they denied the Sioux' request for a reservation, in skillful ways they reduced Sitting Bull's hold on his followers, etc. Early in 1881 Gall separated forever from Sitting Bull, and, taking the large body of the hostile Sioux with him, surrendered to Gen. Miles. On July 19, Sitting Bull with the few who had remained loyal (one hundred and eighty-seven men, women, and children) surrendered at Ft. Buford, but he also was placed under arrest and retained for two years at Ft. Randall, although now that the Sioux War was declared over he was a celebrity admired by the soldiers and deluged with fan mail from all over the world. In the spring of 1883, Capt. Grant Marsh (of *Far West* fame, now commanding the *W. J. Behan*) took Sitting Bull up the river to his permanent home on Standing Rock Agency. It was a trip the captain remembered in detail. The old chief sold hundreds of autographs at a dollar apiece, their value considerably increased by the fact that he spelled his name "Seitting Bull." Capt. Marsh also noted a peculiarity of Indians—they stumbled when trying to walk up a white man's staircase and could make no progress except by crawling on their hands and knees.[14]

5.

The Teton Sioux now had ahead of them the long staircase of civilization, and many of them, including Sitting Bull of course, still had no intention of getting down on their hands and knees, although for some years the struggle between "the forces of civilization" and what the Indian Bureau called "the ancient regime" stopped short of violence. In this struggle, almost necessarily one of the first aims of the Indian agents was to break the power of the

14. *The Conquest of the Missouri,* pp. 415–17.

warlike chiefs and to keep the Indians scattered, the more remote and positive aims were to change the Sioux from hunters into farmers, to see that their children went to school, and to convert them to Christianity.

To break the power of the "hostile" chiefs, agents elevated minor chiefs who had become "friendlies." Sitting Bull was pictured as a sly medicine man who had hidden in his lodge on the Little Bighorn while the Sioux were led to victory on the ridge above by Gall, now a Christian farmer. In fact, the Indian Bureau was so anxious to get Sitting Bull off the reservation that they encouraged exhibitions of him across the country. In 1883, accompanied by the wife and son of the agent at Standing Rock, he was taken on a tour of fifteen cities by Col. Alvaren Allen, who advertised him as "the slayer of General Custer," a tour authorized by the Secretary of the Interior; he took another trip the next year; and in 1885 he was in the Wild West Show of Buffalo Bill, who took a liking to him and sent him back to the reservation with a number 8 white sombrero and a grey circus horse that would sit down and raise one hoof when a pistol was fired.[15]

A good part of the next problem—that of scattering the Indians—was taken care of by the encroachments of farmers, ranchers, and railroads so that by 1889 the once Great Sioux Reservation had been shrunken and broken into five separate reservations in the badland country of what is now southwestern South Dakota.[16] It was a much slower job, however, to scatter the life centered about big villages and to disperse the Teton Sioux harmlessly and presumably profitably on 160-acre allotments, yet something deeper even than geography was separating the Teton Sioux. Many of them saw, or at least sensed, that the course of events since 1876 would not relent until they accepted another way of life; by the whites, these were called "progressives." Those who tried to maintain the old way of life and believed that the buffalo would return were called "conservatives," white party-labels that cannot tell what went on among reservation-Indians. They distrusted each other, spied and told on each other, and enlisted against each other, even against their great chiefs. Crazy Horse was killed probably because of false information given to an Army interpreter by an Oglala, and Sitting Bull was to be shot by Sioux police. Such were the chosen people who had marched as one body past Reno Hill in the sunset of June 26, 1876.

15. Sitting Bull, pp. 256–57.

16. Pine Ridge, Rosebud (not to be confused with the Rosebud in Montana), Standing Rock, Cheyenne River, and Lower Brule. *Warriors without Weapons*, p. 32.

About the time of the surrender of the last hostile Sioux, two other events occurred that took from the old way of life its most basic sources of strength. The great buffalo herd disappeared forever from the plains—the final great buffalo hunt was held in 1882, and the Teton Sioux killed their last buffalo in the following year.[17] Earlier even, in 1881 when Sitting Bull returned from Canada, the Sun Dance was prohibited,[18] and the Sun Dance had been almost as central to their religious life as the Buffalo had been to their economy. As compensations for the long way ahead, they were offered ploughs, compulsory education, and Christianity, and so, let it be said, they were given what nineteenth-century America regarded as the miracles that had produced its own miraculous success—miracles as yet producing no great wonders in the badlands of southwestern South Dakota, although they are distinguishable features of the mixed society of the present-day Sioux. At first, however, their impress was slight. When Sitting Bull and his people finally reached their reservation, they were presented with twelve acres of ploughed land and, so that Sitting Bull would feel what it was like to be an honest industrious American instead of an Indian letting the squaws do the work, he was ordered to pick up a hoe and it is said that he made a few motions with it. In the joke-book of history, this must be rated among the better laughs.

Yet some of the early Sioux, such as Gall, did try farming, a few even were successful, and with the modern developments in dryland farming large fields of winter wheat have made a showing on certain parts of the reservations, fields, however, that are often on land leased from the Sioux by white farmers and on reservations only 12% of which is suitable for agriculture.[19] On old buffalo range, old buffalo hunters have done best with cattle, for a time making it look as if a new prosperity were to succeed the buffalo economy, but this prosperity also quickly disappeared when during the First World War the Sioux were permitted and even encouraged to sell their entire herds. They promptly spent the proceeds, and, concerning the rest of their slow, sad economic history, it is enough to say here that the Sioux have never found a source of wealth as sustained and democratic as the buffalo.[20] Eventually, too, their ancient religion was supplanted; although certain native religious

17. *Warriors without Weapons*, p. 32.

18. And remained under official ban until 1933. *Warriors without Weapons*, p. 91.

19. *Warriors without Weapons*, p. 45.

20. For an account of their modern economic history, see *Warriors without Weapons*, especially pp. 37 ff.

cults are still practiced on the reservations,[21] the majority of the Teton Sioux slowly became converted to Christianity, in many cases and especially at first partly for the reason that they hoped to acquire the superior medicine of their conquerors.[22]

6.

During the 80's, "the ancient regime" took no part in any of this future, yet they waited for something to come, waited in blankets, long hair, and big scattered villages. It was a period in the history of the Teton Sioux with analogies in other histories, a never-never period such as occurs indeed in much personal history when the present is no more substantial than the hope that the future will eventually omit it and continue ahead into the past. It has closer analogies to moments in the history of chosen people who have suddenly been faced with their powerlessness as people but who still believe in the power that chose them. In 1889, the Teton Sioux heard that an Indian Messiah was coming.[23]

The news came from the southwest. A Piaute Indian by the name of Wovoka, also known by the name of Jack Wilson because he had been brought up in a white family of that name, had a vision during an eclipse, a vision in which he was taken to heaven where he saw God and all his own people happily continuing their old way of life in a land full of game. God informed him that the universe was to be divided into three parts, God himself ruling heaven, Wovoka as his deputy handling matters in the west, and the east left in charge of "the governor," President Harrison. God then returned Wovoka to earth to

21. *Warriors without Weapons*, pp. 98–102.

22. *Warriors without Weapons*, pp. 91–92.

23. The following account of Messiah Religion and the Messiah Outbreak among the Sioux is heavily indebted to James Mooney's *The Ghost-Dance Religion and the Sioux Outbreak of 1890, Fourteenth Annual Report of the Bureau of Ethnology to the Secretary of the Smithsonian Institution* (1892–93), Part II. It is seldom worthwhile to quote later works on this phenomenon in Sioux history since they are based, second, third or fourth hand, on this same report. And it is truly a remarkable document, especially when one realizes how soon after the event it was published. Mooney was an Indian ethnologist in the field at the time, interviewing many of the tribes involved and even the Prophet, Wovoka, himself. But as remarkable as the first-hand data he offers is his scientific, sympathetic, and psychological understanding of what he saw. Naturally, a study made so close to the event has its errors, distortions and omissions, and the Ghost Dance is now the subject of a modern study being made by that able historian of the National Park Service, Robert Utley, whose criticisms and suggestions have helped many parts of this book besides this section.

instruct his people to cease quarrelling among themselves and to keep peace with the whites in order to hasten the day of The Great Event. An important part of the preparation for things to come was a dance lasting five days, a time that proved sufficient for mass-hypnosis and fatigue to accumulate to a point where most of the dancers fell in a trance and communed with their departed relatives. The dance, something of an equivalent for the forbidden Sun Dance, was called the Ghost Dance.

The Word went out across the plains, but none heard more eagerly—or tragically—than the Sioux. A Sioux council was called late in 1889, a delegation was sent immediately to the southwest to find out more about the new Messiah, and upon its return in the spring of 1890 the reservations became tense with excitement.

Wovoka's vision had been a Christian-Indian vision compounded out of simple elements of both faiths, an acceptance of a Christian peace on earth for an eternal Happy Hunting Ground. The vision that the Sioux returned with was naturally more their own than the dream of any Indian brought up in a Christian family named Wilson. The Sioux had a Sioux vision—undefeated in spirit but knowing the need for help, help necessarily to be borrowed from the only superior power, their conquerors.[24] At the base of the Sierra Nevadas, they said, was the Son of God still bearing on his body the marks of the crucifixion as signs of His rejection by the whites. So the whites had had their good medicine and had destroyed it. Now the Son of God was returning to avenge their rejection of Him and their injustice to the Indians. The date of the Second Coming was set for some time in 1891.

In the camps of "the ancient regime," there was dancing by day and far into the night. In the center, a young woman stood holding a red pipe pointing to the west, the direction from which the Messiah was to come, and about her the dancers circled in white Ghost shirts thought to be bullet-proof. Each people is always looking for a magic-carpet characteristic of its wishes, and the Indians were not yet completely disillusioned in their quest for something to wear that would turn aside bullets.[25] Although the religious excitement spread through all the Sioux reservations, the real trouble was confined to certain

24. Naturally different tribes and sometimes even different medicine men introduced their own variations in ritual, costume, and creed. Mooney discusses many of them in detail.

25. Mooney argues that the belief in a protective article of clothing probably came from the whites, possibly from the muslin "endowment robe" of the Mormons. As he points out, the Indian customarily went into battle naked above the waist, his "protective medicine" being a claw,

camps such as those of Big Foot, Hump, and Sitting Bull. It can be and has been argued that the craze would have run its course if the management of affairs had been left to the Indian Bureau and if the agents on the reservations had all been experienced, firm, and patient.[26] But, as is often the case, history was played out with a different set of characters from those wished for by historians, and at this moment only the agent at Standing Rock, Maj. James McLaughlin, had unusual qualifications and believed that he could handle the situation himself. Many of the settlers were understandably terrified and appealed for military support, the Christian Indians were alarmed, and there were whites who saw that the occasion could be turned to their advantage. On November 13, the president gave to the secretary of war the responsibility of seeing that an outbreak was prevented, Gen. Miles with headquarters at Rapid City was placed in command, and nearly three thousand troops surrounded the reservations. When the troops moved in, large bands of "hostiles," eventually themselves numbering around three thousand, left their reservations and escaped into the most inaccessible parts of the badlands. Then the tension mounted.

There is no use arguing, at least here, as to whether Sitting Bull believed in the coming of an Indian Messiah or was merely using the new religion to inflame old passions among his people.[27] Probably not even Sitting Bull himself could tell with any accuracy what proportions of belief and mere hope were stirred in him by the news that the whites had destroyed their own good medicine which would now work to return to the Sioux the way of life and the great lands that he regarded as rightfully theirs. Sitting Bull was a medicine man who had had great visions for his people, these visions had some times proved true, he now presided at Ghost Dances, and, when a woman would

---

head of a bird, etc. which could be worn in his hair or hidden between the covers of his shield (pp. 790–91). After such trinkets, the Ghost shirt must have seemed armorial.

26. See DeLand, pp. 446 ff., and Vestal, p. 284.

27. For opposite opinions on this question as well as on the general character of Sitting Bull, consult Major McLaughlin who as the agent at Standing Rock Reservation regarded Sitting Bull as having "all of the faults of an Indian and none of the nobler attributes," and then consult Stanley Vestal who makes him, at least to me, equally destitute of character by trying to make him into the noblest Roman of them all. To McLaughlin, Sitting Bull was using the new religion craftily as a means of enhancing his own power (pp. 180 ff.; pp. 205 ff.), and, to Vestal, Sitting Bull was an innocent and agnostic spectator of the Ghost Dance (pp. 279 ff.).

fall beside him in a trance, he would put his ear to her lips and then astonish the dancers with a long recital about her dead relatives.[28]

When the rumor came that Sitting Bull intended to move his camp off the reservation and closer to the "hostiles" in the badlands, the order went out to arrest him. Maj. McLaughlin insisted that it would be safer to use his Indian Police, but two troops of the 8th Cavalry were moved within supporting distance, although remaining out of sight. At daybreak of December 15, 1890, forty-three Sioux Police and volunteers under Lt. Bull Head, a cool and tough officer, surrounded his cabins, pulled him naked out of bed and got him dressed. He ordered his grey circus horse to be saddled, and seemed to be willing to go until he got outside the cabin which had quickly become surrounded by a large crowd of excited Ghost Dancers. At first they cursed the Metal Breasts. Then one of Sitting Bull's wives chanted a song to him:

> Sitting Bull, you have always been a brave man;
> What is going to happen now?[29]

Catch-the-Bear had an old grudge to settle with Lt. Bull Head, and he went looking for him, shoving his Winchester into the bellies of the Metal Breasts. Sitting Bull stopped by his horse, turned, and then said in a loud voice to his people, "I am not going. Come on! Come on! Take action." Catch-the-Bear dropped Lt. Bull Head who twisted as he fell to get Sitting Bull. It was bloody business between the Sioux—short and like a frenzy. At the sound of the shots, the circus horse sat down and lifted a hoof and they thought that the spirit of Sitting Bull was still there.

Although the fight had lasted no more than a few minutes, fourteen were killed, six of the Sioux police and Sitting Bull and seven of his followers. The remainder of his band, numbering over three hundred, then scattered, but before long most of these surrendered, and only about fifty joined Big Foot's camp. For a while then, it looked as if there would be no further violence. The Second Coming began to appear less imminent than the three thousand white troops, and, although it is not customary in western history to credit the Army with intelligence or human intention, the truth is that Gen. Miles did his best to restore the situation by peaceful means. On the whole, he did a good job— better certainly than any historian who might have been put in charge of the

28. *My Friend the Indian*, pp. 203–4.

29. *Sitting Bull*, p. 304.

same material. If the aim of the Army had been a military victory, it could have been realized fairly easily this time for those were not the Sioux of '76. They were carefully surrounded by white troops, reduced in numbers, disunited, bereft of their sense of superiority, and crowded into an area too small to allow them the power to maneuver that they needed in order to carry on their kind of war. Miles' tactics were to impress them with his strength while at the same time to persuade them through friendly Indians to give up their arms and return peacefully to their reservations, tactics that proved successful except for one bloody moment when all the feelings of the past blotted out any considerations of the present or the future.

7.

Big Foot's camp of Ghost Dancers had left the Cheyenne River Reservation and was heading south, looking for the large bands of "hostiles" that had gathered in the badlands, but these camps had already been persuaded to surrender by Miles' emissaries and were on their way back to their agencies, when Big Foot's camp was intercepted and surrendered, agreeing to give up its arms on the following morning, December 29. Of course, it was tense as the Indians slept that night on Wounded Knee Creek surrounded by white troops and a battery of four Hotchkiss machine guns. Cool observers say, though, that the intentions on both sides were good—that the Indians intended to give up their arms and that the troops intended to escort them to the nearest agency (Pine Ridge). In fact, the commander had provided Big Foot, who had pneumonia, with a warm tent and stove and had sent his personal physician to attend him. He also had separated the women and children from the warriors in case of trouble and had issued strict orders to the troops that women and children should not be hurt.

In the morning the Indians received their orders—to bring out their arms and surrender them—and we might pause even here to think for a moment of what it meant to Sioux warriors to renounce their weapons. When only two rifles were forthcoming the soldiers were instructed to search the lodges, and they were probably not very delicate in going about this job. At the same time, the medicine man, Yellow Bird, walked through the warriors, blowing an eagle-bone whistle and assuring them that the white soldiers would become powerless and that their own "Ghost shirts" were bullet-proof. The women and children came crowding back in the excitement. Everything was close together—women, children, warriors, and soldiers. The moment came— certainly an understandable moment psychologically—when a soldier pulled open an Indian's blanket to search him. A Sioux started the shooting. They were so crowded on top of each other that at first much of it was hand-to-hand fighting. Then the Indians broke and started running up a dry ravine, most of them women and children for all but a few of the warriors were dead in front of their lodges. The Hotchkiss guns poured two-inch explosive shells into the ravine at the rate of nearly fifty a minute, and infuriated soldiers followed, killing for two miles up the ravine. Big Foot's camp, including men, women, and children, had numbered around three hundred and fifty and it would be merciful to estimate that a hundred of them were not killed.

But to the Teton Sioux the number of dead, whatever it may have been, was not the greatest casualty of the Battle of Wounded Knee; speaking of it in retrospect forty years later, a Sioux said: "After the Battle of Wounded Knee all ambition was taken out of us. We have never since been able to regain a foothold."[30] And Scudder Mekeel, modern historian of the Teton Sioux, uses it to mark the end of a historical period, one which he describes as a "complete rejection of white culture and its concomitant evils"; the next period, which still continues, is described as one of "acceptance, passive at least, of white culture."[31]

These divisions of the historical periods of the Sioux are also marked by geometrical lines extending back to the Battle of Little Bighorn. The troops who surrounded the Sioux camp on Wounded Knee Creek and ended even the hope for a return of the old way of life were themselves ruled that day, as were the Sioux warriors who could not renounce their weapons, by overpowering feelings and events of the past. They were troops of the 7th Cavalry.

30. *Warriors without Weapons*, p. 33.

31. "A Short History of the Teton-Dakota," *North Dakota Historical Quarterly*, X (Jan., 1943), 139–40.

CHAPTER 3

. . . .

The Cheyennes

. . . .

"'Brave' hardships, surely"
—*Big Foot, Cheyenne Chief*

The Cheyennes and Sitting Bull's Hunkpapas occupied special positions in the great column that marched up the Little Bighorn in the sunset of the day following the Battle—the Cheyennes led the column and the Hunkpapas protected the rear. Ahead of the Cheyennes lay three long shadows, one that fell upon all Indians, another that pursued those who had been in the Battle, and then the Cheyennes had their own dark way to go.

Even if they had not been specially marked, as Indians they were doomed to be no longer Indians and for a long time not much of anything else. But a shadow harsher in outline was to pursue them and the Teton Sioux. They were marked by too great a victory; for years a humiliated Army was to follow them wherever they were or were rumored to be, and western settlers who regarded all good Indians as dead ones, lived in special dread of the Cheyennes and Sioux with a picture far more vivid than ours of the mutilation on Custer Hill. Particular circumstances, however, and the particular character of the Cheyennes gave their succeeding history its own tragic form.

For instance, the Sioux in defeat have not been deprived of the glory of their victory whereas today few know that the Cheyennes had anything to do with the Battle. Yet on the march they were at the head of the Indian column; their circle was at the lower end of the Indian camp where Custer tried to make his attack; Lame White Man, the most important chief killed in the Battle, fell leading his Cheyennes in a charge that may have been one of the most important in demoralizing Custer's troops; and there are soldiers and historians who rate the Cheyennes as the best cavalry men of the plains. It is not easy to explain how the Sioux have succeeded in completely winning the Battle of the Little Bighorn, obliterating even the Cheyennes. Their superiority in number is only part of the explanation. The Sioux had the gift for glory. They were the United States Marines—or the RAF—of the Plains Indians—they were good and they knew it and had besides this extra something which succeeds in conveying the impression that they did all the fighting. So the Cheyennes have had to suffer the harsh consequences of a victory for which they no longer get any of the credit.

1.

It is not very profitable to argue at this late date over whether the Cheyennes or the Sioux were the better fighters. They were both first-rate, that is clear from their record, but the record also makes clear that, as the Sioux had a gift for glory, the Cheyennes had a knack for defeat. It seems that almost every time the Army of the frontier got around to exterminating a camp of Indians, the Cheyennes happened to be the first they ran into—as at Sand Creek and Washita. And so it was again after the one great victory over the whites in which the Cheyennes participated. During the summer following the Battle of the Little Bighorn the Cheyennes like the Sioux moved back over the buffalo ranges of the Rosebud, Tongue and Powder rivers avoiding any serious trouble with an Army that was slowly preparing to defeat them forever, but the winter was different and part of the old story. Although the Sioux camps had to run, fight, hide, and fight again until many were ready to surrender, only the Cheyenne camp under Dull Knife was surrounded, crushed, and burned; its survivors, some of them naked or covered only with a cartridge belt, ran up the snow-covered hillsides and then started on the long frozen journey to find the camp of Crazy Horse. The cause of this defeat cannot be attributed just to bad luck. The Cheyennes had known for some days that Gen. Mackenzie's troops were in the vicinity, but Last Bull, chief of the Fox fighting society, talked bigger than the chiefs of the tribe and persuaded the camp not to move.[1] So we have another example of a fatal weakness of the Indian—an aboriginal social and political organization in which bands were often more powerful than tribes and tribes more powerful than confederacies. The Cheyennes may individually have been better fighters than the Sioux, but their battle record is not; perhaps their very power as fighters gave too much power to their fighting societies and clearly they did not have leaders at this time comparable to Sitting Bull and Crazy Horse, both of whom camped fairly close to the white troops all winter without making mistakes. Still, when all is said and done, the Cheyennes were hard-luck fighters, lacking something indefinable that leads other fighters who are no better to victory.

1. *The Fighting Cheyennes*, p. 369. This work gives a full account of the defeat which occurred on November 26, 1876 in the Bighorn mountains near the head of one of the tributaries of the Powder river.

2.

A further difference between the Cheyennes and the Sioux appeared in the spring of 1877. The Cheyennes recognized the inevitable sooner and more completely than the Sioux, and by May almost all of them[2] had surrendered for reasons some of which are not hard to surmise—their hostility toward the whites had not been of such long standing as the Sioux', they lacked the Sioux' collective sense of self-confidence, and the defeat of Dull Knife's camp in the winter must have been a frozen memory, although stirring memories of other bitter defeats. In any event, they surrendered in two bands, the smaller of which came to be called the Two Moon Band[3] to Gen. Miles in the north at Ft. Keogh[. . . .]

3.

There is still something else distinguishing the after-history of the Cheyennes from the Sioux—mountains and Ponderosa pine. Although both tribes were plains Indians, they were Indians of the High Plains of the northwest where, as in the paintings of Charley Russell, there is usually a haze of mountains that look cool in the distance and suddenly are cool as they get close. To be close to them means many things—to game and horses, they mean shade, high grass and white water, things that also have meaning to us, and it is not necessary to be a western painter or an Indian deifying the Four Winds to sense that mountains overlooking the plains guard still other meanings more difficult to express. As for the Ponderosa pine, it has special meanings, too, turning black in the distance and naming the Black Hills, but what we would all notice close at hand is that it completely dominates the ground under it, making it open and good to walk on. From east to west, the main mountain ranges to be considered are the Black Hills, the Rosebud Mountains between the Tongue river and the Rosebud, the Wolf Mountains between the Rosebud and the Little Bighorn, and beyond, the Bighorns themselves.

This is roughly the "unceded" land which had been granted by treaty to

2. A small band under White Hawk briefly postponed the inevitable by joining Lame Deer's "irreconcilable" Sioux who were defeated by Gen. Miles in May, 1877. Mark H. Brown and W. R. Felton, *The Frontier Years*, (New York, 1955), pp. 101–2.

3. Two Moon's eminence as a chief was acquired after the surrender. Both Cheyennes and Gen. Miles agree that at the time of the surrender he was a minor figure. *The Frontier Days*, pp. 99, 227.

the Sioux; it was the land which they were fighting to stay on, and, in sur-rendering, many of them believed that a reservation would be established for them there.⁴ Instead, they were returned to their reservations in the badland or semi-badland country of South Dakota, and, although to some one who has lived in the mountains this country looks as if it had been de-signed primarily for snakes and fossils, still it was part of the former home of the Teton Sioux even if they had fought not to be confined on it. With the Cheyennes it was different, both better and much worse. The Two Moon band that had surrendered in the north to Gen. Miles was kept at Ft. Keogh where the Tongue river joins the Yellowstone, so they were still near home. Moreover, in surrendering to Gen. Miles, they surrendered to a soldier who had fought the Cheyennes in the southwest and had a special respect for them. He promised them that, if they would enlist and help him in his wars against the Indians, he would help them get a permanent reservation in their own country,⁵ and in addition Indians at Ft. Keogh were usually given spe-cial immediate inducements to enlist—raisins and a chance to listen to the telephone ("whispering spirit") and to see the telegraph sparking messages ("captured lightning"). Many Cheyennes "held their hands to the sky" and proved to be Miles' best Indian soldiers,⁶ and he did not forget his promise, although it took a long time to fulfill. So for some years Two Moon's band continued their old way of life as warriors, and if they now fought against their former allies, the Sioux, and even against some Cheyennes, still it was fighting and fighting was deeper with them than the color under the scalp. Besides there were brass buttons and raisins and the promise of a perma-nent home in the mountains.

4. Harry Anderson, "Nelson A. Miles and the Sioux War of 1876–77," *The Westerners Brand Book*, Vol. xvi, No. 4 (June, 1959), pp. 26, 32. There is much detailed information about events following the Battle in this article which reduces the magnitude of the role Gen. Miles played in these events considerably from that the General assigns to himself in his own reports. The estimate seems just and impartial, although it would be hard to find either an Indian fighter or an Indian who did not "pull the long-bow" in recounting his own feats. The fact that the prose of most men (Miles, Custer, and Crook along with the others) exceeds their martial exploits does not alter my admiration—which appears later in this chapter—of Miles's treatment of the Cheyennes and of his general attitude toward the Indian question.

5. Verne Dusenberry, "The Northern Cheyenne," *Montana: Magazine of History*, V (Winter, 1955), 27.

6. *The Frontier Years*, pp. 105–17.

4.

This is not what happened to Dull Knife's band after their surrender at Ft. Robinson. The Cheyennes, when they became nomadic plains Indians, had at first ranged with the seasons as far south as Texas and as far north as the Black Hills, but in 1832 William Bent, a trader, on the upper Arkansas river, had married a Cheyenne woman and after that a portion of the tribe stayed in the south, became known as the Southern Cheyennes, and eventually were granted a reservation in Indian Territory (in what is now the state of Oklahoma).[7] Crook and Miles were so busy collecting Indians in the spring of 1877 that Ft. Robinson and Ft. Keogh become overcrowded, and orders were issued to transfer Dull Knife's Northern Cheyennes to the southern reservation. Nine hundred and eighty Indians started south, many of them on foot, and seventy days later 937 arrived at the Cheyenne Agency in Indian Territory.[8]

Then the real misery began. Their arrival overcrowded the southern reservation, there was no hunting range left, the government had not provided extra rations for the newcomers, the rations were no good anyway and the so-called beef was old cow and not much of that. The Northern Cheyennes had to live off the soup of their relatives with whom they were soon quarreling, and for the hope of something on the side the girls began to slip off their chastity ropes and go out with the soldiers. Worse still, it was the south and not their home; wherever they looked, it looked the same. Even biologically the Northern Cheyennes were no longer a part of this environment—within two months after their arrival two-thirds of them were sick with malarial diseases and at the agency there was one physician and no quinine.[9] Although this part of their history after the Battle has no parallel in Sioux history it is a fate they shared with many other tribes—eastern, middle western, and western—who were removed from their homeland and settled among the mosquitoes on land that seemed permanently worthless. There is one big difference, though, between the Northern Cheyennes and the others—the Northern Cheyennes are back on the Rosebud, just east of Custer Battlefield, and they fought their way back, all the way back, 1500 miles.

By early summer of 1878 Dull Knife and Little Wolf, the great Northern Cheyenne warrior, were trying to persuade the agent to let them return home. Little Wolf said to the agent, "These people were raised far up in the north

7. *Cheyenne Autumn*, p. 2.

8. *Cheyenne Autumn*, p. 5.

9. *The Fighting Cheyennes*, pp. 400–401.

among the pines and the mountains. . . . Now, since we have been in this country, we are dying every day. This is not a good country for us, and we wish to return to our home in the mountains."[10] When the prospect of another winter was not far off, Dull Knife and Little Wolf concluded the argument, shook hands with all present, and hoped that they would be allowed to go peacefully. Then Little Wolf added, "I do not want to see blood spilt about the agency. If you are going to send your soldiers after me, I wish that you would first let me get a little distance away from this agency. Then if you want to fight, I will fight you, and we can make the ground bloody at that place."[11] On September 7, 1878, two hundred and eighty-four of the thousand Northern Cheyennes who had marched south from Ft. Robinson left the reservation without permission and headed north. Of this band of less than three hundred, fewer than a hundred were warriors.[12]

This homeward journey of the Northern Cheyennes has been likened many times to the march of the Greeks to the sea, but it needs no analogy and in many ways was a thing in itself. Mari Sandoz has recorded its sufferings in her book *Cheyenne Autumn*, and here all that can be done is to indicate merely the kind of thing it was.

Word that the Cheyennes were loose was the same as word that Cheyennes were on the warpath. The nation was angry and alarmed,[13] and the plains in terror, so the Cheyennes had to fight not only the Army but settlers, buffalo hunters, cowboys and various combinations of these. Going north rather than east or west they should have been easy to head off—they had to cross three railroads over which reinforcements could be rushed and many quick-sand rivers with fords that could be guarded. Even worse was the fact that for hundreds of miles they went over flat country with no place to hide; often they and the Army were in plain sight of each other all day with the Cheyennes fighting in depth, throwing out screens of warriors to protect their moving camp. At night if they were not surrounded they kept on to be ahead of the Army the next morning; if they were surrounded, the women tried to cook something

10. *The Fighting Cheyennes*, pp. 401–2.

11. *The Fighting Cheyennes*, p. 403.

12. *Cheyenne Autumn*, p. 30.

13. Although before the journey was completed American sympathy for the underdog began to assert itself, especially since the top dog was the American Army. The fear was humorously expressed that it was no longer a question of whether the Army would capture the Cheyennes, but the other way around. *Cheyenne Autumn*, p. 128.

and the men fought all night. And always they had the problem of supply. Before long their ammunition ran low, their food was gone, their horses gave out, and they had to supply themselves in flight off the country. The policy of Dull Knife and Little Wolf originally had been to fire on the Army only after the troops had started the shooting and not to kill any settlers, but they had to have beef and horses and it is not possible to make a practice of running stock off ranches without eventually killing some ranchers. Besides, as was so often the case in Indian history, there was a big difference between what the old chiefs said and what the young warriors did, yet the chances are that Dull Knife and Little Wolf probably didn't care much after their own women and children were shot in holes where they were trying to hide. Perhaps between thirty or forty settlers were killed, although the newspapers had the plains covered with scalps and drenched with innocent blood.[14]

It is not customary in histories of Indian warfare to recognize the presence of women except as they are contained in the proposition that one of the great military weaknesses of the Indians was that they usually had their camps with them. For a moment, let us examine this proposition and more simply, try to visualize what it was like to fight fifteen hundred miles with women along, many of them on foot. No doubt there were times when it would have been better for Indians if their women could have been left safely behind, but this was only sometimes the case, and without them this fifteen-hundred-mile fight would been much shorter and with not enough humanity in it to be long remembered. The Cheyennes themselves did not think of their women as ornaments of peace; there is an old saying among them, "No people is whipped until the hearts of its women are on the ground, and then it is done, no matter how great the warriors or how strong the lance."[15] They were beautiful Indian women, and noted among Indians for their chastity, fidelity, and courage. But they were Indian women, and for their own sakes should not be sentimentalized into sweet Victorian types in extra good physical condition. It was their silvery laughter that sounded over Custer Battlefield as they cut off the genitals of the dead, and what they did to captured white women was dreaded almost as much as being passed around among the warriors. They were Indian women, with their own beauty and wonderful in their own kind of ways, and if Gen. Custer had an Indian "wife," he took the daughter of a Cheyenne chief, who, accord-

14. *Cheyenne Autumn*, p. 118.

15. *Cheyenne Autumn*, p. 136 (116?).

ing to legend, did not marry again until after she heard of his death. And, if none of this story is true, still the Cheyennes made it up and expressed something deep of themselves in it.

As the Cheyennes hurried ahead of the soldiers, their women hastily picked currants, chokecherries, and plums, and, when there was no meat, they caught snakes and sand turtles. When the young warriors drove in beef, they pulled the sharp knives from their belts and went to work skinning and butchering, hanging the meat in strips on drying ropes and hardening the hides over fires for the soles of moccasins. When fresh horses were captured, the work was rougher, for even the horses that had been ridden before were not used to Indians and some times danger was so close that about all a woman could do was to crawl on a horse with her papoose and see what would happen. There were women along who were already noted for their exploits in battle—Buffalo Calf Road Woman in whose honor the Indians call Crook's defeat on the Rosebud, "Where the girl saved her brother,[16] and Pretty Walker, the long-legged daughter of Little Wolf who at fifty-seven was still one of the fastest Cheyenne runners. But Pretty Walker's great battle exploit—rescuing a white soldier from the thick of battle because he had given his horse to a squaw too old to run away—while respected was not named or mentioned.[17] Also children were born on the long flight north—a woman would drop behind, crouch in a hole while the troops rode by, and pinch the nose of the baby every time he cried until he learned by strangulation the first Cheyenne law, to be noiseless in danger; at night she did or did not succeed in passing through the troops again and rejoining the camp waiting for her around low fires. Yet there was even a darker time ahead for the Cheyenne women.

5.

Trouble began to develop in the Cheyenne camp as they reached Nebraska, old-time Cheyenne trouble, dissension among the leaders. Dull Knife believed that now they were close at home nothing bad would happen to them; besides winter was not far off and he seemed to remember that he had been told he could return to Ft. Robinson if he did not like it down south. Little Wolf, the warrior, was wiser than the statesman. He said it was bad to divide but worse to stop before they reached home. Somewhere near the Platte river

16. *The Fighting Cheyennes*, p. 336.

17. *Cheyenne Autumn*, p. 18.

they separated,[18] Little Wolf continuing north until he reached the Sand Hills of Nebraska where he camped for the winter. Soldiers and others rode close by without discovering them, for no one left the camp on foot and they rode out to meet all returning messengers in order that there would be no moccasin tracks about, and each stick was charred before it was burned in order that there would be no smoke. In March, Little Wolf broke camp and headed north again until he crossed the Little Missouri where he was spotted by the Indian scouts of Lt. W. P. Clark, one of those unheard-of young Army men who felt deeply about the Indian and had studied his customs, psychology, and speech.[19] Lt. Clark rode out ahead of his troops and said, "I have prayed to God that I might find my friend Little Wolf, and now I have done so." Little Wolf replied, "It is well; we will go with you wherever you say."[20] So Clark took them to Ft. Keogh where they joined the Two Moon Band, and Gen. Miles offered them a chance to enlist. Little Wolf said they had been fighting a long time and were tired, and Gen. Miles said, "Well, think the matter over and see how you feel about it." They thought it over and after some of the weariness was gone, Little Wolf and all the young men enlisted and went back to their old job of fighting in the country that had been their home.

6.

For some time after Dull Knife's band surrendered at Ft. Robinson, things went well with them. They ate and slept their fatigue away; though they were prisoners, they had a good deal of freedom as long as they showed up at night; and there were even dances to which soldiers came bringing presents for the girls. Then in the hard cold of early January, the order came from Washington that they were to be returned to the south immediately. The order was so appalling that Gen. Crook, trying to avert shame from himself and the Army, telegraphed the Indian Bureau demanding that they and not the War Department superintend the move if it had to be carried out.[21] Dull Knife said, "No, I am here on my own ground, and I will never go back. You may kill me here;

---

18. Grinnell says that he heard variant stories from the Cheyennes as to where the bands separated, some giving the location as south, others as north of the Platte (pp. 409–10); Sandoz raises no question about the location, giving it as north of the Platte (p. 114).

19. [blank]

20. *The Fighting Cheyennes*, p. 412.

21. *Cheyenne Autumn*, pp. 190, 193.

but can never make me go back."[22] When all the other Cheyennes refused to go, the new commander at Ft. Robinson, Capt. Wessels ("The Flying Dutchman"), ordered them confined to one barracks and denied them heat, food, and finally water. He tried to get the women and children to leave the building, but none would go except those ordered out by the young men—the families of two warriors who were being held in the guard house and the old women.[23] Since they had cached a little food in the barracks, what was worst at the beginning was the cold and filth—everything had to be done in front of everybody else except that the soldiers occasionally marched the women out behind the stables. Afterwards some of the Indians said that they were eight days without food and water, others that they had no food for five days and were without water for three,[24] but how could people agree precisely on such suffering afterwards? They scraped the ice off the window sills, and the women, when they were taken out behind the stables, tried to collect a little snow in their dresses. Toward the end it became like the preparation for a religious ordeal, like the fasting and ecstasy before a Sun Dance when they run skewers through their breast muscles and then hang from poles until the flesh pulls away. On January 9, Little Shield, one of the soldier chiefs, said, "Now, dress up and put on your best clothing. We will all die together."[25] They all put on such finery as they had—a terrible thing to do considering the cold outside—and the women began to assemble rifles. Supposedly, they had surrendered all their arms, but the women had not been searched very carefully and a few had strapped carbines on their backs under their dresses, a few more had revolvers hanging between their breasts, and others had distributed pieces of rifles to the children who since the surrender had been playing with such toys as triggers and rifle sights. When they assembled all their arms, they had five rifles, nine revolvers, and another that worked part of the time.[26] Then they sang their death songs, kissed each other, and went out through the window.

The soldiers came running in their underwear, looking like white ghosts to the Indians. It was bright outside and easy shooting—five inches of snow and moonlight—with the temperature standing at zero. Those who got as far

22. *The Fighting Cheyennes*, p. 418.
23. *The Fighting Cheyennes* p. 419.
24. *The Fighting Cheyennes* p. 419.
25. *The Fighting Cheyennes*, p. 420.
26. *Cheyenne Autumn*, p. 202.

as the creek drank too much, and those who got across had to go from there on in frozen finery. The bluffs ahead were too much for most of the starved women carrying children. One of Dull Knife's three daughters, who had been called "the Beautiful People" by Lt. Clark, was found part way up the hillside holding somebody else's baby, and when they tried to lift her she was so badly shot she was in pieces. Figures will have to tell the rest of the story: of the hundred and fifty in Dull Knife's band, sixty-four were killed, eight or ten were never heard of again, and the rest were captured; of these, fifty-eight were sent to Pine Ridge reservation and the remaining twenty were returned south to stand trial for the murder of settlers,[27] and, looking for something to say for ourselves, let us add that they were eventually acquitted.

Dull Knife, with his remarkable capacity for bringing grief to his people and surviving himself, quickly separated himself and his small party from the main body of the Cheyennes trying to climb the bluffs, found a hole in the rocks, and starved there for ten more days. Then after nearly three weeks of traveling by night, hiding by day and eating moccasins and rosebuds, he and his family reached Pine Ridge reservation. Dr. V. T. McGillycuddy, in charge of Pine Ridge, was one of the best Indian agents of his time, but he wanted none of these Cheyennes who were joined by Wild Hog and the others acquitted of the murder charge. He complained that they "were of a more war-like nature than our Sioux" and "were mourning continually for their relatives who were killed," and consequently he was only too glad "to accede to a request of General Miles" who both fought and befriended the Cheyennes, that the remnants of Dull Knife's band be transferred to Ft. Keogh. So in 1880, two years after Dull Knife had left the Indian Territory in the south, he and what was left of his followers arrived home. They had made it the long and hard way. Later, when Lt. Clark was gathering material for his book, The Indian Sign Language, Dull Knife, trying to explain to him that in Cheyenne "brave" means not only fearless in conduct but outstanding generally in quality, illustrated by speaking of the journey north and especially of the outbreak at Ft. Robinson and of the days following as "'brave' hardships, surely."

7.

Still, the Northern Cheyennes were in effect prisoners at Ft. Keogh and the mouth of the Tongue River was really not their home—the mountains and the pines were farther back, between the Tongue and the Rosebud. No one

27. The Fighting Cheyennes, p. 426.

knows when they began to slip out of camp and return to this country that is not far from the Custer Battlefield. Perhaps it was Little Wolf himself who started the final move; in 1880 while drunk he killed Starving Elk who long had been paying too much attention to Little Wolf's wives and his daughter, Pretty Walker, and, when any Cheyenne killed one of his own, his people had "to throw him away." In exile, he and a small group of his followers went up the Rosebud until they came to a tributary that led them into the mountains between the Rosebud and the Tongue, and there, about fifteen miles southwest of the present townsite of Lame Deer, they pitched camp.[28] The camp grew, and probably Gen. Miles was glad to have Indians he trusted leave for the back country and reduce the Indian population around Ft. Keogh. Besides, he had promised the Cheyennes that, if they surrendered and fought for him, he would fight for a permanent home for them. Gen. Miles' attitude toward Indians probably should not be confused with that of some of his young officers, such as Lts. Clark and Casey, who in their own time must have been regarded as "Indian lovers" and who to us seem like early modern students of ethnology, but if Gen. Miles was not an anthropologist he was all Army, and for some reason it is easy to forget the number of old-line soldiers who believe the Army is the implement of their country's ideals just as it is easy to forget how often an old-fashioned sense of honor and justice arrives at right conclusions and once there has lasting power to see that something is done. By Executive order dated November 26, 1884 a reservation was set aside for the Northern Cheyennes in the country they had chosen which is close to the Custer Battlefield and takes in the mountains lying between the Rosebud and the Tongue.[29]

Even yet the troubles of the Northern Cheyennes were not over. For one thing, as a late and somewhat arbitrary creation, the Tongue River Reservation, unlike the Great Sioux Reservation, included land in which there were already ranchers, and at best and understandably ranchers regarded strychnine as equally suited for coyotes and Indians. The white settlers for miles around did all they could to get the Cheyennes moved, and finally in 1889 their agent, needing help and without an important friend near, wrote Gen. Miles, then commanding the Division of the Pacific. There is nothing very modern about the military reply; it is without sentiment or sociology, reflecting only one emotion—old fashioned moral indignation:

28. Dusenberry, p. 30.

29. Dusenberry, p. 31.

Headquarters,
Division of the Pacific
San Francisco, California

June 1, 1889

Sir:

Referring to your letter of May 15 in regard to the proposed removal of the Indians I would say that, in my judgment, there is no good reason or justice in doing so.

These Indians surrendered in good faith in the spring of 1877. . . . During the last twelve years they have been entirely peaceable; several of their people have been killed while employed by the Government. They have been a good part of the time self-sustaining; the Government has allowed them a little corner of territory upon which to live, and justice, humanity, and every other commendable reason demands that they should be allowed to live in peace in the vicinity in which they were born.

The congregating of great masses of Indians, as has been done in the Indian Territory and on the Great Sioux Reservation, is not only a blot upon our civilization, but also a black mark upon the map of the United States, and I trust the Government will extend to those people the protecting hand which a peaceably disposed people are entitled to.

They were told that if they remained at peace and did what they were directed to do the Government would treat them fairly and justly. They have fulfilled their part of the compact and it would be but justice for the Government to allow them to remain where it has placed them during the past years. What is more, Indians who surrender their tribal relations, are, under the law of Congress, entitled to take up the land for homes on the public domain, and in this instance, they have undoubted right, legally and morally, to remain where they are now located.

Very respectfully

Your obedient servant
Nelson A. Miles,
Brigadier-General,
U.S. Army[30]

30. Dusenberry, p. 33.

So the Northern Cheyennes were allowed to keep their reservation, although some of them still were not allowed to live on it. Another Cheyenne band had accumulated at Pine Ridge Agency, made up in good part of the two hundred and fifty followers of Little Chief who had voluntarily left Ft. Keogh in 1878 for Indian Territory, had been steadily unhappy there, and had been granted permission to return north in 1881.[31] The agent at Pine Ridge, Dr. McGillycuddy, did not like these Cheyennes any better than he had liked Dull Knife's band. "The Bedouins of the Desert" would not farm or haul freight, they kept his Sioux in turmoil, and every now and then some of them would take off for the summer, making the four-hundred-mile trip to the Rosebud to see their relatives back home. The Cheyenne agent was not much happier than McGillycuddy to receive them, since they came without rations and he had trouble to get enough for his own charges. It was probably Gen. Miles who understood their loneliness and finally did something about it, although a practical reason may also have influenced his action.[32] Gen. Miles, it will be remembered, was put in charge of the operations against the Sioux during the Messiah Outbreak in the winter of 1889–90, and he may have wanted to reduce the number of Indians on the Pine Ridge Agency where much of the trouble was brewing, although, since there were not many Cheyennes on the reservation and they had avoided the Ghost Dance, the chances are that other things were more important in his mind when he allowed them to start happily in midwinter across the four hundred miles of badlands, broken country and deep snow lying between them and Ft. Keogh. Even there they had to wait for the government to send further orders. It was October, 1891 before they were allowed to move to the reservation, a decade after they had left the south for home. At last, though, they were all there, all who were still alive, in the red mountains covered with pines that look black in the distance from the plains.

So, for the Cheyennes, geometrically speaking, there was finally a convergence of the lines that marked all those who survived the Battle of the Little Bighorn. For the Cheyennes, the lines spread over thousands of miles; many of them were broken lines spread over thousands of miles; many of them were broken lines ending abruptly; and all of them were deep, so deep as to outline the Cheyenne life of today.

31. Dusenberry, p. 33.
32. Dusenberry, p. 38.

In 1954, Eugene Fisher, grandson of Little Wolf and then president of the Northern Cheyenne Tribal Council, said:

> "You'd think after sixty or seventy years, there'd be no more bands, there'd be just Northern Cheyenne. But, no, these people still belong to Two Moon's band, or Little Wolf's band, or the Pine Ridge band, or whatever band their folks belonged to.
>
> "Before, we used to have the soldier societies, and that was the important way to tell who a man was. But the Custer battle changed all that—and everything else about us. You might say, it was kind of a revolution. . . ."[33]

33. Dusenberry, p. 40.

Our Marks

. . . .

In Business

. . . .

There is no balance-sheet that tells whether the debt Gen. Custer owes Anheuser-Busch, Inc., is greater than the debt the corporation owes the General, who was a teetotaler. The General's debt is not reduced by the fact that, when the business connection was first established, the memory of the General was a national asset and the company was still pretty much a local brewery. In the long run, they have done very well by each other.

There is some correlation between the profits of this world and its lasting memories. Although the dead are not allowed to take it with them, the dead who continue to live in this world generally go on making money. In a way, they have to earn their keep. Why not? Sometimes business rescues individuals from near oblivion and makes them weekly heroes on TV, as it has done with Wyatt Earp and Bat Masterson. Sometimes it immortalizes a whole class of men by industrializing them. The cowboy, for instance. Apart from Westerns on movie and TV, apart from rodeos and dude ranches and adult consumption altogether, it would take quite an audit to calculate the annual profit in children's cowboy boots, pants, belts, hats, toy revolvers, etc. More frequently, of course, business capitalizes on well established reputations but its investment in them raises the valuation of their stock and adds to their security as well as to that of the investor. So Prudential Insurance advertisements increase our feeling of security about Prudential and even about the Rock of Gibraltar.

1.

Custer's Last Stand has been a big money maker. How much it has made would be impossible to calculate, and it is undoubtedly proper that something should remain misty about the economics of the dead. There are, for instance, small local profits starting with the Black Hills where there is a Custer State Park and a town of Custer that has grown into a motel city famous because Custer's command first discovered gold near there in 1874. In the Black Hills,

State Park lodges, souvenir shops, etc., sell Ed Ryan's story of how at Gen. Custer's request he remained behind with a sick buddy, and in the summer Ed dispenses autographs to eastern pilgrims.[1] Just a few miles from Custer, a massive sculptor makes a hard-earned living from the private contributions and admission fees of those who came to watch him change a mountain into a statue of Crazy Horse.[2] North of the Black Hills, in Medora, North Dakota, the Eaton brothers started one of the first dude ranches, the Custer Trail Ranch. From here on west to the Battlefield the trade picks up—the town of Custer, Montana, the General Custer Hotel in Billings and a mounting number of Custer motels and restaurants (some not too good). Who knows how many cars choose the Custer Battlefield Highway because it has this tradename and not just a number? One hundred and thirty thousand people visit the Field annually, even though they have to turn off an east-west transcontinental road to get there; and it is an important source of income for the permanent residents who live near by in Crow Agency and even in Hardin. This is small stuff, but it all adds up.

As a source of national income, writers have profited from it more than any other large group of investors. Some of these returns have been small—quick articles and stories, novels with rapidly fading royalties, etc.; it has been a natural for the fast-buck writer. But it has also been turned into steady income, even a few historians having made small nest eggs out of the Battle. And when it gets into the movies and TV, as it has done almost since the beginning of screen history, it gets into Big Money. Of course, as we all know, its biggest business affiliation has been with Budweiser beer.

2.

"Custer's Last Fight" began its advertising career at an important moment in the history of advertising and American business in general. Lithographs of it made their first barroom appearances soon after Mr. Busch acquired the Adams' painting[3] and therefore in the very late 80's or early 90's. During the 80's, according to Frank Presbrey, standard authority on the subject, only four American companies (Sapolio, Royal Baking Powder, Pear's Soap and

---

1. See above, [incomplete].

2. See below, [incomplete].

3. Don Russell, "Sixty Years in Bar Rooms; or 'Custer's Last Fight,'" p. 62.

Ivory Soap) advertised on a large scale and "in the highest sense,"[4] but during the 90's, especially after the depression of '93, advertisement and business fast became Big Business. "How pregnant the advertising '90's were with the future of American business may be put with the statement that it was in this period that the foundation was laid with large-scale advertising for such present-day establishments as the Eastman Kodak Company, Sears, Roebuck & Co., the Quaker Oats Company, the Shredded Wheat Company, Postum Cereal Company, H. L. Heinz (which bought Mulvany's painting, 'Custer's Last Rally'), Gold Dust, the National Biscuit Company and others of similar size and prestige. . . ."[5]

Presbrey points out certain general developments in advertising during the 90's that help to explain the early commercial success of the lithograph, "Custer's Last Fight." "By 1896 illustrations had become so much a characteristic of the advertisement that the Western Druggist ventured a prophecy that 'when the history of advertising is written, the present will be known as "the picture period."'"[6] Moreover, because of rapid improvements in methods of reproduction, the "picture" advertisements of the '80s changed from "relatively lifeless" outlines to "the naturalness and greater emotiveness of the half-tone reproduction of humans in action."[7] The concurrent development of another important advertising device, the slogan, gave trademarks to other companies, and to other beers, including "The Beer That Made Milwaukee Famous"; but in the public mind Anheuser-Busch became identified with a picture full of "motiveness" and "humans in action."

It is hardly possible that Mr. Adolphus Busch could have known what an important step he was taking in the history of his company's relations with the public when he first distributed lithographs of "Custer's Last Fight" to bars handling his beer. He had first-hand evidence, of course, for believing that they would stir up some interest for a time, since the Adams' painting had evidently attracted a good deal of attention while it was hanging in the St. Louis saloon. But within a few years he presented the Adams' painting to the 7th Cavalry in a gesture characteristic of early advertisement much of which was a projection of the owner's personality, and in a gesture, too,

4. *The History and Development of Advertising* (New York, 1929), p. 338.

5. P. 360.

6. P. 356.

7. P. 382.

characteristic of the patriotism and generosity of Mr. Busch who had his company wire $100,000 to San Francisco at the time of the earthquake.[8] But the gesture also probably indicates that "Mr. Busch assumed interest in the lithographs had been exhausted," and it is Don Russell's conjecture that, when the interest increased instead, Mr. Busch had to commission Mr. Becker, foreman of the department issuing his lithographs, to make a painting "after" the departed original.[9] Who knows at the time, even in business, which of his gestures is going to be taken as his public image?

"About one million copies have been distributed to bars and taverns through the years."[10] In addition, the success of "Custer's Last Fight" must have entered the thinking of company officials when later they commissioned Oscar E. Beringhaus "to paint a series of oils depicting the romantic growth and expansion of America," a series so notable that "even ardent prohibitionists" acclaimed its art.[11] But it is "Custer's Last Fight" that has become America's best known object of art. At present, about 25,000 copies of it are issued annually, and, significantly, many of these are sent to customers who want to hang them in their recreation and rumpus rooms.[12]

3.

In these days of high-powered research into consumer-motivation, it seems natural to want to make a few friendly speculations concerning the causes of the happy business relations that have long existed between "Custer's Last Fight" and Budweiser beer. Since much of this study deals with the general causes of the Battle's appeal to the public everywhere, these speculations focus on the Battle's barroom success. They are speculations of friends, all of

8. Roland Krebs and Percy J. Orthwein, *Making Friends Is Our Business: 100 Years of Anheuser-Busch* (Cuneo Press, 1953), pp. 1–2.

9. Don Russell, pp. 62–63.

10. For this and other information I am indebted to the advertising agency handling the Budweiser account, the D'Arcy Advertising Company, and in particular to Robert B. Irons who is manager of their account with Standard Oil Company (Indiana) and to James B. Orthwein, vice-president of the agency and son of one of the co-authors of *Making Friends Is Our Business: 100 Years of Anheuser-Busch*. Their responses to my queries were always immediate, full and friendly. Information obtained from them will be acknowledged hereafter simply as "Irons-Orthwein."

11. *Making Friends Is Our Business*, pp. 337, 4.

12. Irons-Orthwein.

whom are familiar with American art, advertising, the West and, in varying degrees, with barrooms.

Joshua Taylor, historian of American art, says that we should start by recalling a period when a saloon was one thing and a barroom another—the barroom with goboons [spittoons] and sawdust on the floors, and walls of the fancy saloon crowded with good to not-so-good examples of what the carriage-trade regarded as the latest style in painting. It is true that, although some pictures early had been given to bars by wholesalers, Anheuser-Busch was the first brewery to specialize in this kind of advertisement,[13] and, in so doing, according to Taylor's theory, helped to make the barroom into a poor man's saloon. Andrew Armstrong, ad man and amateur painter, has much the same theory. He thinks that the lithograph of "Custer's Last Flight" may be an early example of what would now be called "tone-up" advertisement (a distributor walks into a retail establishment and says if you'll use our product we'll give you a fancy lamp and turn this place into a cocktail lounge). John Jamieson says that, when his advertising agency used to handle beer accounts, they always tried to think of something "controversial" to hang on the tavern walls. According to his theory, a customer has a few drinks, points to "Custer's Last Fight," and then announces to the customer next to him, "Do you know that happened out in Nebraska and every son-of-a-bitch was killed and scalped?" The adjacent customer or the one down from him says, "You're crazy. That happened in Colorado where I was born, and my uncle was in it and used to tell me all about it when I was a kid."

One thing for sure, it is an odd advertisement for beer. In the first place, it is the only national event that has become a trademark in the public mind for a large American business. A good many companies have identified themselves with national heroes, for instance the Franklin Life Insurance Company, but this identification is generally based on some quality of the hero, like thrift, which the customer is supposed to link with the company. Other companies, of course, have used historical events in their advertising, but these have generally been related to the company's own history, as the Pennsylvania Railroad's calendars (by Dean Cornwell) depicting important events in the history of transportation and the calendars of western railroads depicting scenes from the history of westward-ho. On the surface at least, it is not easy to see the relations that have proved most lasting between a historical event and a big

13. Irons-Orthwein.

business—the relations between "Custer's Last Fight" and beer—even when the fact that the General was an ardent teetotaler is set aside.

Perhaps a recent development in advertising may give us a glimpse into some of the underlying relations. According to the motivational ad men, advertisement should present not so much the objective merits of the product as the feelings the customer should have in using it. Although "Custer's Last Fight" has no visible relations to beer as a product, it may give general expression to the feelings of the consumer of the product—heroic, on a high eminence, free of family and full of pro patria, ready to fight through all encirclements or, just as good or even better, to be carried out in the attempt.

The attitude of the D'Arcy Agency, which handles the Budweiser advertising account, is perhaps the most illuminating of all. They do not like to get very analytical about the success of "Custer's Last Fight," and about such success it does seem more decent to be reverential than analytical. Reverence itself, however, can be slightly analyzed and divided into at least two elements—a reverence of the holy origins of the mystery and a reverence of its continuing practical efficacy. When asked for an explanation of the success of "Custer's Last Fight," those who should know best are likely to say, "Mr. Busch did it for the 7th Cavalry—and it sells beer."

4.

In attempting to make some rough estimate of the size of the after-image of Gen. Custer and his Last Stand, we may have come across some of the secular although none of the spectral answers to the question of what are the necessary conditions for enduring life in the world as we know it. Although the question is directed only to the lower world, it has overtones that suggest it should be asked in catechetical form.

Question:
  How can a man lose his own life and gain immortality, at least in this world?

Answer:
  History can temporarily elevate this or that man above others, but when the history of the moment floats from under him he will be secure only if he has mingled with our enduring dreams, "dreams" here being used in a modern sense as images not only of romantic desires and longings but of fears, resentments and perversities as well. And it further

appears that the living do not remain deeply involved with the dead unless the living imagine that they see in the dead parts of their own lives—and deaths.

To this should be added, not cynically on the whole, that the dead increase their security here by making good business connections. Immortality on earth, then, seems to depend on three factors: history, our private lives, and business.

. . . .

Shrine to Defeat

. . . .

*Life as we find it is too hard for us; it entails too much
pain, too many disappointments, impossible tasks.
We cannot do without palliative remedies. . . . There
are perhaps three of these means: powerful diversions
of interest, which lead us to care little about our
misery; substitutive gratifications, which lessen it; and
intoxicating substances, which make us insensitive to it.
Something of this kind is indispensable.*
—Sigmund Freud, Civilization and Its Discontents

Sometime fairly long ago we turned from the puzzle of the Battle as
one that probably could never be solved to the mystery of why it has
meant so much to us, hoping that, though the Battle remains classi-
fied forever as a military secret, it might reveal something about our
civilian lives. But the study of the Battle and the exploration of our images of it
have many parallels. At first there is an even greater confusion of artifacts, for
the remains of these few soldiers, described by Benteen as so many seeds of
white corn scattered over the Hill, have been scattered by us through history,
art, literature, painting, song, and casual speech, and have been preserved
throughout the world in museums, public libraries, private collections, barroom windows, juke boxes and rumpus rooms. In both studies, too, abstractions eventually emerge from the artifacts: bodies fall into lines of white markers and their histories assume certain strategies, paintings of them encircle a
pattern, and stories of them follow well-marked plots.

The final question seems naturally to be whether there is any convergence
of the lines we have exposed of ourselves to explain what has been the center
of our interest in this sandy stretch of ground; and the answer was intimated
much earlier by our linear images of the Battle, which despite individual
differences and the changes in artistic conventions of different times, have
been drawn around an encircled circle at the top of a hill. The convergence
repeats itself in our other images.

This internal convergence suggests that, in turning from the mystery of
the Battle, we have ventured into the larger mystery of defeat. If the Battle has
a secret to reveal, it is of the power that defeat has over us and we perhaps

have over it. Our images of it, of course, do not reveal how in fact we will meet defeat, but they show us in the act of preparing to meet it, irrespective of whether our preparations fail us in the crisis. And they tell something of one of our closely guarded domestic secrets—namely, that much of seemingly ordinary and uneventful life is spent in marching and counter-marching over the scenes of previous defeats and in fortifying ourselves against those to come. Great writers from the beginning of our drama have made no secret of the fact that defeat is the issue of our great moments, but the only commanding figure who tried to make a science of defeat found it everywhere inherent in the organism, even in sleep; and, although science, no more than poetry, will never completely discover us, it is a tool of this age, and, like the metal-finders on the Battlefield, may expose artifacts hitherto missed because buried underground.

1.

How hidden we keep certain aspects of defeat from ourselves is suggested even by the fact that many people, including Freudians, think of Freud only as the scientist of sex and suffer something like a Freudian "black-out" in failing to see the role he assigned to defeat. Yet the personal tragedy he observed in life went deeper than his own cancer; it is in the blood-stream of his writing, more extensive than any operable passage such as the one removed for the heading of this chapter.

Private defeat is built in the Freudian mechanics of being. The machinery of the Oedipus complex will not run with sex alone, for with only desire there can be no complex or, for that matter, no outer reality. The complex begins with the defeat of desire, with the first repudiations of the organism which until then is the whole cosmos; even the mother has no separate existence to the child until she is not there when he desires her. Thus, through frustration, rejection and defeat the organism becomes aware of the presence of a thing other than itself, which when multiplied by countless rejections becomes the cosmos, and with defeat life's strategies begin—the maneuverings, diversionary movements and retreats to hold off life which is "too hard for us."

The Freudian strategies mount in complexity, and only partly because defeat is outside waiting for the organism to encounter it; it is also internal to the organism, which is driven by two polar instincts—eros, the life instinct, and thanatos, "the death wish," that craves defeat and destruction. So we maneuver both to avert defeat and to bring it about, and the child, playing "King of the Hill," struggles at first to gain the eminent position and to maintain himself there, but, when it looks as if he cannot be pulled down, he cooperates clumsily in his own downfall.

It would seem, then, that Freud would have approved of the joke we have made of Custer's Last Stand and would have thought that more than its literary form deserved analysis. Probably to him its ultimate success would depend upon its penetration of the obscurities of history to the true causes of defeat, internal and external, and to its compression of them into a single exclamation of discovery: "Holy cow! Too many fucking Indians!"

Of course, we must not start off committed to anyone else's theory of ourselves or of the Battle, or we shall miss all the trails not going our way. For many reasons it seems much better to be always in hope of being surprised by what we find, especially by the surprises that keep repeating themselves and still remain surprising. Of these, fundamentally just two have taken this study beyond the afternoon of June 25, 1876. The first is that officially we have made a National Monument out of a small historical event; the second is that this odd magnification of almost lost reality would lack general significance except for the much larger but related fact that as a people we make shrines of many of our defeats.

2.

The common people of England, says George Orwell, "do not retain among their historical memories the name of a single military victory." Moreover, he adds, English literature is distinct in that its popular battle poems "are always a tale of disasters and retreats" such as Dunkirk and Sir John Moore at Corunna—not even Trafalgar or Waterloo is poetically memorable. "The most stirring battle poem in English is about a brigade of cavalry which charged in the wrong direction."[1]

Like the English, Americans have the freedom, security and predisposition to memorialize defeat. For Dunkirk, we have Corregidor and Bataan and a shattering retreat from the Philippines to the British commonwealth of Australia. We remember Pearl Harbor, although probably not the name of one of the great battles in which we finally defeated the Japanese. And, as the English, we have not forgotten some 600 of our own cavalry who rode into the jaws of death, and we still argue about whether they were charging in the wrong direction.

Orwell attributes the tendency of the English to make Nikes out of their

1. "England Your England."

defeats to "English hatred of war and militarism," and undoubtedly there is something to this explanation, which also accounts for a part of our tendency to memorialize some of our disasters. But Orwell, to whom all knowledge was a branch of political propaganda, takes us down only one trail and not very far down it. For one thing, neither the English nor other people memorialize any or all of their defeats. The English do not commemorate, for instance, their "disasters and retreats" during the American Revolution, and we do not enshrine our retreat from the Yalu River in our un-victorious war in Korea. Furthermore, Orwell's explanation of the private needs that impel us to build public shrines to our defeats took him only where he wanted to go—to the conclusion that we need places of sacrifice to atone for our guilt feelings about war and aggression. Now, it is clearly true that certain of our defeats at certain times are used by many of us for this purpose, Custer's defeat itself being a good example, for, as will be seen later, in recent times it is often depicted as an atonement for the crimes committed by our ancestors (and ourselves?) against Indians and minority groups in general. But it is much clearer that these public defeats, including Custer's and all those mentioned by Orwell, were first political calls to arms to arouse a nation from the illusion that war was not likely ("Remember Pearl Harbor") or that an expeditionary force "could restore the situation" on the frontier or on foreign soil without disturbing the homefolk (Dunkirk). Initially, therefore, they were not endorsements but condemnations of a people's hatred of war, love of peace and preference for beer and darts. But both Orwell's explanation and its opposite, which is at least equally true, seem inadequate and fairly close to the surface, unless public enactments are expressive of nothing deeper than public needs.

Acting on the assumption that more than the surface is involved, let us look carefully at the structure the public made of Custer's Last Stand to see which of its elements are highly distinctive and which are the more common elements of the defeats we enshrine. Two questions are really being raised, the nature of the structure and the need for it—but the two can be treated together, since our structures are both signs of our needs and in some ways, the needs themselves [. . .]

A Maclean Sampler

"This Quarter I Am

Taking McKeon"

A FEW REMARKS ON THE

ART OF TEACHING

In his forty-five years (1928–73) as a member of the University of Chicago's English department, Maclean became a legendary teacher for his courses on Shakespeare and the British Romantic poets, and won the university's Quantrell Award for Excellence in Undergraduate Teaching three times (1932, 1940, 1973). In "'This Quarter I Am Taking McKeon'" (1974), he defines, as much as he ever attempted to, the art of teaching. With typical humor and self-deprecation, he summarizes a career and sketches a self-portrait. He elaborates the theme that "a great teacher is a tough guy who cares deeply about something that is hard to understand."

It has been predetermined that I should talk today on the impossible subject, teaching, in almost impossible circumstances. Anyone here could and probably should get up and give this talk, and all of us would say fundamentally the same few things, even if somewhat differently.

For instance, I am sure that any of us would start off by saying that he never read or heard anything that helped him much with his own teaching. I am retired now, and in looking back I can think of only one such thing that helped me, and I'm not sure it helped, but I admit using it.

I started teaching at Dartmouth College immediately after my graduation there, and, also immediately, one of my classes was inspected by a senior member of the faculty. The same thing was done to one of my classes when I started teaching here, but here instead of saying they were "inspecting" my class they said they were visiting, and sent a woman. But at Dartmouth they sent a man. His name was McCallum and he was tall, red-headed and Scotch,

"'This Quarter I Am Taking McKeon': A Few Remarks on the Art of Teaching" is excerpted from *The University of Chicago Magazine* 66 (January/February 1974): 8–12.

with a long sardonic moustache. He would have resembled Mephistopheles, if Mephistopheles had been Scotch, as he well might have been.

Like most Scotchmen, he took religion very seriously, only he happened to be an atheist, and would not allow the word God to be mentioned in his classes. He was the first great teacher I ever had, but naturally my feelings were mixed about being inspected by someone who did not think very much even of God. Still, I regarded him so highly as a teacher that I was sure he would tell me something about teaching when my class was over that, however harsh, would let me in on the secret to the mystery.

I discovered later that he himself had had no mixed feelings about the coming prospect. He thought the whole business was beneath him—and beneath me, for that matter. But it was some years later when I found out these feelings. In the meantime some hours had passed after he inspected my class and he hadn't called me into his office; and then some days, and finally several weeks.

At times in life unexpected silence is a momentary relief, but it can go on until you can't bear it any longer and finally you have to hear something, no matter what. So finally I made an appointment with him at his office and when I came in he asked, "Yes?" as if he didn't know why I came. I couldn't think of any way to approach the subject gradually, so I asked, "What did you think of the class?" And he asked, "What class?" I said, "My class, the one you inspected." Then he said, "It was all right." We had suddenly run out of conversation, but still I couldn't leave. I was still hoping for the secret that would clear up the life that was to come. Finally I asked, "Don't you have something to tell me that would help me be a good teacher?"

SARTORIAL PEDAGOGY

He thought for a while and then said, "Wear a different suit every day of the week." He had come from Princeton.

I said, "I can't afford that."

"Well, then," he said, "wear a different necktie."

I had been brought up to believe that you made the most in life of what little you had, and, since this is all that has ever been told me about my teaching, I must confess that I wore a different necktie every day of the week until I retired. I never did get up into the daily suit class.

So, as we all know, teaching is something like physics or music. It is mostly biological. It is something you can do—or not do—when you are fairly young.

If you can do it, experience will make you a little better. Then toward retirement you will get a little worse. I have just given a complete log of a teacher. I feel that I have slipped now to where I am about as good as when I started teaching at twenty. In between, there were times when I was a little better. That's it.

If, though, I have heard only one thing that has been directly useful to me as a teacher, I have had the opportunity to watch unusually gifted teachers through the years. I don't know whether this results in anything one can incorporate directly into his own teaching, teaching being such a highly individualized art, but it does make one a better teacher by lifting up the spirit and making one feel elevated about what he has chosen to do in life. Though I retired after teaching in only two colleges, Dartmouth and here, they are two colleges that put great premium upon fine teaching. When I went as a student to Dartmouth in 1920, I was told that a great tradition had only recently died and might at any moment be revived. The tradition was called "horning." Presumably Dartmouth students for generations had rented a barn and stored hundreds of horns in it, and when a teacher was hired who was something less than pleasing, the students would assemble at night at the barn, arm themselves with horns and march around the teacher's house, for all practical purposes terminating his contract irrespective of whether, according to the American Association of University Professors, the contract still had three years to go.

In later years, I came to doubt whether in fact there had ever been such a custom, because when I was a junior I acquired a couple of teachers who I thought might be improved by musical accompaniment, but the barn where the horns were stored could not be found, either in daylight or literally by lantern. But even if it was only a legend, it worked. I even came to suspect it was a legend started and nurtured by the administration, as an effective and cheap device to get some very creative teaching.

At the University of Chicago, of course, one of our chief devices to spur the teacher on to higher effort is the Quantrell Award for Excellence in Undergraduate Teaching. It has also proved to be a very effective device for encouraging teachers to put forth their best efforts, but it is more costly than the Dartmouth method. Whereas the Dartmouth method works by trepidation and musical chairs and mythical horns, the University of Chicago method works by showers of solid blessings amounting to four and sometimes five awards each year of $1,000 each. Although admittedly the Dartmouth method of improving pedagogy was effective, I am sure that those of us who have received the $1,000 tax exempt award think of the University of Chicago's method as the more humane.

. . . .

Partly since the two universities where I have taught have had very different but very effective extracurricular stimuli to get the maximum yardage out of their teachers, I have had the privilege of observing some remarkable teaching in my time, a good deal of it done by some present today.

For some years after I started out on my observation tours I saw nothing in common between one great teacher and another. For instance, Wayne Booth, who gave us this morning one of the few fine convocation speeches I have ever heard, walks into his classroom, takes off his coat, hangs it on the back of the chair, sits on the corner of his desk, which he uses as a launching pad.

But his great master—and mine, too, for that matter—was R. S. Crane, and he couldn't have been more formal. He wore a tall starched collar and I can still see the tip of his gold collar button only partially hidden under the knot of his tie.

Joe Schwab punches a student all over the ring until he finally gets him in a corner and disposes of him. So Joe Schwab teaches like a prize fighter.

But Tom Hutchinson taught like an architect. He began his lectures just as the bell rang and his last word came just as it rang again and, when you looked back over it, all the parts were there in just the right order and size, and it had the beauty that comes from something built in serenity.

So you can teach like a prize fighter and be a great teacher, or you can teach like an architect and be a great teacher, or you can be a great teacher in shirt sleeves or in back of a gold collar button. It seems you can do about anything and be a great teacher.

But if you like to go around watching great teachers, as I used to when I could sit longer in one place than I can now, you will eventually see certain common characteristics emerging amid all the variety of gymnastic techniques. And, on the basis of some of the more obvious of these common characteristics, I am willing to make a rough description of a great teacher just to get started on this part of the subject. Later I hope to refine it, but I'll start by saying that a great teacher is a tough guy who cares deeply about something that is hard to understand.

To vivify what I have just said, I think I'll take one of the most popular and flamboyant of undergraduate teachers in our College's history. I take him in deference to Mr. Bate, whose honorary degree was awarded today in part because he is one of the world's most renowned scholars and teachers of early 19th century Romanticism.

Teddy Linn of long ago had no such distinction as a scholar, but what he lacked in scholarship about Romanticism he made up in being a flamboyant version of Romanticism itself. It was forty-five years ago this autumn when I went to observe his opening class in his favorite course in the English Romantic poets, and I remember the class as if it had been held yesterday. Well, I don't remember the first few minutes of the class, because those of us who hadn't seen him in action before were worried that the cigarette on the edge of his lip would burn his lip in another half-inch, but the cigarette evidently always went out in another quarter of an inch and stuck there the rest of the hour.

Mr. Linn, in his introduction to Romanticism, mentioned no such aged and agricultural figures as Wordsworth, and he said nothing on the opening day about Coleridge and German metaphysics, although Coleridge and Wordsworth came first chronologically. For his opening words, he jumped the first generation of English Romantic poets and went straight for Keats.

Keats was dead, he said, when he was no older than some of them in the class and only a few years older than most of them. He was immortal at an age when they did well to get C plus on a theme in English composition because it had no split infinitives or dangling participles. He said that despite this notable difference, they and Keats were one in that Keats gave the finest expression in all literature of what was best in them. He said when you grew older, as he had, you grew used to things, but youth trembled at the beauty of the earth, even when death stood close by. And he said Keats knew he was dying, and he recited the "Ode to Melancholy" and repeated the final stanza which begins

She dwells with Beauty—Beauty that must die;
And Joy, whose hand is ever at his lips
Bidding adieu.

Then he told them a story, somewhat apocryphal, I am sure, but so spiritually true that I—and I am sure the rest of the class—will never forget it. He told them how Keats had been sent to Rome when it was discovered he was dying of tuberculosis, and how an art student friend of his by the name of Severn nursed him in his last illness. And how one day Severn had gone out shopping, and when he came back he found Keats leaning on his elbow staring at his pillow. And when Severn got closer to the bed he saw that Keats had hemorrhaged while he had been gone and so was staring at his life blood.

Then suddenly Keats either saw or felt that Severn was present, and raised his head, and said, "Look, man, at that red against that white."

"And so," Mr. Linn said, "you will bring in a paper tomorrow on John Keats." There was a long silence, and I am sure Mr. Linn knew how it was going to be broken. Finally, a fraternity pledge raised his hand and asked, "Did you say that paper is due tomorrow?"

"That's right," Mr. Linn said. "Tomorrow. That's just to let you know what big teeth your grandmother has."

Everybody in class had his paper in the next day, and, although I never saw any of them, it's a good bet that none of them was much good. But that wasn't the idea.

I used this incident to illustrate my rough definition before discussing it, especially the ingredients of being tough and caring deeply.

When I say "tough," I realize we are in an age when students seem to be demanding that teachers stroke the silk on their egos while serving them sherry with the other hand, and I have one favorable thing to say about all this—the students don't seem to care whether the sherry is good or not, and after a while they tire of the whole business.

The truth is, no matter what students seem to be saying at the moment, they want things tough, too. A student has to be sick to want a teacher for a pal or a pet. Of course, students don't care to be roughed up just to give somebody else pleasure, and by being tough I don't mean being rude or unsympathetic, although I want to make clear that I do not feel any compunction about being courteous to all people at all times, either in a classroom or anywhere else. You treat students the way you treat other people—the way you think they deserve to be treated.

I would be glad to argue this matter psychologically or even philosophically. Outside, just ahead of the student is the world of lumps-and-bumps. Is day-care what he needs most at this stage of the game to help him be ready? And, if so, just where did we acquire the breast-development to give it to him? But I am not really looking for arguments today. I have included "toughness" in the definition of great teachers because, on observation, I have found it one of their few common characteristics.

Some years ago I had a student by the name of Liz Ginsburg. She was a great handsome, intelligent girl who remains one of my all-time favorites. I hadn't seen her for some time, so when I ran into her I asked, "Liz, what are you doing this quarter?" And she looked at me a little glassy-eyed and said, "This quarter I am taking McKeon," which, as all of us know who have been students of his, is just a refined way of saying, "This quarter McKeon is taking me."

What a great compliment for a great and tough teacher! Would that the campus were alive with large, handsome intelligent girls murmuring, "This quarter I am taking Maclean."

Then I also want to say a little about the part of the definition that has to do with caring deeply about something hard to understand. This is the part without which there is nothing. In this student-oriented age when we are all huddled together with "togetherness," I should like to step slightly apart and say I have seen great teachers who didn't care much about students, including America's first Nobel Prize winner, Albert Abraham Michelson.

There was another eminent scientist who by legend found teaching very disturbing because, as he said, "Every time I remember the name of a student I forget the name of a fish." But, according to the legend, he was also a fine teacher, and, if the account is true, he became the first president of Stanford.

Most teachers like some students for some reason or other, and the reverse is true—most students have a few teachers they like, sometimes for very obscure reasons. But, in the legend, our scientific president of Stanford was a fine teacher because he liked fish, and you can't be one unless you do. And in addition have, as you can see he had, the power of conveying his feelings about fish.

On the other hand, I don't want to push a teacher to a place where he has to publish or perish. After all, if it had not been for students of his, Socrates would have had no bibliography. Perhaps that is why he didn't get tenure. If one becomes contemporary and looks at the list of Quantrell award winners in a disinterested way, he finds that of the 127, perhaps half also have the distinction as scholars. The count could vary five or ten one way or the other, depending upon how one feels about friendship while he is counting, but that roughly is the proportion, and it is roughly the proportion I have seen to exist among the great university teachers I have observed in something over half a century of counting.

TEACHERS' GENES

It is for my half of this proportion that I should like to say a few words. But just to get the cards dealt fairly before we begin this game, let me add that, during the same half century of observation, something less than half of the great scholars have not been great teachers, or even very good ones, a fact which has left the world somewhat short of very good teachers.

Now, as to the particular fraction for which I was going to speak. First of all, we believe that scholarship should and does pervade this university and other great universities. Secondly, we think that in some fundamental senses we are scholars, but, for this to be true, scholarship has to exist in several fundamental senses besides the conventional one that results in a long bibliography.

No matter how we think of scholarship, we must at least think of it as the discovery of truth, and in the conventional sense this discovery should also be a discovery of some significance to our colleagues. It is in this sense that we say that a great university is known for its great scholars and that a person is—if he is—a great scholar and a great teacher.

But a teacher must have a wider range of discovery than this. A teacher must forever be making discoveries to himself—he must have a gene marked "Freshness of the World."

And then he must have another gene that gives him the power to lead students to making discoveries—ultimately, he hopes, to the power of self-discovery. This gene might be marked, "You-Don't-Say-So?" However, many of these stirring discoveries may have been made, indeed should have been made, before by other men and women, and hence are not publishable in a scholarly journal.

Now there is this third gene marked, "The Best and Freshest on the Subject." As a minimum, the great teacher must have a half of this gene—the half that gives him command of the best that is known among his colleagues. However, he may or may not have the other half of the gene which leads him as a minimum to a hankering after immortality in a footnote.

I should like to leave this part of the subject in language that does not echo the "publish or perish" controversy, and so I shall say that the great teacher should care as much as any man for his subject and be able to convey his pleasure in it far better than most.

Perhaps a Freudian way could be found to describe the great teacher that would at least be more interesting than measuring the length of his bibliography. There is no greater commonplace from Freud than that in the beginning we are all Id, the principle of pleasure and lust, and the Ego, the principle of reason and sanity, comes later and is only a feeble outgrowth of the Id, is always subservient to it, and is developed only to protect the Id from the censure of society and to allow it the maximum fulfillment in a world where orgy is a bad word.

But long before I reached the age of retirement I realized the reverse of this can be a second truth. The ego can become so powerful that it can woo the id and make pleasure a servant of reason and sanity. The reason can become so powerful and fancy that it can make love to the id and say, "Look at me. Feel my muscles and see how graceful and beautiful I am. As for gifts, I can bring you samples of the moon. Forget about women's lib and come along and pledge to love, honor and obey me, and consider yourself lucky." I would be willing, then, I think, to consider the art of teaching as the art of perverting nature, as nature is given to us by St. Sigmund, and I would accept, not wholeheartedly I admit, a definition of teaching as the art of enticing the ego to seduce the id into its services.

. . . .

My father, I am sure, however, would have had nothing to do with such a definition. As a Presbyterian minister, he would have remained aloof from any definition that began with seduction and ended with the id. What he would have said would have been something more or less like this: "Teaching is the art of conveying the delight that comes from an act of the spirit (and from here on the Presbyterianism gets thicker), without ever giving anyone the notion that the delight comes easy."

Although I realize the variety of religious experience present here today, I shall end on this Presbyterian note. So teaching will remain as the art of conveying the delight that comes from an act of the spirit, without ever giving anyone the notion that the delight comes easy.

But all I really know about teaching is that, to do it well, supposedly you should change your necktie every day of the week.

"Billiards Is a

Good Game"

GAMESMANSHIP AND

AMERICA'S FIRST NOBEL

PRIZE SCIENTIST

Maclean was particularly proud of his portrait of Albert Abraham Michelson, the first American scientist to win the Nobel Prize. Maclean used to watch Michelson play billiards downstairs in the University of Chicago's Quadrangle Club during Maclean's first year on the faculty (1928). He occasionally said that he thought "'Billiards Is a Good Game'" was one of the best things he'd written.

When I came here in 1928, now more than half the history of the University ago, the University of Chicago was the one institution of higher learning that was thought to exist west of the Appalachians by the populace east of the Appalachians. This widespread recognition was based largely on the names of Leopold and Loeb, Clarence Darrow (who in the eastern mind was also connected with the University of Chicago), A. A. Stagg, and Albert Abraham Michelson, who in 1907 had been the first American to win the Nobel Prize in science. Before arriving on campus, I may also have heard of Arthur Holly Compton, because only the year before he had been awarded the Nobel Prize, but I have the feeling I did not know of him until I saw Mrs. Compton showing him off at intermissions in Mandel Hall.

Michelson and Einstein, however, were the best known scientists of the time—in some ways for almost opposite reasons, although both were physicists. Einstein was the wonder of the world because he had encased the whole

"'Billiards Is a Good Game': Gamesmanship and America's First Nobel Prize Scientist" is reprinted from *The University of Chicago Magazine* 67 (Summer 1975): 19–23.

universe in a simple formula, $E = mc^2$, which we were told, equally wonderful to us, would be very upsetting if we could understand it. Especially to us who could not understand, he was the theorist beyond theorists.

Michelson's wonder was what his head did with his hands, and a few boxes and rotating mirrors. He measured things, especially things that were regarded as unmeasurable, ineffable, and precious as life itself. Among other things, he had measured light and a star. I watched him play billiards nearly every noon for several months before he retired from the University, and, in introducing myself, I could further say with equal truth, "Shake the hand that shook the hand of John L. Sullivan." If I get the right opening, though, I prefer saying, "When young, I watched Michelson play billiards."

Michelson's hands were to make many things that brought light to our universe, but nothing so marked him in the popular mind as his measurement of the speed of light itself. Throughout most of history, light had been thought of as instantaneous and present wherever there was nothing to cast a shadow, and probably throughout all history light will be thought of by poets and the rest of us as the source of body and soul, without which there would be no photosynthesis or food or love or moonlight in which to make love. Without light for a metaphor there would have been little poetry written and no candlelight to write it by. Christ said, "I am the light of the world," and Cardinal Newman's hymn to Him begins, "Lead, kindly light."

Michelson was to measure the speed of light many times (his most accurate figure being 186,285 ± 2½ miles per second) and modern electronic equipment has changed that figure to only 186,282.3960. When in 1878 as an ensign in Annapolis he made his first measurement he spent $10.00 of his own money to assemble his equipment (for $10.00 light measured 186,508 miles per second).

In 1928, three years before his death, everyone said of Michelson, "He measured light," and today he is one of the few Nobel Prize winners whom nearly all educated people can name and give the reason for the award, although Michelson's award actually was based on a wide spectrum of experiments. His youngest daughter showed her father's own sense of truth and artistry when she entitled her recent biography of him, *The Master of Light*. Of course, the fact that he was the first American to win the Nobel Prize in science helped to enshrine him both nationally and locally. Nowadays Nobel Prize winners at times seem to come a dime a dozen and every now and then in job-lots, two or three to an award, but for a long time in history there was none and then there was one and he was at the University of Chicago. President Harper himself had started the University on its long string of firsts—the first university to have a summer school, the first extension division organized as part of a university, the first university press to have its own press, and, certainly not least or last, the first university to have women on its faculty and a dean of women. But probably the University's two most unforgettable firsts go to Michelson for the first American Nobel Prize in science (1907) and to Enrico Fermi and his group for the first self-sustained nuclear reaction (1942). To include one of my old students, I'll add Jay Berwanger for the first Heisman Trophy (1935).

In 1928, when I first saw Michelson he was eating lunch at the Quadrangle Club, and I thought instantly of the opening of Carl Sandburg's poem, "I saw a famous man eating soup." One look at Michelson in old age and there could be no doubt that he was famous. He did not eat at the table reserved for the physicists. He ate at a table always reserved for him alone, and he occasionally smiled as he drew on his napkin. The waitress told us he drew sketches of the faculty he did not care to eat with. She said they all had long noses.

Few of us in these present days of unfamous and infamous men have any idea of what it was like to be one of the two or three most famous physicists of the early twentieth century and to eat your soup at a table reserved for you alone. The meaning of the words "elite" and "aristocratic" have been lost, except in their profane senses, and it is doubtful if we would recognize an aristocrat if there were one and we happened to see him. But at the first general open meeting in 1900 of the American Physical Society (of which Michelson was vice-president seven years before his Nobel Prize), its president, Henry Rowland, addressed his fellow members as follows:

> . . . We meet here in the interest of *a science above all sciences* which deals with the foundation of the Universe . . . with the constitution of matter from which everything in the Universe is made and with the ether of space by which alone the various portions of matter forming the Universe affect each other. . . .

> . . . We form a small and unique body of men, a new variety of the human race as one of our greatest scientists calls it, whose views of what constitutes the greatest achievement in life are very different from those around us. In this respect we form an aristocracy, not of wealth, not of pedigree, but of intellect and of ideals.

In case present-day readers might feel this prose is running over with self-anointed oil, they should start jotting down the names of some of the late-nineteenth and early-twentieth century physicists whom they and the world remember: Madame Curie and her husband, Pierre (radium and radioactivity), Lord Kelvin (as in Kelvinator), James Clerk Maxwell (electromagnetic field), Wilhelm Conrad Röntgen (X-rays), and, to end where we began, Einstein and Michelson. Every once in a while science comes to a place where it meets a bunch of great men coming its way who are big enough to overturn it and then set it on its wheels again but going forever in a different direction.

But his being the first American physicist to win the Nobel Prize still doesn't give us an adequate measurement of how high Michelson stood in the firmament of men apart from other men. Michelson was a Navy man. He had received his basic scientific training at Annapolis and it was better all around and forever after not to forget he had been a naval officer.

Shortly before anyone else in the dining room had finished his lunch, Michelson rose and went downstairs. Before long, I heard that he went down to the billiard room and probably at the same time I heard he was a fine billiard player. Nobody in the University, I was told, was good enough to play with him. Immediately, I started arriving earlier for lunch, and, when he folded his long-nosed napkin, I rose and followed him.

So for at least several months before he left Chicago for good, I sat on one of those high pool-room chairs for ten or fifteen minutes at noon and watched the famous physicist play billiards after he ate soup and sketched the ordinary self-anointed physicists with whom he did not sit. He and I occasionally spoke. Most of our communication, however, was carried on by a lifted eyebrow followed by a nod or shake of the head. He lifted the eyebrow, and I shook or nodded the head.

I had come here in 1928 to start graduate work with an A.B. in English from Dartmouth, and, since I had taught courses there in freshman English for two years after graduation, I was able to start here as a Graduate Assistant, a form of degradation that has since been abolished, at least in the English Department. As the first half of the title suggests, it was bestowed upon certain graduate students, but the second half of the title, "Assistant," gives no idea of how little money and how much servility went with it.

Only a few years later (in 1932), *Vanity Fair*, the magazine of the sophisticates (*The New Yorker* just getting under way), started publishing a series of caricatures by Covarrubias entitled "Impossible Interviews," the one that comes to mind first being between Mae West and Dowager-Queen Marie of Romania. If Covarrubias had seen the young Graduate Assistant in English and the great and aging physicist who was the first American Nobel Prize winner in science gathered each noon around a billiard table he might have included us in his series.

In 1928 there were two ways graduate students in English without money could see their way to an advanced degree, both involving considerable medical risk. Besides "the Graduate Assistant route," which was the scenic detour, there was the more common family way which was to marry a fellow graduate student, the marriage vows often consisting only of promises that each would take his or her turn in working on some job until the other received his or her Ph.D. In 1928 (as in 1975) it always fell out that it was the woman's turn first to give up her graduate studies and become the breadwinner. By the time the male finally fenced in a Ph.D., the female of the species had had so many children and jobs and was so generally worn-out (or dead) that it was too late for her and she could never bear to open a book again, except for pleasure.

The "Assistant" half of a Graduate Assistant needs a little more defining before one can appreciate the spectator as well as the billiard player in the coming scene. A Graduate Assistant, in addition to taking graduate courses, could teach up to three sections a quarter of the required course in English Composition at the rate of $200 per section. Financially, this meant that a Graduate Assistant who taught the full schedule of three sections for three quarters of a school year made $1,800. Since many of our freshman in 1928 were still from the rural Middle West, being a Graduate Assistant teaching three sections of English Composition spiritually meant going home late Friday afternoon, having a couple of shots of Prohibition gin, going to bed right after dinner and reading thirty (students) times three (sections) of one-thousand-word compositions on "How to Fill a Silo." By then, he was too weak to get out of bed, and besides he had to start preparing the graduate courses he was taking.

So the great difference between the two kinds of needy graduate students in English was in how they spent their weekends in bed. As a result of my weekends, I became an expert on corn, but my conversations with the great physicist were still limited to billiards.

For instance, we never mentioned bridge; yet I was soon to discover he hurried down to the billiard room before anyone else left upstairs because he wanted to play bridge but was not a good bridge player. Although he was too good at billiards to play with anybody in the club, none of the bridge players in the room next to the billiard tables wanted him for a partner. He coordinated these two facts by eating early, getting downstairs before anyone else, playing billiards by himself for ten or fifteen minutes, and then, just before the first big scraping of chairs upstairs, seating himself at the bridge table where there was room for just three others. But, though I also watched him play bridge, we never spoke about anything except billiards.

Undoubtedly, then, I would never have exchanged a single word with the Master of Light if I had not been brought up in western Montana, where all my generation spent more time in what were then called Card and Billiard Parlors than in school or at home. In the early part of this century the Card and Billiard Emporium was "the home away from home," and home was only where we ate and slept. Usually, the first table was the billiard table, because in Montana billiards was thought of as the sport of the upper class and was played only by the town's best barbers and the one vice-president of the bank. Then came three pool tables with dead cushions and concrete balls that hairy loggers hit so hard they jumped off the tables. At the rear, enthroned by several steps as at the Quadrangle Club, was the card room, in the center of which was the poker table under an enormous green shade. In the glare of the circle of light were always two or three poker players trying to look clumsy. They were housemen or "shills" waiting for some lumberjack to drop by who had just cashed his summer's check. If you were any good at cards yourself, you could see it was hard work for them to look clumsy.

We high school players were pool players, although we should like to have been billiard players if for no other reason than that each billiard player was so elite he had a woman besides a wife, but we could rarely finance our aspirations. It cost twenty-five cents an hour to play billiards, and only ten cents a game for rotation pool and, as any high school rotation-pool player knows, it is no great trick, when the houseman is not looking, to sneak balls back on the table that have already been sunk and thus to prolong the game.

When I came to the University as a Graduate Assistant then, I was just as good a billiard player as I had had spare twenty-five cent pieces when I was in high school, and still aspiring to be better, I ate my lunch early to get downstairs and watch the club champion.

Michelson was the best billiard player I have ever seen at the University, and I think I have seen all the really good ones, including the barbers at the Reynolds Club. At first I was somewhat embarrassed to see how good he was, because I did not expect to find any academic type as good at a "man's sport" as the best we had in western Montana. But the more I thought about it and the more I learned about Michelson, the less surprised I became. Before long, I comforted myself with the question, "Why not? He's the best head-and-hands man in the world."

So it wasn't just billiards I watched when I arrived early every noon to watch Michelson play billiards. I came to watch his hands. The year 1928 was still in an age which counted men who made machines among its marvels and took for granted that the rest of men could use tools and that women could embroider beautifully. Edison still performed his wonders, but the wonders of Bell and Edison were more or less household utilities. Michelson's head-and-hands made machines almost godlike in properties, designed to tell us how it was with the universe. His favorite creation was his interferometer, with which, among other things, he (and later his collaborator, Edward Morley) had performed an experiment that shook the old universe and gave Einstein a big push toward creating a new one with his theory of relativity.

Before the Michelson-Morley experiment, the common scientific assumption was that the universe consisted of bodies of matter moving through and permeated by a substance that, although invisible, had somehow itself to be material. This substance at first was spelled "aether." Since Michelson tended to believe that the major theories of the universe were already in and that accordingly the chief jobs left to do were to measure what was sailing around in the ether, his head and hands produced his interferometer which split a light wave, sending one half with the orbit of the earth and back again where it met the other half wave length that had been sent on a return trip at right angles to the orbit of the earth. If there were ether out there (unless it were being carried along by the earth as if it were an envelope of the earth), the expectation was that when the two halves of the light wave rejoined they would be "out of phase," since one had held a course parallel to "the ether drift" and the other had crossed it at right angles and returned. The difference between the two half-light waves would indeed be small, but Michelson was sure he could measure it—and measure it he did, again and again—only to conclude reluctantly that there was no difference and that therefore there was no stationary ether "out there" and that light traveled at equal velocity in all directions.

In 1928 we only crudely knew how these negative results of the Michelson-Morley experiment opened the universe to Einstein's theories of relativity and we had even vaguer notions of the kind of machine that left Newtonian physics lying in a heap feebly struggling to get out from under its own ruins.

I had heard, however, something about the interferometer, and, having worked ten or eleven summers in the Forest Service and logging camps, I had enough feeling for tools to make it hard for me to keep my mind solely on billiards. After Michelson would run ten or twelve billiards with a touch so delicate that the three balls could always be covered by a hat, I found myself wondering how he had ever made a machine so delicate its finding would be invalid if it vibrated half a wave length of light, a whole wave length of light being so small that it can't be seen by our most powerful microscope. A fancy, wide-angle billiard would also take my mind off the game, because I knew just from the nature of the experiment that the machine had to turn ninety degrees without vibration (in mercury, I later found) so that any change in the pattern of the light waves could be observed. Perhaps the most American, air-conditioned question I kept asking was, "How the hell in the 1880s did he ever keep the machine in a temperature that probably couldn't vary a tenth of a degree?"

You don't have to have a diagram of the interferometer to realize why it was Michelson's favorite creation or why Michelson must have felt about his interferometer something of the way Galileo felt about his telescope:

> "O telescope, instrument of much knowledge, more precious than any sceptre! Is not he who holds thee in his hand made king and lord of the works of God?"

But even this poetical outpouring isn't as moving a tribute to a machine as the factual statement about the interferometer made by Arthur Stanley Eddington, the English astronomer; it is a machine, he said, that can detect "a lag of one-ten-thousand-billionth of a second in the arrival of a light wave."

A MASTER'S HANDS

No wonder that before long the astronomers tried to enlist Michelson's hands in their service and succeeded. Dissatisfied with their own attempts, they urged him to give them the first accurate measurement of a star. For the first star ever to have its diameter measured accurately he picked a big one with a big name a long way off—Betelgeuse, linear diameter 240,000,000 miles (2,300 times larger than our sun) and 150 light years from the earth.

His hands were legendary long before I ever saw them. As legend, they were part fact and some fiction. For instance, I soon heard he was a fine violinist and a mini-Stradivarius who made his own beautiful instruments, but I think the truth is that, while his Jewish father was out selling pick-handles to California gold miners, his Polish mother kept him indoors to "practice,

practice, practice," with the result that he became a fine violinist and, in his turn, spent half an hour before going to his lab in passing on his love and skill to his daughters. The business, though, about his making violins was just a fictional tribute to his hands.

It is a fact, however, that at the end of his first year at Annapolis he stood at the top of his class in drawing and that all his life he expressed himself by sketches and watercolors. Often in late afternoons if you looked over the wall in front of his beautiful home at 1220 East 58th Street (just behind the Robie House) you could see him in the sunshine and shadow of his yard painting shadow and sunshine.

Many of his last late afternoons in Chicago he spent either in his yard or at the Quadrangle Club. In those days, before so much of the Quadrangle Club was turned into an eating place, there was a beautiful chess room on the second floor, and on late afternoons his slightly stooped shoulders were often reflected in the dark and light squares of ingrained wood. He had been good enough once to play the American chess champion, Frank James Marshall, who however was not overpowered by his unorthodox openings, as most of his opponents were, and is supposed to have remarked that the physicist's game was a little long on imagination and passion.

He also had the reputation of having been a very good tennis player, but I have no memory of ever seeing him play; perhaps at seventy-five he had quit the game, but supposedly he had been very good.

It may not be so surprising as it first seems that he was not a good bridge player, although always wanting to be in the game. It is hard to predict just where there is going to be a gap in somebody's genetic tape, and, before I ever heard the word "genetic," I was learning in the Quadrangle Club that a gene can be very narrow and not include what seems almost necessarily a part of it. For instance, Leonard Eugene Dickson, the outstanding mathematician, who at the time was writing his classic works on the theory of numbers, was sometimes a poor card player. Anton J. Carlson was also not a good bridge player, although he was nationally famous as an exponent of the scientific method in the biological sciences ("Vat iss da evidence?"). In fact, there were quite a few card players in western Montana who would have taken the money from the world-famous intellectuals who gathered at noon in the card room of the Quadrangle Club in those days (and since).

After watching Michelson play bridge for a while, you could predict more or less the kind of mistake he would make, and it was not unrelated to the American champion's description of his chess game. He would make a bid short of game, but, after getting the bid, would see that, if he took and made two long finesses, he could come in with a little slam. Of course, a little slam would make only a few points difference since he hadn't bid it, but he would take the two finesses and not only lose both but lose his bid on an absolutely "lay-down hand." He was a rather small man, as you know, and he would look with almost childlike incredulity at the ruined remains of his daring invention of two long finesses where none was a sure thing.

There may also have been a causal relation between his shortcomings in bridge and chess. As the great head-and-hands scientist, the games that he was really good at involved great skill with a cue, a violin bow, a paint brush or a racket, but chess and bridge required no gift of hands. This is just a guess. The University of Chicago had as yet no Nobel Prize winners by the names of George Wells Beadle and James Dewey Watson to decode the hodge-podge of genetic tape that makes us one, or to explain why Michelson, who when it came to games was a mini–Leonardo da Vinci, with a wide spread of gifts, was not wanted as a bridge partner. It is easier to understand Carlson's case—we certainly don't think of there being much connection between animal experimentation and fifty-two cards and two jokers—and there wasn't.

Dickson, the master of numbers, was sometimes expectedly brilliant in a game where only 13 × 4 numbers were involved; his habitual troubles were at least partly environmental—he had come here by way of Texas. He almost consistently overbid and, when he lost three or four hands in a row, he would slam his cards down on the table and leave the card room in a rage, always denouncing Carlson on the way out. No matter who had misplayed—Carlson, Michelson, or himself—he always denounced Carlson. While the cards were still shivering on the table, he would shout, "Why the hell, Carlson, don't you go back to your lab and feed your dogs? And don't let Irene Castle catch you killing any of them."

Overbidding three or four hands in a row and then blaming the great biologist seemed to put the great mathematician in the right state of mind to race back to his office and resume his classic studies on the theory of numbers.

But be sure that Dickson or no one else ever even mentioned that Michelson did not play bridge well. Michelson was something like the other great University tradition we had in those days (observed in these present days only by James Cate and me)—namely, that the University shield in the floor of the Reynolds Club, in front of the entrance to the cafeteria, should never be stepped on. No one wanted to play with Michelson, but he was Michelson, and no one ever stepped on him and said he did not play bridge well.

At seventy-five, though, he was still the best billiard player in the club. He even looked like a billiard player. In fact, he looked like everything he did well—he looked like a violinist, a water colorist, a chess player and a physicist. And he still looked like an Annapolis-trained naval officer. At seventy-five, he was slight, trim, and handsome. He was quietly dressed, with a high, stiff collar and a small, sharp mustache. He was small all over, and even his hands did not look particularly unusual. In fact, one of the fascinations of his hands was that they looked fairly ordinary. I suppose we are used to thinking of a master's hands as being long and powerful and "esthetic," but the hands of the greatest of all billiard players, Willie Hoppe, were not particularly unusual just to look at, although those of his great rival, Jake Shaefer (the Younger), conformed to the picture in our minds and were like long and powerful bridges. I had learned, though, while working in logging camps, that a man's hands don't always tell how good he is with them.

Michelson was slightly stooped-shouldered (possibly from age), and his small size and slight stoop made him fit the proportions of a billiard table when he was taking a shot, and, when he was standing, he looked as if he were leaning over his cue to chalk it. With a shift of context, of course, the slight stoop and quiet elegance made him look like a violinist, a painter and a chess player.

Like most of the very good "downtown players" at Bensinger's, he seemed to shoot slowly, an obvious illusion if you kept track of the number of points he was making. It would be more accurate, therefore, to say he shot steadily and rhythmically, only occasionally taking more time to study one shot than another. Those who had seen him shoot in his prime said he was best at three-cushion billiards and credited his skill at this wide-angle game to his mastery of physics, but when I saw him play, his long game was his weakness, possibly because his eyesight was not so sharp as it had been.

In 1928 what he was best at was getting the three balls close together and then "nursing" them—that is, making long runs by keeping the balls together with a soft, delicate stroke. When they slowly worked apart, he would bring them together again with a "position shot" that required an understanding of the angle each ball would take when it came off a cushion, together with perfect control of the speed and hence the distance each ball would travel. Speed and angles he had under his control. When I saw him play, he was essentially a control player.

It would be non-scientific to describe him as a great billiard player but he was a very good amateur player. At seventy-five he could have played down-town at Bensinger's, and he was the best billiard player in the history of the University. I saw him run over forty several times, and it was not unusual for him to put a string together of twenty or thirty; he had to start with a tough "leave" if he didn't make five or ten.

Once he handed me his cue and said, "Shoot a few yourself." Considering my general confusion, I thought I did pretty well. In fact, he said, "Not bad." Then he added, "But you use 'English' on too many of your shots." English comes from putting a spin on the cue-ball by hitting it on one side instead of the center so that it comes off the cushion or another ball at an unusual angle. "Once in a while it is necessary to use English," he said, "but it is hard to predict accurately. Cue your ball in the center as often as you can. Don't use something hard to control unless you have to."

Only this once did he hand me his cue and ask me to shoot, so once must have satisfied him that, although I wasn't good enough to play with him, he could turn to me now and then and lift an eyebrow.

Often when he missed a shot, he stood silently studying the green cloth un-til (I think) he had reconstructed the preceding series of shots and had decided where he had started to lose control of the balls. Once he said when he missed a shot, "I am getting old."

Just he and I were present, so he said this to me or himself, but I had to let him know I heard it and I have always been glad I did. I said, "No, no. It was a hard shot, but it was the one you should have taken, and you barely missed it."

"Are you sure?" he asked.

I said, "I am sure. The easy shot would have left the balls spread all over the table. Any of the good players down at Bensinger's would have played it the way you did, and a lot of them would have missed."

EXTENDED EPIGRAM

I think that he was glad I had stopped him from blaming old age, but he was through for the day. He locked his cue into the rack on the wall, and said, either to me or himself or the wall, "Billiards is a good game."

He made sure that his tie was in the center of his stiff collar before he added, "But billiards is not as good a game as painting."

He rolled down his sleeves and put on his coat. Elegant as he was, he was a workman and took off his coat and rolled up his sleeves when he played billiards. As he stood on the first step between the billiard room and the card room, he added, "But painting is not as good a game as music."

On the next and top step, he concluded, "But then music is not as good a game as physics."

As you can see, I have never forgotten this extended epigram, but for many years I thought of it largely as an extended epigram and for some time I thought probably he had shaped it for me, knowing vaguely that I was in English and should appreciate a literary construction that extended across the billiard room to the top of the stairs. As I grew older and more detached from myself, however, I could see nothing in our relations that would have suggested to him what I intended to do with my life, so next I came to assume that it was just a stylish remark he made to himself, because at seventy-five he was still very stylish—in appearance, dress, serenity, and slowness of movement that turned out not to be slowness but the shortest distance between two points, which is one definition of grace.

Always, though, I must have sensed that this extended epigram was more than a reflection of style, because, forty-five years later, by which time I had several subjects I might have talked about, I suddenly decided I would tell the Alumni Cabinet about Michelson's comment on games. I also decided it was time for me to clarify to myself what was missing to me but I always knew was there, so I went over to the President's Archives, got Michelson's file and read his most serious scientific prose. Then, not long afterwards—but unfortunately not until after I gave my talk to the Alumni Cabinet—I discovered and read the humanly and scientifically perceptive biography of him by his youngest daughter. You should read it, too, if you wish to experience for a short time Michelson's universe which moves in beauty playing games. It is not a universe governed by morality or theology but by esthetics, mechanics, and gamesmanship, all shades of one another.

In 1928, then, Michelson was not talking to the wall when he said, after missing a correct but hard shot: "Billiards is a good game, but billiards is not as good a game as painting, but painting is not as good a game as music, but then music is not as good a game as physics."

He was saying much the same thing many years earlier, only more formally, and more beautifully. In 1899, for instance, he began the Lowell Lectures on physics before his Boston audience by speaking first of esthetics:

If a poet could at the same time be a physicist, he might convey to others the pleasure, the satisfaction, almost the reverence, which the subject inspires. The esthetic side of the subject is, I confess, by no means the least attractive to me. Especially is its fascination felt in the branch which deals with light, and I hope the day may be near when a Ruskin will be found equal to the description of the beauties of coloring, the exquisite graduations of light and shade, and the intricate wonders of symmetrical forms and combinations of forms which are encountered at every turn.

In the games that were going on in the universe, the participants were not only the universe and those hoping to understand it, but even the machines that were made to help the understanding. Of one of his machines that Michelson could never quite master, he said:

One comes to regard the machine as having a personality—I had almost said a feminine personality—requiring humoring, coaxing, cajoling— even threatening! But finally one realizes that the personality is that of an alert and skillful player in an intricate but fascinating game—who will take immediate advantage of the mistakes of his opponent, who "springs" the most disconcerting surprises, who never leaves any result to chance—but who nevertheless plays fair—in strict accordance with the rules of the game. These rules he knows and makes no allowance if you do not. When you learn them and play accordingly, the game progresses as it should.

Einstein left behind, not only a formulation of the universe, but a formulation of Michelson's delight in it. His telegram on the one-hundredth anniversary of Michelson's birthday began:

I always think of Michelson as the artist in Science. His greatest joy seemed to come from the beauty of the experiment itself, and the elegance of the method employed.

Although I watched Michelson play billiards regularly at noon for a few months before he retired from the University, I have the feeling now that he never came to know anything about me, except that I put English on too many of my shots and so did not have perfect control of them.

But I am certain that eventually I came to know something important about him, perhaps in part because I taught literature, and certainly in part because I was brought up in pool halls and logging camps—he was an artist and played many games well, especially those involving something like a cue, a brush, a bow, or, best of all, a box with slits and silvered mirrors. In that game he was playing with light and a star.

WORKS CITED

Livingston, Dorothy M. *The Master of Light: A Biography of Albert A. Michelson.* New York: Charles Scribner's Sons, 1973.

Retrievers

....

Good and Bad

Shortly after 1970 when, at the behest of his son and daughter, Maclean began to write what he called "reminiscent stories," "Retrievers Good and Bad" was the first result. He had long wanted to write about his murdered younger brother, Paul, but found himself approaching the subject obliquely through their father and the succession of duck dogs he owned. "Retrievers" shows Maclean's humor in a strong light, and the essay's swift modulation to tragedy at its climax closely anticipates the same movement in A River Runs through It. *Maclean was not satisfied with it, however, referring to it in a letter to Nick Lyons as both a moral and artistic failure. In 1977, after the success of* A River Runs through It and Other Stories, *Maclean finally published the essay in* Esquire *magazine.*

The day I was born, as I was to be often told, my father gave me a dog for a birthday present. Very early in life, then, I was to learn about the power of odd coincidence, because my dog turned out to be a duck dog and my father turned out to be a duck hunter and evidently, at least in my infancy, I did not resemble a duck and the dog did not give a damn about me. We talk painfully about father and mother rejections, but if you are going in for rejections, there is nothing like being the supposed infant owner of an animal and wanting to be loved by it and instead being studied by yellow eyes that wished you were a dead duck. Even so, in many ways and for long periods of the year, the dog belonged more to my mother than to my father or to me.

My father was a Scotch Presbyterian minister. He was intellectual and somewhat poetical and referred to Methodists as Baptists who could read. He thought he was fulfilling his calling by preaching two very good sermons on Sundays and by baptizing, marrying and burying the local Americans of Scotch descent on weekdays. The so-called church work he regarded as

"Retrievers Good and Bad" is reprinted from *Esquire* 88 (October 1977): 22, 30, 32, 34, 36.

woman's work, and so it was my mother who visited the new members of the church and ran the Ladies' Aid and Christian Endeavor and tried to sing louder than anyone else in the congregation.

My father's ideas about a duck dog were highly specialized. He expected the dog to be totally his from the opening morning of duck season until the closing sunset. During the remaining portion of the year, he expected the dog to be taken care of, as the church was, by God and my mother, but in the case of the dog, God with some justification left the work to my mother. So she fed the dog all year until hunting season, she combed and brushed it, and she saw that the dog had a good bed and clean bedding. She even watched—more closely than my father—the coming date of the opening of the duck season; a month before, she would confine the dog to the garage because she knew my father was not unique among mankind in expecting to have a duck dog on opening day even though he hadn't taken care of it until then. Any dog resembling a duck dog, any dog even with yellow eyes, could not venture alone on the streets of my town two weeks or even a month before the opening of the season without being—not exactly stolen—but abducted until November 30. So my mother locked up the dog and then of course she had to walk it.

My mother was a fine working woman, but she had one shortcoming. She ran the church and all that, she had a family to take care of and she was stableboy, as it were, for a succession of large female Chesapeake Bay retrievers. But she was not a dog trainer, and my father on the opening day of duck season expected not only a well-fed and well-kept dog but a perfect retriever. Since he would not train the dogs himself, it may be difficult to understand just how he expected them to show instantaneous perfection, but this is what he expected of hunting dogs and firstborn sons.

My father's interest in the dog business was more theological than scientific, so if a dog did not approach perfection, we got another Chesapeake Bay retriever for the next season. They were always called Fanny, a name I did not like, and the dogs never particularly liked me, but my father always said they were mine. This process went on long after I left home and included dogs that I practically never saw, but it is easy to understand how in over thirty years I came to own a kennel, as it were, of "almost duck dogs" and even one dog that on her own power approached perfection. Then, finally, there was a dog that was not given to me.

I realize that my father and my town were fairly special, but it's a good guess that something like what went on in my town went on in most small towns that were near shooting water. Universal pulsations seem to spread among ducks and duck hunters alike. It is said that far north in Canada, in the marshes where the ducks nest, you can hear increasing restlessness both day and night some weeks before the migrations begin, even if there is no visible sign of the storms that finally set the ducks off. And, at the same time, south of the border, there is a stirring all along main streets when something like a duck dog—even a cocker spaniel—goes by. Doors flutter open, sales are postponed, and customers and salesmen alike, especially hardware salesmen who sell shotgun shells, come out on the walk and suddenly become dog fanciers. It is almost a sure bet, too, that not one of the dogs, even those with good bloodlines, is well trained. It takes time to train a dog—summertime—and in summertime the duck hunters and hardware salesmen I knew went fishing, including, of course, my father, who even tied his own flies. Come autumn, a dog hasn't much choice but to rely on his blood, which, given my experience, is never quite enough.

The almost duck dog whose genetic deficiencies aroused my father most was Fanny II. By the time I acquired title to her, we had moved to western Montana, where there was excellent duck shooting and where for the first time my father was tempted to shoot over his legal limit. Accordingly, he started taking me with him, although I was scarcely as long as the castoff double-barrel shotgun I kept stumbling over and not half so powerful, at least in reverse. Naturally, my father didn't take me along to shoot ducks. I was too young to have to buy a license, and all the ducks over the twenty he shot (twenty was the limit then) I was given to carry. They were mine—along with the dog. The dog, when I try honestly to remember, looked like any other Chesapeake Bay retriever—big, with brown curly hair, yellow eyes, intelligent, professional. We were shooting in an outlet of a lake, quiet water covered with dead reeds, stuff that looked to me like seaweed and muck of that sort. Every time my father dropped a bird in the water, Fanny II would charge out and, swimming high, would shoulder the dead duck aside and, four or five feet beyond, snap a mouthful of floating seaweed. She had a passion for seaweed, and with an almost sexual smile on her face she would return it to my father. Then, still standing right in front of him and still untrained, she would shake all the water out of her coat, most of which he had to absorb.

After a while he asked me if I would take off my clothes and swim for the ducks, and I did, but I hated it. It was all kind of marshy stuff, and I had to pull my legs through ooze a foot or more deep, dragging bubbles behind me, and when I swam I could feel things touching my body. I was exhausted by the end of the day and hoped that my father would soon get rid of the dog. I needn't have worried about my father. He regarded the dog as an anti–duck dog and even as an antichristian. It wasn't the dog's retrieving seaweed that was sacrilege to my father; it was her pushing the dead duck aside. You can be sure that it was the only day we ever hunted with Fanny II.

I tend to remember best the almost duck dogs that enraged my father most. One made him swear—the only time I ever heard him do so. This Fanny was rather late in the succession, and by the time I acquired ownership, I was going with a girl whose home was in Wolf Creek, which is only a few miles from the Missouri River and not too far from its headwaters. Even there it is a big river and looks as big or even bigger than it does six or seven hundred miles farther down. It is still clear but is powerful and full of undercurrents and big bends against cliffs. It was just below the fabled canyon named the Gates of the Mountains by Lewis and Clark.

My father had hunted several seasons with this dog and evidently had found her satisfactory, but he had hunted with her in the quiet oozy outlet where seaweed drifts by that I described earlier. Well, there is no seaweed drifting on the Big Missouri, where we were shooting. The Missouri is one of the main flyways for ducks in America, and when the autumn storms begin in the north, the ducks come whistling out of Canada, hit the Missouri River, follow it to the Mississippi and coast the rest of the way to Louisiana. When they go around those big bends on the upper Missouri, the air is left hurt and shaking, and if you are a duck hunter, the place to be is behind a rock on the cliffside of the bends, because the ducks' speed on the turns almost drives them into the cliffs and into your gun barrel. That is just where my father and I were.

My father was in good form, and we knocked down several ducks so close to shore that we almost could have retrieved them without a dog. Then a stray came by making such faint vibrations that he passed us before we saw him. We both fired, and he hit the water at least halfway across the river, but the dog had seen him and started out. The trouble was she was used to retrieving in quiet water, and she should have run down the river bank a lot farther before starting to swim for the duck because the current carried the duck a long way before the dog caught up with it. In fact, the duck by then was nearer the other bank, so the dog gave an extra snap of her neck to set the duck securely in place and then just kept going—for the other side.

I have a theory—probably not subscribed to by academic geneticists—that just as Chesapeakes are coded for retrieving, Scotchmen are coded for profanity. Not obscenity, just profanity. I have known quite a few Scotchmen in my time, including my father's brother, so this has to be taken at least as a considered opinion. I always felt that my father lived a somewhat unnatural and unhappy life because he could not swear, but once, to my knowledge, he showed his genetic tape.

He leaned his shotgun against the rock and stood up, scaring off a big flight that had started to make the bend, but he never noticed it. "Goodness!" he said, which is as far as he usually descended into the abyss. Then he said, "My goodness." Then he exploded: "Do you see that damn dog over there?" It was a hell of a long way off, but I could see the bitch lying on a sandbar with what looked like a big fat mallard between her paws. I believe that if my father thought his gun could have carried the river, he would have given the dog both barrels. After a good rest she came swimming back, without the duck, and if you are interested in things that give the appearance of being a long way off, take a good look at a duck you have shot that's lying dead forever on the other side of the Missouri.

Fortunately, the dog handled most of the rest of the ducks fairly well, but she carried four or five more across the river and left them there—which was enough to spoil the day for my father. I am glad to say, though, that the experience left no lasting marks on any of us. That evening my Wolf Creek girl and I had several good laughs, and a little later in life we were married and lived happily for many years. My father forgave the dog and hunted with her for a number of seasons—but always on quiet water. It might have been simpler if he had trained her to recognize that he was the center of the universe and that all things falling into the water were to be returned to him, he being, as it were, the Creator. It wouldn't have been hard.

Our almost-perfect duck dog was our last Chesapeake—as if genetics had arranged itself in dramatic and climactic order. She was bigger than our other dogs and more imperial. When my father started me fly-fishing, there were only about a dozen flies that any trout fisherman carried with him—plain and royal coachmen, grey hackles with red or yellow bodies, brown hackles and my favorite—if only for its name—Queen of Waters. To me, this dog was Queen of Waters. I wish that she could have found it in her heart to return a little of the feeling I had for her, but she did not care for me particularly or for my father or even for my mother or ducks or even dead ducks. She was my first encounter with a strict professional. She loved only one thing—she loved to do the thing she could do, which was to bring in dead ducks.

She made that Missouri River look like an irrigation ditch. Sometimes, while the rest of the world lies turning in bed and counting sheep, I lie turning in bed and counting the ducks she brought in for us the first day we worked her on the Missouri. It was as cold as hell and the ducks were being projected from Canada as if from a rocket base, but she missed nothing that skidded upon the waters. We were hunting with two other parties, each of which had a spaniel, and by nine o'clock in the morning both spaniels were through. The big water and the undercurrents and the cold had finished them off. There could be five dead ducks floating down the river and the dogs would only put a foot in the water and whine. Finally, their owners took them back to the car and wrapped them in blankets. Even in the bitter cold of the late-afternoon shooting, the Queen of Waters was still retrieving the ducks for my father and me and the other two parties. It was so cold by then that long icicles hung from her brown curls. I can still hear her rushing by me for the river, tinkling like a glass chandelier in a windstorm, and I can go to sleep with this sound in my ears.

This dog was great even when she goofed. Actually, I can remember her goofing only once, and then she almost killed my father, me and herself. Not just one or two of us—the works. She swung only in the larger orbits. This was the first season she had been shot over, and we were shooting on a slough on the Blackfoot River. There were a good many ducks on the water when we sneaked into our blind around daybreak, and we got three of them when they rose off the water. The dog hit the slough as if she had come out of a cannon, but even so, she hadn't got the three ducks to shore before another flight circled, started to light, then saw the dog and took off before my father had a shot. This is a good slough, and for an hour or so after daybreak there is a big movement of ducks over it, so it is best not to send your dog out on the water until the flights start easing off. Well, the Queen of Waters, although still but a large pup, was doing her thing and in the process she scared another flight that had started to settle. Finally my father fumbled in the pockets of his hunting jacket, pulled out a long piece of stout cord, softly called her and tied her to him, from her collar to his leg. Then he looked shyly at me to see if I had been watching.

This slough is in deep woods, and usually you hear the ducks coming in before you see them. I didn't even hear the ducks this time, but I saw the dog stiffen and I kept raising my eyes. I saw my father swing his gun to his shoulder and then I saw a duck swerve out of the flock, and in a moment you could project the duck's curve to the water. The moment you could, the dog could, too, and the cord held. She started for the water like a supercharged dray horse, hauling my father's leg through the reeds. My father didn't freeze on the trigger because the gun was a semiautomatic and if he had frozen on the trigger he would have fired only once. Instead, he must have gone into a state of convulsions, and his gun was blazing. One shot went through the reeds and laid down a swath as if he were mowing hay. Then he just missed me and then he just missed the dog and once, I am sure, he almost shot himself. It scared the hell out of me, but I lived to verify the accuracy of the old western description of a charge of shot going past your head as "busting a hole in the breeze." Shakily, I got my father unwound from the reeds and the dog and the cord and his gun, but even before I had totally completed this operation and certainly before I had quit shaking, I heard the spraying of water on reeds, and there was the dog with the duck.

She was a magnificent creation and had a privilege not granted to many mortals—of living long enough to approach perfection. Then, shortly after these things happened to the dog, my brother was murdered. I try to say it the way it was—without premonition, never to be explained and never to be as-similated. It had no past and it never went on and turned into something else. It just was—suddenly, shockingly and forever.

After the funeral my father and mother and I spent several weeks at our cabin on the lake. It was early May, and the forest floor of the cathedral of thousand-year-old tamaracks was covered with dogtooth violets, which are re-ally lilies. Around the lake they are often called glacier lilies, probably because it is only about twenty miles from our lake to the glaciers. We thought they were the most beautiful and fragile flowers we would ever see, and we tried not to walk on any of them.

My father aged rapidly. He never hunted ducks again and had to give up most of his trout fishing. His feet dragged when he walked, as if his leg muscles had atrophied, so he could not fish the big rivers any more or even the creeks that were hard to get to. Mostly, he fished in the lake in front of our cabin in a flat-bottomed boat he had made many years before. If it was bright, he wore no hat, and his almost-red Scotch hair paled until it became part of the sunlight. If it was at all cool, he wore one of my brother's fishing jackets, and soon after my brother's death he adopted his dog. My brother's dog was a handsome springer spaniel called Quake because my brother had got him as a pup in 1935, the year of the earthquake in Helena. My brother had been a fine shot with a scatter-gun, and Quake was a very good duck dog—not as professional a duck dog as the Queen of Waters, but in the end the best dog of all.

This dog and my father greatly changed each other's lives. The dog and my father were inseparable, whereas before, my father cared to be with dogs only during the hunting season. As for the dog, I am sure there are other cases like his, but he was the only dog I ever saw that became another dog for love of another man. For my brother he had been a duck dog, and now for my father he became a fishing dog, if one can speak of such a species. He would sit all day in the boat on the seat next to my father and peer into the impenetrable water. He not only loved but admired my father greatly—I am sure he thought the whole fishing thing was completely under my father's control, as I did when I was the dog's age and believed my father could come up with a fish whenever he was so minded. After staring a respectable length of time into the water without seeing anything but pieces of sunlight, he would bark at my father, and when my father caught a fish, the dog would lick my father's whole face, though my father still needed part of it to see how to unhook the fish.

To the others in my family, the dog was something of a sacred object that had prolonged my father's life and helped to steady the rest of us. He was a fine dog, and after him, my father had no other dog.

Logging and Pimping

....

and "Your Pal, Jim"

*"Logging and Pimping and 'Your Pal, Jim,'" the short story
positioned between the two novellas in* A River Runs through
It and Other Stories *(1976), was written in the early 1970s,
before the two novellas. In it the reader glimpses a long-ago world
of logging camps before chain saws and other power equipment,
places where a boy could prove himself a man. Maclean first
announces a theme that occupies him in his novellas and* Young
Men and Fire: *an abiding, pervasive respect for those expert with
their hands and the tools of their trade.*

The first time I took any real notice of him was on a Sunday afternoon in a bunkhouse in one of the Anaconda Company's logging camps on the Blackfoot River. He and I and some others had been lying on our bunks reading, although it was warm and half-dark in the bunkhouse this summer afternoon. The rest of them had been talking, but to me everything seemed quiet. As events proved in a few minutes, the talking had been about "The Company," and probably the reason I hadn't heard it was that the lumberjacks were registering their customary complaints about the Company—it owned them body and soul; it owned the state of Montana, the press, the preachers, etc.; the grub was lousy and likewise the wages, which the Company took right back from them anyway by overpricing everything at the commissary, and they had to buy from the commissary, out in the woods where else could they buy. It must have been something like this they were saying, because all of a sudden I heard him break the quiet: "Shut up, you incompetent sons of bitches. If it weren't for the Company, you'd all starve to death."

At first, I wasn't sure I had heard it or he had said it, but he had. Everything was really quiet now and everybody was watching his small face and big head and body behind an elbow on his bunk. After a while, there were stirrings

"Logging and Pimping and 'Your Pal, Jim'" is reprinted from *A River Runs through It and Other Stories* (Chicago: University of Chicago Press, 1976).

and one by one the stirrings disappeared into the sunlight of the door. Not a stirring spoke, and this was a logging camp and they were big men.

Lying there on my bunk, I realized that actually this was not the first time I had noticed him. For instance, I already knew his name, which was Jim Grierson, and I knew he was a socialist who thought Eugene Debs was soft. Probably he hated the Company more than any man in camp, but the men he hated more than the Company. It was also clear I had noticed him before, because when I started to wonder how I would come out with him in a fight, I discovered I already had the answer. I estimated he weighed 185 to 190 pounds and so was at least 35 pounds heavier than I was, but I figured I had been better taught and could reduce him to size if I could last the first ten minutes. I also figured that probably I could not last the first ten minutes.

I didn't go back to my reading but lay there looking for something interesting to think about, and was interested finally in realizing that I had estimated my chances with Jim in a fight even before I thought I had noticed him. Almost from the first moment I saw Jim I must have felt threatened, and others obviously felt the same way—later as I came to know him better all my thinking about him was colored by the question, "Him or me?" He had just taken over the bunkhouse, except for me, and now he was tossing on his bunk to indicate his discomfort at my presence. I stuck it out for a while, just to establish homestead rights to existence, but now that I couldn't read anymore, the bunkhouse seemed hotter than ever, so, after carefully measuring the implications of my not being wanted, I got up and sauntered out the door as he rolled over and sighed.

By the end of the summer, when I had to go back to school, I knew a lot more about Jim, and in fact he and I had made a deal to be partners for the coming summer. It didn't take long to find out that he was the best lumberjack in camp. He was probably the best with the saw and ax, and he worked with a kind of speed that was part ferocity. This was back in 1927, as I remember, and of course there was no such thing as a chain saw then, just as now there is no such thing as a logging camp or a bunkhouse the whole length of the Blackfoot River, although there is still a lot of logging going on there. Now the saws are one-man chain saws run by light high-speed motors, and the sawyers are married and live with their families, some of them as far away as Missoula, and drive more than a hundred miles a day to get to and from work. But in the days of the logging camps, the men worked mostly on two-man crosscut saws that were things of beauty, and the highest paid man in camp was the man who delicately filed and set them. The two-man teams who pulled the saws either worked for wages or "gyppoed." To gyppo, which wasn't meant to be a nice-sounding word and could be used as either a noun or a verb, was to be paid by the number of thousands of board feet you cut a day. Naturally, you chose to gyppo only if you thought you could beat wages and the men who worked for wages. As I said, Jim had talked me into being his partner for next summer, and we were going to gyppo and make big money. You can bet I agreed to this with some misgivings, but I was in graduate school now and on my own financially and needed the big money. Besides, I suppose I was flattered by being asked to be the partner of the best sawyer in camp. It was a long way, though, from being all flattery. I also knew I was being challenged. This was the world of the woods and the working stiff, the logging camp being a world especially overbearing with challenges, and, if you expected to duck all challenges, you shouldn't have wandered into the woods in the first place. It is true, too, that up to a point I liked being around him—he was three years older than I was, which at times is a lot, and he had seen parts of life with which I, as the son of a Presbyterian minister, wasn't exactly intimate.

A couple of other things cropped up about him that summer that had a bearing on the next summer when he and I were to gyppo together. He told me he was Scotch, which figured, and that made two of us. He said that he had been brought up in the Dakotas and that his father (and I quote) was "a Scotch son of a bitch" who threw him out of the house when he was fourteen and he had been making his own living ever since. He explained to me that he made his living only partly by working. He worked just in the summer, and then this cultural side of him, as it were, took over. He holed up for the winter in some town that had a good Carnegie Public Library and the first thing he did was take out a library card. Then he went looking for a good whore, and so he spent the winter reading and pimping—or maybe this is stated in reverse order. He said that on the whole he preferred southern whores; southern whores, he said, were generally "more poetical," and later I think I came to know what he meant by this.

So I started graduate school that autumn, and it was tough and not made any easier by the thought of spending all next summer on the end of a saw opposite this direct descendant of a Scotch son of a bitch.

But finally it was late June and there he was, sitting on a log across from me and looking as near like a million dollars as a lumberjack can look. He was dressed all in wool—in a rich Black Watch plaid shirt, gray, short-legged stag pants, and a beautiful new pair of logging boots with an inch or so of white sock showing at the top. The lumberjack and the cowboy followed many of the same basic economic and ecological patterns. They achieved a balance if they were broke at the end of the year. If they were lucky and hadn't been sick or anything like that, they had made enough to get drunk three or four times and to buy their clothes. Their clothes were very expensive; they claimed they were robbed up and down the line and probably they were, but clothes that would stand their work and the weather had to be something special. Central to both the lumberjack's and the cowboy's outfit were the boots, which took several months of savings.

The pair that Jim had on were White Loggers made, as I remember, by a company in Spokane that kept your name and measurements. It was a great shoe, but there were others and they were great, too—they had to be. The Bass, the Bergman, and the Chippewa were all made in different parts of the country, but in the Northwest most of the jacks I remember wore the Spokane shoe.

As the cowboy boot was made all ways for riding horses and working steers, the logger's boot was made for working on and around logs. Jim's pair had a six-inch top, but there were models with much higher tops—Jim happened to belong to the school that wanted their ankles supported but no tie on their legs. The toe was capless and made soft and somewhat waterproof with neat's-foot oil. The shoe was shaped to walk or "ride" logs. It had a high instep to fit the log, and with a high instep went a high heel, not nearly so high as a cowboy's and much sturdier because these were walking shoes; in fact, very fine walking shoes—the somewhat high heel threw you slightly forward of your normal stance and made you feel you were being helped ahead. Actually, this feeling was their trademark.

Jim was sitting with his right leg rocking on his left knee, and he gestured a good deal with his foot, raking the log I was sitting on for emphasis and leaving behind a gash in its side. The soles of these loggers' boots looked like World War I, with trenches and barbwire highly planned—everything planned, in this case, for riding logs and walking. Central to the grand design were the caulks, or "corks" as the jacks called them; they were long and sharp enough to hold to a heavily barked log or, tougher still, to one that was dead and had no bark on it. But of course caulks would have ripped out at the edges of a shoe and made you stumble and trip at the toes, so the design started with a row of blunt, sturdy hobnails around the edges and maybe four or five rows of them at the toes. Then inside came the battlefield of caulks, the real barbwire, with two rows of caulks coming down each side of the sole and one row on each side continuing into the instep to hold you when you

Rev. John Norman Maclean and Clara (Davidson) Maclean
with their sons, Norman (*left*) and Paul, about 1911.

Norman Fitzroy Maclean in an undated studio portrait from his college years. Maclean graduated from Dartmouth College in 1924.

Paul Maclean in a photograph
by Norman Maclean, late 1930s.
Norman was an enthusiastic
amateur photographer.

(clockwise from top left)
Paul Maclean, Jessie Burns Maclean,
and Norman Maclean at Seeley Lake,
Montana, 1932.

Rev. John Norman Maclean, no date. Photograph by Norman Maclean.

Paul Maclean at Seeley Lake, Montana, in 1937, the year before he was murdered in a Chicago alley. Photograph by Norman Maclean.

Jessie Burns Maclean, 1934. Photograph by Norman Maclean.

(*opposite*) Norman Maclean (*right*) with George Croonenberghs at Diana Lake, Montana, 1949. Croonenberghs tied flies for Norman and Paul, and served as fishing instructor and period adviser for the 1992 movie *A River Runs through It*.

Body retrieval in Mann Gulch, Montana, August 6, 1949.
The Mann Gulch fire haunted Maclean until his death and
was the subject of his 1992 book, *Young Men and Fire*.
Photograph by Dick Wilson.

Robert Utley at the Custer Battlefield
Monument, 1950. Courtesy of Robert
Utley.

Marie Borroff in an undated photograph. Courtesy of Marie Borroff.

Nick Lyons at Hunter College, 1980. Courtesy of Nick Lyons.

Norman Maclean in the cabin
at Seeley Lake, about 1960.

Maclean teaching English 237, his
popular course on Shakespeare, at the
University of Chicago, January 1970.
Photograph by Leslie Strauss Travis.

Seventh Cavalry grave markers at Custer Battlefield, photographed by Norman Maclean in August 1933.

One of the original markers in
Mann Gulch, Montana, for the United
States Forest Service Smokejumpers
who perished there on August 5, 1949.
Photograph by Alan Thomas, 1992.

(overleaf) Norman Maclean, Chicago,
1975. Photograph by Joel Snyder.

jumped crosswise on a log. Actually, it was a beautiful if somewhat primitive design and had many uses—for instance, when a couple of jacks got into a fight and one went down the other was almost sure to kick and rake him with his boots. This treatment was known as "giving him the leather" and, when a jack got this treatment, he was out of business for a long time and was never very pretty again.

Every time Jim kicked and raked the log beside me for emphasis I wiped small pieces of bark off my face.

In this brief interlude in our relations it seemed to me that his face had grown a great deal since I first knew him last year. From last year I remembered big frame, big head, small face, tight like a fist; I even wondered at times if it wasn't his best punch. But sitting here relaxed and telling me about pimping and spraying bark on my face, he looked all big, his nose too and eyes, and he looked handsome and clearly he liked pimping—at least for four or five months of the year—and he especially liked being bouncer in his own establishment, but even that, he said, got boring. It was good to be out in the woods again, he said, and it was good to see me—he also said that; and it was good to be back to work—he said that several times.

Most of this took place in the first three or four days. We started in easy, each one admitting to the other that he was soft from the winter, and, besides, Jim hadn't finished giving me this course on pimping. Pimping is a little more complicated than the innocent bystander might think. Besides selecting a whore (big as well as southern, i.e., "poetical") and keeping her happy (taking her to the Bijou Theater in the afternoons) and hustling (rounding up all the Swedes and Finns and French Canadians you had known in the woods), you also had to be your own bootlegger (it still being Prohibition) and your own police fixer (it being then as always) and your own bouncer (which introduced a kind of sporting element into the game). But after a few days of resting every hour we had pretty well covered the subject, and still nobody seemed interested in bringing up socialism.

I suppose that an early stage in coming to hate someone is just running out of things to talk about. I thought then it didn't make a damn bit of difference to me that he liked his whores big as well as southern. Besides, we were getting in shape a little. We started skipping the rest periods and took only half an hour at lunch and at lunch we sharpened our axes on our Carborundum stones. Slowly we became silent, and silence itself is an enemy to friendship; when we came back to camp each went his own way, and within a week we weren't speaking to each other. Well, this in itself needn't have been ominous.

Lots of teams of sawyers work in silence because that is pretty much the kind of guys they are and of course because no one can talk and at the same time turn out thousands of board feet. Some teams of sawyers even hate each other and yet work together year after year, something like the old New York Celtic basketball team, knowing the other guy's moves without troubling to look. But our silence was different. It didn't have much to do with efficiency and big production. When he broke the silence to ask me if I would like to change from a six- to a seven-foot saw, I knew I was sawing for survival. A six-foot blade was plenty long enough for the stuff we were sawing, and the extra foot would have been only that much more for me to pull.

It was getting hot and I was half-sick when I came back to camp at the end of the day. I would dig into my duffel bag and get clean underwear and clean white socks and a bar of soap and go to the creek. Afterwards, I would sit on the bank until I was dry. Then I would feel better. It was a rule I had learned my first year working in the Forest Service—when exhausted and feeling sorry for yourself, at least change socks. On weekends I spent a lot of time washing my clothes. I washed them carefully and I expected them to be white, not gray, when they had dried on the brush. At first, then, I relied on small, home remedies such as cleanliness.

I had a period, too, when I leaned on proverbs, and tried to pass the blame back on myself, with some justification. All winter I had had a fair notion that something like this would happen. Now I would try to be philosophical by saying to myself, "Well, pal, if you fool around with the bull, you have to expect the horn."

But, when you are gored, there is not much comfort in proverbs.

Gradually, though, I began to fade out of my own picture of myself and what was happening and it was he who controlled my thoughts. In these dreams, some of which I had during the day, I was always pulling a saw and he was always at the other end of it getting bigger and bigger but his face getting smaller and smaller—and closer—until finally it must have come through the cut in the log, and with no log between us now, it threatened to continue on down the saw until it ran into me. It sometimes came close enough so that I could see how it got smaller—by twisting and contracting itself around its nose—and somewhere along here in my dream I would wake up from the exertion of trying to back away from what I was dreaming about.

In a later stage of my exhaustion, there was no dream—or sleep—just a constant awareness of being thirsty and of a succession of events of such a low biological order that normally they escaped notice. All night sighs succeeded grunts and grumblings of the guts, and about an hour after everyone was in bed and presumably asleep there were attempts at homosexuality, usually unsuccessful if the statistics I started to keep were at all representative. The bunkhouse would become almost silent. Suddenly somebody would jump up in his bed, punch another somebody, and mutter, "You filthy son of a bitch." Then he would punch him four or five times more, fast, hard punches. The other somebody never punched back. Instead, trying to be silent, his grieved footsteps returned to bed. It was still early in the night, too early to start thinking about daybreak. You lay there quietly through the hours, feeling as if you had spent all the previous day drinking out of a galvanized pail—eventually, every thought of water tasted galvanized.

After two or three nights of this you came to know you could not be whipped. Probably you could not win, but you could not be whipped.

I'll try not to get technical about logging, but I have to give you some idea of daylight reality and some notion of what was going on in the woods while I was trying to stay alive. Jim's pace was set to kill me off—it would kill him eventually too, but first me. So the problem, broadly speaking, was how to throw him off this pace and not quite get caught doing it, because after working a week with this Jack Dempsey at the other end of the saw I knew I'd never have a chance if he took a punch at me. Yet I would have taken a punching from him before I would ever have asked him to go easier on the saw. You were no logger if you didn't feel this way. The world of the woods and the working stiff was pretty much made of three things—working, fighting, and dames—and the complete lumberjack had to be handy at all of them. But if it came to the bitter choice, he could not remain a logger and be outworked. If I had ever asked for mercy on the saw I might as well have packed my duffel bag and started down the road.

So I tried to throw Jim off pace even before we began a cut. Often, before beginning to saw, sawyers have to do a certain amount of "brushing out," which means taking an ax and chopping bushes or small jack pines that would interfere with the sawing. I guess that by nature I did more of this than Jim, and now I did as much of it as I dared, and it burned hell out of him, especially since he had yelled at me about it early in the season when we were still speaking to each other. "Jesus," he had said, "you're no gyppo. Any time a guy's not sawing he's not making money. Nobody out here is paying you for trimming a garden." He would walk up to a cut and if there was a small jack pine in the way he would bend it over and hold it with his foot while he sawed and he ripped through the huckleberry bushes. He didn't give a damn if the bushes clogged his saw. He just pulled harder.

As to the big thing, sawing, it is something beautiful when you are working rhythmically together—at times, you forget what you are doing and get lost in abstractions of motion and power. But when sawing isn't rhythmical, even for a short time, it becomes a kind of mental illness—maybe even something more deeply disturbing than that. It is as if your heart isn't working right. Jim, of course, had thrown us off basic rhythm when he started to saw me into the ground by making the stroke too fast and too long, even for himself. Most of the time I followed his stroke; I had to, but I would pick periods when I would not pull the saw to me at quite the speed or distance he was pulling it back to him. Just staying slightly off beat, not being quite so noticeable that he could yell but still letting him know what I was doing. To make sure he knew, I would suddenly go back to his stroke.

I'll mention just one more trick I invented with the hope of weakening Jim by frequent losses of adrenalin. Sawyers have many little but nevertheless almost sacred rules of work in order to function as a team, and every now and then I would almost break one of these but not quite. For instance, if you are making a cut in a fallen tree and it binds, or pinches, and you need a wedge to open the cut and free your saw and the wedge is on Jim's side of the log, then you are not supposed to reach over the log and get the wedge and do the job. Among sawyers, no time is wasted doing Alphonse-Gaston acts; what is on your side is your job—that's the rule. But every now and then I would reach over for his wedge, and when our noses almost bumped, we would freeze and glare. It was like a closeup in an early movie. Finally, I'd look somewhere else as if of all things I had never thought of the wedge, and you can be sure that, though I reached for it, I never got to it first and touched it.

Most of the time I took a lot of comfort from the feeling that some of this was getting to him. Admittedly, there were times when I wondered if I weren't making up a good part of this feeling just to comfort myself, but even then I kept doing things that in my mind were hostile acts. The other lumberjacks, though, helped to make me feel that I was real. They all acknowledged I was in a big fight, and quietly they encouraged me, probably with the hope they wouldn't have to take him on themselves. One of them muttered to me as we started out in the morning, "Some day that son of a bitch go out in the woods, he no come back." By which I assumed he meant

I was to drop a tree on him and forget to yell, "Timber!" Actually, though, I had already thought of this.

Another good objective sign was that he got in a big argument with the head cook, demanding pie for breakfast. It sounds crazy, for anybody who knows anything knows that the head cook runs the logging camp. He is, as the jacks say, "the guy with the golden testicles." If he doesn't like a jack because the jack has the bad table manners to talk at meal time, the cook goes to the woods foreman and the jack goes down the road. Just the same, Jim got all the men behind him and then put up his big argument and nobody went down the road and we had pie every morning for breakfast—two or three kinds—and nobody ever ate a piece, nobody, including Jim.

Oddly, after Jim won this pie fight with the cook, things got a little better for me in the woods. We still didn't speak to each other, but we did start sawing in rhythm.

Then, one Sunday afternoon this woman rode into camp, and stopped to talk with the woods foreman and his wife. She was a big woman on a big horse and carried a pail. Nearly every one in camp knew her or of her—she was the wife of a rancher who owned one of the finest ranches in the valley. I had only met her but my family knew her family quite well, my father occasionally coming up the valley to preach to the especially congregated Presbyterians. Anyway, I thought I had better go over and speak to her and maybe do my father's cause some good, but it was a mistake. She was still sitting on her big horse and I had talked to her for just a couple of minutes, when who shows up but Jim and without looking at me says he is my partner and "pal" and asks her about the pail. The woods foreman takes all our parts in reply. First, he answers for her and says she is out to pick huckleberries, and then he speaks as foreman and tells her we are sawyers and know the woods well, and then he replies to himself and speaks for us and assures her that Jim would be glad to show her where the huckleberries are, and it's a cinch he was. In the camp, the men were making verbal bets where nothing changes hands that Jim laid her within two hours. One of the jacks said, "He's as fast with dames as with logs." By late afternoon she rode back into camp. She never stopped. She was hurried and at a distance looked white and didn't have any huckleberries. She didn't even have her empty pail. Who the hell knows what she told her husband?

At first I felt kind of sorry for her because she was so well known in camp and was so much talked about, but she was riding "High, Wide, and

Handsome." She was back in camp every Sunday. She always came with a gal-
lon pail and she always left without it. She kept coming long after huckleberry
season passed. There wasn't a berry left on a bush, but she came with another
big pail.

The pie fight with the cook and the empty huckleberry pail were just what I
needed psychologically to last until Labor Day weekend, when, long ago, I had
told both Jim and the foreman I was quitting in order to get ready for school.
There was no great transformation in either Jim or me. Jim was still about the
size of Jack Dempsey. Nothing had happened to reduce this combination of
power and speed. It was just that something had happened so that most of the
time now we sawed to saw logs. As for me, for the first (and only) time in my
life I had spent over a month twenty-four hours a day doing nothing but hating
a guy. Now, though, there were times when I thought of other things—it got
so that I had to say to myself, "Don't ever get soft and forget to hate this guy
for trying to kill you off." It was somewhere along in here, too, when I became
confident enough to develop the theory that he wouldn't take a punch at me.
I probably was just getting wise to the fact that he ran this camp as if he were
the best fighter in it without ever getting into a fight. He had us stiffs intimi-
dated because he made us look bad when it came to work and women, and so
we went on to feel that we were also about to take a punching. Fortunately, I
guess, I always realized this might be just theory, and I continued to act as if
he were the best fighter in camp, as he probably was, but, you know, it still
bothers me that maybe he wasn't.

When we quit work at night, though, we still walked to camp alone. He still
went first, slipping on his Woolrich shirt over the top piece of his underwear
and putting his empty lunch pail under his arm. Like all sawyers, we pulled
off our shirts first thing in the morning and worked all day in the tops of our
underwear, and in the summer we still wore wool underwear, because we said
sweat made cotton stick to us and wool absorbed it. After Jim disappeared for
camp, I sat down on a log and waited for the sweat to dry. It still took me a
while before I felt steady enough to reach for my Woolrich shirt and pick up
my lunch pail and head for camp, but now I knew I could last until I had said
I would quit, which sometimes can be a wonderful feeling.

One day toward the end of August he spoke out of the silence and said,
"When are you going to quit?" It sounded as if someone had broken the silence before it was broken by Genesis.

I answered and fortunately I had an already-made answer; I said, "As I told
you, the Labor Day weekend."

He said, "I may see you in town before you leave for the East. I'm going to quit early this year myself." Then he added, "Last spring I promised a dame I would." I and all the other jacks had already noticed that the rancher's wife hadn't shown up in camp last Sunday, whatever that meant.

The week before I was going to leave for school I ran into him on the main street. He was looking great—a little thin, but just a little. He took me into a speakeasy and bought me a drink of Canadian Club. Since Montana is a northern border state, during Prohibition there was a lot of Canadian whiskey in my town if you knew where and had the price. I bought the second round, and he bought another and said he had enough when I tried to do the same. Then he added, "You know, I have to take care of you." Even after three drinks in the afternoon, I was a little startled, and still am.

Outside, as we stood parting and squinting in the sunlight, he said, "I got a place already for this dame of mine, but we've not yet set up for business." Then he said very formally, "We would appreciate it very much if you would pay us a short visit before you leave town." And he gave me the address and, when I told him it would have to be soon, we made a date for the next evening.

The address he had given me was on the north side, which is just across the tracks, where most of the railroaders lived. When I was a kid, our town had what was called a red-light district on Front Street adjoining the city dump which was always burning with a fitting smell, but the law had more or less closed it up and scattered the girls around, a fair proportion of whom sprinkled themselves among the railroaders. When I finally found the exact address, I recognized the house next to it. It belonged to a brakeman who married a tramp and thought he was quite a fighter, although he never won many fights. He was more famous in town for the story that he came home one night unexpectedly and captured a guy coming out. He reached in his pocket and pulled out three dollars. "Here," he told the guy, "go and get yourself a good screw."

Jim's place looked on the up-and-up—no shades drawn and the door slightly open and streaming light. Jim answered and was big enough to blot out most of the scenery, but I could see the edge of his dame just behind him. I remembered she was supposed to be southern and could see curls on her one visible shoulder. Jim was talking and never introduced us. Suddenly she swept around him, grabbed me by the hand, and said, "God bless your ol' pee hole; come on in and park your ol' prat on the piano."

Suddenly I think I understood what Jim had meant when he told me early in the summer that he liked his whores southern because they were "poetical." I took a quick look around the "parlor," and, sure enough, there was no piano, so it was pure poetry.

Later, when I found out her name, it was Annabelle, which fitted. After this exuberant outcry, she backed off in silence and sat down, it being evident, as she passed the light from a standing lamp, that she had no clothes on under her dress.

When I glanced around the parlor and did not see a piano I did, however, notice another woman and the motto of Scotland. The other woman looked older but not so old as she was supposed to be, because when she finally was introduced she was introduced as Annabelle's mother. Naturally, I wondered how she figured in Jim's operation and a few days later I ran into some jacks in town who knew her and said she was still a pretty good whore, although a little sad and flabby. Later that evening I tried talking to her; I don't think there was much left to her inside but it was clear she thought the world of Jim.

I had to take another look to believe it, but there it was on the wall just above the chair Jim was about to sit in—the motto of Scotland, and in Latin, too—*Nemo me impune lacesset.* Supposedly, only Jim would know what it meant. The whores wouldn't know and it's for sure his trade, who were Scandinavian and French-Canadian lumberjacks, wouldn't. So he sat on his leather throne, owner and chief bouncer of the establishment, believing only he knew that over his head it said: "No one will touch me with impunity."

But there was one exception. I knew what it meant, having been brought up under the same plaque, in fact an even tougher-looking version that had Scotch thistles engraved around the motto. My father had it hung in the front hall where it would be the first thing seen at all times by anyone entering the manse—and in the early mornings on her way to the kitchen by my mother who inherited the unmentioned infirmity of being part English.

Jim did most of the talking, and the rest of us listened and sometimes I just watched. He sure as hell was a good-looking guy, and now he was all dressed up, conservatively in a dark gray herringbone suit and a blue or black tie. But no matter the clothes, he always looked like a lumberjack to me. Why not? He was the best logger I ever worked with, and I barely lived to say so.

Jim talked mostly about sawing and college. He and I had talked about almost nothing during the summer, least of all about college. Now, he asked me a lot of questions about college, but it just wasn't the case that they were asked out of envy or regret. He didn't look at me as a Scotch boy like himself, not so good with the ax and saw but luckier. He looked at himself, at least as he sat there that night, as a successful young businessman, and he certainly didn't think I was ever going to do anything that he wanted to do. What his being a socialist meant to him I was never to figure out. To me, he emerged as all laissez-faire. He was one of those people who turn out not to have some characteristic that you thought was a prominent one when you first met them. Maybe you only thought they had it because what you first saw or heard was at acute angle, or maybe they have it in some form but your personality makes it recessive. Anyway, he and I never talked politics (admitting that most of the time we never talked at all). I heard him talking socialism to the other jacks—yelling it at them would be more exact, as if they didn't know how to saw. Coming out the back door of the Dakotas in the twenties he had to be a dispossessed socialist of some sort, but his talk to me about graduate school was concerned mostly with the question of whether, if hypothetically he decided to take it on, he could reduce graduate study to sawdust, certainly a fundamental capitalistic question. His educational experiences in the Dakotas had had a lasting effect. He had gone as far as the seventh grade, and his teachers in the Dakotas had been big and tough and had licked him. What he was wondering was whether between seventh grade and graduate school the teachers kept pace with their students and could still lick him. I cheered him up a lot when I told him, "No, last winter wasn't as tough as this summer." He brought us all another drink of Canadian Club, and, while drinking this one, it occurred to me that maybe what he had been doing this summer was giving me his version of graduate school. If so, he wasn't far wrong.

Nearly all our talk, though, was about logging, because logging was what loggers talked about. They mixed it into everything. For instance, loggers celebrated the Fourth of July—the only sacred holiday in those times except Christmas—by contests in logrolling, sawing, and swinging the ax. Their work was their world, which included their games and their women, and the women at least had to talk like loggers, especially when they swore. Annabelle would occasionally come up with such a line as, "Somebody ought to drop the boom on that bastard," but when I started fooling around to find out whether she knew what a boom was, she switched back to pure southern poetry. A whore has to swear like her working men and in addition she has to have pretty talk.

I was interested, too, in the way Jim pictured himself and me to his women—always as friendly working partners talking over some technical sawing problem. In his creations we engaged in such technical dialogue as this: "'How much are you holding there?' I'd ask; 'I'm holding an inch and a half,' he'd say; and I'd say, 'God, I'm holding two and a half inches.'" I can tell you that outside of the first few days of the summer we didn't engage in any such friendly talk, and any sawyer can tell you that the technical stuff he had us saying about sawing may sound impressive to whores but doesn't make any sense to sawyers and had to be invented by him. He was a great sawyer, and didn't need to make up anything, but it seemed as if every time he made us friends he had to make up lies about sawing to go with us.

I wanted to talk a little to the women before I left, but when I turned to Annabelle she almost finished me off before I got started by saying, "So you and I are partners of Jim?" Seeing that she had made such a big start with this, she was off in another minute trying to persuade me she was Scotch, but I told her, "Try that on some Swede."

Her style was to be everything you wished she were except what you knew she wasn't. I didn't have to listen long before I was fairly sure she wasn't southern. Neither was the other one. They said "you all" and "ol'" and had curls and that was about it, all of which they probably did for Jim from the Dakotas. Every now and then Annabelle would become slightly hysterical, at least suddenly exuberant, and speak a line of something like "poetry"—an alliterative toast or rune or foreign expression. Then she would go back to her quiet game of trying to figure out something besides Scotch that she might persuade me she was that I would like but wouldn't know much about.

Earlier in the evening I realized that the two women were not mother and daughter or related in any way. Probably all three of them got strange pleasures from the notion they were a family. Both women, of course, dressed alike and had curls and did the southern bit, but fundamentally they were not alike in bone or body structure, except that they were both big women.

So all three of them created a warm family circle of lies.

The lumberjack in herringbone and his two big women in only dresses blocked the door as we said good-bye. "So long," I said from outside. "Au revoir," Annabelle said. "So long," Jim said, and then he added, "I'll be writing you."

And he did, but not until late in autumn. By then probably all the Swedish and Finnish loggers knew his north-side place and he had drawn out his card from the Missoula Public Library and was rereading Jack London, omitting the dog stories. Since my address on the envelope was exact, he must have called my home to get it. The envelope was large and square; the paper was small, ruled, and had glue on the top edge, so it was pulled off some writing pad. His handwriting was large but grew smaller at the end of each word.

I received three other letters from him before the school year was out. His letters were only a sentence or two long. The one- or two-sentence literary form, when used by a master, is designed not to pass on some slight matter but to put the world in a nutshell. Jim was my first acquaintance with a master of this form.

His letters always began, "Dear partner," and always ended, "Your pal, Jim."

You can be sure I ignored any shadow of suggestion that I work with him the coming summer, and he never openly made the suggestion. I had decided that I had only a part of my life to give to gyppoing and that I had already given generously. I went back to the United States Forest Service and fought fires, which to Jim was like declaring myself a charity case and taking the rest cure.

So naturally I didn't hear from him that summer—undoubtedly, he had some other sawyer at the end of the saw whom he was reducing to sawdust. But come autumn and there was a big square envelope with the big handwriting that grew smaller at the end of each word. Since it was early autumn, he couldn't have been set up in business yet. Probably he had just quit the woods and was in town still looking things over. It could be he hadn't even drawn a library card yet. Anyway, this was the letter:

> Dear partner,
>   Just to let you know I have screwed a dame that weighs 300 lbs.
>
>   Your pal,
>   Jim

A good many years have passed since I received that letter, and I have never heard from or about Jim since. Maybe at three hundred pounds the son of a bitch was finally overpowered.

An Incident

"An Incident," published here for the first time, is a "hometown
talk," as Maclean called it, that he gave in Missoula in May 1979
to conclude a four-day conference on the topic "Who Owns the
West?" In it he addresses the craft of writing fiction, using A River
Runs through It as his example. He organically defines plot
and character, quoting a long passage from River—his "Incident"
—to illustrate his definition and the artistic and self-destructive
sides of his long-lost brother, Paul.

There are three special reasons why I wanted to be in Missoula now,
besides the ever-present one of wanting to see old friends and the
mountains again, which are also friends—not only the remotely
beautiful Squaw Peak or Mt. Lo Lo but always Reservoir Hill and Mt.
Jumbo. These two are plain and bare admittedly, but they are close and warm
and good practice-mountains for a boy to grow up on. Eventually a boy works
his way up to Mt. Sentinel, and starts fires in the grass there and spends the
rest of his life looking uphill over his shoulder afraid that somebody will catch
him. But my favorite mountain has to be Mt. Jumbo, at least at this time of
year. Then the sun covers its exposed sides with early flowers, especially near
the moisture of its gulches. My father always took me for a walk to freshen up
between his morning and evening sermons, and my mother took me whenever she could get me at this time of the year for a slow walk a little way up Mt.
Jumbo to see the flowers on the edges of moisture. I was up there this morning. It is yellow and purple and white with balsam roots, larkspurs, and service
berry bushes overpoweringly in bloom.

There was a difference in my family about how I should be brought up. My
father wanted to bring me up as a tough guy, and my mother wanted to bring
me up as a flower girl. Since both of them had a profound effect on my character, I seem to have ended up as a tough flower girl.

The mountains, too, I shall always remember from long ago when, in more
vigorous times, Squaw Peak was called Squaw Teat and Mt. Lo Lo was thought
to be named after the famous international whore, Lo Lo Montez, not as Bud

"An Incident" is the transcript of a talk given at the conference "Who Owns the West?" held in
Missoula, Montana, May 9–12, 1979.

Moore, the old Trapper, would have us believe, after some old Trapper who died somewhere back there and whose name was LouLou. Such is the leveling effect of time and trapping upon great mountains.

I had another special reason for wanting to get to Missoula now. I wanted to start finishing something I started here two springs ago when I talked for John Badgley and the Institute of the Rockies at the old Florence Hotel.

Since I had the impression the talk went well, I began to have an idea. My talk had been about how my father had kept me home from the early grades of school and taught me to read and write, and how some of the things he taught me about writing were visibly present in my stories even though I did not start writing them until I was 70. I talked mostly about style, including rhythm, because that is mostly what he taught me. Then I read from one of my stories to prove that stylistically my father was present in it. The idea I began to develop undoubtedly had something to do with the fact that after my father got through with me I went on to spend my total professional life in teaching literature and writing. So I thought to myself, "Why don't you start pulling yourself together by writing a book on the job of writing stories, drawing illustrations from your own stories?" Then, last spring, I was invited to speak before the faculty and students of Montana State University, so I took advantage of another intelligent captive audience to talk about another aspect of the narrative art and again illustrate it from my own stories. Only at Bozeman I jumped to the other end of the ladder of the narrative art from style, which deals with such bricks and straw and mortar as words, sentences and paragraphs. In Bozeman, I talked, not about the building material, but about the blueprint, the architecture of the whole, referring to it loosely sometimes as the structure of the whole or the plot. It's whatever holds the other elements together and presides over them and tells them what to be.

Tonight, I would like to talk about an element of the story that is between the blueprint of the whole and the style. Tonight, it will be about the art of constructing incidents, of embodying the plot in interesting and particular events and characters.

It is not particularly a verbal art—despite outside opinion, a great deal of the art of narrative writing is non-verbal, and I divide my writing days accordingly. In the mornings I write, then I work around the house, take a walk or go fishing, or both, freshen up, so to speak, but before I go to bed I take a bath, not a shower, and I sit in the tub until the water gets cold. I am not sitting there looking for pretty sentences; I am trying to think and feel through what I am going to write next morning. It's hard enough to write without having at the

same time to start to think about what you are going to write—I do most of
that in the bathtub, and call it "the bathtub part of stories."

The art of making incidents belongs largely to the bathtub, but I think I can
save time in telling you what I mean by an incident and its relation to the story
as a whole if I start turning from generalities to a particular incident. The one
I have selected is understandably from the story you probably know best if you
know any of my stories, the title story of A River Runs through It.

I can't talk about an incident, though, without being able to relate it to the
story as a whole, and, since at Bozeman I talked about the art of constructing
the whole, I will quote here a short summary I made there of the overall form
of this story.

"The major obligation of a story is *always* to be a story. This is true even if
it is the most personal story one will ever tell, as this one is mine. This is the
story of my brother who was murdered. It was my brother who was a master
of the art of fly-fishing, perhaps the finest in the Northwest. It is a story of his
father and brother who were expert fishermen—not as good as he was but
perhaps necessarily more thoughtful because they did not have his genius.
Our chief claim to be in the story is that we loved him and loved to watch him
fish. It is a story of my brother who had another side to him—at least we
heard he had, and maybe most of the time we believed he had but we were
never sure, and were never to be sure. We knew, though, he was a gambler
and had a packstring of women and we heard he was behind in the big stud
poker game at Hot Springs and beyond a doubt in Montana it is not good to
be behind in a stud game at a hot springs. In our Scottish family, the family and religion were the center of the universe, and, like Scots, we did not
believe we should praise each other but should always love and be ready to
help each other, only we never seemed able to help my brother, being hesitant because we were not often sure he needed help—in fact, were not sure
we understood him, and we were also hesitant because we looked clumsy
when we tried to be of help, and he looked like what he was, an artist whose
Scottish pride was offended by a clumsy offer of help. So, in the end when he
was murdered, we did not know whether it had been just a case of his being
stuck up in an alley and beaten to death or whether he was paying some debt
he owed in his other life.

"In the end all we knew—really knew—about him was that he was beautiful and dead and we had not helped. And, through him all we came to know
about mankind my father summed up when he said, 'It is those we live with
and love and should know who elude us.'"

Something like this, crudely stated, is a summary of the story. "Anything that goes into the story from reality or the imagination must be with it and for it."

From what has just been said about the whole, a large organic part of it would be an incident consisting of a movement of characters and events giving a sense of completeness in itself and at the same time moving the plot on to its ultimate destination, something like a station of the cross, where there is a pause in the movement of the soul on its long journey. Although it didn't always seem so to me, it now seems almost "a must" that a major incident in this story should consist of a movement of events that reveals both sides of my brother's character—the beauty of his person and of his art and of his mastery of it and of the earth where he performed it—and then goes on to reveal the other side of his character, its ambiguities and darkness and our helplessness in trying to lighten them. Such a movement has some kind of completeness in itself, as the movement from daylight to darkness has, just as in life the movement leading to the discovery that "a person has another side to him" seems to be a little story in itself, sometimes a shocking one. But an incident has to be more than a movement of events from one of its opposite sides to the other. In this story, at least, it is three-dimensional, for between beauty and darkness comes the ordinary, the real of every day. For any number of reasons, every day reality must be there, ultimately, I suppose, because it is there in life. It is the transition between beauty and darkness, making both believable, and assuring the reader he is not reading just poetical fantasy or a ghost story. In this story it must be there for an added and perhaps non-artistic reason—it must be there because I wrote it, I who believe that hilarity and tragedy and ordinary daylight are all necessary for salvation. It may also be there not just because of my philosophy but for my pleasure—for the pleasure I find in seeing the world so full of a number of things.

It should be clear now how these somewhat complete incidents can also be parts of this whole. As the incidents succeed each other the beauty enlarges, takes on different forms, and appears in different places, and at the same time the ambiguities clear up and the darkness deepens until at the end of the story all three—beauty, everyday reality, and darkness—merge into one and a river runs through them, "the them" now spoken of as "it." Tragically, the only ambiguity left at the end is the forever unanswered question of whether my brother needed help and whether we might have helped him.

A fact I have only once alluded to tonight is that I have been a schoolteacher most of my life, although it must be a fact reflected in most of what I do and think. For instance, when I am fishing and I look upstream and see a fisher-man on the other side coming downstream I wait until he gets nearly opposite to me—then I take one look and say to myself, "C minus." I want people to learn something when I talk, and that also goes for when I tell stories. In this first collection of my stories, I wanted to show what men and women could do with their hands and heads in the world of the woods before bull-dozers, "cats," and power saws started doing it for them. I wanted to preserve glimpses of people at work when I was young, partly because they might be worth preserving as small pieces of both the history of the West and the his-tory of art. To me, what men and women can do with their hands and heads is often as beautiful as mountains and can be more so. Thus, just watching a sawyer at work in the woods is to me an art experience, and it should not there-fore be surprising to you that even in the shortest of my stories there is a good deal about the art of being a sawyer before power saws and before axes became just heavy-headed wedges to open a cut in a log that has pinched. In the story "USFS 1919," you should get a good idea of what a man had to know and do to be a member of a crew in the early Forest Service when the world was still a world of hands and horses and White logging boots made in Spokane. When I was young I saw Bill Bell pack mules. No one has ever seen anyone better.

One of the compliments I appreciated most about "A River Runs through It" came from a doctoral candidate in biology here at the University who sent word to me that he considered the story "A River Runs through It" one of the finest manuals yet written on the art of fly-fishing in the Northwest. I hope it is. The art of fly-fishing furnishes material for nearly every incident of the story, and the order and arrangement of the main incidents is partly deter-mined by the order of teaching fly-fishing. Thus the earliest fishing incident is largely a lesson from my father on how to cast with a flyrod on a four-count rhythm, and the last time my brother is seen he is using his great skill in land-ing a big trout. That spans the art of fly-fishing, from getting your fly out on the water to getting the fish in the basket. The in-between aspects of the art are depicted in in-between incidents showing how to read water to tell where the fish are, how to pick the right fly, how to set a hook, and so on.

The glimpses of the history of western Montana and of art in these stories are not released from the obligation of being parts of the story. They are essential parts. My brother manifests his power and grace in his mastery of all elements of the art of fly-fishing. T. S. Eliot might have called fly-fishing his "objective correlative"—it externalized his beauty and it also was one of the centers of our family love, objectifying our feelings. The need of the story to portray my brother as a complete master of his art also gives the story-teller a rich opportunity to vary the narrative and its scenic effects—from the roar of fast water west of the Divide, where rainbow and cutthroat look for antagonists, to the quieter water east of the Divide, preferred by the more meditative brown and eastern brook trout. Always there is a change of scene and for some good fishing and artistic reason.

The incident I will read from is the one in which my brother is first seen fishing. It is important that he so impress us with his power and grace that later we can never doubt his beauty no matter what else we come to see about him. But this first fishing incident concludes with out first direct view of his dark side, which earlier had only been hinted at—we see him now arrested and in jail. In between these two views of him, an ordinary, everyday husband and wife in overalls sit down in astonishment to watch him cast. They are the transition between the beautiful and the dark and assure us both are real. So the incident is three-dimensional and has its kind of completeness in the story.

What we learn about the art of fly-fishing in this incident are two advanced ways of flycasting, advanced because we have already learned about the basic four-count cast from my father accompanied by my mother's metronome. The first advanced cast is "the roll cast," the cast needed when casting in front of a big rock or tree and we can't lift our line behind us. I have always found it a difficult cast, so my brother is standing beside me and gently instructing me on how to get more distance out of it. When he finally starts fishing himself, he is casting a special cast pretty much of his own invention. He called it "a shadow cast" and it was a scenic and spectacular thing to watch, and not many besides him could make it work. When we first see him fishing, then, he "is doing his thing," and catching fish.

Just prior to his shadow casting, he has tried to help me with my roll cast. We have gone from Helena to the Big Blackfoot and to the beautiful canyon above the red wooden bridge at the mouth of the Clearwater. I am fishing a big blue hole and am just in front of a big rock so I can't let the line go behind me. My brother has gently told me that I am not casting far enough out to reach the big ones. He adds, if I brought the line into me on a diagonal on the water instead of straight toward me, the line would be a more resistant base to my cast and would add several yards to it. Then he gently disappears and I add several yards to my cast and catch a hell of a big one. This one was my big one for the day, so let's watch him from here on.

———————————

Even when I bent him he was way too long for my basket, so his tail stuck out.

There were black spots on him that looked like crustaceans. He seemed oceanic, including barnacles. When I passed my brother at the next hole, I saw him study the tail and slowly remove his hat, and not out of respect for my prowess as a fisherman.

I had a fish, so I sat down to watch a fisherman.

He took his cigarettes and matches from his shirt pocket and put them in his hat and pulled his hat down tight so it wouldn't leak. Then he unstrapped his fish basket and hung it on the edge of his shoulder where he could get rid of it quick should the water get too big for him. If he studied the situation he didn't take any separate time to do it. He jumped off a rock into the swirl and swam for a chunk of cliff that had dropped into the river and parted it. He swam in his clothes with only his left arm—in his right hand, he held his rod high and sometimes all I could see was the basket and rod, and when the basket filled with water sometimes all I could see was the rod.

The current smashed him into the chunk of cliff and it must have hurt, but he had enough strength remaining in his left fingers to hang to a crevice or he would have been swept into the blue below. Then he still had to climb to the top of the rock with his left fingers and his right elbow which he used like a prospector's pick. When he finally stood on top, his clothes looked hydraulic, as if they were running off him.

Once he quit wobbling, he shook himself duck-dog fashion, with his feet spread apart, his body lowered and his head flopping. Then he steadied himself and began to cast and the whole world turned to water.

Below him was the multitudinous river, and, where the rock had parted it around him, big-grained vapor rose. The mini-molecules of water left in the wake of his line made momentary loops of gossamer, disappearing so rapidly in the rising big-grained vapor that they had to be retained in memory to be visualized as loops. The spray emanating from him was finer-grained still and enclosed him in a halo of himself. The halo of himself was always there and always disappearing, as if he were candlelight flickering about three inches from himself. The images of himself and his line kept disappearing into the rising vapors of the river, which continually circled to the tops of the cliffs where, after becoming a wreath in the wind, they became rays of the sun.

The river above and below his rock was all big Rainbow water, and he would cast hard and low upstream, skimming the water with his fly but never letting it touch. Then he would pivot, reverse his line in a great oval above his head, and drive his line low and hard downstream, again skimming the water with his fly. He would complete this grand circle four or five times, creating an immensity of motion which culminated in nothing if you did not know, even if you could not see, that now somewhere out there a small fly was washing itself on a wave. Shockingly, immensity would return as the Big Blackfoot and the air above it became iridescent with the arched sides of a great Rainbow.

He called this "shadow casting," and frankly I don't know whether to believe the theory behind it—that the fish are alerted by the shadows of flies passing over the water by the first casts, so hit the fly the moment it touches the water. It is more or less the "working up an appetite" theory, almost too fancy to be true, but then every fine fisherman has a few fancy stunts that work for him and for almost no one else. Shadow casting never worked for me, but maybe I never had the strength of arm and wrist to keep line circling over the water until fish imagined a hatch of flies was out.

My brother's wet clothes made it easy to see his strength. Most great casters I have known were big men over six feet, the added height certainly making it easier to get more line in the air in a bigger arc. My brother was only five feet ten, but he had fished so many years his body had become partly shaped by his casting. He was thirty-two now, at the height of his power, and he could put all his body and soul into a four-and-a-half-ounce magic totem pole. Long ago, he had gone far beyond my father's wrist casting, although his right wrist was always so important that it had become larger than his left. His right arm, which our father had kept tied to the side to emphasize the wrist, shot out of his shirt as if it were engineered, and it, too, was larger than his left arm. His wet shirt bulged and came unbuttoned with his pivoting shoulders and hips. It was also not hard to see why he was a street fighter, especially since he was committed to getting in the first punch with his right hand.

Rhythm was just as important as color and just as complicated. It was one rhythm superimposed upon another, our father's four-count rhythm of the line and wrist being still the base rhythm. But superimposed upon it was the piston two count of his arm and the long overriding four count of the completed figure eight of his reversed loop.

The canyon was glorified by rhythms and colors.

I heard voices behind me, and a man and his wife came down the trail, each carrying a rod, but probably they weren't going to do much fishing. Probably they intended nothing much more than to enjoy being out of doors with each other and, on the side, to pick enough huckleberries for a pie. In those days there was little in the way of rugged sports clothes for women, and she was a big, rugged woman and wore regular men's bib overalls, and her motherly breasts bulged out of the bib. She was the first to see my brother pivoting on the top of his cliff. To her, he must have looked something like a trick rope artist at a rodeo, doing everything except jumping in and out of his loops.

She kept watching while groping behind her to smooth out some pine needles to sit on. "My, my!" she said.

Her husband stopped and stood and said, "Jesus." Every now and then he said, "Jesus." Each time his wife nodded. She was one of America's mothers who never dream of using profanity themselves but enjoy their husbands', and later come to need it, like cigar smoke.

I started to make for the next hole. "Oh, no," she said, "you're going to wait, aren't you, until he comes to shore so you can see his big fish."

"No," I answered, "I'd rather remember the molecules."

She obviously thought I was crazy, so I added, "I'll see his fish later." And to make any sense for her I had to add, "He's my brother."

As I kept going, the middle of my back told me that I was being viewed from the rear both as quite a guy, because I was his brother, and also as a little bit nutty, because I was molecular.

Since our fish were big enough to deserve a few drinks and quite a bit of talk afterwards, we were late in getting back to Helena. On the way, Paul asked, "Why not stay overnight with me and go down to Wolf Creek in the morning." He added that he himself had "to be out for the evening," but would be back soon after midnight. I learned later it must have been around two o'clock in the morning when I heard the thing that was ringing, and I ascended through river mists and molecules until I awoke catching the telephone. The telephone had a voice in it, which asked, "Are you Paul's brother?" I asked, "What's wrong?" The voice said, "I want you to see him." Thinking we had poor connections, I banged the phone. "Who are you?" I asked. He said, "I am the desk sergeant who wants you to see your brother."

The checkbook was still in my hand when I reached the jail. The desk sergeant frowned and said, "No, you don't have to post bond for him. He covers the police beat and has friends here. All you have to do is look at him and take him home."

Then he added, "But he'll have to come back. A guy is going to sue him. Maybe two guys are."

Not wanting to see him without a notion of what I might see, I kept repeating, "What's wrong?" When the desk sergeant thought it was time, he told me, "He hit a guy and the guy is missing a couple of teeth and is all cut up." I asked, "What's the second guy suing him for?" "For breaking dishes. Also a table," the sergeant said. "The second guy owns the restaurant. The guy who got hit lit on one of the tables."

By now I was ready to see my brother, but it was becoming clear that the sergeant had called me to the station to have a talk. He said, "We're picking him up too much lately. He's drinking too much." I had already heard more than I wanted. Maybe one of our ultimate troubles was that I never wanted to hear too much about my brother.

The sergeant finished what he had to say by finally telling me what he really wanted to say. "Besides he's behind in the big stud poker game at Hot Springs. It's not healthy to be behind in the big game at Hot Springs.

"You and your brother think you're tough because you're street fighters. At Hot Springs they don't play any child games like fist fighting. At Hot Springs it's the big stud poker game and all that goes with it."

I was confused from trying to rise suddenly from molecules of sleep to an understanding of what I did not want to understand. I said, "Let's begin again. Why is he here and is he hurt?"

The sergeant said. "He's not hurt, just sick. He drinks too much. At Hot Springs, they don't drink too much." I said to the sergeant, "Let's go on. Why is he here?"

According to the sergeant's report to me, Paul and his girl had gone into Weiss's restaurant for a midnight sandwich—a popular place at midnight since it had booths in the rear where you and your girl could sit and draw the curtains. "The girl," the sergeant said, "was that half-breed Indian girl he goes with. You know the one," he added, as if to implicate me.

Paul and his girl were evidently looking for an empty booth when a guy in a booth they had passed stuck his head out of the curtain and yelled, "Wahoo." Paul hit the head, separating the head from two teeth and knocking the body back on the table, which overturned, cutting the guy and his girl with broken dishes. The sergeant said, "The guy said to me,

'Jesus, all I meant is that it's funny to go out with an Indian. It was just a joke.'"

I said to the sergeant. "It's not very funny," and the sergeant said, "No, not very funny, but it's going to cost your brother a lot of money and time to get out of it. What really isn't funny is that he's behind in the game at Hot Springs. Can't you help him straighten out?"

"I don't know what to do," I confessed to the sergeant.

"I know what you mean," the sergeant confessed to me. Desk sergeants at this time were still Irish. "I have a young brother," he said, "who is a wonderful kid, but he's always in trouble. He's what we call 'Black Irish.'"

"What do you do to help him?" I asked. After a long pause, he said, "I take him fishing."

"And when that doesn't work?" I asked.

"You better go and see your own brother," he answered.

Wanting to see him in perspective when I saw him, I stood still until I could again see the woman in bib overalls marveling at his shadow casting. Then I opened the door to the room where they toss the drunks until they can walk a crack in the floor. "His girl is with him," the sergeant said.

He was standing in front of a window, but he could not have been looking out of it, because there was a heavy screen between the bars, and he could not have seen me because his enlarged casting hand was over his face. Were it not for the lasting compassion I felt for his hand, I might have doubted afterwards that I had seen him.

The girl was sitting on the floor at his feet. When her black hair glistened, she was one of my favorite women. Her mother was a Northern Cheyenne, so when her black hair glistened she was handsome, more Algonkian and Romanlike than Mongolian in profile, and very warlike, especially after a few drinks. At least one of her great grandmothers had been with the Northern Cheyennes when they and the Sioux destroyed General Custer and the Seventh Cavalry, and, since it was the Cheyennes who were camped on the Little Bighorn just opposite to the hill they were about to immortalize, the Cheyenne squaws were among the first to work the field over after the battle. At least one of her ancestors, then, had spent a late afternoon happily cutting off the testicles of the Seventh Cavalry, the cutting often occurring before death.

This paleface who had stuck his head out of the booth in Weiss's cafe and yelled "Wahoo" was lucky to be missing only two teeth.

Even I couldn't walk down the street beside her without her getting me
into trouble. She liked to hold Paul with one arm and me with the other
and walk down Last Chance Gulch on Saturday night, forcing people into
the gutter to get around us, and when they wouldn't give up the sidewalk
she would shove Paul or me into them. You didn't have to go very far
down Last Chance Gulch on Saturday night shoving people into the
gutter before you were into a hell of a big fight, but she always felt that
she had a disappointing evening and had not been appreciated if the guy
who took her out didn't get into a big fight over her.

When her hair glistened, though, she was worth it. She was one of the
most beautiful dancers I have ever seen. She made her partner feel as if he
were about to be left behind, or already had been.

It is a strange and wonderful and somewhat embarrassing feeling to
hold someone in your arms who is trying to detach you from the earth
and you aren't good enough to follow her.

I called her Mo-nah-se-tah, the name of the beautiful daughter of the
Cheyenne chief, Little Rock. At first, she didn't particularly care for the
name, which means, "the young grass that shoots in the spring," but
after I explained to her that Mo-nah-se-tah was supposed to have had
an illegitimate son by General George Armstrong Custer she took to the
name like a duck to water.

Looking down on her now I could see only the spread of her hair on
her shoulders and the spread of her legs on the floor. Her hair did not
glisten and I had never seen her legs when they were just things lying on
a floor. Knowing that I was looking down on her, she struggled to get to
her feet, but her long legs buckled and her stockings slipped down on her
legs and she spread out on the floor again until the tops of her stockings
and her garters showed.

The two of them smelled worse than the jail. They smelled just like
what they were—a couple of drunks whose stomachs had been injected
with whatever it is the body makes when it feels cold and full of booze
and knows something bad has happened and doesn't want tomorrow
to come.

Neither one ever looked at me, and he never spoke. She said, "Take
me home." I said, "That's why I'm here." She said, "Take him, too."

She was as beautiful a dancer as he was a fly caster. I carried her
with her toes dragging behind her. Paul turned and, without seeing or
speaking, followed. His overdeveloped right wrist held his right hand

over his eyes so that in some drunken way he thought I could not see him and he may also have thought that he could not see himself.

As we went by the desk, the sergeant said, "Why don't you all go fishing?"

I did not take Paul's girl to her home. In those days, Indians who did not live on reservations had to live out by the city limits and generally they pitched camp near either the slaughterhouse or the city dump. I took them back to Paul's apartment. I put him in his bed, and I put her in the bed where I had been sleeping, but not until I had changed it so that the fresh sheets would feel smooth to her legs.

As I covered her, she said, "He should have killed the bastard."

I said, "Maybe he did," whereupon she rolled over and went to sleep, believing, as she always did, anything I told her, especially if it involved heavy casualties.

By then, dawn was coming out of a mountain across the Missouri, so I drove to Wolf Creek.

In those days it took about an hour to drive the forty miles of rough road from Helena to Wolf Creek. While the sun came out of the Big Belt Mountains and the Missouri and left them behind in light, I tried to find something I already knew about life that might help me reach out and touch my brother and get him to look at me and himself. For a while, I even thought what the desk sergeant first told me was useful. As a desk sergeant, he had to know a lot about life and he had told me Paul was the Scottish equivalent of "Black Irish." Without doubt, in my father's family there were "Black Scots" occupying various outposts all the way from the original family home on the Isle of Mull in the southern Hebrides to Fairbanks, Alaska, 110 or 115 miles south of the Arctic Circle, which was about as far as a Scot could go then to get out of range of sheriffs with warrants and husbands with shotguns. I had learned about them from my aunts, not my uncles, who were all Masons and believed in secret societies for males. My aunts, though, talked gaily about them and told me they were all big men and funny and had been wonderful to them when they were little girls. From my uncles' letters, it was clear that they still thought of my aunts as little girls. Every Christmas until they died in distant lands these hastily departed brothers sent their once-little sisters loving Christmas cards scrawled with assurances that they would soon "return to the States and help them hang stockings on Christmas eve."

Seeing that I was relying on women to explain to myself what I didn't understand about men, I remembered a couple of girls I had dated who had uncles with some resemblances to my brother. The uncles were fairly expert at some art that was really a hobby—one uncle was a watercolorist and the other the club champion golfer—and each had selected a profession that would allow him to spend most of his time at his hobby. Both were charming, but you didn't quite know what if anything you knew when you had finished talking to them. Since they did not earn enough money from business to make life a hobby, their families had to meet from time to time with the county attorney to keep things quiet.

Sunrise is the time to feel that you will be able to find out how to help somebody close to you who you think needs help even if he doesn't think so. At sunrise everything is luminous but not clear.

Then about twelve miles before Wolf Creek the road drops into the Little Prickly Pear Canyon, where dawn is long in coming. In the suddenly returning semidarkness, I watched the road carefully, saying to myself, hell, my brother is not like anybody else. He's not my gal's uncle or a brother of my aunts. He is my brother and an artist and when a four-and-a-half-ounce rod is in his hand he is a major artist. He doesn't piddle around with a paint brush or take lessons to improve his short game and he won't take money even when he must need it and he won't run anywhere from anyone, least of all to the Arctic Circle. It is a shame I do not understand him.

Yet even in the loneliness of the canyon I knew there were others like me who had brothers they did not understand but wanted to help. We are probably those referred to as "our brothers' keepers," possessed of one of the oldest and possibly one of the most futile and certainly one of the most haunting of instincts. It will not let us go.

When I drove out of the canyon, it was ordinary daylight.

I cannot end without mentioning another special reason that brought me to Missoula at this time of year. It was in early May when my brother was buried here.

So we conclude our conference on the West by recalling, I hope not inappropriately, memories of it full of pain and joy, and everyday reality.

The Woods, Books,

....

and Truant Officers

The title of Maclean's essay "The Woods, Books, and Truant Officers" reflects his penchant for triadic structures, which is appropriate in an essay that reviews Maclean's devotion to rhythm in language. In the essay, Maclean describes his home-schooling regimen (during the mornings of his elementary school years) and his father's influence over Maclean's language, even claiming him as "co-author of the title of this book, A River Runs through It." The essay reads as a companion to Maclean's first book, and in it he offers close readings of the Twenty-third Psalm and the opening sentence of USFS 1919 that illustrate his professorial dedication to prose rhythms.

Just how much I learned from my afternoon schooling in the woods, you are to judge, especially if you are experts at what I am talking about. I dedicated A River Runs Through It and Other Stories to my children and also to experts. I meant these stories in part to be a record of how certain things were done just before the world of most of history ended—most of history being a world of hand and horse and hand tools and horse tools. I meant to record not only how we did certain things well in that world now almost beyond recall, but how it felt to do those things well that are now slipping from our hands and memory. I meant when I said we fished with an eight-and-a-half-foot rod weighing four and a half ounces that it was a rod and not a pole and that it was four and a half ounces and not four, and if it had been four ounces it would have been an eight-and not an eight-and-a-half-foot rod; and I also meant that when the rod trembled in our hands our hearts trembled with it.

But it is the morning part of my schooling that should be of most concern to us collectively, for it was in the morning that my father helped with the writing part of this book. The morning was divided into three hourly periods. We started at nine and ended at noon, and each of the three hours was divided into two parts, one of 45 minutes when I studied in my room across the hall

"The Woods, Books, and Truant Officers" is reprinted from *Chicago* (1977).

from his, and 15 minutes when I recited to him in his study. I cannot tell you how much of life 15 minutes can be when you are six, seven, eight, nine, or ten years old and alone with a red-headed Presbyterian minister and cannot answer one of his questions and he won't go on to the next and there is no one else in the room he can turn to and ask and it is going to be the same way tomorrow.

But I can tell you that none of these three hourly periods was devoted to show-and-tell or to the development of personality, mine or his. They were devoted exclusively to reading and writing; while the kids my age in school were learning their ABC's, he was trying to teach me how to write the American language. John Stuart Mill boasts that his father taught him to read Greek when he was so young that English almost became his second language. I have been a little slower to develop, being 73 before I thought I could write the American language as my father tried to teach it to me.

Three basic things he pounded into me long ago about this book that I started to write after reaching my Biblical allotment of three score years and ten.

(1) Being a Scot, he tried to make me write economically. He tried to make me write primarily with nouns and verbs, and not to fool around with adjectives and adverbs, not even when I wanted to write soul stuff. At nine o'clock, when the first period began, he would assign me a 200-word theme; at the end of the ten o'clock period he would tell me, "Now rewrite it in 100 words"; and he concluded the morning by telling me, "Now, throw it away." Sometimes in my study room alone I shed as many tears as I sacrificed words. In the next period, to brace me up, he would say, "My boy, never be too proud to save a single word."

(2) To perceive clearly another characteristic of the writing in this book, you will have to realize that both my father and my mother were first-generation immigrants. Indeed I am told that when my father came to this country he had a heavy Scottish burr, but it had disappeared by the time I first remember him. Great as his pride was in his Scottish background, it had to make way for his love of his new land, and, as a small sign of his love, he tried to remove his burr and speak American. He despised Presbyterian ministers who came from Scotland and floated from church to church in this country trying to pick up a living by keeping on the move. My father swore that they were all fourth-raters in Scotland, where they couldn't make a living, and that they made a pitiful living in America only by exaggerating their Scottish burrs so their congregations would think they were the original Church of Scotland. By

the time I can remember my father, he had no burr, but his speech, although flawless, was more English than American—and he knew it. So, like many other first-generation immigrants, he put upon the shoulders of his first-born son the job of becoming completely an American. I was taught to listen and then listen some more to American speech—its idioms and turns of phrase, its grammatical structures, and its rhythms. Then, I was told that I should take these pieces of American speech and put them together into something at least fresh and interesting and at times into something strange and beautiful if I could. You can start looking for this characteristic of style with the opening sentences of my stories: "I was young, and I thought I was tough, and I knew it was beautiful, and I was a little bit crazy but hadn't noticed it yet." "I was young" . . . "thought I was tough" . . . "was a little bit crazy" . . . and "hadn't noticed it yet" are all ordinary pieces of American speech, but they allow something to sneak in unnoticed that is not a part of ordinary speech but is key to the whole feeling of the story, "I knew it was beautiful." In addition, these pieces, when put together in their grammatical structures and rhythms, should fit together in no ordinary manner.

One of my editors admitted to me that he spent two evenings looking through the Bible and Biblical concordances for the source of the title of the book, A River Runs Through It. But its source, as far as I know, is in such an ordinary farmer's expression as "a creek runs through the north forty," listed to beauty perhaps by the substitution of "river" for "creek" and "it" for "the north forty." The liquid R's that begin and end "river" are to be contrasted to the grunting K's that begin and end "creek"; and the farmer's "north forty" (forty acres being a 16th of a square mile or section of land) is to be contrasted to the substituted "it" which is the "it" of the world to come and the "it" of Shakespeare, as in, "If it be now, 'tis not to come." Also, the farmer's ordinary phrase is without rhythm, made up, except for "forty," of staccato one-syllable words, whereas the two syllables of "river" turn "A river runs" into running rhythm, the rhythm running over three alliterative R's. So my father is also co-author of the title of this book, A River Runs Through It.

(3) My final acknowledgement is that it was my father from whom I first learned rhythm, perhaps without his or my quite knowing it. Every morning we had what was called "family worship." After breakfast and again after what was called supper, my father read to us from the Bible or from some religious poet such as Wordsworth; then we knelt by our chairs while my father prayed. My father read beautifully. He avoided the homiletic sing-song most ministers fall into when they look inside the Bible or edge up to poetry, but my

father overread poetry a little so that none of us, including him, could miss the music.

Although since retirement I seem to have turned to the narrative art, most of the courses I have taught have been in poetry, and unlike teachers of poetry who devote most of their courses to the psyche and society, I always devoted a big portion of each course in poetry to rhythm—quantitative and qualitative, accentual and intonational and superimposed rhythms.

Twice a day when I was very young I heard my father read such English as: "The Lord is my shepherd; I shall not want. He maketh me to lie down in green pastures; he leadeth me beside the still waters. He restoreth my soul; he leadeth me in the paths of righteousness for his name's sake. Yea, though I walk through the valley of the shadow of death, I will fear no evil; for thou art with me; thy rod and thy staff they comfort me."

And so to the end of the 23rd Psalm, by the way with only two adjectives, *green* pastures and *still* waters, both of them immortal, which is the right way to use adjectives if you can't stay away from them. As for rhythm, it may be said that I learned rhythm early on bended knees.

Of course, when I was between six and ten and a half I didn't know anything about superimposed rhythms; I only knew when I heard my father read the 23rd Psalm that I could hear the still waters moving and pausing and the Lord comforting me. Now, since I have long been a teacher, I can say that it is a wonderful example of superimposed rhythms, although I always try to remember in making an analytical statement like that to remember the still waters and the Lord's comfort. Still, I can count at least three concurrent rhythms in the harp of David. There is, perhaps most obviously, what we can call quantitative rhythm, a patterned recurrence of speech groups of almost the same length or quantity. Concurrent with this quantitative rhythm is a second rhythm; in each quantitative unit there is a repetition of or a coming close to the same grammatical structure, which we shall call a grammatical rhythm—the repetition of subject, verb, and predicate in that order. Let us listen to just these two at first, the patterned recurrence of length and grammatical structure: "The Lord is my shepherd; I shall not want. He maketh me to lie down in green pastures; he leadeth me beside the still waters." But listen now to the lovely variants of patterns so that the song is a song and not a sing-song of mechanical repetition. In "thy rod and thy staff they comfort me," the subject still comes first but instead of being just one word as "I" or "He" or two words as "The Lord," it is now six words. "Thy rod and thy staff, they," and so the verb is only one word and the predicate only one, "comfort me."

And what about other such lovely variants, as "Yea, though I walk through the valley of the shadow"?

These two rhythms, what we have called quantitative and grammatical rhythms, are deep in Hebrew poetry, but present also in the King James translation is the modern base rhythm of English poetry—accentual rhythm, or, as we used to say in school, "the stuff that scans," where what recurs is what we called "feet" when I was young, although I believe now in high school and even college feet go nameless and perhaps unnoticed. The foot is a unit of two or more syllables that are disproportionately stressed, and, when the first syllable is relatively unstressed and the second stressed it is called an iamb and when the first two syllables are relatively unstressed and the last one stressed it is called an anapest. Furthermore, when the rhythmical pattern is a patterned recurrence of either or both of these feet, we shall call it here falling-rising rhythm, and we shall not bother about the opposite, rising-falling, made up of trochees and dactyls, because the King James version of the 23rd Psalm is in falling-rising rhythm, made up of iambs and anapests, which are often changing place for variety and richness, both being falling-rising rhythms and easily interchanged. The first line of the psalm opens and closes with an iamb and two anapests in between:

Thĕ Lórd / iš m̃y shép / hĕrd: Ĭ sháll /
nŏt wánt.

The psalm ends with a line that likewise has two anapests in the middle and an iamb at the end (with a feminine ending) but opens with two iambs instead of one:

Ănd Í / wĭll dwéll / ĭn thĕ hóuse /
ŏf thĕ Lórd / fŏrévĕr.

There are, then, at least three kinds of rhythms going on at the same time in this translation of David's psalm—quantitative, grammatical, and accentual—and three rhythms all at once are a lot of rhythm for a little poem that is marked as being six lines long, and especially since there is always the danger of poetry becoming too poetical. Important for us, too, there is always the danger of prose seeming to be poetical at all. It is perhaps enough to say here that the 23rd Psalm does not bang out its rhythms, but hovers about them, sometimes stating them precisely so the ear knows what it is listening for, then drifting off into the dim shadows of rhythms, and then bouncing back into sunshine rhythm again.

The questions raised by rhythm in prose are too big to go into here, so I will not start any arguments but instead just state a few of what to me are axioms about rhythm and prose. You don't have to believe them but you can bet they're true. (1) All prose should be rhythmical. (2) One should practically never be consciously aware of the rhythms of prose; one should be aware only that it is a pleasure to read what one is reading. (3) There are, of course, exceptions to my statement that prose rhythms should not be noticeable—there are times indeed when rhythms should be both seen and heard, as for instance, when one is fooling around and showing off. I will quote again the opening sentence of the story "USFS 1919," which I used earlier as a sentence made out of American idioms, but it comes back now as an example of a sentence having the three kinds of rhythms of the 23rd Psalm—quantitative, grammatical, and accentual. "I was young, and I thought I was tough, and I knew it was beautiful, and I was a little bit crazy but hadn't noticed it yet." It is a showoff sentence, and the rhythms go with it, but I couldn't go around writing many sentences like that in a row without getting challenged. (4) The fourth and final axiom is that there are places in prose where the reader not only will accept but expects a great deal of rhythm—where he will notice an absence of rhythm and take it as a deficiency not only in the writing but in the author. If an author writes out of a full heart and rhythms don't come with it then something is missing inside the author. Perhaps a full heart.

The Pure and the Good

· ·

ON BASEBALL AND

· ·

BACKPACKING

*"The Pure and the Good: On Baseball and Backpacking" focuses,
as does "The Woods, Books, and Truant Officers," on Maclean's
personal and pedagogical interest in rhythm in language. In
this essay, he analyzes the old ballad "Lord Randal" to define
four overlapping rhythms that together create the ballad's music.
Maclean also reviews some core aesthetic principles, calling his first
book "love stories" that include his "love of seeing life turn into
literature," citing USFS 1919 as an illustration of this view. Along
the way, he compares "a fair number of professional literary critics"
unfavorably to baseball fans.*

I must have been a little confused when I agreed to talk on this subject,
"The Pure Good of Literature." A member of the Association of Departments of English (ADE) Executive Committee that planned the program,
no less a person than Arthur Coffin, asked me whether I would as I was
walking to the platform to talk to his students at Montana State University in
Bozeman. "Pure" and "good" are words that don't come through to me clearly
at normal altitudes, but Bozeman is such a beautiful town, with the Spanish
Peaks behind it and the Bridger Mountains in front, that the pure and the good
seem possible there, so I said yes, and went on to the platform to talk about
something very different.

Next morning, though, I was troubled enough to look Arthur up before
leaving the Gallatin Valley to ask whether I had heard him right, and he repeated himself in daylight and went on to say that maybe I didn't know but
since I had retired from teaching there had been a steady decline in the enrollment of students in English. He stated this in such a way as to suggest some
relation of cause and effect, so I remained sufficiently confused to be here this
morning to speak, in New York of all places, about the pure and the good.

"The Pure and the Good: On Baseball and Backpacking" is reprinted from *Associations of Departments of English Bulletin* 61 (May 1979): 3–5.

There isn't a chance, though, I will say anything timely to affect the job market. I began teaching in 1928 during the Great Boom but just before the Great Depression and, although I always had a job during the Depression, I never once in all those years got a raise in rank or salary. So I have taught in good times and bad times, without greatly affecting the economy.

Something tells me that this may be true of many of us. All we can do at any given time is to teach what we see as best in literature and, I may add, in ourselves. It is also true, however, that in literature, as in life, we may come to take things for granted when times are good, or may do the opposite—through affluence, get fancy and lose sight of the fundamentals in a sea of aesthetics. In either event, it probably makes sense to take a fresh look at ourselves when things are not good to be sure we are at our best.

For instance, it pays from time to time to see whether, as teachers, scholars, and critics of literature, we are as good as professional baseball writers or even as baseball fans. Baseball fans are among our leading exponents of the art-for-art's-sake school of criticism—to them the art of baseball is a thing in itself and sufficient unto itself. They love it deeply and are very learned about it. The difference between a double steal and a delayed steal is primer stuff to them, and, as critics, they all know it is a disfigurement of the art to try a steal of any kind when your team is three or four runs behind. They know what they are talking about, and they are willing to stand up all night to get a ticket to see the big game. I have just written a small book of stories that was widely enough reviewed to entitle me to the opinion that a fair number of professional literary critics don't even know what kinds of questions to ask about a book. There are people in the grandstands of our profession who wouldn't be allowed in the bleachers of baseball. And many of our students in poetry can't tell an anapest from third base.

I am old-fashioned. I believe that one must know something about craftsmanship to come to know and love an art in its purity. We just must assume that one of our greatest loves is of the things men and women make with their hands and hearts and heads. We must assume that some of these beautiful things are hard to make and that therefore it will probably be hard to know as much as we should about an art in order to love it as we should. Even the ordinary baseball fan operates on these assumptions.

But many of our students in poetry courses—even in graduate courses—can do nothing, for instance, with the rhythm of poems. Reading a poem to them is like going to the senior prom and not being able to dance. But they have to know some things about craft before they can see and feel some of the complex beauty that has given immortality to such a seemingly simple old ballad as "Lord Randal." To see its beauty they must see that part of it is in its complex rhythm and in the suitability of its rhythm to a musical form such as the ballad, and in particular to "Lord Randal." At the end, they should be able to write a paper showing that it has at least three rhythms superimposed on its base English accentual rhythm of falling-rising syllables—carefully varied iambs and anapests—as "o where hae ye been, Lord Randal, my son." But they should be able to go on from there and show that the music only begins with qualitative rhythm, that quantitative rhythm is concurrent with the qualitative, that above the patterned syllables are larger verbal units of half lines and whole lines falling into patterns, as in Hebrew verse, and that the four-line stanza itself eventually becomes a foot, with the first two lines being a question and the last two lines the answer. This patterned repetition of grammatical structure we might call grammatical rhythm, and with it comes another kind of rhythm, a patterned recurrence of pitch or key, the question asked in the first two lines by the anxious mother in a high female key and the answer in the last two lines in the low masculine tones of her dying son.

So in this old-time immortal ballad there are at least four rhythms harmonizing with one another: the qualitative patterned recurrence of stressed syllables; the quantitative rhythm of recurring half lines, whole lines, and four-line stanzas; the repeated grammatical structures within these quantitative units; and finally a patterned change of key within each stanza from high key in the first two lines to low key in the last two.

> "O where hae ye been, Lord Randal, my son?
>   O where hae ye been, my handsome young man?"
> "I hae been to the wild wood; mother, make my bed soon,
>   For I'm weary wi' hunting, and fain wald lie down."
>
> "Where gat ye your dinner, Lord Randal, my son?
>   Where gat ye your dinner, my handsome young man?"
> "I din'd wi' my true-love; mother, make my bed soon,
>   For I'm weary wi' hunting, and fain wald lie down."

Such a lovely old poem, forever fresh and forever carrying with it its own musical accompaniment.

Let us leave the baseball fans behind in the bleachers. Ultimately, of course, literature does not play a game unless it is the game of life, and life is impure—it flops around and has spasms and in between it runs too straight, routinized by jobs and families and what the neighbors think. What then can be pure or good about it?

From here on I speak for myself, while hoping I speak for others. As I look back at my life now that I have been allowed to pass considerably beyond my biblical allotment of three score years and ten, I find times when it lifted itself out of its impurities of spasms and routines and became, usually briefly, as if shaped by a poet or storyteller. When the time was short and intense, like one of Wordsworth's "Spots of Time," it became, alas for a moment only, a lyric poem. If it went on through time and took in characters and events, it became a story. Now, looking back at my life, I see it largely as a sheaf of unarranged poems and stories with a few threads binding them together. I don't remember much of what happened in between. What I remember most about my life is its literature.

I don't want at my age to go metaphysical, but I doubt that there are, outside us in X, assortments of ready-made poems and stories and that we just happen along and find roles in them. It takes a poet and a storyteller to make a poem and a story. Even if such literary works are lying ready-made outside us in X, it takes a poet and a storyteller to recognize them when they come along.

As perhaps several of you know, I turned to writing stories of my own life to fill a gap left by my retirement and the death of my wife. I had the good fortune of having been brought up in the early part of this century in the woods of western Montana and of not having to go to school until I was nearly eleven. My collection of stories is called *A River Runs Through It*, and they are love stories: stories of my love of craft—of what men and women can do with their hands—and of my love of seeing life turn into literature.

The reaction to these stories suggests that at times I may have succeeded. One of the stories, entitled "USFS 1919," is about my third summer in the early United States Forest Service, when I was seventeen years old, but older than the Forest Service. It is, if anything, overloaded with the excitement of learning how to do things in the woods of northern Idaho and how it feels to do them, of how, for instance, to fight forest fires and how it feels when the heat is so great that the only oxygen left is less than fourteen inches from the ground. But now in my hometown of Missoula, Montana, I am something of a hero to the big-legged boys and girls who are backpackers—they stop to congratulate me because an excerpt from this story was published in the *Backpacking Journal*. The excerpt contains a brief sketch of the history of the art of packing horses, mules, and camels—of its origins in Asia, its travels across Africa and from there by way of the Arabs to Spain, where it picked up much of its present terminology (such as *manty* and the *cinch* of a saddle), and from Spain to Mexico and from Mexico to squaws and from squaws to us. To the big-legged boys and girls of my hometown, no greater honor can befall a living writer than to have something published in the *Backpacking Journal*, especially if it tells how to throw a diamond hitch.

But I have had several letters about this story from some girls from Brooklyn that pleased me even more. The overall plot of my Forest Service story is that of a boy in the woods who for the first time sees his life turning into a story, and the girls from Brooklyn, where supposedly one tree grows, wrote to tell me that they liked my story of the boy in the Forest Service in northern Idaho in 1919 because that very summer (1976) the same thing had happened to them—for the first time ever they had seen their own lives turn into a story. I don't know what had happened to them—perhaps they had fallen in love with some boy in a summer camp in upstate New York—but what was even more important to them is that for the first time they had seen their lives have a complication and a purgation.

No doubt, much of their power to make such an observation is genetic, but I am sure some of it can be taught. If I did not think so, I would not have spent fifty years of my life trying to teach literature, in good times and in bad times.

Black Ghost

....

"Black Ghost," found in Maclean's papers after his death, seems the inevitable beginning of Young Men and Fire because it reveals the book's autobiographical sources of Maclean's obsession with the 1949 Mann Gulch fire. Maclean links his own experience being chased by a wildfire, alluded to in USFS 1919: The Ranger, the Cook, and a Hole in the Sky, with his initial visit to Mann Gulch about a week after the August 5, 1949, blowup. In this powerful story, Maclean's encounter with a burned, blinded deer in Mann Gulch recalls a nightmarish image (the "black ghost") from his own adolescent race against a "blowup." "Black Ghost" suggests the second life Maclean imagined for himself: that of a career Forest Service employee, possibly a wildland firefighter, even a Smokejumper.

It was a few days after the tenth of August, 1949, when I first saw the Mann Gulch fire and started to become, even then in part consciously, a small part of its story. I had just arrived from the East to spend several weeks in my cabin at Seeley Lake, Montana. The postmistress in the small town at the lower end of the lake told me about the fire and how thirteen Forest Service Smokejumpers had been burned to death on the fifth of August trying to get to the top of a ridge ahead of a blowup in tall, dead grass. In the small town at Seeley Lake and in the big country around it there are only summer tourists and loggers, and, since the loggers are the only permanent residents, they have all the mailboxes at the post office—the postmistress, of course, has come to know them all, and as a result knows a lot about forests and forest fires in a gossipy way. Since she and I are old friends, I have a box, too, and every day when I came for my mail she passed on to me the latest she had heard about the dead Smokejumpers, most of them college boys, until after about a week I realized I would have to see the Mann Gulch fire myself while some of it was still burning.

I knew, of course, that a fire that big would be burning long after it had been brought under control. I had gone to work for the Forest Service during World War I when there was a shortage of men and I was only fifteen,

"Black Ghost" reprinted from *Young Men and Fire* (Chicago: University of Chicago Press, 1992).

four years younger than Thol, the youngest of those who had died in Mann Gulch, so by the time I was his age I had been on several big fires. I knew, for instance, that the Mann Gulch fire would be burning for a long time, because one November I had gone back with my father to hunt deer in country close to where I had been on a big fire that summer, and to my surprise I had seen stumps and fallen trees still burning, with smoke coming out of blackened holes in the snow.

But even though I knew smoke would probably be curling out of Mann Gulch till November there came a day in early August when I could not listen to any more post office gossip about the fire. I even had a notion of why I had to go and see the fire right then. I once had seen a ghost, and the ghost again possessed me.

The big fire that had still been burning late into the hunting season had been on Fish Creek, the Fish Creek that is about nine miles by trail, as I remember, from Lolo Hot Springs. Fish Creek was fine deer country, and the few homesteaders who had holed up there made a living by supplementing the emaciated produce from their rocky gardens with the cash they collected from deer hunters in the autumn by turning their cabins into overnight hunting lodges. Deer, then, were a necessary part of their economy and their diet. They had venison on the table twelve months a year, the game wardens never bothering them for shooting deer out of season, just as long as they didn't go around bragging that they were getting away with beating the law.

Those of us on the fire crew that had been sent from the ranger station at Lolo Hot Springs were pretty sure that the fire had been started by one of these homesteaders. The Forest Service had issued a permit to a big sheep outfit to graze a flock of a thousand or so on a main tributary of Fish Creek, and you probably know—hunters are sure they know—that sheep graze a range so close to the ground that nothing is left for a deer to eat when the sheep have finished. Hunters even say that a grasshopper can't live on the grass sheep leave behind. The fire had been started near the mouth of the tributary, on the assumption, we assumed, that the fire would burn up the tributary, which was a box canyon, all cliffs, with no way of getting sheep out of it. From a deer hunter's point of view, it was a good place for sheep to die. The fire, though, burned not only up the tributary but down it to where it entered Fish Creek and could do major damage to the country. We tried first to use Fish Creek as a "fire-line," hoping to stop the fire at the water's edge, but when it reached thick brush on one side of the creek it didn't even wait to back up and take a run before it jumped into the brush on the other side. Then we were the ones who had to back up fast. At this point, Fish Creek is in such a narrow and twisted canyon that the main trail going down it is on the sidehill, so we backed up to the sidehill trail, which was to be our second line of defense.

I was standing where the fire jumped the trail. At first it was no bigger than a small Indian campfire, looking more like something you could move up close to and warm your hands against than something that in a few minutes could leave your remains lying in prayer with nothing on but a belt. For a moment or two I could have stepped over it and fought it just as well from the upstream side, and when it got a little bigger I still could have walked around it. Instead, I fought it where I stood, for no other reason than that all of us are taught to be the boy who stood on the burning deck. It never occurred to me that I had alternatives. I did not even notice—not until I returned the next day—that if I had stepped across the fire I would have been on a side of it where the fire would soon reach a cedar thicket whose fallen needles had made a thick, moist duff in which fire could only creep and smolder.

The fire coming up at me from the creek in the bunch and cheat grass stopped for only a moment when it reached the trail we were hoping to use as a fire-line. The grass on either side of the trail did not make such instant connections as the brush had on the sides of the creek. Here the fire rocked back and forth like a broadjumper before it started toward the takeoff. Then it jumped. One by one, other like fires reached the line, rocked back and forth, and they all made it.

I broke and started up the hillside. Unlike the boys on the Mann Gulch fire, who did not start running until they were nearly at the top, I started running near the bottom. By the testimony of those who survived, they weren't scared until the last hundred yards. My testimony is that I was scared until I got near the top, when all feelings—fright, thirst, desire to stop for a moment to pray—became indistinguishable from exhaustion. Unlike the Mann Gulch fire, though, the fire behind was never quite a blowup; it was never two hundred feet of flame in the sky. It was in front of me, though, as well as behind me, with nowhere to go but up. Above, it was little spot fires started by a sky of burning branches. The spot fires turned me in my course by leaping into each other and forming an avalanche of flame that went both down and up the mountain. I kept looking for escape openings marked by holes in smoke that at times burned upside down. Behind, where I did not dare to look, the main fire was sound and heat, a ground noise like a freight train. Where there were weak spots in the grass, it sounded as if the freight train had slowed down to cross a bridge or perhaps to enter a tunnel. It could have been doing either, because in a moment it roared again and started to catch up. It came so close it sounded as if it were cracking bones, and mine were the only bones around. Then it would enter a tunnel and I would have hope again. Whether it rumbled or crackled I was always terrified. Always thirsty. Always exhausted.

Halfway or more toward the top I heard a voice beside me when the roar of the main fire was reduced for a moment to the rattle of empty railroad cars. The voice sidehilled until it was on my contour and said, "How're you doing, sonny?" The voice may have come down with a burning branch, or it may have belonged to a member of our pickup crew whom I had never seen before. The only thing I noticed about him at first was that he didn't slip because he wore a good pair of climbing boots with caulks in them.

In answer to his question of how sonny was doing, I answered, "I keep slipping back," pointing back but not looking back. I also pointed at my shoes.

I was in my second summer in the Forest Service, so I knew what good climbing shoes were and how hobnails in them weren't enough to make them hold on hillsides, especially on slick, grassy hillsides, but I was young and still trying to escape such harsh realities as growing up and paying half a month's wages for a good pair of shoes. Consequently, I had gone to an army surplus store and bought a pair of leftover shoes from World War I. They were cheap shoes and wouldn't hold long caulks so I had rimmed them with hobnails, and hobnails soon wear as smooth as skates. The ghost in the caulks climbed straight uphill and never slipped, but I had to weave back and forth in little switchbacks and dig in with the edges of my soles.

Being sorry for myself made me feel that I couldn't go any farther; being terrified made me feel exhausted; waiting for the ghost in caulked shoes to help me made me feel exhausted; being so thirsty that I couldn't form words to ask for help made me feel exhausted. As a fire up a hillside closes in, everything becomes a mode of exhaustion—fear, thirst, terror, a twitch in the flesh that still has a preference to live, all become simply exhaustion. So upon closer examination, burning to death on a mountainside is dying at least three times, not two times as has been said before—first, considerably ahead of the fire, you reach the verge of death in your boots and your legs; next, as you fail, you sink back in the region of strange gases and red and blue darts where there is no oxygen and here you die in your lungs; then you sink in prayer into the main fire that consumes, and if you are a Catholic about all that remains of you is your cross.

The black ghost that could walk in a straight line came closer to me and took a look. I looked back but out of fright. The black ghost had a red face. In more leisurely times he could have been an alcoholic, but certainly much of the red now was reflection from the flames. "Could I be of any help?" the red face asked, becoming a voice again.

I thought I was beyond help, but I swallowed the thirst in my throat to find a word and said, "Yes." When I was able, I said, "Yes, thanks."

The black ghost came closer, the red in his face burning steadily. Then suddenly in his face there was a blowup, a reflection of something either behind him or in him, and he slapped me in the face.

"My God," I said, and reeled sideways across the hillside. All I knew while I staggered was that if I fell I might never get up. I burst into tears even while I was staggering, but came to rest standing. When I could recover my breath and hold the hot air in my lungs, I cried out loud, especially when I realized that all that could save me now was my army surplus boots. Still in tears, I proceeded to climb almost straight uphill almost without slipping until I reached the contour where I had been outraged. Here I stopped and went looking for what had done it, but he was far up the hill, peering down at me from the mouth of a cave that now and then opened in a red cliff of flame.

This is all I know about the violent apparition that was just ahead of the fire. It must have been a member of the fire crew that had been picked up in the bars of Butte. I had never seen him before and have never seen him since. Maybe he was a Butte wino demented by thirst. Maybe he was a Butte miner with tuberculosis whose lungs were collapsing wall to wall from the heat of the air they were trying to breathe. It is even possible something was working on him besides the fire as he tried to keep ahead of it, something terrible that had been done to him for which he had to get even before his consignment to flames. In either of these cases, at just the right moment I may have appeared out of smoke, young and paralyzed and unable to do anything back if he did what he wanted to do, so he did it.

Above, the crevice in the red cliff opened now and then. From its entrance a figure retreated and ascended into the sky until he hung like a bat on the roof of a cave. He was always watching me, but I don't know what he hoped to see. Finally, he was hanging upside down by his claws.

I have no clear memory of going up the rest of the ridge, except that when I reached the top I had to put out the fire that smoldered in my shoelaces. I didn't think of the crew or where I might find them. I didn't think of the ghost. After I reached the top of the ridge, for a time I couldn't think of anything behind me. I thought of things ahead, the nearest of which was a hunting lodge up the main fork of the Fish Creek where my father and I had stayed the last two hunting seasons. It was run by a woman, Mrs. Brown, who looked something like my mother but more like an Indian with brown crow's-feet in the corners of her eyes. In addition, she was a fine shot so that if one of her guests didn't get a deer she would run out for an hour or two the last morning and shoot one for him. I thought, if I follow the ridge upstream and then drop into the creek bottom where her cabin is, Mrs. Brown will be able to do something for me, even if I am in pretty bad shape. I thought she might even shoot a deer for me, and then I thought, no, that's wrong—I don't need a deer, but go anyway. You need something.

Now that I had started thinking again I became exhausted again. Mrs. Brown can help men who cannot help themselves, I thought, and I am exhausted beyond comprehension. It took me until nearly dark to get within a quarter of a mile from her cabin. Then I put exhaustion out of mind and ran the last quarter of a mile to get there in time, although time was just a hangover from the past with no present meaning. I did not collapse, but I rocked on my feet from the suction of air she caused when she opened the cabin door.

She did not ask a question. She said quietly, "Come in and lie down. You look very white." I was baffled. I was sure I was black. "No," she said, "you're very white."

She felt the water in the pail but it was evidently lukewarm, so she went down to the creek and dipped out a cold pail. Then she said, "I told you to lie down." She still hadn't asked a question. If you have spent your life in a cabin, you know that there are times when you have to do things before you try to find out what things are all about.

She washed me in cold water again and again, taking my pulse each time she did. Then finally she took my pulse again, nodded her head, and threw a whole dipper of water on me to signify my convalescence period was over. She buttoned my shirt and said, "When you go deer hunting this autumn, you'll get your limit."

Not until then did she try to find out what had happened to me and how I had got there. "Did you try to stop the fire?"

"Mrs. Brown?" I asked. "Mrs. Brown, did you start it?" I finished asking.

"You'll have no trouble getting your limit next deer season," she reassured me.

I knew that she wasn't going to say anything more and that I'd better not ask anything more.

"For a preacher," she said, "your father is very handy with a rifle."

I said, "He's also good with a scatter-gun."

Then she said, "I'll write him tomorrow and let him know what happened."

I said to her, "Skip it. He knows I can take care of myself."

I wasn't sure I should have come to her for help, now that I didn't need help anymore. Even tough women who are good with the rifle get motherly when it's all over.

She advised me, "Stay here and take it easy until tomorrow. Then go back to Lolo Hot Springs and report to the ranger station there."

After a pail and a half of cold water I no longer needed an Indian mother, and I wanted to make this clear. I said, even if she was a good shot, "Thanks, I'll stay over tonight, but tomorrow I'll go back to the fire and see if I can find the crew." I didn't add that mostly I wanted to see where the fire had jumped the trail and I had started up the ridge ahead of it, fear being only partly something that makes us run away—at times, at least, it is something that makes us come back again and stare at what made us run away.

Although I was very tired the next morning, I hurried to where the fire had jumped the trail. It was not until I stared that I realized if I had stepped across a little fire and been on the side of it where the cedar duff was that I would not have had to race a giant uphill for my life or been stopped by a ghost along the way.

I have several times returned to that spot on the trail. The autumn of the same year of the fire I said to my father, "Let's hunt another season at Mrs. Brown's in Fish Creek." It was while hunting in Fish Creek that November that I saw smoke coming out of black holes in the snow.

· · · ·

While I listened to the postmistress in the record heat of early August of 1949, my memory turned to snow with smoke curling out of it. When the smoke started mixing at night with my dreams, I locked my cabin and drove the 150 miles to Wolf Creek and picked up my brother-in-law, who had fought a few days on the Mann Gulch fire as a volunteer. He and I borrowed a Dodge Power Wagon from the Oxbow Ranch, because we knew it would be tough going ahead. Then we drove up the dirt road on the east side of the Missouri until we came to the Gates of the Mountains and to Willow Creek, the creek north of Mann Gulch where the fire was finally stopped on its downriver side. The road went up the creek for a way and then dead-ended, and it and the creek had been used by the crew—on the whole, successfully—as fire-lines. Only occasionally had the fire jumped both of them, and where it had the crew quickly controlled it again. By the time we reached the fire the crew had put it out for several hundred yards back of the road or creek, sawing down the still-burning trees and either burying them with dirt or pouring water on them when they were near the creek. Since there was no danger of the fire jumping the lines again, the crew had moved on, leaving the fire to burn itself harmlessly in its interior.

It was a world of still-warm ashes that had incubated once-hot poles. The black poles looked as if they had been born of the gray ashes as the result of some vast effort at sexual intercourse on the edges of the afterlife. When the vast effort was over, it was discovered the poles were born dead and the ashes themselves lived only because the winds moved them. It was the amphitheater of the afterlife where passion had destroyed life, but passion devoid of life could be reborn. A little farther into the fire a black pole would now and then explode and reproduce a progeny of flames. A cliff would tear loose a tree it had kept burning in a secret crevice and then toss the sacrifice upon the rocks below, where the victim exploded into flames and passion without life. On the fire-lines of hell sexual intercourse seems to be gone forever and then brutally erupts, and after a great forest fire passes by, there are warm ashes and once-hot poles and passion in death.

Not far up the creek my brother-in-law stopped the Power Wagon. Ahead, the creek came close to the road, and standing in the creek was a deer terribly burned. It was drinking and probably had been for a long time. It was probably like the two Smokejumpers, Hellman and Sylvia, who did not die immediately and could never put out their thirst, drinking at every chance until they became sick at the stomach.

The deer was hairless and purple. Where the skin had broken, the flesh was in patches. For a time, the deer did not look up. It must have been especially like Joe Sylvia, who was burned so deeply that he was euphoric. However, when a tree exploded and was thrown as a victim to the foot of a nearby cliff, the deer finally raised its head and slowly saw us. Its eyes were red bulbs that illuminated long hairs around its eyelids.

Since it was August, we had not thought of taking a rifle with us, so we could not treat it as a living thing and destroy it.

While it completed the process of recognizing us, it bent down and continued drinking. Then either it finally recognized us, or became sick at the stomach again.

It tottered to the bank, steadied itself, and then bounded off euphorically.

If it could have, it probably would have said, like Joe Sylvia, "I'm feeling just fine." Probably its sensory apparatus, like Joe Sylvia's, had been dumped into its bloodstream and was beginning to clog its kidneys.

Then, instead of jumping, it ran straight into the first fallen log ahead.

My brother-in-law said, loathing himself, "I forgot to throw a rifle into the cab of the truck."

The deer lay there and looked back looking for us, but, shocked by its collision with the log, it probably did not see us. It probably did not see anything—it moved its head back and forth, as if trying to remember at what angle it had last seen us. Suddenly, its eyes were like electric light bulbs burning out—with a flash, too much light burned out the filaments in the bulbs, and then the red faded slowly to black. In the fading, there came a point where the long hairs on the eyelids were no longer illuminated. Then the deer put its head down on the log it had not seen and could not jump.

In my story of the Mann Gulch fire, how I first came to Mann Gulch is part of the story.

From *Young Men and Fire*

Chapter 8 from Young Men and Fire *opens the second of the
book's three parts and contains one of Maclean's major statements
about art, including the "slow time" of art. He defines his belief
in tragedy as the ultimate literary form and the tragic aspirations
of the book he is writing—a haunted, haunting "fire report" that
defies generic classification. He also firms up the many analogies he
sees between the fate of Custer's Seventh Cavalry at Little Bighorn
and those young Smokejumpers from Missoula who died in the
blowup. These analogies suggest that in* Young Men and Fire
*Maclean finally wrote the book he could not complete with Custer
as his subject in the 1960s.*

We enter now a different time zone, even a different world of
time. Suddenly comes the world of slow-time that accompanies grief and moral bewilderment trying to understand
the extinction of those whose love and everlasting presence
were never questioned. All there was to time were the fifty-six speeding minutes before the fire picked watches off dead bodies, blew them up a hillside
ahead of the bodies, and froze the watch hands together. Ahead now is a world
of no explosions, no blowups, and, without a storyteller, not many explanations. Immediately ahead we know there is bound to be a flare-up of public
indignation and the wavering candlelight of private grief. What then? It could
be a slow fade-out of slow-time until all that's left of the memory of Mann
Gulch are cracking concrete crosses on an almost inaccessible hill and a memorial tablet with the names to go with the crosses beside a picnic ground at
the mouth of the next gulch upriver.

After the autumn rains changed ashes into mud slides, the story seems
to have been buried in incompleteness, pieces of it altogether missing. As a
mystery story, it left unexplained what dramatic and devastating forces co-
incided to make the best of young men into bodies, how the bodies got to
their crosses and what it was like on the way, and why this catastrophe has
been allowed to pass without a search for the carefully measured grains of
consolation needed to transform catastrophe into tragedy. It would be natural

Excerpt reprinted from *Young Men and Fire* (Chicago: University of Chicago Press, 1992), chap. 8.

here, looking for at least chronological continuity to the story, to follow the outcries of the public and at the same time to try to share some part of the private sufferings of those who loved those who died. But always it would have to be conceived as possible, if an ending were sought in this direction, that there might be a non-ending. It is even conceivable that most of those closely connected with the catastrophe soon tried to see that it got lost; when the coming controversies and legal proceedings were added to all the rest of it, clearly the whole thing got so big it frightened people. They wanted it to go away and not come back.

Even so, there may somewhere be an ending to this story, although it might take a storyteller's faith to proceed on a quest to find it and on the way to retain the belief that it might both be true and fit together dramatically. A story that honors the dead realistically partly atones for their sufferings, and so instead of leaving us in moral bewilderment, adds dimensions to our acuteness in watching the universe's four elements at work—sky, earth, fire, and young men.

True, though, it must be. Far back in the impulses to find this story is a storyteller's belief that at times life takes on the shape of art and that the remembered remnants of these moments are largely what we come to mean by life. The short semihumorous comedies we live, our long certain tragedies, and our springtime lyrics and limericks make up most of what we are. They become almost all of what we remember of ourselves. Although it would be too fancy to take these moments of our lives that seemingly have shape and design as proof we are inhabited by an impulse to art, yet deep within us is a counterimpulse to the id or whatever name is presently attached to the disorderly, the violent, the catastrophic both in and outside us. As a feeling, this counterimpulse to the id is a kind of craving for sanity, for things belonging to each other, and results in a comfortable feeling when the universe is seen to take a garment from the rack that seems to fit. Of course, both impulses need to be present to explain our lives and our art, and probably go a long way to explain why tragedy, inflamed with the disorderly, is generally regarded as the most composed art form.

It should be clear now after nearly forty years that the truculent universe prefers to retain the Mann Gulch fire as one of its secrets—left to itself, it fades away, an unsolved, violent incident grieved over by the fewer and fewer still living who are old enough to grieve over fatalities of 1949. If there is a story in Mann Gulch, it will take something of a storyteller at this date to find it, and it is not easy to imagine what impulses would lead him to search for it.

He probably should be an old storyteller, at least old enough to know that the problem of identity is always a problem, not just a problem of youth, and even old enough to know that the nearest anyone can come to finding himself at any given age is to find a story that somehow tells him about himself.

When I was a young teacher and still thought of myself as a billiards player, I had the pleasure of watching Albert Abraham Michelson play billiards nearly every noon. He was by then one of our national idols, having been the first American to win the Nobel Prize in science (for the measurement of the speed of light, among other things). To me, he took on added luster because he was the best amateur billiards player I had ever seen. One noon, while he was still shaking his head at himself for missing an easy shot after he had had a run of thirty-five or thirty-six, I said to him, "You are a fine billiards player, Mr. Michelson." He shook his head at himself and said, "No. I'm getting old. I can still make the long three-cushion shots, but I'm losing the soft touch on the short ones." He chalked up, but instead of taking the next shot, he finished what he had to say. "Billiards, though, is a good game, but billiards is not as good a game as chess." Still chalking his cue, he said, "Chess, though, is not as good a game as painting." He made it final by saying, "But painting is not as good a game as physics." Then he hung up his cue and went home to spend the afternoon painting under the large tree on his front lawn.

It is in the world of slow-time that truth and art are found as one.

. . . .

The hill on which they died is a lot like Custer Hill. In the dry grass on both hills are white scattered markers where the bodies were found, a special cluster of them just short of the top, where red terror closed in from behind and above and from the sides. The bodies were of those who were young and thought to be invincible by others and themselves. They were the fastest the nation had in getting to where there was danger, they got there by moving in the magic realm between heaven and earth, and when they got there they almost made a game of it. None were surer they couldn't lose than the Seventh Cavalry and the Smokejumpers.

The difference between thirteen crosses and 245 or 246 markers (they are hard to count) made it a small Custer Hill, with some advantages. It had helicopters, air patrol, and lawsuits. It had instant newspaper coverage and so could heighten the headlines and suspense as the injury list changed from three uninjured survivors, two men badly burned, and the rest of the crew missing, to the final list on which the only survivors were the first three. The headlines flamed higher as all the burned and all the missing proved dead.

The Forest Service knew right away it was in for big trouble. By August 7 chief forester Lyle F. Watts in Washington appointed an initial committee to investigate the tragedy and to report to him immediately, and on August 9 the committee flew over the area several times, went back to Mann Gulch by boat, and spent three hours there. Like General Custer himself, who liked to have reporters along, the investigating committee took with them a crew of reporters and photographers from Life magazine. The lead article of Life's August 22, 1949, issue, "Smokejumpers Suffer Ordeal by Fire," runs to five pages and includes a map and photographs of the fire, the funeral, and a deer burned to death, probably the deer that Rumsey and Sallee saw come out of the flames and collapse while they were ducking from one side of their rock slide to the other.

Accompanying the Smokejumpers on their August 5 flight was a Forest Service photographer named Elmer Bloom, who had been commissioned to make a training film for young jumpers; Bloom took shots of the crew suiting up and loading, of the Mann Gulch fire as it was first seen from the plane, and of what was to be the last jump for most of the crew. There are five frames from his documentary reproduced in Life, and for all my efforts to find the film, this is all I have ever seen of it. I did find an August 1949 letter from the regional forester in Missoula to the chief forester in Washington saying in effect that the film was too hot to handle at home so he was sending it along. Nobody in Washington can find it for me. I'm always told it must have been "misfiled," and it may well have been, since there is no better way in this world to lose something forever than to misfile it in a big library.

It is hard to believe the film could be anything other than an odd little memento, but very early the threats of lawsuits from parents sounded in the distance and the Forest Service reversed its early policy of accommodating Life's photographers to one of burying the photographs they already had.

The leader of the public outcry against the Forest Service was Henry Thol, the grief-unbalanced father of Henry, Jr., whose cross is closest to the top of the Mann Gulch ridge. Not only was the father's grief almost beyond restraint, but he, more than any other relative of the dead, should have known what he was talking about. He was a retired Forest Service ranger of the old school, and soon after the fire he was in Mann Gulch studying and pacing the tragedy. Harvey Jenson, the man in charge of the excursion boat taking tourists downriver from Hilger Landing to the mouth of Mann Gulch, became concerned about Thol's conduct and the effect it was having on his tourist trade. His mildest statement: "Thol has been very unreasonable about his remarks and has expressed his ideas very forcefully to boatloads of people going and coming from Mann Gulch as he rides back and forth on the passenger boat."

The Forest Service moved quickly, probably too quickly, to make its official report and get its story of the fire to the public. It appointed a formal Board of Review, all from the Forest Service and none ranked below assistant regional forester, who assembled in Missoula on September 26, the next morning flew several loops around and across Mann Gulch, spent that afternoon going over the ground on foot, and during the next two days heard "all key witnesses" to the fire. The *Report of Board of Review* is dated September 29, 1949, three days after the committee members arrived in Missoula, and it is hard to see how in such a short time and so close to the event and in the intense heat of the public atmosphere a convincing analysis could be made of a small Custer Hill. In four days they assembled all the relevant facts, reviewed them, passed judgment on them, and wrote what they hoped was a closed book on the biggest tragedy the Smokejumpers had ever had.

In this narrative the *Report* and the testimony on which it was based have been referred to or quoted from a good many times, and an ending to this story has to involve an examination of the *Report*'s chief findings. But the immediate effect of the Forest Service's official story of the fire was to add to its fuel.

By October 14, Michael ("Mike") Mansfield, then a member of the House of Representatives and later to be the distinguished leader of the Democratic senators, pushed through Congress an amendment to the Federal Employees' Compensation Act raising the burial allowance from two hundred dollars to four hundred dollars and making the amendment retroactive so it would apply to the dead of Mann Gulch.

The extra two hundred dollars per body for burial expenses did little to diminish the anger or personal grief. By 1951, eight damage suits had been brought by parents of those who had died in the fire, or by representatives of their estates, "alleging negligence on the part of Forest Service officials and praying damages on account of the 'loss of the comfort, society, and companionship' of a son." To keep things in their proper size, however, it should be added that the eight suits were filed by representatives of only four of the dead, each plaintiff bringing two suits, one on the plaintiff's own behalf for loss of the son's companionship and support, and the other on behalf of the dead son for the suffering the son had endured.

Henry Thol was the leader of this group and was to carry his own case to the court of appeals, so a good way to get a wide-angle view of the arguments and evidence these cases were to be built on is to examine Thol's testimony before the Board of Review, at which he was the concluding witness.

Thol had become the main figure behind the lawsuits not just because he alone of all the parents of the dead was a life-long woodsman and could meet the Forest Service on its own grounds. Geography increased his intensity: he lived in Kalispell, not far from the Missoula headquarters of Region One and the Smokejumper base. In addition, Kalispell was the town which had been Hellman's home. Thol knew Hellman's wife, and his grief for her in her pregnancy and bewildered financial condition only intensified his rage. There is also probably some truth in what Jansson told Dodge in a sympathetic letter written after the fire: Jansson says that Thol, like many old-time rangers, felt he had been pushed around by the college graduates who had taken over the Forest Service, so he was predisposed to find everything the modern Forest Service did wrong and in a way designed to make him suffer. In his testimony every major order the Forest Service gave the crew of Smokejumpers is denounced as an unpardonable error in woodsmanship—from jumping the crew on a fire in such rough and worthless country and in such abnormal heat and wind, to Dodge's escape fire. The crew should not have been jumped but should have been returned to Missoula; as soon as Dodge saw the fire he should have led the crew straight uphill out of Mann Gulch instead of down it and so dangerously paralleling the explosive fire; Dodge should not have wasted time going back to the cargo area with Harrison to have lunch; when Dodge saw that the fire had jumped the gulch and that the crew might soon be trapped by it, he should have headed straight for the top of the ridge instead of angling toward it; and so on to Dodge's "escape" fire, which was the tragic trap, the trap from which his boy and none of the other twelve could escape.

The charge that weighed heaviest with both Thol and the Forest Service from the outset was the charge that Dodge's fire, instead of being an escape fire, had cut off the crew's escape and was the killer itself.

While the fire was still burning, the Forest Service was alarmed by the possibility that the Smokejumpers were burned by their own foreman. The initial committee of investigation appointed by the chief forester in Washington was headed by the Forest Service's chief of fire control, C. A. Gustafson, who testified later that he had not wanted to talk to any of the survivors before seeing the fire himself because of certain fears about it which he wanted to face alone. In his words, this is what brought him into Mann Gulch on August 9. "The thing I was worried about was the effect of the escape fire on the possible escape of the men themselves."

Jenson, the boatman who took tourists downriver to Mann Gulch, makes probably the most accurate recording of Thol's opinion of Dodge's fire. He said he had heard Thol say, "There is no question about it—Dodge's fire burned the boys." And the father didn't blur his words before the Board of Review. "Indications on the ground show quite plainly that [Dodge's] own fire caught up with some of the boys up there above him. His own fire prevented those below him from going to the top. The poor boys were caught—they had no escape."

The Forest Service's reply to this and other charges can be found in the conclusions of the *Report of Board of Review*. The twelfth and final conclusion of the *Report* is merely a summary of the conclusions that go before it: "It is the overall conclusion of the Board that there is no evidence of disregard by those responsible for the jumper crew of the elements of risk which they are expected to take into account in placing jumper crews on fires."

The Board also added a countercharge: the men would all have been saved if they had "heeded Dodge's efforts to get them to go into the escape fire area" with him. Throughout the questioning there are more than hints that the Board of Review was trying to establish that a kind of insurrection occurred at Dodge's fire led by someone believed to have said, as Dodge hollered at them to lie down in his fire, "To hell with that, I'm getting out of here!" As we have seen, there were even suggestions that the someone believed to have said this was Hellman and that, therefore, the race for the ridge was triggered by the second-in-command in defiance of his commander's orders.

Rumors still circulate among old-time jumpers that there was bad feeling between Dodge, the foreman, and his second-in-command, Hellman, although I have never found any direct evidence to support such rumors. There seems somehow to be a linkage in our minds between the annihilation near the top of a hill of our finest troops and the charge that the second-in-command didn't obey his leader because there had long been "bad blood between them." Custer's supporters explain Custer's disaster by the charge that his second-in-command, Major Reno, hated the general and in the battle failed to support him, and it is easy to understand psychologically how a narrative device like this can become a fixed piece of history. It relieves "our" leader and all "our" men from the responsibility of having caused a national catastrophe, all except one of the favorite scapegoats in history, the "second guy."

Back in the world where things can be determined, if not proved, the suit of Henry Thol reached the United States Court of Appeals for the Ninth Circuit, where Warren E. Burger, later chief justice of the United States Supreme

Court, was one of the lawyers arguing against the retired United States Forest Service ranger's charge that his son would have made the remaining sixty or seventy yards to the top of the ridge except for the negligence of the United States Forest Service. Despite the number of times "United States" occurs in that sentence, nothing much happens because of it.

The court of appeals in 1954 upheld the decision of the district court for the district of Montana. Both courts therefore ruled that the Federal Employees' Compensation Act could constitutionally exclude nondependent parents from receiving damages from the federal government beyond the burial allowance. The decision was also upheld that Mansfield's amendment was constitutional in making itself retroactive so that it would apply to the dead of Mann Gulch. Therefore, after the parents had buried their boys, they received another two hundred dollars.

. . . .

For a time it looked as if the four hundred dollars would put an end to the story. A court decision built on two hundred dollars plus two hundred dollars per body silenced the parents; they could not pursue their charge of negligence unless the decision of the court of appeals was reversed by our highest court. To the average citizen the government holds nearly all the cards and will play them when the government is both the alleged guilty party and judge of its own guilt.

For instance, late in 1951 (December 12) in Lewistown, Idaho, Robert Sallee made a second statement about the Mann Gulch fire to "an investigator for the United States Forest Service," and less than a month later (January 1, 1952) Walter Rumsey in Garfield, Kansas, made his second statement to the same official investigator. The Forest Service was preparing its two key witnesses just in case, going so far as to bring them back to Mann Gulch for a refresher course. Their second statements follow closely their first, which were taken only a few days after their return to Missoula from the fire (both dated August 10, 1949). In fact, their later statements follow their first statements word for word a good part of the way, so the alterations stick out like sore thumbs, which is still a good figure of speech at times. Two assurances were drawn from Rumsey and Sallee: they now protested at length that if those who died had followed Dodge's appeals to lie down with him in his own fire (as they themselves hadn't), they, like Dodge, would have been saved. Moreover, they now insisted at length that in escaping over the hill they had followed the up-gulch edge of Dodge's fire "straight" to the top of the ridge and so Dodge's fire could not have pursued those who were burned toward the head of the gulch, since they and his fire would have been going roughly at right angles to each other.

Some official documents about the fire, then, were retouched and given the right shading. More of them probably were just buried—some were even marked "Confidential" and were held from the public as if these fire reports endangered national security. Still others were scattered among different Forest Service offices from the headquarters of Region One in Missoula to the national headquarters in Washington, D.C. The Mann Gulch fire was so scattered that about a quarter of a century later the first mystery I had to solve about it was to find out where it had disappeared. It was like a burial at sea—it was hard afterwards to find the bodies in the wash, and I couldn't have done it without the help of men and women of the Forest Service who felt the burial had been indecent. It's a different world now anyway from what it was before the passage of the Freedom of Information Act in 1966, but I lived most of my life before that date and I can remember it being a loud laugh at Regional Headquarters in Missoula when an energetic, outspoken journalist tried persistently to get access to the documents there on the Mann Gulch fire. With eight lawsuits in the docket brought against the Forest Service for negligence in the deaths of thirteen of the West's finest, the Forest Service was not opening its heart or its files for all to see. As far as the files marked "Mann Gulch Fire" were concerned, mum was the word.

The reasons why parents, relatives, and close friends hoped for silence are naturally very different from the government's. The Forest Service sought silence; the parents were reduced to it, although in sad ways they may also have sought it. On the whole, they were not people of means and could not afford to appeal their case to the Supreme Court, even if they had wished, and, except for Thol, they must have had small understanding of their own case and therefore an underlying reluctance to pursue it. Most important of all probably is the secrecy of the grief and moral bewilderment suffered at the death of one of ourselves who was young, had a special flair, a special daring, a special disregard for death, who seemed, both to himself and to us, to be apart from death, especially from death leaving behind no explanation of itself either as a sequence of events or as a moral occurrence in what-kind-of-a-universe-is-this-anyway. It is the frightened and recessive grief suffered for one whom you hoped neither death nor anything evil would dare touch. Afterwards, you live in fear that something might alter your memory of him and of all other things. I should know.

A few summers ago, thirty years after the fire, I sent what I hoped was gentle word through a common friend to a mother of one of the Mann Gulch dead asking if I could talk to her, and she returned through the common friend gentle word saying that even after all these years she was unable to talk about her son's death. I thought next I would try a father, and he came in dignity, feeling no doubt it was a challenge to him that he must meet as a man, and he talked in dignity until I began to tell him about his son's death. I had assumed that he knew some of the details of that death and, as a scientist, would care for other details that would help him participate in his son's last decisions, very thoughtful ones though tragic. As I mistakenly went on talking, his hands began to shake as if he had Parkinson's disease. He could not stop them, so there is no story, certainly no ending to a story, that can be found by communicating with the living who loved the young who are dead, at least none that I am qualified to pursue. A story at a minimum requires movement, and, with those who loved those who died, nothing has moved. It all stopped on August 5, 1949. So if there is more to this story for me to find, I shall have to find it somewhere else.

The silence, of course, could never be complete. Some things do remain— worn-out things, unconnected things, things not in the right place or clearly of another time: a worn-out fishing jacket, a few unrelated letters written by him, a few unrelated letters written to him, a childhood photograph that is hard to imagine as his, a picture in which something may be right.

A movie supposedly based on the Mann Gulch fire can still be seen now and then as a rerun on television. In 1952, while litigation was still in progress, Twentieth Century–Fox released *Red Skies of Montana*, filmed at the Smoke-jumper base in Missoula and on a fire just outside of town. The cast included Richard Widmark, Constance Smith, Jeffrey Hunter, and Richard Boone. At the beginning of the plot a foreman on a forest fire lights an escape fire, as Dodge did when the flames closed in; then he lies down in his own fire and the likeness to Dodge continues—his own men "do not heed him" and he alone survives only to live in disgrace.

At the end of the movie, though, there is another fire and the movie foreman again lights an escape fire. This time his crew heeds him, and everybody lives happily ever after.

Our story about the Mann Gulch fire obviously makes it hard on itself by trying to find its true ending. Here is this movie that lives on to rerun several times a year on TV and so has attained some kind of immortality by easily adding to small broken pieces of truth an old, worn-out literary convention. This added, life-giving plot is the old "disgraced officer's plot," the plot in which the military leader has disgraced himself before his men, either because his action has been misunderstood by them or because he displayed actual cowardice, and at the end the officer always meets the same situation again but this time heroically (usually as the result of the intervening influence of a good woman). By the way, this plot has often been attached to movies and stories about Custer Hill. Perhaps this is a reminder to keep open the possibility that there is no real ending in reality to the story of the Mann Gulch fire. If so, then let it be so—there's a lot of tragedy in the universe that has missing parts and comes to no conclusion, including probably the tragedy that awaits you and me.

. . . .

This coming part of the story, then, is the quest to find the full story of the Mann Gulch fire, to find what of it was once known and was then scattered and buried, to discover the parts so far missing because fire science had not been able to explain the behavior of the blowup or the "escape fire," and to imagine the last moments of those who went to their crosses unseen and alone. In this quest we probably should not be altogether guided by the practice of the medieval knight in search of the holy grail who had no clear idea of what he was looking for or where he might find it and so wandered around jousting with other knights who didn't know what they were looking for until finally he discovered he was home again and not much different from what he had been when he started except for some bruises and a broken lance. I early picked up bruises in my wanderings, but I tried to shorten the length of the search by pursuing several quests concurrently. As early as 1976 I started the serious study of the Mann Gulch fire by trying to recover the official documents bearing on it and at the same time reacquainting myself with the actual ground on which the tragedy had occurred. For an opener I took a bruising boat trip down the Missouri River to Mann Gulch. Even earlier I had started with the archives in Missoula because, both as headquarters of Region One of the Forest Service and as the location of the base of the Smokejumpers sent to the fire, it was the center of the Forest Service's operations against the Mann Gulch fire. My opening jousts with both the archives and the ground went in favor of my opponents, whoever they were. My brother-in-law, Kenneth Burns, who was brought up within a few miles of Mann Gulch and was then living in Helena, said he would have no trouble borrowing a boat and taking us down the Missouri from Hilger Landing to the mouth of Meriwether Canyon where, as you'll remember, there is an almost vertical trail to the top of the ridge between Meriwether and Mann Gulch. Charles E. ("Mike") Hardy, research forester project leader at the Northern Forest Fire Laboratory in Missoula and only recently the author of a fine study of the beginnings of research in the Forest Service (*The Gisborne Era of Forest Fire Research: Legacy of a Pioneer*, 1983), had this early interested me in a scientific analysis of the fire and had been good enough to make the trip with us to give me a close-up view of his theories at work. Although we did not quite make it to Mann Gulch on this trip, I am grateful to Mike for starting me in the right direction.

A cloudburst was already waiting to challenge us at the top of the ridge. From the bottom of Meriwether Canyon we could both see and hear it making preparations for a joust with us. As we tried not to fall backwards to where we started in the canyon, we could hear the storm rumble and paw the ground. When we neared the top, it tried to beat us back by splintering shafts of lightning on gigantic rocks. There was a lone tree near the top, only one, and in case we had any foolish ideas of taking refuge under it a bolt of lightning took aim and split it apart; it went down as if it had been hit by a battle-ax. Trying to reach the rocks, we were held motionless and vertical in our tracks by the wind. Only when the wind lessened for a moment could we move—then we fell forward. With the lessening of the wind the rain became cold and even heavier and forced us to retreat from the battlefield on top. The rain fell on us like a fortified wall falling. By the time we reached the bottom of Meriwether, we were shivering and demoralized and my brother-in-law probably already had pneumonia.

All this was like a demonstration arranged to let us know that Mann Gulch had power over earth, air, and water, as well as fire. As the wind continued to lessen, the rain increased and fell straight down. It was solid now everywhere. It knocked out the motor in our borrowed boat, and we couldn't get it started again; after a while we didn't try anymore, and it took several hours to pole and paddle our way back to Hilger Landing. My brother-in-law was seriously sick before we got there; he would never go back to Mann Gulch. So for some time Mann Gulch was mine alone if I wanted it, and for some time I left it to the elements. I turned to the archives because I knew they would be dry and no wind would be there and the air would be the same air the stacks had been built around and nothing but a book or two had been moved since. The signs would demand "Silence" and even the silence would be musty, and for a time anything musty had an appeal.

The Forest Service archives in Missoula were about as hard to get anything out of as Mann Gulch. Although there wasn't much trouble gaining access to the Regional Library, there wasn't much stuff in its files on the Mann Gulch fire, and what was there was the ordinary stuff. Yet surprisingly even some of that was marked "Confidential."

I hadn't thought there would be much in the files, because you can't dip very far into the Mann Gulch story without becoming suspicious that efforts have been made to scatter and cover the tragedy. Besides, you are not far enough advanced in your thinking to do research on the Forest Service if you don't know ahead of time that the Forest Service is a fairly unhistorical outfit, sometimes even antihistorical. So when I first looked under "Mann Gulch Fire," the cupboard was practically bare, but before long I met the great woodsman W. R. ("Bud") Moore, who was then director of the Division of Aviation and Fire Management for Region One of the Forest Service. He is outspoken and devoted to the Forest Service and expects every American citizen, except the president of the United States, to be likewise. He sent out orders to round up all stray documents bearing on Mann Gulch that could be found in the region and make them available to me. They add up to a small but interesting file and contain most of the documents in my collection marked "Confidential." But all told, the Mann Gulch fire turned to ashes without depositing much in the offices of Region One of the United States Forest Service, and I had to make three visits to the Forest Service's Office of Information in Washington, D.C., before I had a good working collection of documents on the Mann Gulch fire.

It is harder to guess ahead of time how you will be received by those in charge of government documents than to guess what you will find in them. Ahead of time, I had guessed I would be sized up as a suspicious character up to no good: I was alone and peeking into government files and into Mann Gulch itself, which long since had been put out of sight and was better that way. Although Forest Service employees, I figured, would always be watching me with a fishy eye when I was around and even more so when I wasn't, there were not nearly as many spies as I had expected. They were mostly old-timers, and some of them had worked in the office long enough to know that some funny PR business had gone on at the time of the Mann Gulch fire. Most of the Forest Service employees who had a corner of an eye on me belonged to that element in most PR offices who are never important enough to be trusted with any of the organization's real secrets—they just know genetically that big organizations have shady secrets (that's why they are big). Also genetically they like shady secrets and genetically they like to protect shady secrets but have none of their own. I gather that government organizations nearly always have this unorganized minority of Keepers of Unkept Secrets, and one of these, I was told, went so far as to write a letter to be read at a meeting of the staff of the regional forester reporting that I was making suspicious visits to Mann Gulch and reportedly and suspiciously arranging to bring back with me to Mann Gulch the two survivors of the fire. According to my source of information, after the letter was read the regional forester went right on with the business at hand as if nothing had interrupted him. And as far as I know, nothing had.

On the other hand, many of the men in the Forest Service whose main job is fire control are unhistorical for fairly good reasons. There have been millions of forest fires in the past; the Indians even set them in the autumn to improve the pasture next spring. What firefighters want to know is the fire danger rating for today, and as for me, I am not as important to them as the fuel moisture content for that afternoon. They are tough guys and I like them and get along with them, although I am careful about telling them stories of the olden days when at times it took a week or more to assemble a crew in Butte, transfer them to the end of the branch railroad line going up the Bitterroot, and then walk them forty or fifty miles across the Bitterroot divide to get them to a fire on the Selway River in Idaho. I tried to be careful and meek and not end any such stories with a general observation such as "Fires got very big then and were hard to fight." Firefighters prefer to believe that no one before them has ever been on a big fire.

Although it took more years than I had expected to get the information I wanted about the Mann Gulch fire, I know of only a very few instances where my difficulties were consciously made more difficult. To reassemble what was left of this fire, I needed the help of many more present members of the Forest Service than I can acknowledge in the course of this story, women as well as men. You must always remember the women, even if you are pursuing a forest fire, especially if you are pursuing it in a big institution. The new age for women had not yet worked its way through the walls of the Forest Service; still maybe it had a little. The women I worked with were in charge of the documents, the maps, and the photographs, and without them there would have been practically no illustrations in this book, or, for that matter, practically nothing to illustrate. Their attitude toward me was possibly a combination of women's traditional attitude toward men touched by an added breath of confidence in themselves coming from the new. They were certainly good and they knew it. When I entered their offices, whether in Washington or Missoula, they looked up and seemed to say, fusing two worlds. "Here's a man with a problem. What can we do to help him?"

Since I started to write this story I have seen women start taking over some of the toughest jobs in the Forest Service. I didn't believe I would ever see it, but now there are even a few women Smokejumpers. I can bear witness. One of them lives just a few blocks from me in Chicago. Her father is a faculty member of the University of Chicago—he is a distinguished statistician and one of the best amateur actors I have ever seen. She is a remarkable young woman—attractive, brainy, and tough. They tell me at the Missoula base for Smokejumpers where she is stationed that she is up there with the rest of her crew (which means men) in the training races run in full jumping gear or hard-hat equipment.

Several times in this story of the Mann Gulch fire I have tried to find places where it would be permissible to say that the story of finding the tragedy of the Mann Gulch fire has been different from the tragedy of the Mann Gulch fire. Tragedy is the most demanding of all literary forms. Tragedy never lets you get far away from tragedy, but I do not want you to think I spent ten years in sustained pain writing what I wanted to write about the Mann Gulch fire. A lot of good things happened along the way. Some things got better, and I met a lot of good people, some of them as good as they come.

It's hard to say when the pleasures and pains of writing start and end. They certainly start before writing does, and they seem to continue for some time afterwards. I met Bud Moore before I started to write, and he has become one of my closest friends. He and I soon discovered that both of us had worked in the Lochsa when we were boys and when the Lochsa was thought to be accessible only to the best men in the woods. Lewis and Clark had nearly starved there. Running into somebody who has worked in the Lochsa in the early part of the century is something like running into a buddy of yours who served on the battleship *Missouri* in World War II at the time General MacArthur was on it. Those of us who worked on the Lochsa early in this century regard ourselves as set apart from other woodsmen and our other countrymen in general.

I had started writing this story before I met Laird Robinson, but was still heavy in research and was wandering around the Smokejumper base looking for any odd items I might have overlooked. Laird had been a foreman in the Smokejumpers and had injured himself landing on a fire and twice had tried a comeback but finally had to accept he was through as a jumper. He had been made a temporary guide at the Smokejumper base until they got him placed in a line of work that would lead him toward the top. He was in his early thirties and in the woods could do anything, and among other things he wanted to know more about the Mann Gulch fire. He put a high premium on friendship, and we soon were close friends and doing a lot of our digging into Mann Gulch together, as you will see from the course of this story. It is a great privilege to possess the friendship of a young man who is as good or better than you at what you intended to be when you were his age just before you changed directions—all the way from the woods to the classroom. It is as if old age fortuitously had enriched your life by letting you live two lives, the life you finally chose to live and a working copy of the one you started out to live.

I tried to be careful that our friendship did not endanger Laird professionally, and there were times when it seemed that it might. We were well along in our investigations when evidence appeared suggesting that Rumsey and Sallee had been persuaded by the Forest Service's investigator to change their testimony regarding the course of the fire at its critical stage. Persuading a witness to change his testimony to what he did not believe to be true was to me a lot more serious charge than scattering or burying documents that might bear on the threat of a lawsuit. So when I knew that I would have to try to find this investigator if he was still alive, I told Laird, "If you don't like the way this thing is headed now, just step off it before you get hurt. I can see it might hurt you, but there's no bravery in it for me because it can't hurt me."

Laird said to me, "Forget it. On my private list, friendship is highest." He said, "Anyway don't worry about me. The Forest Service and I can take care of ourselves."

So one of the pleasures of writing this story has been listening to the talk of first-class woodsmen, some old and some young.

Interview with

. . . .

Norman Maclean

*In 1986 Maclean was interviewed at his Seeley Lake cabin by
writer and teacher Nicholas O'Connell for* At the Field's End:
Interviews with Twenty-two Pacific Northwest Writers
*(University of Washington Press, 1998). The interview shows
a relaxed and candid Maclean, speaking about his two lives
and geographies, his published book and work in progress, his
father and brother, and his work habits. Though he occasionally
repeats metaphors and anecdotes from his published works, the
interview takes us close to Maclean's heart and mind and voice.*

When did you start fly-fishing?

I was about six when we came to Montana, and almost immediately we
started going on these vacations and my father started teaching me to fly-fish.
My father was a Presbyterian minister and always had at least a month off in
the summer. We would camp out for a month on some big river, the Bitterroot
or the Blackfoot.

Do you still fly-fish?

No, I don't. I hope that's a temporary answer. A couple of years ago I hurt
my hip and I haven't been able to work very well since then. I quit fishing but
I'm getting better. I hope I'll still be able to fish a little before I quit for good.
It's hard though. I don't think I'll ever be very good at it again. I've lost my
sense of balance, and I can't stand up on those big rocks and I can't fish that
big hard water. And that's the only fishing I like to do, fishing the big rivers.
If you want big fish, you fish big water.

I miss it a lot. I suppose I get some second-hand pleasure by writing
about it.

What has fly-fishing taught you about the nature of grace?

It's taught me many, many things about grace. I think it's one of the most
graceful things an individual can do out in the woods. It's very difficult art to
master. My father thought it had the grace of eternal salvation in it.

Reprinted from Nicholas O'Connell, ed., *At the Field's End: Interviews with Twenty-two Pacific Northwest Writers* (Seattle: University of Washington Press, 1987, 1998), 211–29.

In "A River Runs Through It," you wrote, "Good things come by grace, grace comes by art and art does not come easy." Is that true of writing?

Oh, yes. It's conceivable that someone could find it smirky and pleasurable on some kind of level, but I think it's a highly disciplined art. It's costly. You have to give up a lot of yourself to do it well. It's like anything you do that's rather beautiful. Of course some people can do it seemingly by genes and birth, but I don't think nearly as often as one would think. I think it always entails terrific self-discipline.

Why did you start writing fiction so late in life?

I can't answer that, but I'll make a couple of stabs. There will be a certain amount of truth to them, but no one ever knows why he tries something big in life.

One stab is that in the literary profession, which was my life profession, it was always said that no one began serious writing late in life. That was kind of a challenge. I thought, "As soon as I retire, I've got some serious things I'd like to write, and I think I know enough about writing to do them well. We'll see how they come out."

Just the fact that you would ask me such a question is part of the reason why I started. I wanted to answer it. But it must have been deeper than just showing off.

When you teach literature, you're so close to it, and yet in some ways so far. If you don't have a lot of extra energy, you don't have time to do what a lot of teachers claim they always want to do but seldom do, and that is both write and teach. I suppose I said it too, but being Scotch I was thick-headed and so I tried it.

It's very costly to start writing when you're so old as I am. You don't have any of the daily discipline built up. Some writers get up every morning and it's like shaving to them. They can do it without thinking.

In "A River Runs Through It," you talked about God's rhythms. I wondered what you meant by that.

One of my fascinations about my own life is that every now and then I see a thing that unravels as if an artist had made it. It has a beautiful design and shape and rhythm. I don't go so far as some of my friends, who think that their whole life has been one great design. When I look back on my life I don't see it as a design to an end. What I do see is that in my life there have been a fair number of moments which appear almost as if an artist had made them. Wordsworth, who affected me a great deal, had this theory about what he calls "spots of time" that seem almost divinely shaped. When I look back on my own life, it is a series of very disconnected spots of time. My stories are those spots of time.

Did you feel a real need to write about these spots of time?

I've given up everything to write them. I'm now getting so old I don't know whether I can write much more. I knew when I started, of course, that starting so late I wouldn't get much done, but I hoped to get a few things done very well. It's been very costly, though, and I don't know whether I would recommend it. I've sacrificed friends. I've lived alone. I work on a seven-day-a-week schedule. I get up at six or six-thirty every morning. I don't even go fishing up here any more.

When you're this old, you can't rely on genius pure and undefiled. You've got to introduce the advantages of being old and knowing how to be self-disciplined. You can do a lot of things because you can do what the young can't do, you can make yourself do it. And not only today or tomorrow, but for as long as it takes to do it. So it's a substitute, alas maybe not a very good one, for youth and genius and pure gift. And it can do a lot of things, but it's very, very costly. Sometimes I wish that when I retired I'd just gone off to Alaska or Scotland and played croquet on the lawn.

Do you want to write many other things?

I'm too realistic to entertain such thoughts. Even when I began, which was right after I retired, I knew I could never become a great writer, if for no other reason than I didn't have time. When I started, I agreed to myself that I would consider I'd accomplished my mission if I wrote several substantial things well. And I haven't lost that sense of reality; in fact it deepens as I grow older and see I was right.

I am now trying to finish a second long story based upon a tragic forest fire. I've been on that for some years, and I hope within the next six or seven months to have it completed. But I have been hoping that for some years now. I'm being enticed into making a movie of "A River Runs Through It." If I do those two fairly big things, then I won't try anything very big again.

Do you write every morning?

I don't write every morning, but I keep my writing schedule. I'm the only one who keeps me alive now. I don't have a family living with me any more. I have two homes, here and Chicago. I have a lot of accounting and just plain housework to keep both those places going.

And even when you just make a small success, there are many people who want to see you. So I spend more time than I should seeing people and writing letters. I still go on four to six talking tours each year.

Your book has only three stories in it, but because they're so well written, it's made you more renowned than writers with four or five novels.

Yes, I would grant that, but there are probably a variety of reasons for that. To some at least, the book is a kind of model of how to begin a story and how to end a story, and it is taught as such. When people are good enough, they try to teach it as an example of prose rhythms. It has a special appeal to teachers of writing, and of course it has a great appeal to fly-fishermen, for many of the same reasons: it seems expert at what it is doing. I've had biologists write me and tell me it's the best manual on fly-fishing ever written.

Did you enjoy writing it?

I don't know how to answer that. Writing is painfully difficult at times, and other times I feel like I have a mastery over what I'm trying to do, and of course there's no greater pleasure than that. But when you feel that words still stand between you and what you want to say, then it's a very unhappy business.

Where did you learn to tell stories?

When I was young in the West, most of us thought we were storytellers. And of course we all worshipped Charlie Russell, partly for his painting, but also because he was a wonderful storyteller. I feel I learned as much about storytelling from him as I did from Mark Twain or Wordsworth or any professional writer. The tradition behind that of course was the old cowboy tradition—coming into town with a paycheck, putting up in a hotel, and sitting around with a half a dozen other guys trying to out-tell each other in stories. Whoever was voted as telling the best story had all his expenses paid for the weekend.

The storytellers' tradition is a very, very deep one in the West. It probably doesn't exist very much any more, but then you don't have the great sources of stories. You don't have bunkhouses for loggers and cowpunchers any more. They live in town with families. They don't sit around at night and tell lies to each other. So part of it has been lost.

I learned as much, even technically, about storytelling from Charlie Russell's stories as I did, say, from Hemingway. He [Russell] was still alive and kicking until I was in my twenties. He was an idol of Montana, much more so than now. He's an idol now of course, too, but then we worshipped him, and with good cause. His stories are only two to ten pages long, but if you want to learn how to handle action economically and just have every sentence jumping with stuff, take a look at him. Marvelous storyteller.

A volume of his called *Trails Plowed Under* is just a miraculous piece of narration. Good title, isn't it? That title pervades not only his paintings, but all of his stories. All the time he was writing and painting he had this feeling that "the West that I knew is gone." There's always a nostalgia hanging over his paintings and stories.

When you were writing your stories, how did they change as you turned them into fiction?

They changed long before I started writing them. I'm not sure that after a few years I could tell what happened from what I say happened, which is fortunate if you want to be a storyteller. I had a drenching of storytelling in all the years when I was in the Forest Service and logging camps, and so it's easier for me to tell a story about what happened than telling it exactly as it happened. They became stories long before I told them.

Did you have to make them longer when you wrote them down?

No. From the time my father gave me my first lessons in writing to the end of my training in writing, I always had teachers whose chief criterion was literary economy—use of the fewest words possible.

When you were writing your stories, did you write them down all at once, or bit by bit?

I know pretty well ahead of time what I'm going to do in the whole story, and often I come home after going for a walk in the afternoon and take a bath before dinner; in the bathtub I sit in the hot water till it gets cool, trying to figure out what I'm going write the next day. The next day I'm concerned with saying it. That's probably highly individual. A lot of guys when they sit down don't know where they're going. They even use the act of writing to make them find out what they're going to write about.

Do you work over the stuff that you've written a number of times?

Yes, three or four times.

Sentence by sentence, paragraph by paragraph?

I suppose so, but that would vary. I'm a great believer in the power of the paragraph. I can't say that I always write by paragraphs, but I often do. I think that paragraphs should have a little plot, should lead you into something strange and different, tie the knot in the middle, and at the end do a little surprise and then also prepare you for the next paragraph.

Why did you choose to write those particular stories?

The title story, "A River Runs Through It," was the big tragedy of our family, my brother's character and his death. He had a very loving family, but independent and fighters. We were guys who, since the world was hostile to us, depended heavily upon the support and the love of our family. That tends often to be the case with guys that live a hostile life outside.

There was our family which meant so much to us, and there was my brother who was a street fighter, a tough guy who lived outside the mores of a preacher's family. We all loved him and stood by him, but we couldn't help him. We tried but we couldn't. There were times when we didn't know whether he needed help. That was all and he was killed. I slowly came to feel that it would never end for me unless I wrote it.

The others? Well, they're all spots of time. Spots of time become my stories. You get that very openly in the Forest Service story. That's the plot. They go out and it's spring, and the things that they do and their order are determined by the job. There's no human preference indicated. The first thing you did was clear out the trails from the winter, dead trees and all that fallen-down stuff. Then you made some new trails, then pretty soon fire season came and you fought fires. It was determined by the seasons and the nature of the job.

The plot starts that way and then things begin to happen in such a way that human decisions are determining and changing this natural order of things. It's the change in the causes that order the events which is the story.

I'd had a good training when I was young in the woods. My father didn't allow me to go to school, kept me home for many years until the juvenile officers got me, and as a result I had to work in the morning, but the afternoons were mine. All the guys my age were in school, so I went out in the woods alone. I became very good in the woods when I was very young. I trained myself, both in the logging camps and in the sawmills. I was going to know the wood business from the woods to board feet.

When World War I came along they were looking for young guys or old men to take the place of the foresters who were getting grabbed up as soldiers. So I was in the Forest Service when I was fourteen. And it became a very important part of my life. I almost went into it; I thought until I was almost thirty that I was going to go into the Forest Service as a life profession.

All these things are important to me: my family, the years I spent in the logging camps, the years I spent in the Forest Service.

Why are these stories about your life in Montana, rather than about teaching in Chicago?

I've written many things about Chicago and teaching, some of my best things in articles, stories, talks, discussions about teaching. I wrote a story about Albert Michelson, who measured the speed of light and was the first American scientist to win the Nobel Prize. Strangely, when I was quite young I came to know him intimately. I was just a kid from Montana, a half-assed graduate student and teacher in English, and I was knocking around with this guy who was regarded as one of our two greatest scientists (Einstein being the other). Now I suppose Nobel Prize winners are a dime a dozen, but in those days we had only two in the whole country; he was one of them, and Theodore Roosevelt was the other. I was very touched, as a young boy from Montana, to be trusted with the acquaintanceship of such an outstanding, strange and gifted man. I think my story about him is one of the best things I ever wrote.

Did anyone help you in editing the stories in A River Runs Through It?

I'm a loner in respect to writing. First I should go back to my origins. My schooling was lonely. My father taught me himself, and the prime thing he taught me was writing. I studied by myself and reported to my father three times every morning. I was brought up as a lonely kid and that's continued. Now that everybody has gone off to town after Labor Day and there's nobody on this side of the lake, I'm just coming into my own here. That's the way I am, and it's pervaded my writing.

Having said that, though, I always try to turn, somewhere short of publication, to four or five friends to read over the manuscript. Two or three are from the University of Chicago, and then the first woman full professor at Yale in the English Department, who was a student of mine in her day. She's a great critic. Then three or four from the woods.

I have this three-fold cadre of critics. I give it to them before it becomes a manuscript to be submitted. I listen a great deal to what they say. They're tender with me, but they know me from a long, long time back and I suppose they know what to say and what's useless to say.

What did your father have you read when he was teaching you?

I think the most important thing was what he read out loud to us. He was a minister, and every morning after breakfast we had what was called family worship. And family worship consisted of his reading to us. We'd all sit with our breakfast chairs pulled back from the table and he would read to us from the Bible or from some religious poet. He was a very good reader, and if he had any faults as a reader it was that he was kind of excessive, as preachers often are. But that was very good for me because in doing that, he would bring out the rhythms of the Bible. That reading instilled in me this great love of rhythm in language.

Now when I teach poetry or prose I can teach it quite analytically. When I was at Stanford, I had a long session analyzing prose rhythms with their advanced creative writing class. That's not easy to do, partly because the rule of prose rhythms is that you better not have them show very much. And most of the time you better not have them show at all. Any time you or I or anybody else who has any taste at all suspects that the writer's trying to write pretty, then he's dead. That guy is just as dead as a dead snake.

If you are a writer whose prose falls into rhythm you have to be very, very careful. Most of the time you just approach rhythms and then drift away from them, and then drift back towards them, not really going into any rhythmical passages except as the tension mounts, as the passion increases.

If you look at the last page of "A River Runs Through It," you can scan it as if it were written in accentual rhythm. But when you're on the sand bar with the whore and that goddamn brother-in-law of mine, you don't hear any rhythms although they're there. They're very faint. They come close to rhythm and then drift out. My ordinary style is better than ordinary speech, but not so much you would notice it.

In that story, were you more conscious of the differences in rhythms?

It depends upon the kind of emotional level you're operating on. "A River Runs Through It" is my notion of high, modern tragedy. It's tragedy and deep feeling, and I tried to write about how men and women do things with great skill and loving kindness, with their hands and their hearts, both at the same time. Fishing is such an example. But rhythm is there even when I stop and tell you how you put hobnails in a shoe and why you put them where you put them, and how you pack a horse. I like to tell you about things that men and women can do with their hands that are wonderful. I write about them very carefully. All the time I'm on a level above ordinary speech because what I'm trying to tell you is above ordinary speech. I'm trying to tell you how you do things expertly. When I do that, the language goes up a little bit.

And certainly when you come to the great tragic moments, when you're just pouring out your heart, you don't have to worry about your rhythms; they'll be there if you're at all a rhythmic person.

So the ear has a great deal to do with your writing?

Yes. It goes along with the art. The great fly-tier from Livingston, Dan Bailey, said, "The bookshelves are full of books on how to fish, but only Maclean tells you how it *feels* to fish."

Could these stories have been set anyplace other than Montana?

Montana is very dear to me. You talk about a man without a country, but I'm a man with two countries. Montana's always been one, no matter where the other one is.

So you wrote the stories because the area was important to you?

It's my homeland. I love it, I've always loved it and I always will. When I tell my doctor I'm getting old, that I better close up that place in Montana, that it's getting too tough for me to run, he says, "If you do, Norman, you'll die." So here I am.

Why was it important that you get every detail of those stories correct?

Again, I could answer "because my father told me so." But I'll jump to the other extreme. If you are interested at all, as I told you I was, in whether there are designs and shapes in the passage of events, then design is very important to you. It's very important whether the design or shape or form of a series of events is really in the thing or whether it's something that you, the artist, have manufactured. It's important to me that there is a design and shape to quite a few things that we do in our life. So I'm very, very careful. I don't want to be cheating; I want to get the design as exactly as I can, in itself, not from me.

So you see it as something outside of yourself?

I want to. I'm not always able to. I have to admit that I'm not always sure there is a design and shape to things. Sometimes I think I must be the cause of the designs of things, but I don't really think that is always true. I think that there have been designs and shapes in my life, and I've been almost apart from them. I was a character of them, but I wasn't the author of them.

So in what sense are your stories true? Do you tell them exactly the way they happened?

No, I always allow myself a literary latitude. Often things don't happen fast enough in life. Literature can condense them. I wrote the story on the Forest Service as if it happened all in one summer. But it happened in two or three summers. I didn't consider that a violation at all.

Everything in the story happened to me in the Bitterroots. In the story I have a big fight. The fight was actually in a Chinese restaurant, but in the story I had it in the Oxford, a restaurant and gambling joint in Missoula. It's been there for sixty or seventy years and a lot of us Missoula guys were brought up in there. And they said, "God, how could you put the Oxford up there in Hamilton?" I don't think it made much difference in terms of the story. I felt at home in the Oxford, and I didn't feel at home in Chinese restaurants. Little things like that, mostly for the sake of hastening the story on, of sharpening it.

But you're still true to the spirit of the stories?

I hope so. As I told you, I'm engaged now with several others in trying to make a script out of "A River Runs Through It."

They're always saying, "You make it too tragic. A movie audience, unlike a literary audience, won't accept that much tragedy." It's just too bad if they won't. I didn't ask to write this script. It wasn't my idea. I'm unbending about this, just totally unbending. I'm not going to compromise.

How was your education in Montana different from the one you got back East?

It wasn't a very good education. In 1920 when I was going to go to college neither my father nor I had a very high opinion of the University of Montana. The state was still dominated by the Anaconda Copper Mining Company [ACM]. You had to watch what you said about them and about politics. They owned the whole state and they'd just crush you out of existence if they didn't like you.

At the time I worshipped the chairman of the English Department at the University of Montana. His name was H. G. Merriam. The ACM was out to get him night and day, but never did. He came to be recognized as a kind of martyr, sacred to the history of Montana.

I wanted no part of being a sycophant for rich companies, and the education was not very good at the time. Now I think both state universities in Montana are fine schools.

What sorts of things did you learn in the woods as compared to the things you learned in school?

I learned what little math and science I know, in surveying. The only branch of mathematics I remember anything at all about is trigonometry, the thing that we needed in surveying. In respect to biology, I learned a good deal of what I know in a very wonderful kind of way—through direct observation. I suppose fishing, as much as anything, helped me, the close observation about what fly should be used. In a backwoods kind of homey way we were good naturalists. Although home-spun observation has big gaping holes in it, it also has rich parts that you hardly get anymore. If you didn't know a caddis fly when you saw one, and you didn't know whether they spawned in shallow water or deep, you just weren't going to get any fish on certain days. And you developed from that a sense of their beauty. It's odd, but insects are an important part of life to me.

Did you have a hard time getting adjusted to the East Coast?

I suppose so. I don't know if I ever did get really adjusted. But they were very kind to me. I think the East is very different from what most Westerners think it is, at least the Westerners of my time. They thought of the Easterners as socialized jerks, snooty, kind of removed from life.

I didn't find that at all. They were very kind to me. They were very interested in me, much more so then than now probably, because I was one of
the early guys from the West going back East. So I was supposedly kind of
an oddity from the high brush. But they were better than I ever thought they
would be.

Why did you come back to Montana?

Because I didn't want ever to leave, and never left. Very, very early I formed
this rough outline in my mind of this life I have led. I love Montana with almost
a passion, but I saw I couldn't live here really if I was going to be a teacher;
I'd have to be degraded and submit to views that I couldn't accept. I felt that
this was imposed upon us from the outside—that wasn't our true nature. I
tried to figure out a way to continue this two-world thing that I had begun by
going East.

And that's probably the chief reason that I quit teaching and then went
back to it. I figured teaching probably was the only way I could live in the two
worlds. I could teach in the East, and that would give me a chance to come
back a fair number of summers and retain a permanent footing in a homeland
that I knew so well. I thought that out as I was doing it. I just didn't stumble
on the life I have lived.

Did you come to like Chicago?

I love Chicago. My wife was very wonderful in helping me come to feel that.
I was very provincial in a lot of ways. She was gay and loved life wherever she
lived. She really worked me over in our early years in Chicago. I was insolent
and provincial about that city. She made me see how beautiful it was, made me
see the geometric and industrial and architectural beauty.

You can't look for Montana everywhere. There are all kinds of things that
you should be looking for. There's no architectural beauty in any big city that
equals the modern architectural beauty or the industrial beauty of Chicago.
You see this great big crane, a giant in the sky, picking up things as gracefully
as a woman picks up a child. So that's the way our early married life went. She
tried to get me to see many kinds of beauties.

In a lot of ways I think that helped me immensely in writing about Montana. I think many Montana stories are limited by being too provincial. They're
about roundups and cattle rustlers and whatnot. That isn't even up-to-date.

I was concerned when I wrote about Montana to write with great accuracy about how it really was, but at the same time to show fundamental concerns with universal problems of existence: here is a member of a family who

doesn't always abide by the rules and regulations of his society, and he's living something of an underground life and he's getting desperate about it and he needs help. Can't we do something to help him? And you can't find anything that will help him.

I received over 100 letters about that story, saying, "I have a brother just like that, and I can't find anything to do that will help him." From New York City, Jewish girls in New York City.

Seeing the kinds of problems that run through the hearts of sensitive and intelligent people, no matter where they are, will give an enrichment and enlargement to those problems present in any region.

Chicago is very much a home to me, too. I probably couldn't do without either home; my life depends on both of them. I don't feel that because I love both places I'm living the life of a schizophrenic. I feel that they work for each other. I can see more about each one, because of the other.

Why do you like living in the mountains so much?

There's something about mountains that does strange things to us mountain people. We were brought up in the mountains and always looked at people from the plains as deformed. We took mountains to be the natural state of affairs. I still do. I look at plains and I think, "Christ Almighty, once there were mountains here and then something came along and knocked them over. How could something like this be a natural product of the universe?"

I remember the first time I got disabused of that. When I was up here one summer at Seeley Lake, an old farmer from the Dakotas came out here to visit. He'd never seen the mountains before. This poor old bastard had been living out on the flat plains all his life, hadn't really seen any good country. He lasted about two or three days here before he hurried back home. He was terrified of the mountains. He was afraid they were going to fall on top of him and kill him. As he hurriedly left, we were stumped. We thought we were doing him a favor showing him this country.

Did the stories in A River Runs Through It *help connect your life in Montana with your life in Chicago?*

Often the way things that seem disparate and different are unified is by art and beauty. When you see it and are moved by it, you are about as close as you can get to putting the whole shebang together. Somewhere it says all things merge into one and a river runs through it.

Is there a prejudice among East Coast publishers against Western stories?

Not until recently have the Western writers ever gotten a good break from the publishers in New York. I feel that deeply. If I heard that one of the New York publishers was coming across Grizzly Basin I'd be out there and shoot him on sight. They are a filthy bunch.

I had the good fortune of a dream coming true. I'm sure every rejected writer must dream of a time when he's written something that was rejected which turns out to be quite successful, so that all the publishers who rejected him are now coming around and kissing his ass at high noon, and he can tell them where to go.

Alfred A. Knopf, probably the most celebrated of all publishing companies in this country, rejected *A River Runs Through It*. Two or three years after it was rejected, I got a letter from an editor at Alfred A. Knopf asking me if Alfred A. Knopf couldn't have the privilege of getting first crack at my next novel.

Well, well, well. I don't know how this ever happened, but this fell right into my hands. So I wrote a letter. It's probably one of the best things I ever wrote. I understand it's on the wall of several newspapers in the country. I can remember the last paragraph:

"If it should ever happen that the world comes to a place when Alfred A. Knopf is the only publishing company left and I am the only author, then that will be the end of the world of books."

I really told those bastards off. What a pleasure! What a pleasure! Right into my hands! Probably the only dream I ever had in life that came completely true.

Have your stories done anything to change the prejudices against Western stories?

I hope so, but a change like that has to be very broad. You talk about New York publishers, and in a way there is no such thing; there's this bastard and that bastard. It takes a lot of things to affect a good many of them. It may be that the most important thing is not that they're accepting more Western writing, but that Western writers are getting broader-based themselves, more generally interesting and more generally concerned about problems of mankind instead of just cattle rustling.

It's a much healthier situation now. Not very much happened for many years, but now things are happening. You have a guy like Ivan Doig writing. I don't care how much of a New Yorker you are, you better realize you're reading a helluva good writer when you read Ivan Doig.

What was the reaction to A River Runs Through It back East?

There were four or five New York publishers who turned it down. On the other hand, New York reviewers, from the very beginning, have thought very highly of it. *Publishers Weekly* was very warm-hearted about it. There were probably 600 reviews of it, and I think I read only one poor review. Reviewers consistently have been very warm-hearted, irrespective of the reason. So I have no kick about reviewers.

Who were some of the writers that you've learned from?

The Bible. Wordsworth. Very early, through my father, Wordsworth became a favorite poet of mine. He's influenced my life a great deal. When I was in the woods I always carried a copy of his selected poems with me. I think poets have influenced me more than prose writers. Gerard Manley Hopkins has influenced my poetical side, and I think some of it comes out in my prose. I like his passion. I think Browning is the best English poet after Shakespeare. I learned a tremendous amount from him about how to handle dramatic dialogue, dramatic speech and character.

Same way about Frost, who had a lot of influence on me. He was an occasional teacher at Dartmouth when I was there, so I had the privilege of being in classes that he taught. I liked him even before I went to Dartmouth. He talked straight to you, and often poetry was there, or something close to it.

What did Frost teach?

Creative writing. We had evening classes in a great big basement room with a wonderful fireplace in it. He'd just walk in front of the fireplace in circles. As a teacher he was like a poet: he composed nothing but monologues. Nobody ever stopped him.

How about Hemingway?

Hemingway was an idol of mine for a while, as he was for practically all of us of that generation. He and I were about the same age. Unlike a lot of people who thought a lot of Hemingway, I still think a great deal of him. Now Hemingway is in disrepute as a kind of fake macho guy. I realized that he did put on kind of a show, but on the other hand I don't see how you could be a real American writer unless you knew Hemingway well, and had learned a great deal from him. He was a master of dialogue of a certain kind, that very tight crisp kind. He was a master in handling action, too. He was almost as good as Charlie Russell. In a page or even a paragraph he could tell you the most complicated action. So I don't fall into the school of so-called modern critics who dislike Hemingway.

According to The Westminster Shorter Catechism, *which you mention in "A River Runs Through It," man's chief end is to glorify God and enjoy him forever. Did writing the stories help you to do that?*

I don't know whether I can answer that. I suppose that in any conventional sense I'm a religious agnostic. There are things that make me feel a lot better.

I don't particularly find them in a church. I find them in the woods, and in wonderful people. I suppose they're my religion.

I feel I have company about me when I'm alone in the woods. I feel they're beautiful. They're a kind of religion to me. My dearest friends are also beautiful. My wife was an infinitely beautiful thing. I certainly feel that there are men and women whom I have known and still know who are really above what one could think was humanly possible. They and the mountains are for me "what passeth human understanding."

Selected Letters

Letters to Robert M. Utley,

....

1955–1979

....

Maclean first contacted Robert M. Utley in May 1955, querying him about his master's degree thesis on George Custer. That contact led to a friendship, conducted mostly via mail, that lasted about a quarter of a century. When Maclean talked Utley into collaborating with him for an article about Edward S. Luce (included earlier in this volume), he described their collaboration as "a mail-order marriage." Maclean acted as writing tutor to the young Utley, and the up-and-coming western historian acknowledged Maclean's influence on his second book, The Last Days of the Sioux Nation *(1963). The correspondence also reveals Maclean wrestling with his Custer manuscript, eventually abandoning it and turning to writing "reminiscent stories." Utley has had a distinguished career as a National Park Service historian, publishing over fifteen books, including, most recently,* Lone Star Lawmen: The Second Century of the Texas Rangers *(2007). Maclean was a proud and loyal friend, lauding every new book and writing to him once in the 1970s, "You knew how to write a book before you knew how to write."*

May 11, 1955
Dear Lt. Utley:

Jim Hutchins[1] of Columbus tells me that I ought to write you about one of my interests in the Custer story—namely, the use of Custer and the Battle in "literature" from 1876 to the present. I am using "literature" in a very broad sense to include not only poems, dramas, novels, but radio and televisions scripts, etc. (and painting and music as well). Jim says you wrote your

1. One of the gang of "Custer Hill" sleuths, James S. Hutchins was one of the most prominent Custer historians of the mid-twentieth century. He authored several studies, including *The Army and Navy Journal on the Battle of the Little Bighorn and Related Matters, 1876–1881*; *Boots and Saddles at the Little Bighorn*; and *The Papers of Edward S. Curtis Relating to Custer's Last Stand*. This and other annotations to the letters are by the volume editor.

dissertation[2] on this subject or on one closely allied to it but he wasn't sure to what university you submitted it (he thought it was the University of Indiana). Is it on file in some university library, for, if so, I probably can get it through the inter-library exchange and not put you to any bother? If it isn't publicly obtainable I hope that you are planning to publish it soon (or at least a condensed version of it). Let me know if you have any such plans. [. . .]

Very sincerely yours,
Norman Maclean

May 21, 1955
Dear Bob,

Thanks for your good letter. I've already sent for the thesis. $3.75 for shipping charges! God damn, it better be good at that price.

Some of our interests must coincide, but I doubt if they are identical. If they are, I'll tell you after reading the thesis. I'll tell myself first, though. I think I am going to do something on Custer, but I'm not going to do anything that has been done or is in the process of being done. For me to spend 4 or 5 years of my life on Custer is to take a long leave of absence from English scholarship. I will not do so, you may be sure, unless I am convinced that I can do something on Custer that is worthwhile and different. I think that I come to Custer and the Battle with a somewhat different background, training and set of interests from those who have worked on him so far. But I may be wrong in thinking this way, and if I am I'll go on about my business—the sooner the quicker.

If you get to Chicago before the end of June, be sure to let me know. I'll be out in Montana for the summer—I have a cabin on a lake near Missoula, but I'll be back again in September. Don't go through without looking me up.

I'll write you about that $3.75 after reading the thesis.

Sincerely,
Norman Maclean

Seeley Lake, Montana
July 16, 1955
Dear Bob:

I finally caught up with your letter, or maybe it was the other way around, but in any case I was mighty glad to get it. Thanks, Bob, for the permission to

2. In fact, it was a thesis, titled "The Custer Controversy," submitted for Utley's master's degree in 1952 from Indiana University.

microfilm your thesis, and I was very interested in your plans to expand it. The chapter on the 20th-century historians, of course, is a "must" and ought to be very interesting. [. . .] [T]his bunch interests me very much, and I hope that you won't be too long delayed in getting your chapter on them in shape.

In respect to your proposed chapter on the evolution of the Battlefield, I think that I ought to give you an item of information that I picked up on the Hill when I was there several weeks ago. They have a new historian by the name of Rickey[3] and I was on his tail to get some jobs done around the Museum that would make the road to research easier, but he told me that he couldn't get to them for some time because his first *assignment* was to write a history of the Battlefield. I hope that this assignment doesn't interfere with your plans, but, lest it should, I think it a matter of simple decency to tell you about it. [. . .]

Like yourself, I've read part (about half) of *Custer's Luck*[4] and am not nearly so impressed as the professional reviewers. The reviews that I have read have gone all out, but the need for a book on Custer that at least seemed to be impartial was bigger than a barn door. Then, too, this was a fortunate year for Stewart, with the air full of Davy Crockett and the American legendary hero. On the other hand, the book has some power to it. Of what I've read so far, I like best the opening part which puts the Battle in the large context of that part of American history involving the Indian problem. He thus comes to the Battle with the power and interest of America behind it. [. . .] I thought Stewart's appraisal of the Indian problem was cool, realistic, and complex. (I ought to add, though, that I don't know Indian history well enough to be a good judge of it.) I also think that Stewart writes well. On the whole, he moves right along—not fancy, but clear and a good eye for colorful detail. At times he can't free himself of detail, as in the over-long chapter on "The Montana Column," but I'd rather have someone err even by being too detailed than not detailed enough.

Now, for the other side. (1) He's too long getting to Custer. (2) When he does, he doesn't seem to know the elementary facts. On p. 167 where he first describes him, he makes 3 or 4 mistakes, if I can trust my memory. [. . .] [I]n the Civil War, Custer wasn't "originally assigned to the Balloon Corps,"

3. Don Rickey Jr., a National Park Service historian and author of *Forty Miles a Day on Beans and Hay* (1963), a profile of the enlisted soldier's life ca. 1866–91.

4. Edgar I. Stewart's *Custer's Luck* (1955; repr., 1971), a detailed chronicle of the Seventh Cavalry's entire Little Bighorn campaign.

but to the 2d Cavalry, or am I too old to rely upon my memory? There are other statements in that short paragraph that I would challenge if I had my sources around, and on the opposite page (p. 166) Stewart gives 1872 as the date of the Stanley expedition and "the next year" (that would be 1873) as the date of the Black Hills expedition. I may only be revealing my ignorance, not Stewart's, but I'll confess to you that in my ignorance I've believed that the Stanley expedition was in 1873 and the Black Hills expedition in 1874 (with no campaign in 1875), and I've believed this for a long time. At this point, I decided I'd quit reading Stewart for a while, let my mind clear up, and do some work about the cabins for a week or so. [. . .]

Well, Bob, I didn't mean to unload so many pages on you, but Custer was never one for short marches. Write me if you get time.

Sincerely yours,

Norman Maclean

Seeley Lake, Montana,

Aug. 22, 1955

Dear Bob,

Here it is only a couple of days before I am going to break camp for the summer and I haven't answered your last good letter. There are a couple of other things I haven't done either. No work on Custer. Almost no work on a paper which is to be delivered at the Modern Language Assoc. at Xmas but which has to be written by the end of Sept. I don't know exactly what happened to the summer, but it was very nice. For a change, I was in good health. Also had good luck fishing with my boy, who is big enough to want to take overnight trips into the back country and fish glacier lakes where, as the freshman composition student would say, "the hand of many has never set foot." Anyway, I can't be very abject about not answering your letter sooner when all that I can say in the way of apology is that my health and the fishing have been good.

I'll spend a week at my wife's old home near Helena and while there I always spend a day at the State Historical Museum talking to Ross Toole,[5] the Director and Editor of the *Montana Magazine of History* (it has a new title which I forget) and Mike Kennedy, his chief assistant. I have known Ross and the

5. K. Ross Toole, editor of *Montana: The Magazine of Western History*, 1951–58, author of the influential *Montana: An Uncommon Land* (1959), and Andrew B. Hammond Professor of Western History at the University of Montana from 1965 to 1981.

whole Toole family for many years, and think that he is a remarkable fellow in every way, and I want him to know about you as one of the most promising young western historians on the horizon. I shall be sure to tell him about you in a general way, but have you anything in mind of article-size that you could work up during the next year and that might catch the eye of the editor of the *Montana Magazine*? For instance, I'm going to tell him about Hutchins' and Cartwright's[6] discovery of the site of the Bozeman Party fight of 1874 which I hope I can convince editor and authors could be made into an interesting article. I perhaps also should add that when I talked to Ross in early July I told him that the spring issue of 1956 should feature Custer and the Battle (because of the spring of 1876), and he agreed. So that might give you an idea. My guess is that a history of Custer historians would be too special in its interest for the *Magazine*, but maybe not. [. . .]

It occurs to me you may feel that since writing me a couple of letters you have been subject to a lot of paternal pushing around. This is probably the case. I can't help being what I have been for nearly the last 30 years, and in my defense I will say on that after a considerable amount of practice I have become pretty good at spotting young people with promise and at seeing they get tough training and some contacts and "breaks" to make the next steps easy.

Expect to see Kuhlman[7] on the way back and to spend a day on the Hill with the Luces.[8] You have probably heard by now that they are not leaving in November, but are to remain until next May. I wish, though, that they would stay until he was 70. There will never be another combination up there to match them—in dedication, ability, and color. I'll certainly agree with you that the Major is "unforgettable." My God, Bob, I just had an "idea" after writing this sentence. If the spring number (1956) of the *Montana Magazine* is going to feature Custer and the Battle, and if the Major is going to retire in May, 1956, shouldn't there be a little article on them? As a minimum, the

6. R. G. Cartwright, a Lead, South Dakota, high school athletic coach and "Custer Hill" sleuth who spent years studying and reconstructing the Little Bighorn Battle.

7. Charles Kuhlman, University of Nebraska historian and farmer near Billings, Montana, who became a Custer expert and, after sixteen years of research, published the influential *Legend into History* (1951), a benchmark study of the Battle of Little Bighorn.

8. "The Hill" refers to the "Last Stand" core—a sagebrush slope and enclosed cemetery—of Little Bighorn National Monument. Major Edward Luce and wife, Evelyn: he served for many years as superintendent of what then was still called Custer's Last Stand National Monument.

main facts and a hail and farewell—or, something more extensive, like a *New Yorker* profile, that would try to recreate them as people. Are you any good at characterization? Seemingly objective and light but underneath tender and deeply appreciative [. . .]

Sincerely,

Norman Maclean

November 3, 1955

Dear Bob,

I'm very sorry that I have been so long in answering you, but I don't feel that I have been responsible for the delay. I hope, therefore, that a complete explanation will take the place of an apology.

I saw Ross Toole and Mike Kennedy in Helena during the last week in August, as I told you I would. When I got back to Chicago on the 6th or 7th of September there was a pile of stuff I had to dig through, but I notice the date of my first letter to Ross is September 14 so I wasn't sitting on the oars. I wrote him because, as I told him, I have learned with a certain number of lumps on my head that what I thought I heard an editor say in conversation was not what he later remembered saying. So I put down in black-and-white my understanding of our conversational agreements back in Helena and I asked him and Mike to O.K. or alter them before I made any moves (including writing you). [. . .]

Concerning the tribute to the Major, they said that they recognized its appropriateness, but they also said that such a thing was hard to write and when it was not well written it was very poor reading matter. I agreed that such a thing could be very flat, and in making this admission I trapped myself. So they then said that they would include the tribute if I wrote it. I next told them about you and how you were the man for the job, and I hope and think I impressed them with your qualifications as one of the coming historians of the west, but I couldn't shake myself altogether free. The matter was left in this way: the tribute to the Major is my responsibility, whether it is written by me, or by someone else, or by me and someone else.

Bob, what about doing this thing together? I don't know yet what co-authorship would mean in detail, but I have the general feeling that together we could do a good job on the former "Sarg" of the 7th. In fact, a really good job. But if you feel co-authorship is impossible on a thing like this, will you try it yourself? [. . .]

The Major and Mrs. Luce were in Chicago recently and stayed with us—
the occasion being several awards and medals in his honor. [. . .]

Sincerely yours,

Norman Maclean

[P.S.] I think it is pretty hard to detach a chapter from a large narrative and
expect it to be self-sustained and to have all the power it has in its context. I
had the same problem when I came to publishing part of my thesis. I thought
I would pull out a chunk, make a few verbal changes at the beginning and end,
and be all set. Instead, it took me a whole winter—one of the hardest things
I ever wrote. In one way or another I had to move most of my thesis into the
one piece from it. On the other hand, page after page of your thesis suggests
interesting articles. [. . .]

November 15, 1955

Dear Bob:

Just a hasty note telling you how glad I am to learn that we are going to
work together in applying the Shinola to the Major. I'm sure we'll do a good
job on him. [. . .]

Mighty glad to hear that you're getting parts of your thesis into print. It's
a damn good thesis, Bob, as I have told you before, and don't be impressed
by my reservations concerning the self-sufficiency of its individual chapters. [. . .]

Sincerely yours,

Norman

January 4, 1956

Dear Bob:

[. . .] I guess the time has come for us to get down to business, so this
morning I scratched off a tentative outline [of the Luce profile]. Regard it
merely as a punching-bag, something to condition ourselves on.

[. . .] I wrote him several weeks ago and told him you and I were going to
do this article on him, and told him I would be asking him for lots of information. In his reply, he gave me his life in one coy paragraph. I realize this is
embarrassing for him, but he's got to sober down and give us several pages of
general vital statistics and also more detailed matter on particular points we
decide to develop. [. . .]

O.K., I'm willing to assume that it's my responsibility to write the first draft of the article. I am assuming, however, that we will not submit the article until it suits both of us. [. . .]

Sincerely,

Norman

May 9, 1956

Dear Bob:

As you know, I think your thesis is a dandy but I don't believe I should try to find some coy and involved way of telling you that I don't think this piece comes off.[9] Unlike your thesis, it is *narrative* history, its intention being to make acts and men of the past come to life in the present. I suppose that ultimately this is the most important kind of history, and yet it is the history most dependent upon something else—art, the creative imagination and skill in writing. That is, it is possible to be great as a historian of ideas, as several of my friends are, and not be able to create characters, feelings, and events. I hope you will become eminent in many kinds of history, but your present weakness is narrative.

Some of your major difficulties arise, I think, because you had an interesting narrative idea but one which would require a mastery of narrative technique to execute successfully. "The idea" was to present a whole campaign ending in a tragic climax, not by following it chronologically step by step, but by cutting into it at dramatic moments. In other words, by representing, as it were, only the stations of the cross. Such an attempt presents many problems, and I'll start with a technical one, what is called the problem of "exposition." By "exposition" I mean the problem of working into a narrative while it is still going ahead incidents and events that occurred outside or before the situation being narrated. Thus you jump from Ft. Abraham Lincoln to the mouth of the Rosebud, which is your second scene or station—but many events occurred between these two scenes that you judge the reader must know about for the narrative as a whole to be intelligible. The ancient dramatists had a chorus or prologue which told the audience what they needed to know to understand what he was about to see, and you also are without any technical devices to handle this problem. For instance, your scene at the mouth of the Rosebud begins by you, the author, retracing the route to tell the reader what he ought to know. With merely the problem of "exposition" in mind, you should look

9. Utley eventually titled this "piece" about two Cheyenne boys "Suicide Fight," and it was published in the American History Illustrated series (vol. 6, December 1971, 41–43).

again at the opening scenes of Hamlet and Othello and see how the needed information about the past is incorporated into (not dragged into) the drama
of the present.

A more serious difficulty arises from your intention of flashing the campaign to the reader in 27 pages—the problem of creating emotional interest
and unity. My guess is that the unity, given the shortness of the account, must
be primarily emotional rather than intellectual, since there is not space to give
at each important moment of decision the conflicting pieces of information
and misinformation, etc. needed to make the battle an intellectual puzzle, like
a mystery novel. The best you can hope to do is to keep the main lines of action
intellectually coherent, and this I think on the whole you have done. But there
is nothing the reader can attach his emotions to, nothing human he can iden-
tify himself with and follow throughout with mounting interest. It could have
been a single figure like Custer; or a human relationship, such as the tensions
between Custer, Reno,[10] and Benteen;[11] or a set of characters with a common
and unusual point of view—such as the non-coms. But it has to be something
human and continuous and unfolding. [. . .] When and if you look again at
the opening scenes of Hamlet and Othello, will you note how they are pointed
at Hamlet and Othello, even though *neither character has yet appeared*? They are
the characters for the reader to watch although they haven't been seen. One
of the crucial aspects of the art of narration, as well as the graphic arts, is the
art of proper focus.

Proportion or size is also important. Things are worth so much, and have
so much weight, and I think your scales are off at times. Thus you take 2 ¼
pages to describe the start of the expedition but less than a page to recreate
what to the reader is its eternal moment. [. . .]

I turn finally from some of the problems of *constructing* narrative to some
of the problems of *writing* it. Perhaps the most basic thing I have to say is that
there is a vast difference between *saying* or *stating* what an action, character,
or emotion is and *creating* that action, character or emotion. Thus you tend to
say that Custer "responded *icily*," "Wallace looked at Godfrey *apprehensively*,"

10. Major Marcus A. Reno, second in command under Custer at Little Bighorn, whose three
companies charged to the south of Custer's, met heavy resistance, and retreated back across the
Little Bighorn River. Later court-martialed and accused by many of cowardice.

11. Captain Frederick Benteen, third in command under Custer, and who hated him. Studying the battlefield two days after the June 25, 1876, battle, he declared that the Seventh Cavalry
had reacted in "clear panic." See *Killing Custer* (1994), by James Welch.

"The squaws were at their *ghastly* work of mutilating the dead," etc. But to say it is ghastly does not make it so, or make the reader feel it so. De Rudio, if I remember correctly, said he could hear the *silvery voices* of the squaws as they mutilated the dead, and when he said that he was a fine historian and artist.[12] T. S. Eliot is always talking about "the objective correlative," the action, speech, gesture, reaction that serves as a sign for the emotion or character or state of mind and will create it in a way in which the mere naming of the emotion or character will not. I shall refer to our little Valentine to the Major [Edward S. Luce], not because I am sure it is successful, but because I am sure of why most of it was written the way it was. In this piece, which attempts to create something of the character of the Major, it is never once said (if my memory is correct) that he is such and such a kind of man (tough, sentimental, colorful, devoted, etc., etc., or any combination of these). It tries to create him, not out of adjectives and adverbs, but out of actions and reactions and remarks that are *characteristic* of him. Thus, if you want to create Custer replying *icily*, you drop the icily, and have him replying, "If the saddle fits, put it on." [. . .]

This is, in a lot of ways, a hell of a letter to send to a friend for a wedding present. But then there are ways in which it is not. If a present should be the best thing one can give, then for better or worse, the best thing I can give you are some of my views about writing which I have taught now for 32 years. A teacher, too, ultimately is supposed to know something about people—the hardest kind of people in the world to know something about, those who have promise. You may be sure that if I hadn't picked you as someone with great possibilities, I would never have written you at such length or with such directness. A teacher soon learns to save himself by treating the mediocre gently and briefly.

As my Presbyterian father would say, "May happiness and success attend you."

Sincerely,

Norman

12. Lt. Charles C. DeRudio, of Troop A, Reno Battalion, survived the Battle of Little Bighorn and in its immediate aftermath endured thirty-six hours of "exciting adventure on foot to regain the command" after quitting Little Bighorn valley. His recollections were subsequently alluded to in the published account of another officer who survived with him.

May 26, 1956

Dear Bob,

Thanks very much for finding time amid the general festivities of the moment to drop me a note. And I'm also glad if any of my comments were of use to you. I was a little troubled by them. It is tough business criticizing someone's writing when you don't know him, for, no matter what any of us say, we all have a sentimental attachment to our writing and to a degree take any criticism of it as a personal affront. For a number of reasons, I always have every thing I write criticized by a *variety* of people whom I respect, but, damn it, Bob, each criticism is a slight stab in the heart, and I can't always tell which causes the greater pain—the criticism that I think is erroneous or the one that really has me nailed to the cross. Still, I'm a deep believer in the school of lumps and bumps. I was initiated into it by Father who was a Presbyterian minister and committed to the view that the right way was the hard way. He used to make me take a page of each paper I wrote for him and justify every word I had used. Perhaps the training was too tough and constricting, and it's a cinch I still feel him looking over my shoulder as I write, but still there's much to be said for the feeling that creation and criticism are not unrelated acts.

I was also a little troubled by the fact that I was bearing down on you so much for conventional phrasing. I don't want to encourage you into a style where every sentence is unique and brilliant—such a style creates the worst possible effect in that the reader gets the impression the writer is more interested in *the way* he says something than in *what* he is saying. Actually, I think I might write an essay someday "On the Art of the Cliché," an art ignored by the criticism of the last 30 years or more which talks altogether of the unusual word, the brilliant image, etc. (so the modern critics talk only of images such as Eliot's one about the evening stretched across the sky like a patient etherized upon the table). But a little of this stuff goes a long way, even in lyric poetry, and actually it is easier to write this way, once you have caught on to a few tricks, than to move people's hearts by simple constructions. [. . .]

Sincerely,

Norman

Oct. 20, 1956

Dear Bob,

I'm going to be so indebted to you that I'll have [to] steal the author's line to his wife in the foreword ("without whose aid and inspiration this work would not have been possible, etc.") and transfer it to you, and even it won't be sufficiently accurate or sentimental. [. . .] I can already see this whole autumn quarter is blown out of the water as far as my getting any work of my own done. In fact, I'm not even getting time to prepare my teaching decently. I doubt if I ever told you that, in addition to my full time duties in the English Department, I am chairman of the Committee on General Studies in the Humanities which was authorized some four years ago to give bachelor and master programs for those who wanted a wider view of humanistic activities than can be obtained in a specialized department. We started with nothing—but a certain amount of political opposition—yet four years later we are one of the largest departments in the Humanities Division and this year have a 100% increase over last year, and the students are really good, and naturally I can't help but be pleased. Also, crucified. God damn it, Bob, I can't run one of the largest departments in the Division and keep up a full schedule of teaching in the English department and get any reading—let alone research [word written over] (I can't even spell the word any more) of my own done. [. . .]

Sincerely,

Norman

July 7, 1959

Dear Bob,

I don't know where to begin, it's been so long since I've written you—perhaps with an explanation of the fact, which I suppose essentially is that I've started to write on Custer & the Battle and when I'm through each day the last thing I can do with the remaining time is write some more.

The University gave me an extra quarter off this year, for the first time in 31 years—so with the summer, my regular quarter off, I've five months or so free (or at least the mornings thereof, for part of the deal was that I continue at least in a minimum way my administrative chores which bring me over to the University about three or four afternoons a week). Still, I'm very grateful, and I'm not sure with complete time off I could accomplish more. I'm getting pretty old to write a book—sometimes I'm not sure I have the physical stamina—and four to five hours a morning morning after morning has me whipped. Also it's very lonely, and I'm glad to get over to the University now and then just to hear a human voice.

Oddly, I have started with the last section first—the part on the after-life of the Gen. and the Battle. I had several reasons for doing so, but probably the crucial one was that I thought I could just about finish a first draft of it in the 5 months off and it would be good to have some self-contained unit completed so that it could be looked at with fishy eyes and I could decide whether I had something worth going on with. Bob, I'll need you real bad next autumn to save me from error, to remove my clichés, and to give me an overall estimate of what I am trying to do conceptually. In the mean time, I have been using you a lot, and between now and the fall I'll have to call directly to you for help.

As for instance now. Bob, as an expert in the legend of the Gen. & the Battle, if you had to trace a curve of the public reaction from the event itself to the present, what would it be like? That is, in your thesis [. . .] you were dealing at least primarily with controversies over the Battle & the conduct of Custer, Reno, etc., as it went on among the pros or semi-pros, but how much effect [did] these controversies have upon the public? I'd say off-hand almost none. [. . .] [A]ctually I find that there has been very little change in the juveniles to the present day in respect to the "Boy General" pictures it gives of Custer, and, although some of the authors know more and some less and some almost nothing of the events, still they are roughly the same in respect to the large picture in its emotional design and color—Custer was a fun-loving boy with whom the boy-hero identifies himself.

With adult novels, I find the picture changes abruptly, from the Last of the Cavaliers to a disobedient little son-of-a-bitch to even an ego-maniac. [. . .] [I] would say that literary and eventually public opinion were determined by what might be called "scholarship"—plus the general cynicism of the times—especially about heroes, courage, the Army, etc. Also, the modern feeling about minority groups and our treatment of them has helped to alter this picture of Custer and when two Jews write the script for the movie "Sitting Bull" the Indians are the heroes who were attacked by a well-disposed nation only because this green ego-maniac disobeyed the orders of Grant, president of a peaceloving nation.

As for poems, I know lots of them that were written early, and they are all of one sweep and one color and I can't remember any of them that do other than make the Battle heroic, and therefore seem uncontaminated by any disputes among historians about 'theme.' The truth is, I'm not aware of many poems by modern serious poets on this subject. Are you? Archibald MacLeish's "Wildwest" (inspired by Neihardt's "Black Elk's Memories of Crazy Horse") is about Crazy Horse, representing him as owning and loving the country which was taken from him by railroad speculators, but it never mentions Custer or the Battle directly.

As for paintings (as I know them), they become more historically accurate and Jim Hutchins portrays Custer very close to the way he looked, but they still seem to me essentially romantic in their treatment. Custer is always the center and focal point of the design [. . .] the culmination of the Hill, the other figures are grouped about him, and, although his dress is fairly realistic, he is a romanticized figure.

In other words, my tenuous conclusions which I wish you to criticize are these: (1) That not until the 1930s (after the death of Mrs. Custer) did so-called "scholarly" discussion of Custer & the Battle seriously affect literary and public opinion—then they radically altered it so it is represented or induced by adult novels and magazine articles presumably of a historical nature; (2) that as far as juveniles are concerned, they just go on essentially as before[. . . .] Likewise, highschool and college text-books, of which I have had a study made, also show no curve of change. (3) That paintings also remain on the side of the hero, even if they emphasize the Indians more and make the equipment more realistic.

God Almighty, Bob, I've made this letter all about myself and my problems—after working 3 months straight on Custer, I'm getting ego-centered myself. How the hell are you? And what is the status of that story about the 2 Cheyenne boys that touched me so? And what about the big study on the Ghost Dance?[13] I have a long footnote about it, assuring the reader of its progress and hailing its quality and regretfully admitting that I've had to take my account essentially from Mooney[14]—although, Bob, that report is the work of a very intelligent and modern mind and I'm glad it's you and not me who is competing against it. Still, I've got this one page footnote staking out your claim as the forthcoming author of the definitive study on the subject—as I remember, there's a son-of-a-bitch up in Michigan who has aspirations on this subject, and I thought I'd better get you in ahead of time. [. . .]

Yours,

Norman

13. "Ghost Dance," an early reference to what was later titled *The Last Days of the Sioux Nation* (1963), Robert Utley's second book, which Maclean had considerably influenced.

14. James Mooney's pioneering *The Ghost-Dance Religion and the Sioux Outbreak of 1890* (1896), published only six years after the Wounded Knee massacre, was for a long time the most influential study of that tragedy and the Wovoka movement that, in some respects, precipitated it.

July 20, 1959

Dear Bob,

Thanks so much for your prompt reply. I guess I was lonesome—God damn this daily writing is a lonely business—and needed some one to give me some advice, some confirmation, some tips and a kick or two to keep me going. Anyway your letter helped a lot and I needed it right then.

I also heard what you said about "ritual drama" to which I shall make as short a reply as I am able. (1) The account you are probably referring to is probably in the Chicago Brand Book,[15] but the account is of a talk I gave without notes even and it is [an] account written by someone else and I did not see it until it was published. (2) When I read it, a lot of it was also beyond my comprehension, a fact, though, that has been helpful to me. (3) I think, however, that what I said at the meeting was received with some enthusiasm [. . .] and they are a pretty hard-boiled bunch of boys; (4) I think that it will be cleaner when I write it, but I don't say that you will like it—I don't know whether you will or not; (5) You ought to be pleased, though, to learn that in a book of say 650 pages I don't contemplate more than 40 pages or so devoted to an analysis of the Battle as "ritual drama"—and that in a separate section near the end where it can be skipped over if it seems exhausting.

As for the likelihood that I won't attract many Custer "addicts" as readers, you're probably right, although to tell the truth—even if it sounds like so much crap—I haven't thought much about readers. I'm 56 and at odd times have thought about the General and the Battle from several points of view—military, literary, artistic, anthropological, and psychological; in them I have found manifestations of most of the things (except feeling) that I have some interest or proficiency in. So the book (if I ever carry it through to completion) will in some senses be a very personal one and so far as I think of it I think of it more in connection with myself than with any set of readers. It could well be such an odd dish that it might not be attractive to any but a few off-beats, and, if so, then that's the way it has to be, for, even from a practical point of view, I haven't any chance of success by writing a purely military history of the Battle, or any justification. I have a fair opinion of myself as a (possible) military historian, but I certainly do not put myself in the same league as you and Jim. [. . .]

15. The Chicago Brand Book, an occasional publication of a group of Chicago-area western history aficionados. One of Maclean's talks before the group was published in their October 1958 issue.

God Almighty, it is almost five o'clock and time for me to pick up my wife & go home. And I'm tired (even my hand)—I've been writing all day. [. . .]
Best to you and Lucille,
Norman

March 23, 1960
Dear Bob,
It sounds splendid, and I hope that you did not altogether waste your time in writing me about the plan of your book and in a sense justifying its reason for being or coming-to-be. It occurred to me after I had asked you for such a letter that I was being somewhat professorial—I guess more of my life than I imagined has been conditioned by doctoral candidates in search of a dissertation so that almost automatically I ask these questions: What's your problem? Why do you think it is an important one? What do you have to contribute to it that hasn't already been said?

Well, anyway, you came through your exam with flying colors, and I can justify myself in putting you through it only by assuring you that automatically I ask myself the same questions, even in my daily teaching—although I can't pretend that I answer my own questions to my own satisfaction as often as I would like. [. . .]

In answer to your question about how my own writing has gone, the answer is not a line since last September. For the punishment I take during the autumn and winter, however, I am getting out of teaching again this spring (although I have to continue my administrative duties). It will take me another two weeks to clean off my desk but I hope by then to start bringing back feebly what I once had in mind and to get to work again.

It might interest you to know that one of the first drafts I wrote last summer was a chapter on the Sioux—from the Battle of the LBH to the present day, *all in 20 or 25 pages*. I especially dreaded showing you this one, but your letter indirectly takes some of the fear away. [. . .] [Y]ou may feel that the author [i.e., Maclean] did some pretty good guessing, given the fact that one week he was guessing about the Sioux, the next week about the history of advertisement, the next about the history of battle-field painting, etc., etc. Jesus Christ, just to think of last summer amazes me—and depresses me. The part I was working on then—and, alas, haven't finished—is more than some one of my capacities (and age) should tackle. The part is on the after-life of the Battle and the General, and I can't know all the things I ought to know to write it. Every chapter—sometimes every section of a chapter—involves an entirely different subject-matter. And if I go on talking this way any longer I'll never get up courage enough to try to finish the job. And as you well ought to know by now, writing is largely a matter of courage, or not knowing any better.

Good luck,
Norman

Chicago
Aug. 2, '61
Dear Robert,

I am still hoping to get away to Montana next week, although my wife's recovery is very slow. In any event, both for your sake and mine, I thought I ought to find time to read your mss. now, and I did, and, Robert, it is beautiful. Also, it is true, my guess is down to the more-or-less last detail and certainly in the general attitude it takes toward the subject.

It is one of the few studies I have read of the struggles between Indian and white that view these struggles as complex and compassionate. I am sick of black-and-white struggles between red-and-white men. Apart from the truth of reality, which is complex as I know it, black-and-white never arouses the moving emotions. I am talking in a sense about the difference between propaganda and poetry. Your account of Wounded Knee, for instance, is a tragedy, not a manifesto, and leaves one thinking about life, not just Indians and cavalry, thinking about the course of events, shaped by a few good guys and a few bad guys but mostly by mixed humanity, good and bad luck, pneumonia, somebody with a big mouth, being crowded too close, having to give up something you can't, etc. And what I am trying to say about Wounded Knee I mean to say about your view of the whole struggle.

Your writing also is the most mature I have ever seen it. The sentences are clean, swift and sure. I, who am supposed to be noted for comma-picking, have done very little, as you will see. I only wish my own style was as sanitary, or that I enjoyed it as much. I also want to speak of a part of writing that in a way is not verbal—the putting the thing together part by part so that the thing as a whole has a lift. As you have it now, the order and development seem inevitable—as if there were no other way of doing it—and this of course is the right kind of order. [. . .]

If I go to Montana, I'll stop at the Battlefield for a couple of days to do some checking—chiefly in the Museum. I don't even know the names of the new Superintendent & Historian. Would you (1) send me these names and (2) write them a brief note, telling them that I'll be there around the 15th and that I'm more or less on the level.

Best of luck,
Norman

Dec. 20, 1961
Dear Bob,

[. . .] I won't get a better Xmas present than your kind words about the chapter of my mss you read. I run out of faith in it from time to time, and this autumn I have not been able to make myself work on it at all. It is a very strange and introspective thing to call a history or something of that sort. At times, from its nature I get very involved in it, and then I have long periods when I can't bear to think of it. Then it seems too personal, too hard to do, and altogether too odd.

Yes, Bob, I shall be glad to send you some of it, and will do so, possibly next week or at least after I get my exams and papers marked, etc. I wouldn't send any of it to you last year when nothing was so important, so it seemed to me, as for you to finish your own mss [*Last Days*]. You had it rolling, and you shouldn't be interrupted by other peoples' problems, or at least no more than could be helped. But perhaps for the moment you are cooling off between major opuses and would not be prevented from doing something important of your own by looking at a few chapter[s] of my junk. And there's no one whose judgment I value more. [. . .]

Best wishes to you and Lucille for the coming year and all the years to come.

Norman

Jan. 4, '62
Dear Bob,

I want very much to take advantage of your offer to put your fishy eye on my mss, for I have lived with it too long alone—or at least long enough. I must confess (I think I've already confessed to you) that I regarded an initial stretch of loneliness necessary since this is a pretty introspective study of a battle, one involving a study of topography of certain exposed portions of the surface of the soul (if I may use such a word) more than of the terrain on the eastern bluffs of the LBH 11 miles south of Hardin. But, though introspective in slant, it is naturally supposed to be a slant into reality, and there is always a danger that a certain length of loneliness can turn into an escape from reality. You are one of the few whose judgment I need now before I go on—perhaps before I can go on.

On the other hand, I don't want my needs to interfere too much [with] your time when you are so productive yourself, and accordingly I am not going to dump the whole mss on you now. I am sending you 5 of the last 6 chapters—plus a tentative outline of the whole study I made this summer in order that you will get some notion of the whole and the context into which these chapters fit. I wish I could send you one more chapter—the concluding one on the "Shrine to Defeat," but I was not able to complete it this summer. This is the second time I've tried to write this chapter, and ironically I seem to be defeated by Defeat. But I think I explained to you when you were here what I am trying to do in this chapter. Essentially, I am trying to show that our psychological need to deal with defeat is an ultimate common magnetic power that has drawn so many people to this rather small encounter in military history. The chapters I am sending you (which are those that just precede this final chapter) of course have much to do with the last chapter. The four different "plots" analyzed in these chapters become in the last chapter four different psychological ways by which defeat is commonly handled by the generality of mankind. [. . .]

It is probably too early yet for you to have heard from the publisher about the Ghost Dance [Last Days]—but no news from a publisher can be good news, as I certainly hope it turns out to be. Let me know when you know, for I feel almost like a god-father about your book and hope to be one of the first to wish it a long and prosperous life.

Sincerely,

Norman

Feb. 2, 1962

Dear Bob,

I'm delighted to hear that the Ghost Dance, etc., has been accepted by the Yale Press. They'll do a fine job for you, Bob, first off just as print. Editorially, they will respect your judgment and intention far more than a commercial publishing company would. [. . .]

And thank you in return for your criticisms of my [Custer] mss. I agree with them, almost without exception. As for your major criticism—that I don't really stand up and announce what I'm doing—I accept that in a way even deeper than you mean it—or, at least, would care to say it to an old friend. I do think I say (perhaps too many times in the total mss) that the Battle is important to me primarily for what it reveals about our psychological terrain—I put you in a real bad spot by asking you to read a series of chapters near the end, and it is in the earlier chapters where I try to make most explicit what the major intentions of the study are. Even so, I am sure I should make the later sign-posts clearer. But my deepest trouble is in trying to find out the underlying psychological significance of the Battle. Alas, I didn't start writing this thing by knowing ahead of time what I meant to say, except in a very general way. To some one like me, the soul is nothing which is very clear in outline, yet the history, literature and art about the Battle increasingly seemed to me to have more than historical, literary and artistic significance, although I try to start with these. But now, as you know, I believe that in these historical, literary and artistic patterns is revealed something of man's common mechanisms in dealing with defeat, and the problem of defeat I think is possibly as central in one's psychological [sic] as sex. I think I've already told you that I try to bring the separate insights together in a last chapter called "Shrine to Defeat" and I think I've also told you that I've tried this summer and last to write this chapter but I can't complete it. Although I came close to doing it this summer, still I couldn't finish it and probably nearly all of what I wrote will have to be rewritten—and, worse, still re-thought. I begin to wonder if I'm defeated by defeat, but I keep sticking with it because I know that until I get it out of me there is no use going back and re-working earlier parts.

I'll enumerate some of the difficulties that are troubling me, if for no other reason than to ask indirectly for your sympathy. (1) I've cornered myself into a realm of speculation in which I do not see clearly or move with certainty. Who am I to get involved with the soul? (2) The particular area I have been led to seems especially guarded by secrecy. Defeat, like sex, is hard to think about. It is one of the unmentionables that most people do not like to name. (3) At the other end, the bottom end of the ladder, are the data (historical, literary and artistic) which led to my speculations. But I do not want to see more in the data than are there, and I do not wish to write a personal essay. (4) On the other hand, in this little body of data about this little Battle I do believe there is a body of general significance. I say "body" because I feel they are related to one another, and are not just revealing of this or that individual. Perhaps I could put it this way. Not every thing, God knows, that can be learned about defeat is imbedded in these data, but imbedded in the bones is a body of knowledge, not a monumental work, but a little essay (perhaps somewhat sardonic) on defeat, and until I can write it I am only wasting my time trying to rewrite the chapter that led me there. Pray for my soul, and, in return, I will promise you that if I ever get this thing all written I will thereafter write only when I know and not write in order to try to find out something I want to know.

Perhaps by the middle of April I'll try once more. Right now, I don't have the time, energy or fortitude. And thanks again for your time and discernment and care.

Best wishes,
Norman

Jan. 23, 1963
Dear Bob,

Thanks very much for your letter and the copy of the reviews of your last book,[16] both of which I am acknowledging immediately but from the hospital where I have been for 3½ weeks, although I am hoping to get out this weekend. Nothing serious, though, I believe. During the last six or seven years I have had attacks of what seems to be dysentery that gets beyond any kind of control—my God, this one started back in November. [. . .]

During the last few days when I have been feeling better I have given a little thought to the remains of Custer that are in my possession. I hardly need tell you that for the last 3 years I have done nothing of importance to add to them. In the last year I have had only 2 or 3 months of good health. The year before my wife was sick all the time and in the hospital for 3 months—and still lives a pretty feeble existence. Then the year before that I was sick so the story of my story of Custer is that for a couple of summers [1959, 1960] I got a lot done—since then it might as well have been his grave-marker. But I am determined in the next month or so to face up to what reality there is, and decide either to go back to work on it or write it off for good. I'm sure I've quoted one of Matthew Arnold's lines to you, since it is such a favorite of mine—"Born between two worlds, one dead and the other powerless to be born." Well, that's Custer and me, but I am going to do something about it. The mathematical odds are that I'll quit it. I don't know anything about it any more, it doesn't interest me, I have no one around here to turn to who is interested in it. Even the geography is uncongenial. But if my health comes back and my wife remains reasonably well, who knows? It's wonderful what foolish and uninteresting things one can do when one is healthy and so is his family.

Well, Bob, I had better put an end to this letter soon or I'll be having a

16. *Custer and the Great Controversy*, Utley's first book.

relapse. But not before telling you again of my admiration for what you have done and my hopes for what you will do.

As ever,

[no signature though the letter is handwritten]

[P.S.] God, Bob, if you lived close I'd even finish that book on Custer. Such is your power over me.

April 5, 1963

Dear Bob,

[. . .] Long ago I told you that I hope for a kind of dual audience for my study—the Custer cultists and a larger audience interested also in larger literary, cultural and psychological problems, so the question I have asked about your study [presumably *Custer and the Great Controversy*] might throw some light on my problem, for, although I have hoped for a dual audience, I have always known the danger of not hitting one target when aiming at two. To the Custer cultist, the literary, psychological stuff may very well sound like so much bull shit, and to the reader interested in this all the military detail, etc. may be for the birds and the hobbyists and the boys who want to play Indians.

Anyway first day off I also read your letter and comments on the three or four chapters I sent you over a year ago, and I want you to know that I take them very much to heart. In essence, they said that I wasn't making clear what I was doing, and I acknowledge the general justness of this criticism. In fact, if I hadn't come to some such realization myself before you voiced it for me, I probably would have made more progress than I have during the last two summers, when I have written nothing that meets my approval. There are, I suppose, 2 extreme kinds of composition. The first is the kind that you have fairly well worked out in your mind before you write—as Sheridan, who when he was asked how the next comedy was coming, answered, "It's all finished; all I have to do is write it." The other extreme form is when something is bothering you and you start writing to find out why. All of us, undoubtedly, have tried our hand at both, but the Custer thing is definitely something that bothered me for a long time and so some years ago I started writing. I think I had to, and I'm sure now that I have to go on, if for no other reason than that I have so much time invested in it (even though often I wish I had never started in this mess). But I'm wised up on a couple of things now. One is that it helped for the first couple of summers to write "just as it came to me," guided from the outside by nothing much more than a topic outline of the whole, and some of these early parts are, I think, good. I won't call the last 2 summers [a] waste, although, as I said, what I wrote then is not good. This year I'm not going to write until I can say to myself what I think—what I think the whole is and what are its parts. Be consoling, Bob, and patient. I face one or two tough alternatives. First of all, I don't have any models for the kind of "history" I am trying to write; I don't have any models of methodology (at least, none that suit me) and I have no compendium of truths to rely upon, and yet I aspire for something sounder, more objective than "so it seems to me." I like to think that in a month or so I'll clarify and systematize my premonitions—and then be able to proceed, not to something as strange and searching as I once hoped it would be, but at least to something unified and of proper size.

The other possibility is considerably darker, although I'll try not to say it that way. It may be that I started something that is too big for me. I occasionally think of what Einstein said of chemists. "The trouble with most chemists," he said, "is that chemistry is too hard for them." Either way, the next month is bound to be a tough one for me, and I would appreciate it if you could say something consoling, even if it were irrelevant, as it would have to be. [. . .]

Yours,

Norman

July 30, 1963

Dear Bob,

I have been sick most of the time since we talked over the telephone last spring—an infection of the kidneys & prostate gland (just to let me know I am getting old). [. . .]

I try not to be depressed, but, God damn it, two of my last three summers have been obliterated by sickness—this summer by [my] own sickness and the summer before last by my wife's illness when she was in the hospital threatened with TB.[17] I had hoped to be finished with the Custer thing by now, but I some times think the curse is on it, and if that is an overdramatic reaction, it is a sober fact that the glow is off it. When I do work on it now—and I still try to—it seems out-of-date, whereas once I felt it was ahead-of-the-times or at least fresh and new. But I have met so many disappointments in connection with it that I shall try to view it philosophically—perhaps fatalistically, would be a better word. I think in respect to it I have no choices any more. Just

17. Jessie Burns Maclean's illness in fact proved to be emphysema.

as a matter of character I have to try to go on with it, even if the time for it is passed and even if I can't get the permission of circumstances. It is interesting, though, isn't it that I am so constantly threatened with defeat in trying to write about it? [. . .]

Best wishes to you and yours,
Norman

July 10, 1966
Dear Bob,

[. . .] I don't think that I have ever talked to you about the Committee on General Studies in Humanities, but I feel more personally involved in it than in anything else I have done professionally. As its name implies, it is a committee for students interested in humanistic studies who (at least for a certain time in their development) do not wish to confine their training to just literature, history, philosophy or art but would like to approach problems with a perspective that relates and combines several humanistic disciplines. If I say so myself, it has proved to be very successful and selective and has been built up to think of itself as the 7th Cavalry. For instance, every graduating senior this year either received a Woodrow Wilson Fellowship, or a Danforth, or a fellowship from some first-class graduate school or went in the Peace Corps. Although we have kept ourselves guardedly small, our graduates receive more honors than do the whole graduating classes of many colleges. Like Custer, we think we can beat all the God damn Indians. Well, anyway, it is probably at its finest moment now, and so I have resigned as chairman. Fifteen years, given my political theory, are normally five years longer than anyone should administer anything. The committee would get a booster-shot from new leadership, and I am tired of the job and want to do something else. I have only two more years before I reach the retirement age of 65. I didn't mean that I want to start crawling into my hole and getting ready to hibernate. For that, I'll wait until the snow falls. Actually, I am trying to crawl out of my hole and look around in the late autumn—and, among other things, write you and Jim [Hutchins] a letter.

I don't think, though, that I'll ever take up Custer again—at least, seriously. He was one more life than I could live, and he didn't tie up with any of my others. But, who knows? I might change my mind as I start giving up some of these other lives and looking around for other identities. [. . .]

Best wishes to you and yours,
Norman

May 18, 1971
Dear Bob,

[. . .] Believe it or not I may start back on Custer this summer. Well, if not exclusively on Custer at least it involves him among others. I think I see a certain type of "leaders of horse" from Alexander the Great to Patton, and it interests me—God, it's even somewhat analytical—and so maybe is the fact that I feel like going back to work again. Anyway, I feel a lot better than I have for a few years, and I am looking around for something (not too big) to start me going again. [. . .]

I am always proud of you,
Norman

Dec. 15, 1972
Dear Bob,

[. . .] May be I'll do a paragraph trying to bring myself up-to-date. In December, I shall reach my Biblical allotment of 3 score years plus 10 (Jesus, isn't that appalling?). I am 5 years beyond retirement age but I am still teaching and actually feel better than I have for the last 8 or 10 years. A good time to quit, don't you think? As my son, John, said to me recently (he claims now he didn't), "Dad, why don't you quit when may be you are more or less even?" On the hypothesis that I am, I think that I'll resign next month to be effective in June when I have finished the school year. I'd rather not teach than not to teach well.

Then I'll try a little writing. The summer before last I started some "stories" based on my memories of hunting and fishing and working in logging camps and for the Forest Service when I was young and when Montana and Idaho were younger than they are now. I think that the "stories" are pretty good. The one I worked on last summer [what became USFS 1919] I didn't get finished. It is on the year when I was 17 years old and the United States Forest Service was 14. It got long and difficult (almost novelette size and I had to start it 4 times before I liked the feel of it), but I hope to finish it this winter quarter when I don't teach. Some time I may send you the 2 shorter ones I wrote the first summer (the subtitle of one of them is "Logging and Pimping") and when I get the Forest Service "story" finished I'll take a hard look at all 3 of them and decide whether I want to pursue this direction any further. I have other things in mind, including an odd, half-formed article on Custer. [. . .]

As ever,
Norman

Oct. 23, 1974

Dear Bob,

I'm going to ask you a favor, but without much apology, since in my time you have asked the same favor of me. Can you find time to read something I have written—a story about a 100 pages long?

Shortly before my retirement I began to write reminiscent stories. My children wanted me to, and I also wanted to. I felt it was important as one grew old to clarify himself about his life—to see if it ever took on patterns or form and, perhaps more important, to clarify one's attitude about life, especially about his own. In my stories so far I always have a second intention—that of giving a historical representation of how we once did things that we now do very differently, and, important, how it *felt* to do them. The historical part is not supposed to be just background. I believe that how things were done and how we felt doing them should be in the story, should be part of the story.

To date, I have written 3 such stories—one short and the other 2 long, one 100 pages and the one I am finishing will be 10 or 15 pages longer. The short one is called "Your Pal, Jim & Whoring and Pimping" and is a story in which is embedded the knowledge of what it was like to be a logger when it was still hand and horse and before anyone had heard of a chain saw and "a cat." Also, in a world when nothing was so important as work—where even whoring and fighting weren't as important.

The second story is longer—about 100 pages—and is the one I should like to send you. It is called "USFS 1919," and is based on my third summer in the Forest Service (all told, I put in 12 or 13). It is the story of a boy of 17 seeing for the first time his life change into an art form and becoming briefly a story. The title suggests its second intention—to portray what we did in the early Forest Service, how we did them, and how it felt to do them—again in a world of hand and foot and horse—and no roads.

The story I am finishing up now is in memory of my brother, who was one of the great fly fishermen of his time and who was murdered when he was 32. Its secondary intention should be clear, to give someone a knowledge of and feeling for the art—from rods and flies to casting, to "reading water," to landing (and losing) fish. I should have a first draft ready to go to the typist in another month. Naturally, it means a great deal to me, but I have tried hard not to make it too personal.

In any event, when I finish it I believe I should stop, look and listen, and maybe ultimately stop. The 3 stories add up to a certain "body" of writing—a sufficient body to decide whether I am largely wasting the mornings of my remaining years in writing. I would rather spend my time fly-fishing than in writing a mediocre story about fishing, because I am better than mediocre as a fisherman.

If you have time, then, Bob, what I would like is for you to tell me from the hip whether this story of mine on the early Forest Service (which comes closest to your experience, I should think) has interest and merit beyond my family and close students, and, if you think it has, what I might do to try to get it published. If you think it hasn't, I am anxious to know that, too. I am 71, this story and the one I am finishing now are about as well written as I will ever be able to write. I fished well this summer, and, as I said earlier, I'd rather do that or something else than not to write well. [. . .]

You're always welcome,

Norman

Dec. 29, 1974

Dear Bob,

Thank you for your kind words. Don't worry, they were worth much more than the postage. I don't quite know why I started writing in old age, but certainly not with the hope that I would turn out to be a writer. If anything like that was going to happen it would have happened half a century ago. One reason, for sure, that started me off was the hope that I would please my children and some close friends. So thanks again, Bob—you did all I could hope for. You liked it.

In so far as I have thought of publication, clearly I haven't thought in the same direction as you have. You speak of it as being "too long," so you must have thought of its possibilities for magazine publication. Although I find it very hard to write with publication in mind—a real literary limitation of mine—I don't think I ever imagined when I was writing the Forest Service story that it could or would be published in a magazine.

I really don't know what I was thinking about publication when I wrote it; not a book, certainly, because it is too short for that. I guess I wrote it the way I wanted it. Then I went ahead and wrote 2 more—a conventionally short one and one some 20 pages longer than the Forest Service one which I am just finishing now. Together, as far as pages go, they would make a small book, and they are all about long ago in the high hills, and, Bob, I'm a fairly good student of literature, and I don't know any really first-class stories of long ago in the high hills. Ones that are very real and accurate as well as stories.

So I think I'll tie these three stories into a package and try them on one or two big publishing houses, although, as an old-time westerner, I have a complete lack of faith in the eastern literary establishment. They probably can't stand reading more than four or five pages about the son of a Scotch Presbyterian minister working in the Forest Service and logging camps or fishing the big rivers. What could be more boring than the son of a Scotch Presbyterian minister walking around in trees! It should have been the son of a rabbi locked in the bathroom masturbating in his sister's underwear to be literature. And, Bob, I don't know how to write that story (although lots of others do), so I am resigned.

But I have already partly accomplished two things that I wanted to do by writing these stories. I thought it would be important for me in old age to look back on my life to see moments when it took on the beauty of art. I also thought it would be important for me in old age to find out how I had felt about life—and to be doubly sure how I felt about it now. This is a long way from saying that I thought I would find I was a writer. The story I am in the process of finishing now means more to me personally than the others, but I know enough to know that does not mean it is the best thing I have written. It is about my brother who was murdered and who was a master in the art of fly-fishing, so the story is also about the art of fly-fishing as the Forest Service story is also about how we did things in the early Forest Service *and how we felt doing them.* I hope for my brother's sake it is the best thing I have ever written, but it may have meant too much to me to be as good as it should be. [. . .]

Thanks again,

Norman

[from Seeley Lake]

Aug. 28, 1977

Dear Bob:

[. . .] Bob, as long as I have known you, you have known how to write a book. You knew how to write a book before you knew how to write.

And all of them have been very good. You are truly an author.

I have written just one little book (a few pages over 200—a mere chapter for a genuine book-writer like you [. . .]). But it is doing very well. It has been out now for 1½ years and its last 3 months have been its best and the last month the best of all. And Paramount is going to do the long story that is the title for the whole collection, "A River Runs Through It." And last week *Esquire* bought an early story of mine ["Retrievers Good and Bad"] and all the talks I gave this spring are sold for publication. I haven't written anything, Bob, since I retired at 70 that hasn't been or soon will be published. It's something like what you say about your getting honorary degrees—once you get the hang of the thing, they come easy. The hanging took a long time, though, at least for me.

If you get to Chicago, let me know in advance. Stay overnight with me—I have a nice little condominium near the University and live there about 9 months of the year. The other three I spend here in the cabin my father and I built in 1921. I stay alone and write and walk and fish. It is my country and I love it. It is only 16 miles from the glaciers and night before last it snowed, clear to the edge of the lake. It snows every month of the year.

I am now 74, but it is still my kind of country. It was 29° this morning when I got up. [. . .]

Bob, if this letter goes on much longer I'll never write another book, but it was sure nice talking to you.

As ever,

Norman

Nov. 29, 1979

Dear Bob:

I was delighted to hear from you. I was delighted to hear that you were going to quit the God damn government and give yourself over wholly to sin and writing fiction. I don't see why you can't succeed at both—you had a good start when you were young on Custer Hill. One of the earliest things I remember you writing was the story of the two Cheyenne boys charging down the hill just outside Lame Deer to take on the 7th Cavalry drawn up to meet them. Always in your histories, Bob, you have shown unusual narrative gifts— if you feel like trying some narrative not bound by history, you sure have the credentials—and my blessings. After my blessings, however, I have to add a word of caution. As I get older and older I am more and more sure that Plato was right when he said man was highly specialized in his gifts. Who besides Shakespeare has excelled in both forms of drama—comedy and tragedy? And, although Browning was the great master of the dramatic monologue, he wrote pretty dismal dramas, although he tried hard. Historical narrative and narrative sound close, but it is hard to name any who were good at both. H. G. Wells? except that he wasn't much good at either.

But good luck to you and good sailing. [. . .]

Best wishes,

Norman

Letters to Marie Borroff,

....

1949–1986

....

*Marie Borroff, a student of Maclean's at the University of Chicago,
went on to a distinguished academic career at Yale University,
where she taught from 1960 to her retirement in 1994. A scholar
of medieval and twentieth-century English poetry, and a poet
herself, Borroff in 1962 became only the second woman to be
granted tenure in Yale's Faculty of Arts and Sciences, and in 2008
Yale established a professorship in her name. She is famous in the
academic world for her verse translation of and scholarship about*
Sir Gawain and the Green Knight, *and her poems have been
published in the* American Scholar, *the* New Republic, *and the*
Yale Review, *among other journals. A selection of poems written
over a period of more than fifty years, entitled* Stars and Other
Signs, *was published by Yale University Press in 2002 and is
dedicated to Maclean.*

*In his letters to Borroff, Maclean shows himself a tough poetry
critic and tender friend, one who always pushes her to write and
send more poems even as he praises her career as a scholar and
academic leader at Yale. Borroff has said, "My friendship with
Norman was one of the greatest good fortunes of my life. Still is."
In a 1971 letter, he delightfully recounts the discovery, via a student
they both had, of their nearly identical teaching style. As with
Utley, Maclean felt this protégée's career exceeded his own as mentor.*

March 22, 1949
Dear Marie,
I hope that you will forgive me in taking so long to acknowledge your
poems, but for the last five or six weeks I have been down and out, crawling to classes and then back home again and being contagiously unwhole-
some both in transit and at destination. Mr. Crane,[1] too, has been exhaling

---

1. R. S. Crane, influential University of Chicago English professor, and mentor and friend

morbidity, but finally discovered he was suffering from a thyroid deficiency (this has happened before with him). The pills he has been taking for the last several weeks are, I think, correcting his deficiency, and the last two times I have seen him he was most like himself. I, too, am better, and I hope, nearly well, but I give you this medical chart only to assure you that I am writing you about your poems at the first moment I think I can be somewhat objective about them.

I think you describe your own poems in the lines "now sedate / and half-withdrawn, now passionately tender, / seeming to hesitate / upon a gesture of complete surrender." They touch at the same time chords that are feminine with tenderness and yet dignified, almost stoical. And, of course, they are very competent in craft—emotions such as these cannot be aroused without competence.

You are a young poet and so your question is, "where do I go from here?" and so I am going to make some very dangerous observations. With an older poet, the critic pretty much accepts the emotions and thoughts of the poet. The critic accepts these as the confirmation of the poet's personality and his times. But you are young and elastic—and bigger and more exciting than the role you have assigned your poetry. And, although I recognize that the role you have assigned your poetry is not out of keeping with the poetry of your times, I am going to say that the times and the traditions are dying. The poetical transition of the last twenty or thirty years is no longer productive—it has become as sterile as the Romanticism against which it revolted. It has run its cycle, I feel sure, although naturally I have no notion of what will come to replace it. That is the work of the inventive poets. What I am saying is that I want you to think of being of them. I shall say one thing more general—the poetry that endures generally has one quality to it however it adjusts to and/or revels at its own age—it has *excitation*. Name for me the facts that have gained immortality shaded in wistful half-lights.

I am trying to place you at an unfamiliar vantage-point to scrutinize yourself for your next step. In your last years here everyone was pounding technique and craft at you. That presupposes the poem has already gone through many stages of development—and is now being executed. Possibly you came to take these pre-technical stages too quickly and easily, as a result of this

---

of Maclean's. Crane led what became known as the neo-Aristotelian school of literary criticism at Chicago.

technical preoccupation. I am now suggesting you think of such things as this—what would a poetical *soul* be like (forever and at this moment), what would a particular poetical conception be like, is this a poetical insight, etc.? Perhaps I could put it this way concretely—think of Longinus[2] for a while instead of "some technical elements of style," for although ecstasy is probably not possible now, *excitation*, as I said, always is.

From this pre-technical location, I wish you would think of another closely allied matter—"inventiveness." Step number one is that this is really a stirring concept, step number two—what can I add to, do it to get the maximum effect out of it? Too many of your poems, Marie, are too easy, too expected; and I think I should give you some examples. [. . .]

The odd thing is that I think that in thinking of these pre-technical stages you may well get new insights into technique. After all technique is a means, and a revolution in it is usually accompanied by some sort of mutation in what is being said.

It would be pallid of me to pretend I am not criticizing your poetry, but I want you to know that in criticizing it I am sure that I am criticizing the poetry of one of the promising poets of our country. And you know how austerely I believe that promise should not be allowed to get fat. Even so, if you were here I would try to tell you how much I like some of your poems. But it has taken me most of the morning to tell you what I think is even more important—where to stand in order to take the next look. But I admit that it is very dangerous for me to offer such advice, for a poet is ultimately known by where he looks. You might be wisest, therefore, to take this letter—this very long letter—as merely a sign of my very great interest in where you will go and my surety that the way will be marked with success.

Very sincerely yours,

Norman F. Maclean

Jan. 29, 1952

Dear Marie,

I should have answered your letter sooner if during the last two week I hadn't been sick and busy, some times alternately but more often in conjunction. And if this letter is also brief, be sure that I strutted myself over the recommendation to Yale. But why the hell are you going to Yale? This answer is

---

2. Longinus, a classical Roman poet and author of an influential literary treatise, "On the Sublime."

no I didn't know you were going there. Why don't you and Crane introduce me more gently to the grisly facts of life?

If you go there, though, I want you to know two people closely—Mrs. Wimsatt and Norman Pearson. Mrs. Wimsatt is a former student of mine who like yourself went to Yale for graduate work and married one of the distinguished members of the English Dept.—and if you go to Yale you might as well carry through the parallel. Mrs. Wimsatt is just as fine a woman as comes down the pike—in every way. Norman Pearson is a great man in my scheme of things. He is a fine critic, sensitive and searching; you may know him as co-author with Auden of the recent and highly praised anthology of poetry published by the Viking Press. But he is dear to me mostly because I knew him when he thought he was dying (and had reason to think so). It was a privilege to have known him then. His courage and love of life are absolute. I shall write both him and Mrs. Wimsatt shortly before you put in your appearance at New Haven.

I have had time to do only an impressionistic job on your poems. Beauty is a matter of pressure; within it, you have to feel thrusts and strains, and yet be at rest. I thought there was pressure on in these poems. Yes, yes, they are so much better than those made on the Bosphorus[. . . .][3] My only negative criticisms (and these are indeed very impressionistic) probably basically are—the craft and concentration you put in your poems sometimes makes them appear too highly wrought. Be careful of the "ornamental" that is visibly so. [. . .] I can remember when I thought [Gerard Manley] Hopkins was hot stuff and I still teach him because the stuff is so visible, but it's stuff. Try [Matthew] Arnold for a while. You also use repetition of word, phrase, and line until if you don't watch out you will be mannerized, and everything you write will sound like a rondeau. In "a last word" the repetition is crucial; "falling, falling, draw on, draw on" is for my money n.g. But these are only small signs of much but not enough labor. The last act of labor is to remove all signs of labor.

Critics and Criticism: Ancient and Modern[4] is finally off the press and will be on sale early this month. It was my job to make a final compilation of the complimentary copies to be sent, and you may be sure I looked and saw your name was there.

Say, this didn't turn out to be a short letter after all. I guess when I think of

3. Maclean is alluding to a year Borroff spent in Istanbul and the poems she wrote there.

4. *Critics and Criticism* (1952), a landmark volume of literary criticism edited by R. S. Crane. Maclean contributed to and helped edit this volume under Crane's direction.

you I go on and on. I believe in you, and, if you have health, I know you'll have everything else.

Sincerely,

Norman Maclean

Dec. 19, 1957

Dear Marie:

Thanks for the kind words about the paper at MLA,[5] and, since we're in that mood, I heard nothing but good words about yours. I suppose that I should have come back earlier from Montana and heard you and the whole show, but some day, I hope, you will see my country and understand why I always hate to leave it. [. . .]

Glad to know that you enjoy teaching on the flying trapeze as it swings back and forth between Smith and Yale. This is a feat that calls forth a considerable display of humanistic and prosodic skill, but I was sure all along that you would be equal to it. By all means, send a reprint of anything you do, even if it is criticism. You know, of course, what I think of criticism in general, but I'll feel different about it if it's yours.

Best wishes for the coming year. Hope to see you sooner next time.

Norman Maclean

The following letter was occasioned by a mailing of inscribed copies of Marie Borroff's Wallace Stevens: A Collection of Critical Essays. *Borroff's publisher mixed up the addresses.*

Nov. 5, 1963

Marie, my dear,

I always love your books, but it's really your dedicatory inscriptions on the complimentary copies that leave me breathless. On my copy of the *Wallace Stevens* it says: "Yale's Loss is Princeton's gain," and it could be true that my never having been in Yale could be a loss to Yale and at the same time it would also be that my never having been in Princeton could be a distinct advantage to Princeton. As I say, I can imagine both of these things to be true, at least when uttered by a poetess, but what I can't imagine is someone whose ancestors came from the Isle of Mull in the Hebrides packing around a name like "Nina

---

5. Maclean had delivered his talk "Criticism, History, and the Problem of Teaching" at the Modern Language Association's annual meeting in Madison, Wisconsin, in September.

Berberova."[6] It would almost be easier for me to believe I was Shakespeare's "Mr. W.H." Still, I would have kept the copy if Ronald [Crane] hadn't come into my office with his copy of *Wallace Stevens* inscribed with some flattering remarks that couldn't be me but addressed nevertheless "To Norman." So I have captured his copy and am keeping it, and am returning to you under separate cover the copy inscribed to someone who, from the name and from her going to Princeton, sounds like she might be a descendant of Catherine the Great, who certainly came from the north country but was a little too lively to be rated a Presbyterian.

In addition to the copy I am returning, both Ronald and I send our love, even though at the moment he is holding nothing but the bag.

As ever,
Norman

June 30, 1965
Marie my dear,

It isn't very often, at least in my encounters, that love and business coincide in their courses. In fact, I think that Marvell did a poem on the difficulty of this geometry, and could not make the lines of love meet even though omitting the business factor.[7] I should be lucky, then, if I can say what I have to say by letter.

I shall start with business, but only to sound business-like, not because I believe all things start there. I have just heard that Jerome Taylor has resigned from our department to become a dean at, of all places, Kent State. I think that he is a damn fool, but I have a simple theory that Kent State is just where anyone should be who wants to be at Kent State. As for becoming a dean, I always remember Ronald's remark when I told him that Rea Keast had become chairman of the department at Cornell: "Why the hell do most of my best students either die or go into administration?"

---

6. Nina Berberova (1901–1993), Russian émigré writer known for memoirs, criticism, and fiction. Borroff met Berberova when both taught at Smith College. Berberova was a lecturer at Yale from 1958 to 1963, when she moved to Princeton University.

7. The relevant stanza, from Andrew Marvell's poem "The Definition of Love," is

As lines, so loves, oblique may well
Themselves in every angle greet;
But ours so truly parallel
Though infinite, can never meet.

When I heard this news about Taylor, however, I didn't say anything. I just went into my office to write this letter, and first I wrote the date, which is the last day of June, so, if you wish, you may include this letter among your June proposals.

Taylor, as you probably know, was one of those medievalists in our department. The senior one is Theodore Silverstein and the youngest, Arthur Heiserman (Skelton and Satire).

I am sure that the department will wish to make a really major appointment, and, the lady somewhat willing, I should love to propose your name.

Medieval studies have had a big revival here under Silverstein, Taylor and Heiserman, all of whom have great power in attracting top students, partly I believe because, with all their varied interests—linguistic, philosophic, and scientific—they are primarily devoted to medieval literature as literature. [. . .] If I didn't believe that altogether there would be "a conjunction of murder and stars," I wouldn't be writing this letter. Moreover, the fact that you like to do a certain amount of free-wheeling and to teach courses in "Modern Poetry" or "Language and Poetry" would make you all the more welcome here where no one has to feel that his life must be bounded by conventional divisions in literary history. Who knows what Ronald will be teaching next? Perhaps a joint course with you on "Gawain and Tom Jones: A Non-Prosodic Study in Contrasts."

I wouldn't be writing this letter either unless I also believed that the department and the University as a whole are at one of their most flourishing moments. You have been through here recently and have seen for yourself that. [. . .] For the first time in years, I have the feeling that the whole "planisphere" is in orientation; hence the letter I have been longing to write and the questions I have been waiting to ask—could you be moved to go west?

For the moment at least, this is a quite personal communication, but, with the slightest encouragement I would hasten to publicize my feelings and propose you to the department. Who knows? Perhaps the three of us—you and Ronald and I—might teach a joint course on "Gawain, Tom Jones and General Custer: Or, They Died with Their Boots On," a subtitle that hopefully might prove relevant to the teachers of course as well as to its subject-matter.

As ever,

Norman

June 10, 1969

Dear Marie,

This has been a somewhat numb and silent year for me, but I do not want the term to end without letting you know how happy I felt when I learned that you have a Guggenheim and next year off. It is a recognition of the distinction you have already achieved and a booster-shot to send you into higher orbit. Not least important, it gives you a chance to be lazy for awhile. All told, it couldn't have happened to a finer woman, and don't think that you are stealing time if you write a few more lovely poems on the side.

It was last autumn, I believe, when we talked last, and I told you that my wife was very sick. She had been sick for so many years that we had all come to think (her doctors included) that her courage transcended medical reality. In the end, though, she developed cancer and died on December 7, but with her courage still unbroken. I have taught the winter and spring quarters, and at first it was very difficult. Now, though, other [or outer] things have more meaning to me, in particular the joys of others. And so it is nice to write you again. May the Lord continue to shine upon you and bless you.

As ever,

Norman

Feb. 11, 1971

Dear Marie,

[. . .] Yes, I feel much better—actually, better than I have for some years. I am still teaching, although I am beyond normal retirement age, and have been asked to teach still another two years. I probably shall if my health holds up, but I am not sure I want to teach a full load. I have taught a long time, and it would be nice, for instance, to have the winter as well as the summer quarter off.

Speaking of teaching, I had a student some five or six years ago who was a senior in Yale, lived in Chicago, and for some family reasons was allowed to take a quarter of work here. I had him in the old Shakespeare course, and about a third of the way through he stopped after class and, when everybody else had left, he looked at me out of the corner of an eye and asked, "Do you happen to know Miss Borroff who teaches at Yale?" I said, yes, I do—she and I were here together for a good many years. And he said, "I thought so. It is kind of funny, but you teach a lot like the way she does and you even say some of the same things."

He watched me out of the corner of the same eye for the rest of the quarter, and I am sure that he felt he was watching a guy making a living stealing your stuff.

He was probably right, too. All I can say, it is a nice way to make a living. [. . .]

As ever,
Norman

Christmas, 1971:
Marie, my dear,

[. . .] It will be on toward the holidays when this note gets to you, and I hope that they and the coming year and the years to come will be very happy ones for you. You are in full bloom now, with powers and gifts that everyone stops to admire. I am proud that I knew you when you were a girl and I am proud that you are now Director of Graduate Studies at Yale,[8] but don't let administrated [sic] laurels make you forget that when you were young you started to write poems and about the poets.

Bless you,
Norman

July 24, 1972:
Marie, my dear,

Thanks for your sweet letter and lovely poem about swimming on your back in the sun.[9] Marie, instead of (in addition to?) picking out several volumes of the poems of others to publish, don't you think it time to publish a slight opus of your own? You are such a fine critic that you do not allow yourself to write anything but beautiful poems. I myself have seen quite a collection. Beautiful mood pieces where at the end the mood drops several levels in depth—like this one. Then, too, very masterly in technique—also like this one with its triple rhymes. I thought that only one of them was breathing a little hard to be a rhyme—the last line in the last stave. But it's a slight thing and the poem is a beautiful thing and "there are many more besides—more besides." And it is time for you to lose your amateur standing. Do you think your devoted students are going to start collecting them when you retire and publish them posthumously? Something like Wayne

8. In fact, Borroff had been appointed Director of Graduate Studies in English.

9. The poem, "Floating," appears in Borroff's book of poems *Stars and Other Signs* (Yale University Press, 2002).

Booth and Gwyn Kolb did for the Boss?[10] Touching, but not bestowed upon many and nothing to hang around and wait for. It would be nice, though, to get a few devoted students to help you. That's really what the Boss did, and it worked very well. I hope you will take all this as a very strong hint. Otherwise, there is going to be a lot of Maine sea-coast that is going to perish for want of a publisher. [. . .]

Yes, I am back in what you call "my country." It was 50 years ago last summer when my father and I built our first cabin on this lake (see enclosed card).[11] So last summer some of my old fishing pals and I had a Half Century Celebration, and were drunk for miles around.

I have fallen in a regular routine—so much so that the other day I thought it was the wrong day all day long. Before I have thought it was the wrong day for a few hours in the morning and then got straightened around, but Saturday I thought was Friday until late in the afternoon when I went over for the mail and found the Post Office closed. I felt strange and am still having to make adjustments.

In the mornings I "write." I write "stories" or reminiscences or something like that. My children put me up to it. Then, besides my children, I have always had western pals with whom I have always swapped "stories." The oral tradition is still strong here. When I was young, they called it "pulling the long bow." First of all you have to tell a good story, but you are supposed also in the story to record some aspect of western life that is passing on or already gone. I wrote two last summer—a long and somewhat raucous one set in the lumber camps when logging was done only by men and horses and not by chain saws and "cats." The other is much shorter and is about my family and my duck dogs and the Blackfoot and Missouri rivers and my dead brother.[12]

At the University I belong to a club called the Stochastics. It has 40 members, including the President and Provost, but mostly big scientists, with a few

10. "The Boss" = R. S. Crane.

11. The postcard is entitled "Seeley Lake from Double Arrow Lookout." On it, Maclean writes:

> Marie, my dear, this is my first home. You have to like the cold to like it here. I think it is beautiful. Last week it snowed three days in a row—July 17, 18, 19. When the clouds lifted, the mountains had snow to their base. I fished in a cold stream two of the afternoons, and caught my limit. N. M.

12. Maclean is referring to what would become "Logging and Pimping and 'Your Pal, Jim'" and "Retrievers Good and Bad."

222 : SELECTED LETTERS

odd balls like me. We meet once a month, drink too much and have dinner, the chief purpose of which is to sober you up in time to hear a scientific or scholarly paper. It was my time to speak so I decided I'd read them the story about the summers I spent in the logging camps. The secretary of the Club asked me for a title so he could send out notices, and I changed the title and it came out: "Norman Maclean, noted authority, will speak on 'Logging and Pimping.'" I liked the notice so much that I got several copies, and will send you one when I get back to my files. Darling, it really packed them in. The secretary told me it was the largest attendance of the Club in 9 years.

On the slightest provocation, I would send you copies of either or both of the stories.

I am writing one this summer on my early years in the United States Forest Service—when I was 17 and the Service was 14.[13] I have finally got it rolling and I think it will be good, but I am afraid it is going to be too long. Too many things happened when I was in the Service. I don't want the strain of writing some thing that is long. Would that I could, like you, write a beautiful poem.

As always,
Norman

Oct. 20, 1972
Marie, my dear,
Thanks for your note about your mother, and don't be discouraged because your mother is slow in regaining her strength. Once not too long ago I think you told me she is 79, but, even if she were younger, she has been sick. I spent 4 of the first 6 or 7 months of 1970 in the hospital, and I was a good year getting in shape again. They used to try to cheer me up by telling me about an experiment they ran in World War II to see what would happen to young tough guys (all soldiers) who weren't sick but just had to stay in bed for a month. They could eat anything they wanted and as much. The only thing they could not do was get out of bed for a month.

They were over six months recovering.

So, be patient, Marie. You have been saturated with good health all your life, but your mother is your mother and she is tough, too. Things inside me tell me she will be well again. But keep me informed.

So you're giving a course in modern poetry to 80 students. Yale hasn't

13. This story would become the novella USFS 1919: The Ranger, the Cook, and a Hole in the Sky.

changed much since the month I was there when I was a senior at Dartmouth (1924). Then, too, they brought down the fancy university professors to lecture to big classes of undergraduates. I remember Berdan, Tinker and Phelps.[14] Tinker was lecturing—of all things—on the Romantic poets. He had a birth-mark on the left side of his face so he sat so that the undergraduates could see only his right profile. He read poetry well and he read lots of it and made easy remarks about the lives of the Romantic poets. I remember going to see Berdan in his office once. It was in the basement and it was a dark day and he was not a very successful member of the faculty. In the semi-darkness he talked to me for nearly an hour about how individuals come and go but the institution (that is, Yale) goes on forever. All of which turned out to be true. Phelps was a God damn fool who made a lot of money and taught Brown-ing and was highly thought of by the Yale undergraduates. I remember him spending 20 minutes showing his class of 80 what Browning meant by his line referring to his wife as "his moon of poets," so the moon doesn't rotate so the world sees only one side of her. Then very slowly he walked sideways around the lecture room, saying every once in a while, "Please notice, you still can see only my stomach."

Have no fear, Marie, my dear, even if you are to be compared to these early greats of the Yale English Dept., you must truly be great in this setting, even if, as that Yale undergraduate once told me, my teaching suspiciously resembles yours.

It is always nice to hear from you.

As ever,

Norman

Nov. 3, 1972

Marie, my dear,

I was certainly glad to get your letter and to learn that your mother is begin-ning to feel her biceps again. It is a terrible thing to be old and a terrible thing to be sick at any age. I think that she does well to be back in action this soon, and I am real proud of her and you must let me know how things go with her. But to be loved when she is old is to have over half of the battle won. [. . .]

Thanks so much for your comments about my "stories." I am sure your criticisms are well taken: I must have great limitations as a story-teller. Then,

14. Chauncey B. Tinker, William Lyon Phelps, and John M. Berdan were all professors of English at Yale.

too, my only experience has been in the oral tradition, telling stories to my children and always swapping them with my western pals. Even your children or your pals aren't going to listen to you for more than 10 or 15 minutes, so there is great premium on deletion, and especially of all scenery. Besides, they know the scenery. All you have to say is "the Blackfoot river."

Maybe the one I wrote (but did not finish) this summer will please you more, at least on this account. It is about the early years I spent in the Forest Service which, however, was younger than I was. It was only 14, and I was 17, but we had many of the same characteristics. The story is even more raucous than "My Pal, Jim," but it does try to do something that I didn't try to do in the stories you have read—it tries to say directly how I feel about the mountains of Idaho and Montana and to make these feelings a dramatic part of the "story." Not easy, my dear. When you tell "stories," you had better not try to pull the two into one, as possibly is suggested by my opening sentence: "I was young and I thought I was tough and I knew it was beautiful and I was a little but crazy but hadn't noticed it yet." I'll finish it in the winter quarter, when I don't teach. It will probably be 80 pages, but if you don't mind, I'll send you a copy.

Marie, my dear, I am teaching a course this quarter called "Poem, Poet, and Period," and the other day I gave the class each a copy of "Floating" and talked about you and they very much like both "the Poem" and "the Poet." If you have 80 this year in your class on Modern Poetry, next year you'll have at least 100, 20 of whom will be visitors from the Middle West, expecting you to be swimming on your back in Triplets.

By the way, I perhaps should tell you that in my Forest Service story I have a rather wonderful whore-house scene, including a whore who speaks in iambic pentameter.

As a big academic administrator, can't you find some excuse to visit us with no expense to yourself and with great pleasure and profit to us? [. . .]

Be sure to keep me informed about your mother.

As ever,

Norman

Jan. 21, 1973

Marie, my dear,

It does me good to hear from you. There's everything in your letters—brains, warm-heartedness, humor, poetry (not just about poetry but also a little of the same). And, by the way, you haven't sent me a poem for a long time—nothing since "Floating," and you can't have been swimming on your back ever since. I trust I told you I liked "Floating" very much, but you must have tried the breast or crawl stroke since then, so let's take a look at it. Yes, and when I finish (if ever) this story I am working on now I'll join you in trying to get something published. [. . .]

I can't quite figure out the dates from your letter, but you may be in Florida while I write this. I hope so. And I hope the sun shines upon you, and that must be a good place to go floating. Write "Floating II: A Southern Version." And I hope your blessed mother continues to improve. And do you know something else? I am going to Florida this Saturday and spend a couple of weeks with Mr. Kimpton, former chancellor of the University. He has a car down there and we are going to spend most of the time on the Keys, which we both like very much. If I go on much longer in the letter, I'll never get there.

Sure, I'll send you the story I am working on now when I finish it (hopefully before I have to start teaching in the spring quarter). It is going to be quite long (100 pages?) but I think it will be better as well as longer than anything I have done (whatever that means). It's rougher than the others but also I hope more beautiful, or it should be because it is about my early years in the United States Forest Service. Its tentative title:

USFS

The Ranger, the Cook and Wonderland

"And then he thinks he knows
the hills where his life arose . . ."
—*Matthew Arnold's "The Buried Life"*

Next year sounds wonderful. When I get back from Florida, let's get to work planning some performance for you in Chicago.

As ever,
Norman

[postcard]
Seeley Lake, Montana 59868
July 28, 1973
Dear Marie,
I'm glad you like my story on the early Forest Service. Send it along when you can—I'm still working on it, but want to get started on something new

in a week or ten days. The card of Boothbay Harbor is beautiful. You should provide me with every copy of "Floating" and vice versa.

How's your mother?

As ever,

Norman

[postcard]
Seeley Lake, Montana 59868
August 23, 1973
Dear Marie, (I've misplaced your Maine address)

Thanks for your wonderful letter about my story which I shall reply to fully in a day or so. I will disallow for love and friendship, but I also think it's a pretty good story, and it happened long ago. The goat on the postcard is a lot like my goat in the story—looking for trouble from below where it usually comes. I am sorry you can't come to Chicago, but I will continue to love you.

Norman

Seeley Lake, Montana 59868
Sept. 18, 1973
Marie, my dear,

As the final spiritual act, as it were, of the summer, this short letter to you. I just put away the story I have been working on, and I won't pull it out again until I get to Chicago. Instead, after lunch, I'll start folding up the cabin for the winter, and that's always a 3 or 4 (or 5) day job. Then, I'll spend a week or so with my brother-in-law and sister-in-law in Helena, old mining country that I like very much and so do my relatives. We have become pseudo-experts on old mining towns and methods, and tour the back country in a half-ton truck.

Early this summer the vice-president of a Helena bank gave me an old gold pan, and, no kidding, Marie, on the first pan I showed quite a bit of "color." One flake was so large it almost qualified as a "nugget," but didn't quite. Old-timers defined nuggets as follows: they tinkle when you drop them on the pan. I couldn't hear mine, but it's a good-sized flake.

Marie, I know you are an old violinist but I think you would like to go mining. If nothing else, it's kind of wonderful to see the bumps of the world from the open box of a half-ton truck. Ever since I can remember, the half-ton truck has been my favorite mode of transportation.

And how the hell did I get here? Maybe this letter is an act of the spirit, as I said at the outset, but it looks as if it isn't going to have any brains or guiding principles. I was going to start by thanking you for your wonderful criticism of my story and instead started telling you how to tell a nugget. Maybe that isn't so far off the subject anyway, because I certainly value everything you say about what I say. I was especially touched by the fact that you like the movement of the story as a whole—the story of seeing for the first time life becoming a story. Most people to make me feel good, praise this or that piece of it—the forest fire, the fight, etc., but oddly you and Rebecca Roberts, the poet-girl from South Carolina who is here again at the Lake this summer, made me feel best of all about it by seeing what it all meant to me. Rebecca said, "You know, I feel the story is me. I'm 17 years old, too, and for the first time I see my life this summer becoming a story." Bless her heart, I think she is in love with some Sears-and-Roebuck cowboy who works over at the Ranger Station.

But I am grateful, too, for your detailed criticisms and suggestions. And I am especially grateful for your help with my phonetics, which are nil. Now the sentence reads: "On the next map of the Forest Service, it all appeared as one word and a final e had been added which henceforward was pronounced, and the a had been made in Boston. Now, it doesn't mean anything but be sure you pronounce it right: We/tas/se Creek, just as if its headwaters are on Beacon Hill."[15] OK?

I spent a lot more time this summer reworking this Forest Service story than I had intended to—back at the beginning of the summer and again at the very end. I must feel a bit about it the way that you feel about "Floating"—that is has a lot of meaning to you but you haven't got it out quite the way you want it so you can't keep your hands off it. I have another similar feeling about it and "Floating"—they are getting better.

I started another story this summer, but didn't get far with it. As you pointed out in your remarks. My stories go in heavily for "know-how." Nothing is more beautiful to me than people doing things who know how to do them. This story aims before it finishes to give the reader a pretty complete picture of the art of fly-fishing and, so far, that is its title, although of course as usual it has a whore or two in it and as usual my father, who was a fine fly-fisherman, and my brother, who was the best in the northwest. And, negatively, Izaak Walton, who as you may know was a bait-fisherman which, as you may also know, is the bottom of the ladder in the eyes of a good fly-fisherman.

---

15. Borroff explains, "Norman is talking about a creek whose name is now spelled 'Wetasse' and pronounced with three syllables. But it started out simply as 'Wetass,' two words merged in to one, and was later bowdlerized. Norman loved that."

As my father used to tell my brother and me when we were boys: "Izaak Walton is not a respectable writer." I hope to finish it around Xmas, and will send you a copy. [. . .]

Yes, Marie, that's right—send out "Floating" but don't say anything about it unless somebody agrees to publish it. Anyway, that's what I am going to do with USFS 1919.

I was delighted to hear that your mother is back in business, just as feisty and fast-on-her-feet as ever. She is relatively immortal.

I am enclosing a couple of postcards that I know I have sent you before, but this is the way my country looks right now. It gets its particular autumn coloration from the fact that it has the greatest tamarack (larch) stand in the world—and tamarack, as you know, are the only needle-bearing trees whose needles turn yellow in the autumn—and finally drop off. And it is autumn here—in a big way. Yesterday morning it was 19° at my window when I got up. It snowed first on Aug. 31, and 4 days ago it snowed all day. Everything green was white, except the Lake which was black and you couldn't see across it. [. . .]

As ever,

Norman

[P.S.] No wonder I can't get a story finished when I write letters this long.

[postcard]

September 18, 1973

Marie, my dear, the photograph for this card was taken right in front of my cabin. Right in front of my cabin, too, are 2 beaver who have been building a house all summer (see spot marked X). Under the guest cabin in the rear are a skunk and 3 kittens. She was here last year, too, and we have become very good friends. I hope some summer to tame one of her kittens enough to bring it back to Chicago. I would love to walk across the University campus with it following me as a pet. I have several people in mind whom I should like to meet.

April 16, 1976

Marie, dear,

Almost as soon as you left Chicago I did, too—for Washington, D.C., where I am staying with my son and working on the files of the United States Forest Service on a tragic forest fire of 1949 which is to be the base of my next long story.

But I did stay in Chicago for several days after you left and heard everyone say what a smash-hit you had been.[16] Everybody. You are wasting your talents staying in one place and being the first woman professor of anything. You should be riding the circuit like an old-time Methodist minister preaching and giving inspirational messages on the Logos as revealed in the New Testament including the Book of Wallace Stevens and other insurance agents.

I hadn't more than turned around at O'Hare Field and started for town before I missed you, and in another (and very beautiful) town. I still miss you. Don't be gone so long next time.

As ever and ever,

Norman

April 22, 1976

Marie, dear,

I returned yesterday from over a week in Washington and found your sweet letter plus a couple of poems you wrote long ago when you were a red-headed chick teaching in Smith College (I would guess) and using such eastern women's college words as "caudle" (to rhyme with "dawdle"), "native dower" and "deeming." I won't go on, because you can pick them out yourself. But I like the whole poem, and now and then it is flawless and moving:

As I said,	Shaping the inward welter in subjection
this is flawless	Under one will, of hazardous election,
	The accused accuser, to its own impulse traitor,
	Reluctant witness and adjudicator.

But right before these lines is the line

A more instructed selfhood hardly winning.

If you were writing the poem now, of course, it wouldn't show the effect of commuting between Smith and Yale every other day. Maybe you can still make something of it. As you know now, you can't write a tender poem unless it is clean and tough. Do you remember offhand Sir Walter Raleigh's "To His Son"

---

16. Maclean is referring to a lecture on Wallace Stevens that Borroff delivered at the University of Chicago. Borroff recalls that the lecture "must have been an important occasion because someone introduced Norman, who then introduced me. When your introducer is himself introduced, that's heady stuff!"

and James Joyce's "A Flower Given to My Daughter" ["my blueveined child"] and "Ecce Puer"? They mean more to me than any other poems written to children.

Yes, I think that soon you should go back to writing poems with some regularity, in so far as poems are subject to this treatment. You have a gift. The vein is genuine and deep—no one of us knows now how wide it is, but that may make no difference. It has to be mined to be productive. It won't even add to your inner life if it is left buried—it probably will only mess you up. If I were you, I wouldn't wait until I had finished the book on the American poets[17] before trying your own thing for an hour or so a day, even if most of it for a while is just doing your exercises. It's an art, and they can talk all they want to about an art being in your head or heart but a lot of it has to be in your bones so you can do it without thinking of more than a little part of it. Of course, it takes a lot of thinking and fooling around before you can do it that way. You know, you used to put yourself through school teaching the piano. [. . .]

As ever, and ever,

Norman

[P.S.] Isn't that a lovely line, "My blueveined child." Be sure to reread those poems.

Christmas 1980

Dear Marie:

No one can say either of us spent much of 1980 in writing each other, but I think I haven't entirely lost the knack, because I hope by the end of the winter to have fairly well completed the long forest fire story that I long have been working on, and I hope that you can still read, because I don't publish, even on forest fires, without your permission. So by spring, be prepared. It has been hard work.

Marie, while you are still a young chick, do all the big things you are going to do, because beyond a certain age almost anything big is almost too big.

I hope you are continuing with your critical and linguistic studies and I especially like your combination of the two. I will always regard your essays on Frost and Marianne Moore as classics. Did I ever tell you I knew both of them a little—I even took Marianne out a couple of evenings—she was small,

17. Borroff's "book on the American poets" was published by the University of Chicago Press in 1979 as *Language and the Poet: Verbal Artistry in Frost, Stevens, and Moore.*

fey, and impudent, and knew a great deal about baseball, especially about the Brooklyn Dodgers. She really knew a great deal about the Brooklyn Dodgers, and soon you will know a great deal about forest fires. Most of all, don't ever give up your poetry. Maybe your poetic gift is not as deep as the ocean, but it is a clear and beautiful stream. (How is your mother?)

[unsigned]

January 27, 1981

Dear Marie:

The "Dirge for the Living" is one of the best poems you have ever written.[18] It's very moving—it's a masterpiece of the dramatic lyric, of thought going backward in pain through life until suddenly it is stopped by the pain of being alive now. It is very lovely, everything under control—except the next-to-last line, which seems kind of sick itself in its attempt to find a rhyme. The last line, though, is terrific. Absolutely pure.

The "Concerto" is lovely, too—it is a world you do beautifully, of music fading into dreams and of dreams returning from music of long ago and stopping just on the edge of reality. [. . .]

I'm sorry to learn that your critical essays on the American poets have not been best sellers. This in no way alters my belief that they are remarkable essays on individual poets. I suppose that more critical essays have been written on individual poets than on all in all the other fairly obvious subjects for critical essays—on individual poems or groups of poems, of poetical periods, on critical methods, so your essays entered a highly competitive field, but they are among the very best. Do not be down-hearted, Marie, because they have received no immediate large audience. Criticism is a very fashionable thing. Thirty or forty years ago it was all the fashion. It was a mania. Graduate students in English would far rather to have been noted critics some day than noted creative writers. It was unnatural and criticism in recent years has receded back more into the natural water levels. But there is something unnatural in the levels it has receded to—modern aesthetics and criticism has receded to fads, mostly fads, and, darling, you don't belong in any school of structural nuts. There are plenty of others in the Yale Dept. of English who do, but you are above such things [and] when it does recede to sense and

18. Borroff's poems "Dirge for the Living" and "Mischa Levitzki" (referred to below) are both collected in her book *Stars and Other Signs.*

sensitivity you will be floating on top of its waters, but don't ever be foolish enough to think that criticism is more important than creativity. Most of the time it is mostly a foolish fashion.

Thank you again for your lovely poems.

As always, with love,

Norman

January 29, 1985

Dear Marie:

I must start this year off right by reestablishing some band of connection with you, bodily or spiritual. My last glimpse of you (purely spiritual) was on a raft on the white water of the Grand Canyon, and I would like to have been with you, except it probably would be too tough for me now. I still do a little fishing, and all of it is boat-fishing, from a boat on the Blackfoot river, and it is beautiful but a damn poor way to fish. You look ahead and see a stretch of white water coming that after 150 yards eases off into blue, and you know that 150 yards is going to be so fast and rough that you will be lucky to get in just one cast, and then comes the white water, you are turned sideways going down, drop your rod and grab an oar to straighten out, are turned sideways the other way hitting the next trough, now have to drop your oar to save your rod, emerge from the bottom of your boat to float into the blue water without either rod or oar in your hand and without having made a single cast. It's a hell of a poor way to fish, as I said, but I would like to have been with you, even if I saw you only when I went down without the oar passing you coming up with it.

I pause for a breath to see where I go from here. I suppose to your writing and mine, which is also a perilous undertaking, sometimes, taking you up and sometimes down and sometimes without a rod and sometimes without an oar, which at least describes the way my writing goes. I hope, though, by the end of the summer that I will float out on the blue water with a manuscript of a story on a forest fire ready to lay on the publishers.

How does your writing go, both criticism and poetry? I have had great respect for the criticism you were doing when we last followed each other closely—the using the aesthetic to illuminate the linguistic and vice versa. I thought you were one of the very few (if any) who could make one work for the other. But I suppose it and all other illuminating criticism have been put in the shade by the present fad for "structuralism" (which fad Yale has done more than its full share to promote). I find it completely unilluminating about literature and arrogant to the point of being snotty. Darling, fads come and go.

You alone have the possibility of being steady. You go on doing what you know you can do and is worthwhile.

Near the bottom of this page, Marie, I ask you as always to remember you are a poet. Maybe the vein is not a wide one, but it is very pure. As we say out in my country, it is "high-grade ore."

I love you, as I have for a long time.

Norman

Oct. 30, 1986

Dear Marie:

Forgive me for I know not what I do—but I know a lot of what I don't do. I work all the time, from 6:30 in the morning to 12 at night, but on the 'not' side I don't get much writing done of my own any more and I never went fishing once this summer and seldom go for a walk any more and I don't write you any more and I have almost no fun any more and I don't seem to get all my bills paid any more. What I do is get up at 6:30 every morning, weekends included, and go to bed at 12:00, which at least sounds like something positive for a change, but isn't because I still don't get anything done, including writing you. I take a little nap once in a while, but that doesn't freshen me up, because I still don't write you. I'm glad, though, that you still stay awake and keep on revising "Mischa Levitzki, Valse in A Major" because as you say it gets better each time until it has become one of the best—maybe the best—poems you have ever written.

You don't know what a compliment that is because it comes from someone destitute of musical sensitivity. There is not a musical gene in my musical heritage—on either side of my family. Neither my father nor my mother could hum a tune. But your poem deeply touches me—it makes me feel deeply in touch with something deep that has happened and has been translated into sound waves.

That's pretty high up the musical register, though, and I don't know whether it can be made more resonant by further orchestration, so why don't you write me *another* poem for Thanksgiving, if not Thanksgiving then Christmas?

I love you very much, and will follow (if I have the talent) every new step in your musical career.

As ever,

Norman

Letters to Nick Lyons,

....

1976–1981

....

*Nick Lyons taught English for twenty-eight years, first at the
University of Michigan and then at Hunter College in New York
City. In New York he also became a book editor and publisher,
founding in 1982 what has become the Lyons Press, which has
published an impressive list of fly-fishing books as well as works
by writers such as Tom McGuane, Edward Hoagland, Verlyn
Klinkenborg, and Jon Krakauer. Lyons has himself authored
twenty-two books and hundreds of magazine articles during his
long career. He earned a special place in Maclean's heart because
of his enthusiastic review, in* Fly Fisherman *magazine (Spring
1976), of* A River Runs through It and Other Stories.
Lyons's proved the first published review of River, *and he called
it a "classic" of American literature. In his letters to Lyons after
May 1976, Maclean discusses the writing and reception of* River,
*his work on the Mann Gulch fire book, and their common love
of fishing. For Lyons, he became a generous friend and trusted
sounding board, inquiring about Lyons's teaching and then new
publishing career, and always affirming the quality of his fishing
essays.*

May 26, 1976

Dear Mr. Lyons:

I am deeply touched by your review of my stories in the Fly Fisherman's
Bookshelf. I should like to think that the story, "A River Runs Through It," is
somewhere near as good as you say it is, not so much for my sake as for the
memory of my brother whom I loved and still do not understand, and could
not help.

Since you wrote so beautifully about the story, I feel that I must speak
personally of it to you. After my father's death, there was no one—not even
my wife—to whom I could talk about my brother and his death. After my
retirement from teaching, I felt that it was imperative I come to some kind
of terms with his death as part of trying to do the same with my own. This

was the major impulse that started me to write stories at 70, and the first one naturally that I wrote was about him. It was both a moral and artistic failure. It was really not about my brother—it was only about how I and my father and our duck dogs felt about his death.[1] So I put it aside (and have carefully never tried to publish it). I wrote the other stories to get more confidence in myself as a story-teller and to talk out loud to myself about him. The story, which now stands as the first one in the book, is actually the last one I wrote.

I hope it will be the best one (although not the last one) I ever write, and I thank you again for writing beautifully about it.

Very sincerely yours,
Norman Maclean

July 11, 1976
Dear Mr. Lyons:
Your warm-hearted and encouraging letter was waiting for me when I finally arrived here [Seeley Lake, Montana] a week or so ago. As an ex-English teacher, I always have to admire your prose, too. Being an English teacher always leaves its mark. When I'm fishing and look upstream and see somebody fishing downstream, I pause and watch for a cast or two, and then say to myself, "C minus." [. . .]

Your prose should go well with rivers, even with the Madison which at least used to be one hell of a river. The last time I fished it, though, it was covered with bastards from Texas in rubber rafts. I believe, now, however, it can't be fished by raft. The bastards from Texas in rubber rafts have all moved over to the Big Blackfoot—they are in danger of capsizing from collision.

I am enclosing a colored photograph of my home. My log cabin, which my father and I built over half a century ago, is right on the Lake at the extreme left side of the postcard—the Big Blackfoot is 17 miles from here. Drop by some time and I'll take you down, but there are so damn many fishermen on it now you have to bring your own rock with you.

Yes, I hope to write another book, if I can ever get out from under the effects of writing the first. If you write one book, is it ever possible to write two?

May you live to write many and may a river run through them all.
Norman Maclean

1. Maclean is referring to "Retrievers Good and Bad," published finally in *Esquire* in 1977.

Nov. 10, 1976

Dear Nick:

Your letter of 28 October has reached me by what we used to call in bridge, "the approach system"—anything that reaches me in Chicago by way of Seeley Lake through the United States Postal Service can be thought of as approaching gradually.

Nevertheless, I was delighted finally to receive it. I am grateful to you for nominating my story (I am sure it was you) for the Gingrich Award,[2] and I hope only that your committee thinks as much of the story as the chairman does. I suppose by now that she has received most all of the reviews it will have—and it has received a good many of them, but yours is still my all-time favorite. In part, that could be because our lives and interests and professions have overlapped each other a good deal, but I still like to think that primarily it is because as a thing apart it is such a fine review. In respect to your committee, I hope you're as good a rhetorician as a critic.

I was also delighted to hear that you fished the Big Hole in September, but was surprised to hear you say that practically no one besides yourself was [there]. The Big Hole used to be home, sweet home for every son-of-a-bitch from Butte, but I am sure there is still fishing there and I am glad you ran into at least a day of it. At about the same time, I was having some pretty good luck with big ones on a fly I suspect was very much like your "hopper"—with a big dark wing and an absorbent yellow wool body, meant, I am sure, to be fished wet and allowed to sink a few inches. But this September I fished it dry, and had some unusual luck. I'm really a wet-fly fisherman and when I go to a dry it is to something little in the quiet water of the evening, but in recent years I have been fishing a dry a lot—often in the middle of the day—and big, big as a mattress. When they are on the bottom and won't come up, they will come up and at least take a look. We call the fly "Joe's Hopper," but I think that is a local name.

It must be wonderful to have a year off. I envy you (in retrospect). I never had a year off. The University of Chicago does not grant sabbaticals and I must have been young even before the Guggenheims developed the flotation process which led to the smelter which led to the fellowships in the humanities. But I never got closer to one than working in a Guggenheim smelter in East Helena and getting my skin all pitted.

---

2. The Arnold Gingrich Literary Award of the Federation of Fly Fishers. Maclean did not win the award until 1989; Lyons himself won it in 1986.

As for you, take the General's advice and count your blessings.

Yes, my book is in its second printing. I don't know what it means for a book of stories to do well, but I at least think it [has] done well and has been well received. Paramount is negotiating with the Press for an option to make a film of the fishing story, and *People* magazine supposedly is going to run a story on me (provided, I suppose, if they can find some sex to go with the fishing—something I wish I could find, too).

Try fishing that hopper (and a big hair Royal Coachman) fly some time.

Thanks again,

Norman

Dec. 2, 1976

Dear Nick:

It was great, as always, to hear from you, but I haven't received as yet "the two little fishing books" that were written "during several long city winters." That's a hell of a good time to catch fish. I've caught more then often than in the summers. I'll be waiting with interest to see what you use to fish through the ice.

Personally, I used to use that brand of booze I talk about in my first story— named after the sign of the Vigilantes—3-7-77. You get in one of those little houses over a hole in the ice and start the kerosene burner and you are already drugged from the fumes before you start on the 3-7-77.

I am glad that you gave our sales department a booster shot. And me, too. I sure can't kick about the number or kindness of the reviews that the little blue book has received, but I'll be God damned if *Fly Fishing* [*Fly Fisherman*] isn't the only one of what might be called "an outdoor journal" which has reviewed it. I don't even start with "pig-fucker" in referring to *Field and Stream*.

I'm sure, though, that part of the fault lies in the inexperience of the press in dealing with the kind of thing I write, and I know both the Director, Mr. [Morris] Philipson, and the Sales Manager, Mr. [Stanley] Plona, were grateful for the list you sent them of [illegible] points for fly fishermen. I'm grateful too.

In case this turns out to be the letter-before-Christmas, I should like to thank you for the lift you have given me this year and to wish you health and happiness for the coming season and the coming year. May they always rise in the evening.

Norman

Jan. 1, 1977

Dear Nick:

A good way of starting the year off is to tell you how much I have enjoyed your books (which did not arrive until the day before Christmas!). Although they are about fishing, they are almost escape literature for me. Never in my life did I get up at 2:30 A.M. to catch the milk train to try for trout. About the only thing it resembles in my background is duck hunting, and then the only resemblance is the starting hours. I remember I always had a bottle of whiskey under the bed, and took a couple of shots before I got into my long underwear. But by continuing to drink steadily while I was in the blind I kept even, but when I got back to the warm cabin I would almost pass out just from opening the door.

Nick, you're not only a fine writer but you are also a poet, so I wasn't surprised to see that your first publication was a book of poems. Of course, I doubt if one can really write about fishing unless he's at least a half-ass poet, and you're really a poet. I like some of the human ones best—fishing with your boy or taking your wife (who sounds like quite a gal) along. I can remember being like your boy—at the age where I thought I was pretty damn good and so couldn't understand how my father could catch them and I couldn't. I just couldn't see what he had that I didn't have, but it had to be something.

So I like not only your writing but the fragrance of your situations.

Best wishes,

Norman

[P.S.] Speaking of poems, I wrote one the other day—the first in 50 years. What if I end as you began—with a book of them?

FOREVER
Loneliness is not always lonely.
It can go on to ecstasy.
When I am alone in the woods
I am the universe.
What is there
I do not know
Or cannot do?
Do not tell me I cannot live forever.
I already have.

Sept. 10, 1978

Dear Nick:

It was sure good to hear from you again, even though I was saddened to learn that you had returned to publishing. I was glad, though, to find out you were going to continue teaching—you must be a fine teacher—and I hope you will find time (and the energy—God damn it, it is a kind of energy more than time that passes away—) to go on with your brilliant writing and editing. And how about a little fishing now and then?

I almost went out of the fishing business myself about a month ago. I was fishing on the Swan river. It is a beautiful river, one of the most beautiful in the world, running as it does between the Mission Glaciers and the Swan Mountains. It is perhaps more beautiful than if it ran by the Tetons, but, by the same token, it is in very rough country. It has no banks—the banks are all occupied by blue spruce, and as you well know, there is no way, least of all by climbing through the needles, of getting a fly out of a spruce once you have got careless about one back-cast. So, to fish the Swan, you have to ford it lengthwise. I still don't know how I did it, but I never fell so hard. I pulverized a glass rod, and everything inside me that has turned to glass-fiber from old age. For 10 days I put ice packs on whatever I felt still circulated inside me.

I didn't get much farther than the woodpile until yesterday, when I regained enough self-confidence and circulation to try fishing again. Still being plenty subdued, I tried a small stream, probably because of the word "small." But it was a mistake. I had forgotten how much brush you have to crawl under and how many fallen logs you have to crawl over to fish a "small" mountain stream. It was odd. It was my foot that I had hurt most, but once I was back in business it was my knee that hurt worst, and next my shoulder. Today it's my foot again that's worst. I don't quite understand, except maybe by the time you are 75 you have already learned to hurt all over, if given half a chance.

But I caught 5, not big of course but half-decent, and threw back about 25. I admired one especially. He was a cut-throat about 11 inches long, the sole occupant of an open quiet hole with nothing on the bottom of it but a water-soaked snag. He knew and I knew he had one chance, and that was to get under that snag and throw a half-hitch over it. It was kind of wonderful to watch all the tricks he had of making you think he was going some other way when he really was going for the snag. I admired him so much I threw him back when I landed him, even though he was as big as any of the five I kept.

Cautiously, I fished only an hour by prior agreement with myself, but it was real nice to re-establish social communication with fish, even small fish. They know a dead snag when they see one, which is a lot more than you can say about a lot of big men.

I hope you don't have to give up fishing for publishing. [. . .]

This Sabbath morning was the morning I wasn't going to write this week, but here I have spent all of it writing you. Fortunately, there is enough space left on this sheet to wish you happiness and success in your venture of publishing and continued success and happiness in your writing, teaching, and fishing.

Sincerely,
Norman

Nov. 22, 1978
Dear Nick:

I have been asked to speak before the Chairmen of the English Departments in the country on Dec. 28 at the MLA meetings in New York City. I am arriving there the evening of the day before (the 27th) and will leave the day after (the 29th). I suppose I will be very busy at the meetings and seeing old friends and besides I hope to find time to talk to several New York people who have written me about the publication of my next book. Even so, I would like to get a chance to get together with you, if only for 1/2 an hour or an hour before I head back to Chicago. Although I realize the dates over which I have no control fall in the post-Xmas holidays. You have been very good to me and my book and have known only my book.

I was troubled by your last letters, although I don't know whether I can say anything that will be of help. I hate to see you being driven in so many directions—teaching, editing, writing and now publishing. What I have seen of your writing is often brilliant and yet moving (naturally I am especially touched by your stories of fishing with your boy and by the brilliance of your reviews), but in the dispersion of your gifts I am afraid that writing is what will suffer most.

The hell of it is that I don't know what I can say to help. I let it happen to me. In the "Preface" to my stories I confess in the first paragraph that I was 70 years old before I tried something beyond scholarship and criticism—and I don't know whether I was ever divided into as many pieces as you are. I don't know what to tell you, but I'd like to talk to you for a few minutes if you are going to be in the city after Christmas.

You ask in one of your letters if I have made any commitments about the publication of my next big story. None. I have ducked them. A long story for me is a full-time job, especially when I am about 3/5 through it and can't yet see the end and can't quite remember the beginning. At that point in the traffic I feel I should spend my time trying to see a little more light. [. . .] I have friends in the book business who keep advising me that I should look toward Seattle for my next publisher. I know there is a great boom going on there in the writing and publishing of books, and I know *A River* did better in Seattle than in any other city in the country, except my home town of Missoula, Montana. Have you ever been in Seattle—it is a wonderful and beautiful and powerful city. It's an idea anyway. Although New York City is not one of my favorite watering-places, it would be a pleasure to see you there this Xmas.

Very sincerely yours,

Norman

March 8, 1979

Dear Nick:

Enclosed is one of the earliest copies of the paperback edition of my book of stories. I hope you like the cover—it is a reproduction of a photograph taken for me by a young Forest Service Ranger of the portion of Seeley Lake where my cabin is. My cabin is on the edge of the lake (Seeley Lake) near the left edge of the photograph.

To me, of course, it is beautiful, and I hope you like its looks, too. My cabin is only about 16 miles from the glaciers. It snows every month.

I hope also that you will note the first review quoted on the inside of the covers is yours. Thank you again for your kind words which certainly contributed to the book's success.

By the way, have you ever heard from that friend of yours who was wondering if he could get permission to publish the fishing story in a fishing series of his? Only yesterday I received a similar request from someone who plans to put out an anthology of fishing stories.

I hope all goes well with you. We have a long winter.

Norman

March 27, 1979

Dear Nick:

Thank you for your warm-hearted letter. Don't apologize if it is a little late. I know you are always living a two-storey life.

I wish, though, you could find time to write more of your own kind of thing. I am glad that my starting to write in life gives you some kind of comfort. Given good health, you will find time (in the fullness of time) to sit and write in beauty. I myself don't derive great comfort from that thought, if for no other reason than that you can write in beauty now if you could only find time to sit.

It might interest you to know that I think I also wrote quite well when I was young. T. S. Eliot made his big early reputation by winning *The Dial* poetry contest with his *Waste Land*. In that contest, there were three judges and one of them (Carl Sandburg) selected my entry as number one. So as you can see I have never had much luck in winning contests.

I don't look at the past, however, with much regret—or great jubilation. Like most woodsmen I have known, I am a fatalist. I figure it's all or mostly a matter of having your number called. Of course, you have to be ready, as you will. But, Nick, right now you are a beautiful writer. [. . .]

Just keep pegging away until you are 73 and try not to ask questions. For the next 3 years after 73 God might take care of you.

Norman

August 8, 1980

Dear Nick:

The other day I wrote the last sentence of the first draft of the last chapter of my long overdue story on the tragic forest fire. A few hours later I realized it was Aug. 5, the anniversary date of the tragedy (Aug. 5, 1949). This Delphic coincidence, like most omens, can receive opposite interpretations, but I prefer to interpret it as a good omen, indicating that my story is one with the event rather than it is about to go up in smoke.

Anyway, I am using it as an excuse to myself to take a few days off to answer the pile of letters that have been gathering volcanic dust on them (from Mt. St. Helens—including last night) on the table on my front porch.

I've begun with what's most important—I am delighted to learn of your promotion to full professor, since I wrote a letter for you—I'm sure I have a copy of it in my files in Chicago and will send you one when I get back home. I remember among other things saying in it that you were a better writer than Izaak Walton, taking a chance that none of those eastern bastards on your promotion committee had ever read *A River Runs Through It* in which it is quite clear I was brought up in a family of fishermen who thought Izaak Walton was a piss-poor fisherman and writer. Evidently I was right—that's the way my predications about New Yorkers turn out—usually. It's odd, but being a full-professor settles pretty much for good a fair number of life's problems, and so I am delighted you will be free of these problems and can spend more time fishing and being a better writer than Izaak Walton.

As for me, I also took a slight step forward academically this spring. I was awarded an honorary doctoral degree (Doctor of Letters) by Montana State University. It leaves a good feeling to be well thought of in the country one loves and thinks he knows.

As for the future of my new story, Nick, I expect to spend another 3 or 4 months on it before I submit it to a publisher. Then I think I'll try to avoid wasting some of the year of time I wasted with *A River* having it rejected by eastern publishers who after keeping it 3 months would return it with the comment it had trees in it or was just like the stuff they received every day. My son-in-law, whose advice I nearly always follow, says I should get an agent, preferably a Jewish woman with motherly instincts. He's a Jewish boy from Brooklyn, so he sure as hell should know what he is talking about. Who knows? Maybe around the first of the year a Jewish woman who makes good chicken noodle soup might ask you if you would like to read the manuscript of a story about a forest fire entitled, "A Wildfire Runs Through It"?

Norman

Oct. 27, 1980

Dear Nick:

Your letter says it was written on the 15th of August, so that makes over 2 months since I haven't answered it—and it's such a nice, warm-hearted letter, even though you didn't mention coming to Montana until you were back home in New York. And didn't tell me you had been promoted to full professor until a lot more than 2 months after you were.

Anyway, I am delighted that you now are sitting on the top rung of the academic ladder, with what security, if any, goes with the position.

Still, Nick, I think your department promoted you knowing you pretty damn well and knowing that you weren't going to play the political or administrative game. In my letter of recommendation I certainly tried to make clear to them that if they expected to get the maximum yardage out of you they had to let you call your own signals. I predict that you will find fulfillment and happiness in your new and permanent academic position.

I was also glad to hear you also did pretty well fishing in Montana—better, I am sure, than if you had come over to Seeley Lake and I had taken you to the Blackfoot or Swan to fish. I have had a hard time myself believing what I am going to tell you next—I fished only 3 times this summer and was terrible. The fish could see me coming all the way from Chicago. I was worst of all in my sense of timing in setting the hook, and the worse I got the faster I got. I left a wake of gasping trout behind me wondering whether they had been seeing things instead of flies.

But I did work hard on my forest-fire story. I have worked way too long on it already, and I won't be able to live with myself if I don't finish it by the end of this coming winter. Never again will I try to write a story that is historically accurate in every detail. It is clear to me now that the universe in its truculence doesn't permit itself to be that well known. At my age, [I] should have know[n] that, but at my age I no longer have the choice of turning back. I just worked, as remote from my friends as from fish.

Of course you can see it when I finish it—I would feel a big part of it was missing if you didn't. But I won't feel neglected if we both soon realize that it is a very western book and New York is not its Cape Canaveral. As you already know, I start off with a pretty dim view of New York publishers—and they of me. I will omit this opportunity of stating my view of them—five of them turned down A River Runs through It. I can still fish better than that.

As ever,
Norman

June 15, 1981
Dear Nick:
I was real sorry to hear that you are through telling fish stories. You are one of the best of all of them, and in fact you hold your present high academic position to a sworn statement that you are better than Izaak Walton. You had better be careful about making public any such change in intention or you may end up marking papers for popular lecturers with classes over 135.

Oddly, though, I think I can at least partly understand your change of feeling. Maybe I am even worse than you are—I am almost at the point where I have quit fishing (not just writing about it). With me, I think it was mostly a case of coming to a place in life of not being able to do well what I had done fairly well most of my life After I became a chronic heart-patient and several times picked myself out of the sand and didn't know how I got there I discovered I didn't like fishing any more. So it seems there comes a time that marks the end of each thing—even of sacred love.

It hardly seems possible, though, that you should quit telling fishing stories, and it is probably only a passing fancy. But, if the feeling persists, why don't you quit and see what happens? You have already created a highly informed and loving literature about fishing—full of information and love about the water, and what's in it and above it but also about your son who went with you. Let be, if that's what your heart says. I am a great believer in listening to your heart.

As for me, I have just returned from Montana and two days from now I am going to start out again. Last Sunday I was at the University of Montana (Missoula) where I was awarded an honorary doctoral degree (last year at this time I was awarded an honorary doctoral degree at Montana State University, Bozeman). This coming Sunday I will start with a loaded car to spend the summer at Seeley Lake and, for Christ's sake, finally finish my story on the Smokejumper tragic forest fire.

Of course, Nick, you can see it. You are among the few I most want to see it. I haven't even yet thought much of what I'll do with it when I finish it— probably turn it over to an agent, but if I do, after informing him of my great admiration for you and your literary judgment and your kindness to me and with the instruction that, no matter what, you are to see it at your leisure.

But, Nick, I am sure that, after you see it, you will recognize the story and I are even more western than you thought we were. There won't be that kind of one-to-one relation there was between A River, you, and me because of fishing. This is a Smokejumpers story—at all times a story about forest fires and firefighting and at times almost a manual of these subjects. I think it would be the part of caution to assume that we were not made to go firefighting together—we might waste a lot of each other's time trying to help each other. But read it and see for yourself.

I think it will be good.

Norman

Letters to Lois Jansson,

1979–1981

Maclean's letters to Lois Jansson show him deeply at work on what became Young Men and Fire *and his sensitivity to the survivors of the Mann Gulch tragedy even as he probes their memories and pain. Lois Jansson, who died in 2005, was the widow of Robert (Bob) Jansson, the USFS ranger whose district in 1949 included Mann Gulch (about twenty-five miles northeast of Helena, Montana). Maclean believed that Jansson acted heroically during and after the fire; his letters and the book reflect his respect for the man. Lois Jansson became a trusted Montana friend and source of information, and the letters demonstrate Maclean's scrupulous care in his research and rewriting. In them we see him rehearsing pieces of his quest for the truth of what happened in the Mann Gulch blowup. The correspondence ends in 1981 with Maclean reporting to Mrs. Jansson that he has finished a first draft of his Mann Gulch book. In fact, he would never complete the manuscript to his satisfaction and died in 1990 without submitting it to a publisher.*

Sept. 2, 1979

Dear Mrs. Jansson:

Your letter to me, sent first to the University of Chicago, has finally reached me here at my summer cabin at Seeley Lake, and I am grateful for it and very touched by it. Through my study of the documents relating to the Mann Gulch fire, I have become a great admirer of your husband. Of all the many statements made about the fire, I regard his as the most accurate and humanly moving. He probably would not consider himself a remarkably fine writer, and perhaps stylistically he wasn't, but, because of his power to see vividly and compassionately, he is a moving writer. In the story I am writing of the fire, he is certainly one of the leading characters. As an historian, I cannot write with the major aim of pleasing wives and blood relatives, but I think that you will feel proud of your man as I portray him.

The fact is that I am thinking of doing a short character sketch of him in October when I speak in Missoula before a conference of leading experts in the Rockies on fire management (called the Intermountain Fire Research Council—500 or 600 of them, I understand). If ultimately I follow my present outline, I will send you some copies (it is to be published).[1]

So you have written to a family friend.

As to your questions about the documentary bases of the knowledge I have of him, it is based, I think, on all the official documents of his that you mention—I have not only read them, but I possess them.

I have copies of and know pretty much by heart:

1. The 1949 Report of the Board of Review (and Pete Hanson's report on the fire prior to the Board's report).[2]

2. A verbatim transcript of the testimony at the Board of Review (before which your husband appeared twice).

3. Of all your husband's own statements I have: (1) J. R. Jansson Statement, August 23, 1949; (2) Jansson Ground Check Statement, August 31, 1949; (3) Ranger Jansson's Rescue Statement, 8/3/49; (4) Another "Statement" dated Sept. 7, 1951; (5) somewhere around, although I have misplaced it just now, his fine record (for insurance purposes) of his last day in Mann Gulch with Gisborne; (6) and letters from him to Dodge after the fire.[3] I think I have even other things of his around that are out-of-place or misplaced for the moment.

Documents on matters that you allude to but I am not sure about, however, are as follows:

(1) You allude to his unpublished notes and statements about the fire. Do you know whether these contain any important information or opinions about the fire not in his published reports referred to above? If he had to hold back anything important, naturally I would be anxious to know what it was if it could be revealed. I am familiar, of course, with his theory that "the blowup" was caused by firewhirls, and, with some shifting of particulars, I agree with it. I know, especially from his later letters to Dodge, that he thought Dodge

---

1. Subsequently published as "A Man I Met in Mann Gulch," in part a profile of fire scientist Harry T. Gisborne, and reprinted in *Norman Maclean* (1988) in Confluence Press's American Authors series.

2. Maclean is in fact referring to Regional Forester Percy D. Hanson, author of *History of Mann Gulch Fire*.

3. Gisborne was a pioneering forest fire scientist who figures prominently in *Young Men and Fire*. He died of a heart attack on November 9, 1949, while inspecting the site of the Mann Gulch fire. R. Wagner "Wag" Dodge was the foreman of the Smokejumper crew at Mann Gulch.

"acted as he would have." These are the big theories—the cause of the fire and the conduct of the crew.

I don't want to ask you for access to privileged documents and won't—unless, without them, you think I would make serious mistakes about the fire. I doubt very much if, after me, there will be anyone who has had the right combination of training or will take the endless time to try to write another searching account of the Mann Gulch fire.

I expect you to see that I do not miss anything important. My guess is that this is the last time around. [. . .]

Thank you again for your thoughtfulness in writing me. I am an admirer of your prose style, as well as of your husband's.

Very sincerely yours,

Norman Maclean

[P.S.] Yes, I have *Life* Magazine of Aug. 22, 1949—in fact, I have Wag Dodge's own copy.[4] I also have Wag's scrap-book of newspaper clippings.

Sept. 21, 1979

Dear Mrs. Jansson:

I am packing up to leave Seeley Lake for the summer (? I don't know whether "summer" is the right word, since it's in the high 20s nearly every morning), so there are things I want to say I'll have to leave until I get to Chicago. But I couldn't leave without thanking you for your letter of Sept. 5 and of the enclosed reminiscences of your life as a ranger's wife. In many ways, your husband was also a tragic victim of the Mann Gulch Fire—after it and in part because of it his life began to fade out. I was especially moved by your description of his returning home after he led the rescue team into Mann Gulch—carrying the smell of death with him. Contrary to your fears, I appreciated your personal, behind-the-scenes descriptions of him. As for his professional reports on the Mann Gulch Fire, I think I have all of them, but I am counting on you to check on me to be sure I have.

It is not clear from your letters whether the copy you sent to me of the reminiscences is mine to keep or whether I am to return it. If you wish it returned, do I have your permission to have parts of it Xeroxed?

I shall be visiting a little along the way, so it will be early in October before I reach Chicago. [. . .]

---

4. This issue of *Life* magazine featured an article about the Mann Gulch fire, illustrated in part by Peter Stackpole, one of the original staff photographers of *Life*.

Thank you again. I am sure you haven't heard the last of me.

Very sincerely yours,

Norman Maclean

Dec. 20, 1979

Dear Mrs. Jansson:

I am glad that on the whole you liked the talk I gave at the Conference of the Intermountain Fire Research Council, and I am sorry about the very "cry." I meant it in the sense of "he *cried out* in his sleep," not in the sense of "*wept*." The truth is that I don't believe any man connected with the fire ever wept after he was a child.

I gave my copy of the talk to the Secretary of the Intermountain Fire Research Council nearly two months ago presumably for publication in the Proceedings of their Council, so it undoubtedly is too late to make any changes in it now. I promise, though, that if it is ever republished I will remove this unhappy little ambiguity.

I don't want to close this letter at this time of year without wishing you great happiness during the coming season and the coming new year—and all the years to come.

For me, I hope it is the year that I bring the Mann Gulch Fire under control.

Very sincerely yours,

Norman Maclean

Feb. 8, 1980

Dear Mrs. Jansson:

Thank you for your kind words about my stories. I am especially touched by your words since they come from an authority on the world in which they took place.

I was also touched by the montage of personal remembrances they called up for you of times when you were in Wolf Creek or on the Elkhorn. My wife's ashes are scattered on a mountain named after her and by her when she was a girl that overlooks the town of Wolf Creek and the Oxbow Ranch all the way to the entry to the Gates of the Mountains. I am getting too old, alas, to climb up each summer to be with her for a time.

The mountain you ask about at the head of Mann Gulch is Willow Mountain. At its other side is Willow Creek which runs into the Elkhorn just before they run into the Missouri. The last summer when I went into Mann Gulch

I went through the old McGregor Ranch, up Willow Creek and over the divide into Mann Gulch. The Montana Fish and Game Commission, which now owns the McGregor Ranch, leant me a horse to take me to the top of the divide, or I don't think I could have made it. It was well over 100° that day in the Gulch. [. . .]

The Sleeping Giant[5] had nothing to do with the Mann Gulch Fire. The Sleeping Giant is on the other (the west) side of the Missouri.

I am returning the check you sent me for copies of my book. It is my pleasure and privilege to give them to you.[6]

Tell me, is Roger your son? I will send him an inscribed copy.

Very sincerely yours,

Norman Maclean

March 1, 1980

Dear Mrs. Jansson:

I am sending an autographed copy of the *River* for Roger. I am sending it under separate cover and to you, since offhand I don't seem to find his address in the mess around here.

I can't at this distance assure you that I will be in Chicago in late April. I am visiting my son and his family in April in Washington, D.C.—April in Washington being among other things the season of Magnolias and azaleas, given my taste, more beautiful than Washington in cherry-blossom time. So the time of my visit has to correspond to the time of the azaleas and to the convenience of my son and his wife, both of whom work. [. . .]

I can understand your anxiety over the fact that I am writing about the Mann Gulch Fire. Seemingly all those living who had close connections with those in the fire are worried about me. I have to accept that as a fact of scholarship, and go ahead and call the shots as I see them, trusting my own integrity as a person and a life-long training as a scholar. The reasons are at least several why those connected with those who were in the Mann Gulch [fire] do not want it talked about in public. Although I have known the former Mrs. Dodge, wife of the foremen on the fire, since she was a small girl whom my brother and I chased around the chicken coop, she would be very happy now if I would

---

5. A famous mountain profile north of Helena, Montana, and within the Gates of the Mountains Wilderness Area.

6. Maclean sent Mrs. Jansson a copy of *A River Runs through It* inscribed "To Lois Jansson: One of the true and few survivors of the Mann Gulch Fire."

go off in the brush and die. She still lets me fish, though, on the Blackfoot River where it runs through her ranch. Professor Diettert's hands shake when he tries to talk to me. Mrs. Harrison gently but firmly refuses to talk to me. These are perhaps only small matters, but almost nothing large or small has come easy in trying to find out how thirteen young men died in Mann Gulch on Aug. 5, 1949. I sometimes wonder why I go on trying. In one of your letters you quote someone as referring to [your] husband as "a thick-headed Scot," which sometimes has to explain things when all else fails.

Very sincerely yours,

Norman Maclean

May 9, 1980

Dear Mrs. Jansson:

Thanks very much for the slides and the telephone call. My son-in-law is a photographer and so has a projector, so I'll soon be seeing them on the screen. I'm going to speak late this month at a faculty club here on something or other I am doing on the Mann Gulch fire, and may have occasion to use them. Certainly, some time I surely will, and I am grateful to you for giving them to me.

I was also glad about the telephone call and especially glad to hear that your trip was a big success. Northern Idaho and northern Montana are good places to get out of toward the end of a winter. It is also a pleasure for the rest of us who see you as you fly by. I enjoyed very much our evening together.

I'll be going to Montana a little earlier than usual this spring. Montana State University at Bozeman is awarding me an honorary doctor degree at their spring convocation. That's nice of them.

Norman Maclean

June 12, 1980

Dear Mrs. Jansson:

I just got back from Bozeman where I was treated better than I often am in Missoula where it is very doubtful that "the best university in Montana" is located, but it will be some time yet before I get there myself—certainly not in time to catch you on your way to your family reunion in Minnesota. I should leave here in another week or 10 days (if I quit trying to answer my back-mail), but I stop in Helena for a week or so with my brother-in-law and so get to Seeley Lake just in time to open my cabin for the 4th of July and fortify my woodpile against the onslaught of the motor cycle set.

It will be at least the end of the first week of July before I get down to Missoula, and I doubt if I get much farther west than that before I return to Chicago. I *must* complete a first draft of the Mann Gulch story this summer—or else it will have to be published posthumously. I have worked on it now for four years—I don't think I could face another year on Mann Gulch. I'm already almost as bad as your husband was about it—I'll be having nightmares about it unless I get a transfer soon. But I sure would like to see the Priest River Experiment Station very much. We'll see.

It was indeed a pleasure to meet you.

Norman Maclean

July 2, 1980

Dear Mrs. Jansson:

I arrived yesterday at the Lake and found two letters from you waiting for me and a shocking letter from Walter Rumsey's daughter.[7] In case you have not heard of the time Walter was not a survivor. I am enclosing a copy of his daughter's letter to me together with a copy of the obituary notice that accompanied it. I am also doing the same thing for Bob Sallee[8] and Laird Robinson.

I did not know Walter well, but I admired him greatly. He had a kind of Kansas steadfastness and stateliness about him, and of course as a survivor of the fire that spared almost no man or tree he was as much a ghost as a man or as a Kansan. The day I spent in Mann Gulch with him, Bob Sallee and Laird Robinson was one of the best days of my life.

Walt was a great admirer of your husband and spoke of him several times. As I remember, he knew him not only through the Forest Service but through church and work with the young people. Like yourselves, he was a devout but not a parading Methodist.

My instinct is to leave completely unchanged what I wrote about him, except to acknowledge his death in a footnote or in the preface.

I am woefully behind in everything (including my book) or I would thank

---

7. Walter Rumsey, one of the two survivors of the Mann Gulch tragedy. Maclean is referring here to the news of Rumsey's death in a plane crash.

8. Bob Sallee was the other survivor of the Mann Gulch fire and the youngest member of the fated crew. A retired executive in Spokane, Washington, Sallee has since the publication of *Young Men and Fire* granted an occasional interview and been featured in television specials devoted to the Storm King Mountain fire in Colorado and the Mann Gulch fire.

you at greater length for your letters and your sketch of Duncan Moir[9] and for a copy of your husband's letter to the Regional Forester stating (to keep the record straight) his differences from the Forest Service's logistics of the fire. Hard as I must work this summer, I will find time to thank you more fully for them.

Among other troubles, I can't get Oregon's volcano off my cabin.[10] I oiled it late last summer, and the volcanic dust is ingrained in it. I can't get it off.

Very sincerely,

Norman Maclean

Nov. 19, 1980

Dear Lois:

Your grand-daughter doesn't have it quite right for me. For me, it's "How are you and don't tell me. I'm not so fine."

I no more got back to Chicago from the summer, than I had to return to Montana (Billings) to be the banquet speaker at the annual conference of the Montana Historical Society. It was a rush trip and I caught a cold and a month later still have it and am spiritually bedraggled. The autumn is almost gone and I am almost non-productive.

I am also stopped by the fact that I have come to a place in the story of the Mann Gulch Fire where the time of the final succession of events is important—and that leads to an ever bigger question—the question of whether "the Forest Service" didn't alter the actual time of the events to agree with their logistic scheme of events. And this leads to an even larger question—just what credibility can be placed in any of the statements of "the Forest Service" and the witnesses about the fire?

I can't tell you, Lois, how these questions haunt me and alter my basic feelings about the story and for the time being cripple my progress with it. Hell, I'm not a political muck-raker—in so far as I am a writer, I am a writer of stories, generally western stories and generally tragic ones. I am generally a tragic writer because generally my view of things is tragic. What do I want of a story about a house-detective of the Forest Service who sneaks around getting witnesses to alter their testimony? That might be a pretty good story for my son, who is one of the better Washington news reporters, but it's no story for me.

9. Arthur D. ("Duncan") Moir Jr. was forest supervisor, Helena National Forest, at the time of the fire and was a witness before the board of review, having supervised the rescue operation.

10. Mount St. Helens, actually in Washington State, erupted May 18, 1980.

But I can't walk off now and leave it. As you are a Methodist, so I was brought up a Presbyterian, which is about the same thing. I don't quit a job because near the end it gets messy. Lois, maybe you can help to get me going again.

I have lots of problems in facing the possibility that "the Forest Service" tried to alter evidence to make all stories fit their stories. For one thing, I have been trained all my life to start by trying to make sense out of things, as you being a schoolteacher too must have been trained, but I can't make any sense of why they should run the danger of trying to tamper with witnesses and artifacts. Can you?

(1). I can't see where the story as it occurred needed to be tampered with anywhere. I think it is a rather noble and terrifying story of the elite of men coming to disaster by doing what they were trained to do which always before had led to success. I agree totally with your husband in his letter to Wag Dodge (Sept. 1, '49)—sure anybody in the world who knew the results of the fire ahead of time would have done everything differently, he wouldn't even have let his men or himself be dropped into Mann Gulch on Aug. 5, 1949, but knowing what was known about fire-fighting and what was known about the fire in Mann Gulch on Aug. 5, 1949, he, the Ranger of Canyon Ferry, would have done what Wag Dodge did and probably would not have been smart enough to think of "lighting an escape fire." What was wrong with the truth, Lois? Anyone who understood anything about the bitter turns of the universe and of forest fires would have had no trouble in understanding the true story of Mann Gulch. There was no story they could have put out, including the one they did, that would diminish the tragedy for everyone. Why forsake the truth because at times it is almost unbearably harsh?

(2). More specifically, what sense did it make to try to get your husband to change his logistics by 20 minutes so that it would agree with Dodge's story as to when the tragedy ("the accident," as the Forest Service refers to it) occurred? Lois, when Dodge said "the accident" occurred, he was at the upper end of the Gulch only 100 yards from where some of his crew were dying, and your husband was down in the Missouri River riding in a boat. Why shouldn't there be some variation in the timing of the events? Even Dodge could not know exactly—he saw none of the events. His face was in his wet handkerchief and both his face and his handkerchief were buried in the ashes. He didn't know the time until the main fire passed him by and he looked at his watch and it said 6:10, so he said, and who knows whether his watch and your husband's agreed. Anyway, it would seem almost inevitable (unless they conspired afterward) that there would be some difference in the timing of the same events when they were several miles apart and couldn't see for the smoke anyway. An agreement among them as to the exact timing of events in the circumstances would be more suspicious to me than some differences as what seems to me to be the facts.

Lois, why from the Forest Service point of view—from theirs, not yours or mine—was it so important that your husband and Dodge agree almost exactly about the deaths of 13 men none of which anybody who lived saw?

I've come to a place in my story where it doesn't make sense anymore, and (with a cold) I am having a hard time thinking of what to write.

Can you think of any true words that might help me?

Very sincerely yours,

Norman Maclean

[P.S.] Lois, right now I would like to use a sentence from your husband in a letter to "Bob and Wilma," whoever they are, as the frontispiece of my story:

"I think there is a tremendous story in the Mann Gulch episode and I feel that someday it won't hurt us to tell it."

Dec. 10, 1981

Dear Lois:

Thank you very much for the jelly, which I have just finished, which would seem like a good time to thank you for it, except that it is a sadder time than I thought it would be. I like jelly very much, and was unhappy to see it go.

I have finished a first draft of the story, and have put the manuscript aside for several weeks hopefully to gather strength to start the imposing job of revision. I revise a lot (even my life), but this looks like the biggest revising job I ever took on. I'll never again try to tell a story that all the time tries to tell the truth. Often the truth isn't worth what it costs.

But thanks again for your contributions (some of which were truly helpful), and best wishes for the coming season and the coming new year.

Norman Maclean

Acknowledgments

M any years ago, as I wrote and published several articles about Norman Maclean, I made the acquaintance of University of Chicago Press editor Alan Thomas, as well as John N. Maclean and Jean Maclean Snyder. All three supported my work. With John and a party of others, I walked into Mann Gulch on August 5, 1994, the forty-fifth anniversary of the Mann Gulch fire. In March 2000 I finally met Alan and Jean face-to-face, as both kindly took me to lunch and listened to my gushings about Norman and hopes for a book. John and Jean had graciously allowed me access to the Norman Maclean Archive (Department of Special Collections, Regenstein Library, University of Chicago), where I spent five happy days poring through notes, letters, photographs, and the extant chapters (both longhand and typescript) from the Custer manuscript.

I want to thank Alan, John, and Jean for inviting me to serve as editor of the book you are holding. It is a better book than the one I planned most of a decade ago. I appreciate deeply their vote of confidence, and preparing the *Reader* has proven one of the highlights of my scholarly life. It has also allowed me to step close once again to one of my favorite writers. I also thank Marie Borroff and Nick Lyons for answering my e-mail queries and editing me when I needed it. And I especially thank Robert Utley, preeminent historian of the West, who answered many questions for me more than a decade ago, and who more recently has tolerated my occasional phone query and generally supported this book. My thanks go also to William Bevis for his comments on the selection and introduction, and to Jim Hepworth, who was the publisher of an earlier book on Norman Maclean and was supportive of this project. Bill has been a friend and mentor, and expert on Montana letters, for many years; Jim spent an evening at our home several years ago, after a day of fishing, and we talked in depth about Norman and this new book. Finally, I am grateful to Alan Thomas's colleagues at the University of Chicago Press for their work in bringing this book to publication, including Randolph Petilos, Erin DeWitt, Jill Shimabukuro, Joan Davies, Rich Hendel, and Levi Stahl.

O. Alan Weltzien
February 2008

Suggestions for Further Reading

Bevis, William W. "Maclean's River." Chap. 11 in *Ten Tough Trips: Montana Writers and the West*. 1990. Reprint, Norman: University of Oklahoma Press, 2003.

Borroff, Marie. "The Achievement of Norman Maclean." *Yale Review* 82, no. 2 (April 1994): 118–31.

Browning, Mark. "'Some of the Words Are Theirs': The Elusive Logos in *A River Runs through It*." *Christianity and Literature* 50, no. 4 (Summer 2001): 679–88.

Butler, Douglas R. "Norman Maclean's *A River Runs through It*: Word, Water, and Text." *Critique* 33, no. 4 (Summer 1992): 263–74.

Derwin, Daniel. "Casting Shadows: Filial Enactments in *A River Runs through It*." *American Imago* 51, no. 3 (Fall 1994): 343–57.

Dooley, Patrick K. "Work, Friendship, and Community: Norman Maclean's *A River Runs through it and Other Stories* and Josiah Royce's *The Philosophy of Loyalty*." *Renascence: Essays on Values in Literature* 53, no. 4 (Summer 2001): 287–302.

Egan, Ken. *Hope and Dread in Montana Literature*. Reno: University of Nevada Press, 2003.

Ford, James E. "When 'Life . . . Becomes Literature': The Neo-Aristotelian Poetics of Norman Maclean's 'A River Runs through It.'" *Studies in Short Fiction* 30, no. 4 (Fall 1993): 525–34.

Jamieson, Phillip D. "*Young Men and Fire*: Norman Maclean and the Pastoral Vocation." *Theology Today* 52, no. 1 (April 1995): 102–7.

Maclean, John N. *Fire on the Mountain: The True Story of the South Canyon Fire*. New York: William Morrow, 1999.

Maclean, Norman. "Episode, Scene, Speech, and Word: The Madness of Lear." In *Critics and Criticism: Ancient and Modern*, edited by R. S. Crane et al., 595–615. Chicago: University of Chicago Press, 1952.

———. "From Action to Image: Theories of the Lyric in the Eighteenth Century." In *Critics and Criticism: Ancient and Modern*, edited by R. S. Crane et al., 408–50. Chicago: University of Chicago Press, 1952.

McFarland, Ron, and Hugh Nichols, eds. *Norman Maclean*. American Authors series. Lewiston, ID: Confluence Press, 1988. This volume, anthologizing Maclean's occasional writing with interviews and criticism, is indispensable for anyone interested in Maclean before *Young Men and Fire*. It includes ten pieces by Maclean (five of which are included in this *Reader*); two interviews; and seven "Essays in Appreciation and Criticism," including essays by Wallace Stegner and Wendell Berry.

———, eds. *Norman Maclean*. Western Writers series, #107. Boise, ID: Boise State University, 1993.

Proulx, Annie. Foreword to *A River Runs through It and Other Stories, Twenty-fifth Anniversary Edition*. Chicago: University of Chicago Press, 2001.

Utley, Robert. *Custer and Me: A Historian's Memoir*. Norman: University Oklahoma Press, 2004.

Weick, Karl E. "The Collapse of Sensemaking in Organizations: The Mann Gulch Disaster." *Administrative Science Quarterly* 38, no. 4 (December 1995): 628–51.

———. "Prepare Your Organization to Fight Fires." *Harvard Business Review* 74, no. 3 (May–June 1996): 143–47.

Weinberger, Theodore. "Religion and Fly Fishing: Taking Norman Maclean Seriously." *Renascence* 49, no. 4 (Summer 1997): 281–89.

Weltzien, O. Alan. "George Custer, Norman Maclean, and James Welch: Personal History and the Redemption of Defeat." *Arizona Quarterly* 52, no. 4 (Winter 1996): 115–23.

———. "A 'Mail-Order Marriage': The Norman Maclean–Robert Utley Correspondence." *Montana: The Magazine of Western History* 48, no. 4 (Winter 1998): 34–49.

———. "Norman Maclean and Laird Robinson: A Tale of Two Research Partners." *Montana: The Magazine of Western History* 45, no. 2 (Spring 1995): 46–55.

———. "Norman Maclean and Tragedy." *Western American Literature* 30, no. 2 (August 1995): 139–49.

———. "The Two Lives of Norman Maclean and the Text of Fire in *Young Men and Fire*." *Western American Literature* 29, no. 1 (May 1994): 3–23.

Womack, Kenneth, and Todd F. Davis. "Haunted by Waters: Narrative Reconciliation in Norman Maclean's *A River Runs through It*." *Critique* 42, no. 2 (Winter 2001): 192–204.

Wood, R. C. "Words under the Rocks." *Christian Century* 110 (January 20, 1993): 44–46.